Amish Girls Series

~ VOLUME 1 ~

J. E. B. Spredemann

Blessed Publishing

All incidents and characters in this book are completely fictional and derived by the authors' imaginations. Any resemblance to actual incidents and persons living or dead are purely coincidental.

Disclaimer: The herbal information in this book was derived by the author's (J.S.) education and experience as a Nutritional Herbologist, but is written for fictional and informational use only. No herbal information in this book is, in any way, meant as a prescription or medical advice. This information has not been approved by the FDA, AMA, or any other government agency. It is your constitutional right to prescribe for yourself, if you choose to do so. The author assumes no responsibility for the treatments in this book, if you should choose to implement them. Therefore, the government requires the recommendation that you see your health care provider if you have any medical concerns/issues.

Published in California by Blessed Publishing.

http.//amishbooks.wix.com/jebspredemann

All Scripture quotations are taken from the King James Version of the Holy Bible, are not subject to copyright laws, and may be freely copied and/or quoted.

Cover design by J.E.B. Spredemann.

BOOKS BY J.E.B. SPREDEMANN

(*J. Spredemann)

AMISH GIRLS SERIES

Joanna's Struggle

Danika's Journey

Chloe's Revelation

Susanna's Surprise

Annie's Decision

Abigail's Triumph

Brooke's Quest

AMISH SECRETS SERIES*

*An Unforgivable Secret**

*A Secret Encounter**

New! NOVELETTES*

Amish Fairly Tales:

*Cindy's Story**

COMING SOON! - 2014

Leah's Legacy (Amish Girls Series – Book 8)

Learning to Love – Saul's Story (Sequel to Chloe's Revelation – adult novella)*

UNOFFICIAL GLOSSARY OF PENNSYLVANIA DUTCH WORDS

Ach – Oh
Aldi – Girlfriend
Ausbund – Amish hymn book
Bloobier – Blueberry
Boppli – Baby
Bopplin – Babies
Bruder – Brother
Dat, Daed – Dad
Dawdi – Grandfather
Denki – Thanks
Der Herr - The Lord
Dochder – Daughter
Dokter – Doctor
Dummkopp – Dummy
Englischer – A non-Amish person
Ferhoodled – Mixed up, Crazy
Fraa – Woman, Wife
Gott – God
Gut – Good
Gross Dawdi – Great Grandfather
Haus – House
Hullo – Hello
Jah – Yes

Kapp – Prayer Covering
Kinner – *Children*
Kumm – Come
Lieb – Love
Liede – Song
Mamm – Mom
Mammi – Grandmother
Mein Liewe – My Dear
Mudder – Mother
Nee – No
Ordnung – Rules of the Amish Community
Rumspringa – Running around years
Schweschder – Sister
Vadder – Father
Vorsinger – Song Leader
Wunderbaar – Wonderful

Amish Girls Series - Book 1
CUSTOM
Joanna's
Struggle
J.E.B. Spredemann

Joanna's Struggle

J.E.B. Spredemann

Amish Girls Series - Book 1

To our family...

Without your love and support, this dream would have never become a reality.

AUTHORS' NOTE

It should be noted that the Amish people and their communities differ one from another. There are, in fact, no two Amish communities that are exactly alike. It is this premise on which this book is written. We have taken cautious steps to assure the authenticity of Amish practices and customs. Both Old Order Amish and New Order Amish are portrayed in this work of fiction and may be inconsistent with some Amish communities.

We, as *Englischers*, can learn a lot from the Plain People and their simple way of life. Their hard work, close-knit family life, and concern for others are to be applauded. As the Lord wills, may this special culture continue to be respected and remain so for many centuries to come, and may the light of God's salvation reach their hearts.

CHAPTER 1
Mud Sale

"Be not far from me; for trouble is near; for there is none to help." Psalm 22:11

Eleven-year-old Joanna Fisher bounded into the barn calling, "Jonathan. Jonathan. *Mamm* said to...OW!" she cried, as a clod of dirt pelted her arm. From the haymow she heard muffled giggles and impatiently yelled, "Jonathan Fisher, you *dummkopp*. I'm gonna get you for that. *Mamm* will not be happy when she sees that you've gotten my dress dirty again. Especially since," she added, attempting to wipe the debris from her burgundy cape dress, "we're going to the auction. *Mamm* said you need to get ready now."

From behind a haystack she heard a gasp and then a sandy colored head popped up. "The mud sale?" seven-year-old Jonathan exclaimed, climbing down the ladder and darting out of the barn like a bolt of lightning.

Her anger subsided, Joanna giggled softly to herself. "For sure and for certain Jonathan is excited about attending the mud sale."

She sighed deeply and adjusted her prayer *kapp,* a few of her honey brown tresses escaping the tight bun behind her head. *Lord, I'm trying to love my little brother, but sometimes he makes it difficult,* Joanna complained silently to God. She'd been taught in her Amish heritage not just to love her family and friends, but to love her enemies as well. That certainly was *not* the easiest thing to do.

On this beautiful Saturday morning, the sun shone brightly through the sparse poplar trees that lined the Fishers' property. They'd just had a church service, or *Sunday Go-To-Meeting,* as they called it, last week. There would be no meeting this week because they were only held every other Sunday. Joanna loved to attend the services, although sometimes she had trouble staying awake. She didn't feel bad though, because sometimes she would see several of the older folks nod off too, and occasionally *they* even snored until they were nudged by the person sitting next to them.

Three hours was a long time for anyone to sit through preaching, let alone a girl Joanna's age. Her brother Jonathan had an awfully difficult time staying in his seat. One time, unbeknownst to their folks, he made his way up to the front where Bishop Hostettler was preaching. As the bishop delivered his message, Jonathan followed behind him mimicking his every move. No one reprimanded him for his actions as he performed his silly antics. Joanna attributed their folks' passiveness to the fact that they were probably too dismayed to do anything at the time. And, of course, *nobody* wanted to interrupt the bishop's message. When the bishop noticed the amused faces of his flock and that the eyes of his congregation were focusing on something other than him, he turned around to see what was stealing their attention. He then offered to let Jonathan speak, commenting that perhaps the boy had a future in preaching. Sheepishly, Jonathan declined and Joanna never saw him ascend the platform again.

The ministers preached from the Luther Bible, which was in High German, so Joanna could only understand bits and pieces of the sermon. (Most Amish only spoke Pennsylvania Dutch, which had some words similar to German, and English.) She was looking forward to this Sunday when they would rest and visit with friends and family.

Joanna skipped out of the barn and accidentally collided into her father Gideon, who was leading their beautiful auburn horse. "Careful, Joanna, you almost bumped into Cinnamon here."

"Sorry, *Dat*. I wasn't looking where I was go –"

"Tis all right," her dad interrupted, patting her hand, "now go help your *Mamm*, we will leave soon." Joanna hurried to the house.

"Joanna, we could use your help getting the sandwiches ready to take to the mud sale," her thirteen-year-old sister Grace requested. "And fill up the thermos with hot coffee." Joanna did as told, and then placed the items into their large picnic basket.

"*Mamm,*" Joanna inquired of her mother, "are ya takin' anything to sell today?"

"*Jah, denki* for reminding me. I need to go down to the cellar to get some more jellies and jams. It's a *gut* thing that the Lord blessed us with extra fruit and vegetables last harvest," her mother answered.

When everything was finally ready, all six members of the Fisher family loaded the buggy and headed for the mud sale. Joanna could barely contain her excitement. She couldn't wait to see her best friend Chloe. The two girls enjoyed perusing the many booths almost as much as being in one another's company.

Maybe now would be a good time to ask, thought Joanna.

"*Dat, Mamm,*" she said, hesitating, "do you mind if I get an after-school job so I can earn some extra money?"

"Do you think you'll have any spare time, with all your chores and what not?" her mother queried, sending a pointed look that didn't reassure Joanna.

"I can do my chores as soon as I get home from school, and I'll have some extra time during the summer after the harvest is over. I *have* been doing a good job with my chores, ain't?" Joanna hoped they'd agree.

Her dad answered, "Well, you *have* done your chores diligently...Just what kind of work did ya have in mind to do, Joanna?"

"Oh, I'm not sure just yet." Joanna thought. "Maybe I can help take care of a *boppli,* or do some housework for one of our *Englischer* neighbors like Ruth Yoder does." She hoped mentioning the deacon's daughter would help her plight.

"We'll talk about this later. Right now your *vadder* and I need to discuss the auction," her mom replied, turning back to the front, indicating the discussion was over.

As her mother and father conversed, Joanna and her siblings sat quietly in the back seat of the buggy. Well, most of them did. Jonathan dug into his pocket with one of his grubby little hands and pulled out a tree frog. An imaginary battle ensued with the small green amphibian and Jonathan's index finger. *Mamm* turned around several times in an attempt to shush the young boy, but her efforts were futile and she eventually allowed him to indulge in his merriment.

Cinnamon trotted along at an even pace as they rode past farm houses, barns, silos, and pastures. The fresh scents of spring wafted through the air and Joanna breathed in deeply. *Soon, I'll be able to take off my shoes and run barefoot through the meadow,* she mused. *Oh, to feel the cool, soft, green blades of grass beneath my feet again after being in these miserable shoes all winter.*

Many *Englischer* cars impatiently passed their buggy on the road, some of them honking their horns. The fast, large metal contraptions were sometimes intimidating from the inside of a horse-drawn buggy, especially the huge semi-trucks that nearly blew them off the road. The Amish preferred a simpler, slower-paced lifestyle which, for the most part, Joanna agreed was better. Sure, the Plain People had to work harder than others but that was the life they had chosen. Separation from the world is what they called it, a lifestyle set-apart. The best part about it though, in Joanna's opinion, was the closeness of their tightknit community. Their People loved and cared for one another and it was evident in every aspect of life.

Joanna hummed softly as they came into the Ronks firehouse parking lot and up to one of the hitching posts. Several of the young Amish men often offered their help at the small volunteer fire department. Once, the firemen were called out to a fire at her uncle's metal shop. One of the sparks shot out from the welder and ignited some hay nearby, instantly setting the shop ablaze. There were several Amish men working for the fire department that day, so news of the fire spread quickly. Not too long after the incident, the men of the community rallied together and built a new barn for her uncle in a single day.

The familiar sights and sounds of the mud sale brought excitement, especially for the children. It had been a whole year since Joanna's entire family last attended one, even though there were several throughout Lancaster County. They are called "mud sales" because they take place in the late winter and early spring when the frozen ground begins to thaw, sometimes turning the ground into mud. The money raised at the sales benefited the volunteer firehouse, to make sure they were supplied with the necessary equipment to serve their surrounding communities.

"Come on, Joanna," her brother Isaac called. "Stop your daydreaming and let's go."

As Joanna stepped out of the buggy, her eyes scanned the crowd for any signs of Chloe. Her friend was nowhere to be seen. *She must not be here yet,* Joanna thought disappointedly.

Her dad seemed to have read her thoughts and chuckled. "Don't worry Joanna, she'll be here soon. Let's look around and see what they have for sale today. Keep an eye out for a *gut* saddle. We'll need one for the mare that I plan on purchasing at the auction."

"*Ach,* really, *Dat*?" Joanna squealed. "How will we bring her home?"

"I thought that Isaac would like to ride her back to Paradise," Gideon replied. "She'll need to get used to his touch, especially since she'll be pulling his new courting buggy that we're picking up from the Hostettlers' next week."

By the enthusiasm in his voice, Joanna perceived that her father was proud of her sixteen-year-old brother Isaac. He would be the first of the Fisher children to enter into adulthood and, hopefully, join the Amish church. Eventually, he'd be married and have *bopplin* too. Joanna smiled at the thought, although she had no idea whom her brother might be interested in courting.

"There you are, Jo," Chloe Esh called from the next table over which sold home baked goods. She quickly made her way through the crowd toward Joanna carrying a whoopie pie for each of them, passing Amish and *Englisch* alike. Children ran to and fro amidst the large crowd. "Can you believe all the people this year?"

"It seems like every year there're more *Englischers, jah*?" Joanna replied, as she gave her friend a quick hug and accepted the delicious treat.

"*Jah*, and Plain folks, too," Chloe mumbled around a bite. She eagerly pulled on Joanna's arm. "Let's go see the new pony cart Eli Yoder just bought. Maybe he'll give us a ride in it."

"I want to look at the quilts too, but we can do that later. First, let me tell *Dat* where we'll be," Joanna spoke, and then turned to her father. "Chloe and I are going to walk around a bit, then meet up with her *mamm*. Remember, I'm riding home with the Eshes."

"Make sure you're home for the evening meal," her father reminded her, as he and her mother leisurely strolled to the next vendor's table. "Have a *gut* time."

"My *dat* said to be lookin' for a *gut* saddle," Joanna informed Chloe as they turned to walk in the direction of the quilts. "He's getting a new horse today to pull Isaac's courtin' buggy."

"*Ach*, I wonder who he'll be courtin'," Chloe said dreamily.

Oblivious to Chloe's musings, Joanna continued, "I can't wait – a new horse to ride. I hope the horse is black. The black ones are so pretty, especially when they're racing."

"Joanna Fisher! Don't tell me you've been racing Barley without me," Chloe heralded.

"Shh...we don't want to let everyone know our secret. Besides, you know I never race without my best friend," Joanna whispered, surveying the area for Amish folk that may have overheard. Hopefully, Deacon Yoder was nowhere nearby. "Let's go look at the jams and jellies now. I helped *Mamm* make some plum jam – your favorite," Joanna said proudly.

The girls pushed their way through the crowd toward the brightly decorated jam table. "Hello, Sarah Yoder," Chloe hollered, waving to Eli's mother.

"How are you girls doing this fine morning?" the kind woman asked.

"We're doin' *gut*. Ain't so, Chloe?" Joanna replied, nudging Chloe gently.

"*Jah*, how are you?" Chloe politely asked Sarah, although her eyes flitted elsewhere.

"Well actually, I'm all done in. We've been here since before sun-up," Sarah answered, then rubbed the back of her flaxen-haired daughter. "I think Annie and I are ready for a nap."

"Where are the little ones? Did they stay home today?" Chloe wondered aloud.

"*Jah*, Ruth is watching them today," Sarah responded.

"Has anyone bought my *mamm*'s jam yet?" Joanna questioned.

"Yes, a few, but there're plenty more yet," Sarah Yoder answered, as she examined the table full of delicious home-canned jams and jellies. "They usually sell like hotcakes, so I'm sure we'll be raisin' lots of money today." Most of the Amish in Joanna's district donated their time and talents to help out, along with others in the surrounding communities.

"Joanna and I better get going if we want to see the pony cart and the quilts," Chloe announced, leading Joanna toward the quilts.

"Have a *gut* time girls," Sarah called, as they walked off.

The girls walked up to a grand display of handmade Amish quilts. Joanna and Chloe eyed the various designs with wonder, trying to decide which of the creations their favorite was. Some of the quilts were simple patch work designs and others were amazingly intricate in detail. Joanna decided the Ocean Wave pattern quilt was her favorite design. Perhaps she'd make one for a friend's wedding gift someday.

"Look at this," Chloe remarked, fingering a brightly colored Hearts All-Around quilt, "it's beautiful."

"*Jah*, it looks perfect. Not a stitch out of place. I hope I can quilt this *gut* someday," Joanna responded.

"*Jah*, me too," Chloe agreed, her mouth still agape.

"Hey, there's Philip King, the herb *dokter*. I wonder why *he's* looking at the quilts," Joanna thought aloud.

"I heard that," Philip King replied, chuckling.

"Heard what?" Chloe asked, feigning innocence.

"I happen to be purchasing a quilt for my friend's wedding over in Hickory Hollow next week, for your information. And as of now, the three of us are the only ones that know about it, and I expect you two to keep my secret." Philip winked.

"Of course we will," they chorused and winked backed. The girls knew how quickly news could spread. The Amish community was certainly not immune to gossip. *Sometimes the People all the way over in other states like Indiana and Ohio know what is going on in our back yard,* Joanna thought. Yes, they would keep tight-lipped about Philip's gift.

"We need to find him a wife," Chloe whispered softly in Joanna's ear.

"*Jah,* a wife indeed," Joanna whispered back, smiling broadly.

"What was that, girls?" Philip raised his dark brown eyebrows.

"Nothing," they replied in unison, which sent them into a fit of giggles.

"Well, I'd better get going...back to my herb search." Philip King smiled and walked off slowly.

I wonder why that nice, good-looking man hasn't married, Joanna pondered.

A couple of hours later, Joanna and Chloe had been to just about every vendor booth. They both agreed that the quilt table was their favorite – aside from the horses at auction, of course. The sun stood just above the trees to the west and several families, including Joanna's, had already left for home.

"Chloe...Chloe..." the girls heard Chloe's mother calling in the distance.

"*Ach*, that's *Mamm* calling. We'd better go," Chloe chided.

"You go ahead, and I'll be there in a bit. I need to use the bathroom," Joanna pleaded.

"Okay, but don't be long. I think they want to leave soon," she replied and ran off.

The restroom wasn't too far a walk, thank goodness. As Joanna turned the corner, she felt a firm grasp on her elbow and it startled her. She saw a huge shadow behind her. "Don't make a sound or you *will* regret it," a man with a deep, raspy voice whispered in her ear. He then pointed in the opposite direction. "Now, we're going to walk quickly and get into that blue truck over there. Do you hear me, young lady?"

She nodded briefly, glancing at the old rusted blue truck. *What should I do? Run? I can't, his grip is too strong.* Joanna thought desperately. *Scream!* she told herself. But when she opened her mouth no sound would come out. Frightened and shaking, Joanna complied with his wishes and headed toward the truck in silence...

CHAPTER 2
Where's Joanna?

"What time I am afraid, I will trust in thee."
Psalm 56:3

"We've got to get on the road now; it's getting dark," Chloe's father reminded.

"I still don't see Joanna anywhere...she should have been back by now. I told her not to be long." Chloe was beginning to worry.

"*Ach*, don't fret," Mary replied. "She probably just ran into one of the other *kinner* and lost track of time. I'll go with you to find her."

When Chloe and her mother skimmed the restroom, Joanna was nowhere to be seen. "Well, she's not in there. Let's keep looking, she couldn't have gone far," her mom decided, heading toward the nearly empty parking lot. "Look, there's Philip King. Maybe he has seen her."

"Hello, ladies. Getting ready to head back to Paradise soon?" Philip asked, congenial as always.

"*Jah, hullo*, Philip," Mary Esh responded. "Have you seen Joanna Fisher recently? Chloe left her at the restroom about thirty minutes ago and now it's starting to get dark. She's supposed to ride home with us." Most families didn't like to travel on the main roads at night. There had been many buggy accidents among the People after dark. The lanterns on the buggies were not very bright, and some of the Amish didn't use many reflectors.

"No, I haven't seen her since earlier today when she was with your daughter. Let me put my purchases in my buggy, then I'll help you look for her," Philip promised with a tinge of concern on his face.

True to his word, Philip returned promptly with another Amish man and two Plain Mennonite friends to help with the search.

After an hour, Joanna was still nowhere to be found. The crowd had thinned out quite a bit and the situation did not look promising. The search team had looked everywhere with no sign of Joanna.

"Do you think we should contact the authorities?" one of Philip's Mennonite friends suggested.

"Well, she may be at home as we speak...I will use the telephone to see if she went home with someone else." Peter Esh pulled some coins from his pocket, and then proceeded to locate a pay phone. Unless absolutely necessary, the People did not like to involve the *Englisch* authorities in their affairs. Instead, they chose to trust God, however difficult that might be.

Ring...ring...ring...ring...ring...the telephone sounded in the Fishers' barn.

"Did you hear something, Esther?" Gideon Fisher asked as he sat reading his Bible.

"No, I didn't hear anything. I have too much going on, tryin' to make dinner and what not, to pay attention. But that doesn't mean *you* didn't hear anything," Esther replied, smiling.

"*Jah*, you heard the telephone, *Dat*," Isaac said, as he walked down the stairs from his room. "I was on the balcony and I heard it, but it stopped ringing already."

"I wonder who would be calling the shop at this time of the day. Probably some *Englischer* who wants to order a table," Gideon voiced his thoughts. "Well, I suppose if it is important they'll call back later."

A few minutes later, Peter walked back to the group. "I called Gideon Fisher's shop, but there was no answer. We will pray and trust God for Joanna's safety. We've done all we can. It is time to go home now," Chloe's father stated, his voice resigned.

"Yes, we will trust God...He knows best," Philip offered. Hoping in God was never a lost cause.

"We will stop by the Fishers' place to see if she's there," Peter announced.

"Dear *Gott*," Chloe prayed quietly, "please let Joanna be safe."

Dear Gott, *please help me*, Joanna begged silently, as she rode along in an ugly, beat-up, blue pick-up truck with the burly stranger. She really wanted to trust God, but she was scared.

"You don't need worry your perty little head about a thing, darlin'. Just as long as you behave yourself and do as I say, everything will be fine – just fine," the stranger warned, as he put his hand on her knee.

Joanna winced. She hated feeling his rough, calloused hand on her dress. Somehow, she knew he wasn't telling the truth. An ugly feeling settled in the pit of her belly, heightening her sense of fear. She had to get away, and fast. What could she do? They were traveling down the highway so fast it made her stomach queasy. She'd only been in an *Englischer* car a few times. She much preferred the gentle trot of a horse and buggy, but now was not the time to think about that. "Dear *Gott*, please help me escape," she silently pleaded once more.

"Okay, here's the plan," the stranger stated matter-of-factly. "We're going to walk into Wal-Mart and head straight to the bathroom. And I mean straight – no looking around, no dawdling, no talking." By his stern voice and piercing gaze, Joanna knew he meant business.

She nodded.

"As soon as you go into the little ladies' room, you change into these." He handed her a closed brown paper bag, then continued, "Leave your hair up, but take off that white thing on your head and replace it with this ball cap," he said, pointing to her white prayer *kapp*, as it was called. The man handed her a scruffy-looking baseball cap, similar to the ones some boys wore in *rumspringa*. "I want you to put the clothes that you're wearing back into that paper bag and throw it into the trash can. Got it?"

Joanna nodded silently, too frightened to speak. *How can I throw away the first dress Mamm helped me make? She'll be so disappointed.*

Curiosity got the best of her and Joanna peered into the bag, spying a pair of denim blue jeans along with a green and brown plaid shirt. *I'll look like one of the boys in* rumspringa *with this on! Why does he want me to look like a boy?* she wondered naively. *This man is certainly* ferhoodled.

"No peekin' in the bag," he grumbled, causing Joanna to startle.

As they pulled into the Wal-Mart parking lot, Joanna became even more nervous. She did not want to put on the masculine clothing. How was she going to escape? *This may be my only chance,* she quivered at the thought, *I have to do it right.*

They quickly walked into the store. *Should I tell somebody that works here? What if they don't believe me?* This was getting scary.

"All right, you've got two minutes. You'd better make it quick..." the stranger cautioned.

"But I ne-ne-need to use the restroom, too," she stuttered.

"Okay, three minutes, but no more. I'll be waiting right over there." He pointed to a rack of magazines. "And no funny business," the man whispered, and then walked off.

Joanna had no idea what "funny business" meant, but she walked into the restroom all the same...

CHAPTER 3

An Answer to Prayer

"Behold, God is my salvation; I will trust and not be afraid..." Isaiah 12:2a

Gideon Fisher sat at home in his chair reading *The Budget*, the Amish/Mennonite newspaper, until he heard his *fraa* call, "Supper is ready".

He gazed up at the battery-operated clock on the wall and asked, "Esther, has Joanna come home from the Eshes' house yet?"

From the kitchen he heard Esther say, "*Ach, Nee.* No."

Gideon ran his fingers through his brown wavy hair, something he did only when he was worried or impatient. "*Ach.* I told Joanna to be back for the evening meal. Why hasn't she returned?"

Esther chided, "You're so impatient, *Mein Liewe*. Don't fret, she probably just lost track of time. She'll be back soon."

Dat shook his head unbelieving. "*Nee.* Joanna would've been back by now – I also told Peter Esh to make sure she gets back in time for supper. Peter wouldn't go against my wishes. It wonders me if maybe something has gone wrong. We need to be certain sure. I'm goin' to send Isaac to Peter's to check on Joanna."

Esther chuckled nonchalantly. "As you wish, Gideon."

Joanna couldn't believe her eyes as she walked into the Wal-Mart restroom. It was Naomi Fast, a Plain Mennonite driver that her parents sometimes hired! It was so good to see a familiar face. *Thank you, Gott,* she prayed and sighed in relief.

"Joanna? Is something wrong?" Naomi must have noticed the alarm on her face.

"The-the-there's a man, and he took me. He wants me to put these boy clothes on and ride with him..." she could speak no more, as she broke down into sobs.

Right away, Naomi realized that Joanna had been kidnapped. "Shh...it's okay," Naomi said, attempting to comfort her. "That man isn't going to take you anywhere. This is what we're going to do." Naomi thought for a second, sending up a quick prayer for wisdom. "Okay, I'm going to walk out of the restroom and you will follow right behind me. After I get my cart, you stay close by my side where he won't be able to see you." Naomi gingerly peeked out the bathroom door and noticed the man that Joanna described was thumbing through a magazine. "Let's go now," she said, moving quickly.

Joanna stayed close to Naomi's side, just as she was instructed to do. She was tempted to look back at the *ferhoodled* man, but too scared to do so. As soon as they were out the door, they ran straight to Naomi's car, leaving her purchases behind in the cart. They jumped in and locked the doors. Naomi turned the key and they took off swiftly.

Meanwhile, the gruff man that had abducted Joanna must have noticed something was amiss, because they saw him run out of the store to his truck. *Oh no, he must have seen us,* Naomi thought, realizing the potential danger they were in. *I've got to lose this creep. Please help us, Lord Jesus.*

Isaac saddled Barley and raced to the Eshes' home. Soon the rambling white two-story house came into view. It was an older home constructed mostly of wood with some stone around the base. The rectangular building had two other smaller buildings attached to it where Chloe's paternal grandparents and great grandparents resided. These small dwellings were called the *Dawdi* and *Gross Dawdi* houses. Typically, an Amish father's parents and grandparents lived in the small houses, while their son or grandson lived in the large main house, and would take care of them until they passed on.

As soon as Isaac arrived at the Esh place, he jumped off Barley, too preoccupied to tie him to the hitching post. He walked up to the Eshes' door and pounded on it. "Peter Esh! This is Isaac Fisher – open the door." No one answered, so he pounded even louder but still received no response. "Peter Esh. Peter Esh," he called out as he walked to the barn and around the property.

There were rows and rows of corn, wheat, and barley growing on the plain and partly up the Eshes' hill as well. A row of trees lined the edge of the property. Isaac muttered, "No one's home. I don't see their buggy anywhere. They must still be at the mud sale. *Ach*, but it's dark already."

"Is somebody out there?" said an elderly gentleman's voice from one of the small dwellings.

"*Ach,* I hope I didn't wake you, Daniel Esh," Isaac replied respectfully to Chloe's grandfather, and then proceeded to ask, "Do you know if Peter and his family are back from the mud sale yet?"

"No, they have not returned yet. Is everything all right?" the kind man asked.

"*Dat* is worried about Joanna. She hasn't returned...we were hoping she'd be here," Isaac answered. "I'm sure she'll show up soon enough. Have a *gut* evening," Isaac said optimistically, not wanting to alarm the older gentleman, then turned and promptly headed back to his horse.

Immediately after turning onto the busy street, Naomi spotted a police officer behind her in the rear view mirror. She began turning the steering wheel back and forth, causing the vehicle to swerve all over the road. Joanna hadn't seen the police car and wondered what on earth Naomi was doing. Had she gone *ferhoodled* too? The cop turned on his bright, swirling red and blue lights and Naomi pulled over.

A brown haired, brown eyed, tall man in a black uniform stepped out of the black and white car behind them. The stalwart officer cautiously walked to Naomi's car window and she quickly explained the situation to the officer. He pulled out a small notebook, hastily wrote down some information, and then looked behind him. Right away, the officer flew to his car and took off after the ugly blue truck as it zoomed past, the loud scream of the siren piercing Joanna's ears.

The policeman had asked Naomi to pull over to the side of the road and wait for his return. Joanna watched the scene up ahead of them as the officer accosted her abductor and placed him in handcuffs. Shortly thereafter, she saw a second squad car haul the man away. After Naomi answered the officer's questions satisfactorily, they were free to go home. Both Naomi and Joanna gave out a sigh of relief, and then smiled at each other.

"Oh Naomi, *denki* so much for saving me," Joanna cried, as Naomi drove toward home. It was completely black outside now and Joanna was certain her family was worried over her disappearance.

"Don't thank me," Naomi replied, "thank God. He answered our prayers. He's the one who made sure that I was in that bathroom when you came along. I'm glad we have a God who loves us and takes care of us."

"*Jah*. Thank *Gott*, for sure and for certain," Joanna agreed, as Naomi pulled the car into the lane where Joanna's house was located. Joanna peered out the window, taking comfort in the familiar surroundings. Home had never looked so wonderful. "It's so *gut* to be home. *Denki, Gott,*" she whispered, as unbidden tears slipped down her cheeks once again.

She looked up and noticed several buggies. She never even stopped to think about *all* of the people that might be fretting over her disappearance. Bishop Hostettler's buggy, Chloe's family's, and even Philip King's buggy was there. "*Ach*, all the buggies...*Dat* must be worried," she said, as they stepped out of the car.

"Esther, did you call Naomi Fast?" Gideon Fisher quizzed as he peered out the door, recognizing Naomi's car. "I wonder if she heard the news about..." His eyes squinted. "Joanna! She has our Joanna with her!" he exclaimed at the sight of his daughter, while rushing outside.

"*Dat*!" Joanna sobbed. Oh, how wonderful-*gut* it was to be held in her father's strong protective arms! Gideon glanced at Naomi with concern on his face.

"Jo," Chloe called, hugging her so tight she could barely breathe. "What happened to you? Where did you go?"

Joanna said nothing. Noticing her obvious exhaustion, her father carried her inside and set her on the couch. The small group of friends and family eyed her curiously.

"Joanna, please tell us what has happened, *Liewi*," Mamm prodded gently.

"I – I..." Joanna fought for the words, but was still too shaken to share the ordeal. She glanced around at the familiar inquisitive faces of friends and neighbors and took comfort in the concern shown for her. She shivered as chills ran down her spine, and *Mamm* patted her back comfortingly.

Gideon Fisher turned to his eldest daughter and said, "Grace, get some hot peppermint tea for your sister." Grace nodded and headed toward the kitchen.

"Tis all right, Joanna," Bishop Hostettler spoke up, and then turned to the onlookers. "Let us leave the family, so they can get some rest, *jah*? Tis late and the girl is clearly exhausted...things always look better in the morning. Joanna is safe at home now and that is what matters." With that, one by one, the families left for their own homes.

"Naomi Fast, would ya mind stayin' awhile?" Gideon requested, and then called toward the kitchen, "Grace, bring a cup of tea for Naomi also." Naomi nodded in agreement.

"I'd be glad to help any way I can," the kind lady offered, then proceeded to answer Gideon's and Esther's questions. As she sat down on the couch, she recounted everything Joanna had shared with her regarding the incident, up to the point when they pulled into the Fishers' lane. Naomi herself even looked shaken by the ordeal.

"Let God be praised," Gideon proclaimed. "Our lost sheep has been found and she is safe in the fold again."

"How can we thank you?" Esther enquired gratefully.

"I'm just glad that God gave me guidance and showed me what to do," Naomi said, putting a hand on Joanna's arm. "This is one brave girl you have here," she said, smiling.

"*Jah,* very brave," *Mamm* and *Dat* agreed.

CHAPTER 4
Visiting

"Honor thy father and thy mother: that thy days may be long upon the land which the Lord thy God giveth thee." Exodus 20:12

Joanna yawned as she opened her eyes to see the beautiful sun rays streaming through her window. She had a room of her own so she didn't need to worry about waking anyone. Joanna shared the upstairs with her siblings, but there were four separate bedrooms so each of them could have their own privacy. She felt blessed to have one of the front bedrooms because the house had a small balcony out the front, which was rare for houses in her community. Oftentimes, she would walk out her door to behold God's glory in the night sky. The bedroom next to hers was Grace's, which also had access to the balcony. Across the hall from her bedroom was Isaac's room, and across from Grace's room is where Jonathan slept, with a set of steps to the downstairs between the two boys' rooms.

She took off her heart-shaped prayer *kapp*, gently brushed her waist-length hair, and then placed the covering back on her head. She removed her nightgown and changed into her plain dark green dress and full-length white apron. When Joanna opened her door, she was overwhelmed by the smell of eggs, bacon, and fresh baked bread. *Goodness. I must have slept too long. Why didn't anybody wake me to help prepare the food?* She wondered. As Joanna slowly ambled down the stairs, she could see her mother and Grace busily preparing breakfast.

"Good morning, *mein dochder*. Did you sleep well?"

"*Jah*, I slept well, *Mamm*," Joanna said. "Why didn't anybody wake me up to help make breakfast?" she asked, expressing her thoughts.

"You were pretty worn out last night after the ordeal. We thought you could use a little extra rest," Esther explained.

"*Denki, Mamm*." She smiled. "Would you like me to help set the table?"

"*Jah*, that would be *gut*," her mother replied.

Just then, Gideon, Isaac, and Jonathan came in from the barn. "Somethin' smells *wunderbaar*," Gideon commented, stomping the mud off his boots at the back porch. "Boys, you'd better take your boots off outside," he said to his sons.

"Sit down, Gideon, and have some hot coffee," Esther offered.

"Scrambled eggs – my favorite!" Jonathan exclaimed with a look of sheer delight on his face. He slid into the kitchen in his socks and nearly ran into his oldest sister, who stood in front of the stove preparing the eggs. As soon as she turned to the sink, Jonathan sneakily stuck a fork into the pan and shoved a bite into his mouth.

Grace turned back to the eggs just as Jonathan was about to steal a second bite. "*Ach*, Jonathan! What are you doing now?" She quickly shooed him out of the kitchen, threatening him with a wooden spatula. He popped the second bite into his mouth, and then scurried away with a mischievous grin.

"Here's the fresh milk from Daisy and Buttercup," Isaac said, handing the warm jars to his mother.

"*Denki*," she thanked her eldest son, and then called to the girls. "Is everything on the table?" The girls nodded and they all sat down.

Gideon bowed his head to signal he was about to pray. The family all bowed their heads as well, and then waited in silent reverence. After a short while, Gideon cleared his throat and the family once again lifted their heads. The prayers said at the table were usually prayed in silence, but on occasion they would speak aloud.

As the food was passed around the table, the Fisher family discussed their plans for the day. "We won't be leaving the farm today. *Mammi* Miriam has asked us if we would join her and *Dawdi* John for the noon meal," Gideon explained. "I told them we would love to. They're expecting us at eleven, so we can help with the preparations." Smiles lit up the table like the kerosene lantern that hung overhead.

"May I go fishin' with *Dawdi* John?" Jonathan asked excitedly. He, Isaac, Gideon, and John often made the short trip to the pond by foot. Many times they would bring back a large trout or two that Esther would prepare for dinner. Jonathan could taste the fish already.

"Let's see if *Dawdi* is up to going today, then we'll decide," his father replied. "And if we do, you have to promise not to eat the bait this time." Gideon chuckled at the remembrance. By the time the men arrived at the pond, the cheese and dough balls they used for bait were conspicuously missing. He figured they had just forgotten the bait at the house until Jonathan smiled broadly and they quickly identified the cheddar cheese stuck to his front teeth.

"Maybe we can pick some flowers, if they're in bloom yet," Grace suggested.

"Well, we can figure out all the details when we get there. Right now, let's clear the table and get the dishes washed," Esther said, in her usual practical tone. The men left the table and went outside while the ladies proceeded to clean up, anxious for the time when they would walk to the *dawdi haus*.

"*Kumm.* Come on in," *Mammi* Miriam said with a smile as bright as the sun, as the family walked into the house. Joanna and her sister went to the kitchen, and noticed the table was already set.

"May we help with anything?" Joanna offered.

"*Ach, nee.* I already have everything ready. I'm just waiting on the roast and vegetables in the oven," *Mammi* Miriam replied, and then thought to herself. "I think there are some flowers blooming in my garden right now, though. Will you girls take this vase and go pick some to set on the table?" The girls nodded, and then went outside in search of some of God's most beautiful creations.

Meanwhile, the men folk went to the small living room. The room was sparsely decorated with only a small green sofa, a wooden rocking chair that had been a hand-made gift from Gideon, and a coffee table. A small brick fireplace provided a focal point and adorned the corner of the room. The men conversed about the weather and other areas of interest, while the women did likewise in the kitchen.

After the meal was over, the men headed outside. "Miriam, I'm going down to the pond with the boys. Hopefully, we'll be bringing back supper," *Dawdi* John said, as he went for his fishing pole.

The women folk now sat in the small living room, as *Mammi* Miriam walked briskly to her bedroom. "I have something to show you," Miriam said enthusiastically. It sounded as if *Mammi* was rummaging through her hope chest.

"I wonder what it could be..." Joanna thought aloud. The girls looked at each other, and then at Esther who was curious herself.

Miriam finally appeared with a large colorful blanket in her arms. The girls and Esther gasped in unison. "Oh, Miriam, it's absolutely gorgeous," Esther complimented.

"Do you think so? It's for Isaac...to set up his home someday," *Mammi* Miriam said with misty eyes. "It's not finished yet, but it should be in time."

Joanna and Grace both gaped at the beautiful quilt, as they gently fingered the small stitches. Joanna thought of all the quilts that she and Chloe had perused at the mud sale and decided this was every bit as gorgeous as those. "Look at all the bright colors – just like the flowers in your garden, *Mammi.* I think the Double Wedding Ring pattern is my favorite," Grace stated.

"Then I'll just have to make one for you too...when your time comes, that is," *Mammi* Miriam replied, smiling. Joanna noticed that Grace blushed after *Mammi*'s comment.

"Now, we mustn't let Isaac know about *Mammi*'s surprise," Esther warned. Both girls nodded, indicating their agreement to keep the secret.

Miriam returned after putting the quilt away in her bedroom. "Now, who would like a slice of apple pie?" she asked, then headed to the kitchen. She proceeded to remove two large pies from the oven. "We'll just enjoy a little dessert until the men get back from fishing, *jah*?"

Joanna breathed a sigh of relief when the family returned home for the evening. Neither *Dawdi* nor *Mammi* had asked her about her abduction and for that she was thankful. The sooner she forgot about the whole ordeal, the better.

Barrett Winston stepped in line behind the other prisoners. It felt good to be out in the fresh air after being cooped up in his small cell. He looked around and noticed the high chain-link fences with coiled razor wire on top. *No escaping here,* he thought.

When they reached the center of the yard he was confronted by a fellow inmate. "Hey Winston, how much time you got?"

"Twenty years," Barrett growled back.

"Twenty years, what'd you do?" the large muscular inmate asked.

"None of your business, Jones. Now run off and find yourself a little dolly to play with," he responded feistily.

A short, tattooed, dark-haired prisoner joined the two men. "I'll tell you what he did, Jones. I heard he's in here for child abduction. He's one of those sickos that does wicked things to innocent little children."

"Children?" Jones clenched his fists and popped his knuckles, summoning a few other inmates. "Do you know what we do to worthless losers like you?" Barrett gulped and braced himself for what was inevitably coming next.

CHAPTER 5
Back to School

"Lo, children are an heritage of the LORD: and the fruit of the womb is his reward." Psalm 127:3

The beautiful, old one-room schoolhouse sat at the top of a small hill. It sported a fresh coat of white paint, which the men in the community had recently completed, along with a few repairs. A set of swings and several handmade see-saws were available in the school yard for the children to play on. The many trees around provided a nice shaded area for a picnic lunch, or a haven from the sun.

Grace and Joanna marched silently to the one-room schoolhouse as Jonathan ran up ahead to meet his friends. They and the other scholars from Paradise attended every year when it wasn't planting or harvesting season. Even though Isaac was sixteen, he no longer needed to attend school. He now stayed home to help out his father in his woodworking shop, and would sometimes volunteer his time to make repairs on the schoolhouse. Amish children were only required to attend school up until the eighth grade, assuming a vocational education thereafter.

Joanna was grateful for a moment of peace. It had only been two days since her abduction had taken place. Since then, she vowed that she'd never go anywhere alone again. In fact, the thought of leaving the house this morning frightened her. At times like this, she was thankful for her brothers and sisters.

"*Hullo*, Joanna – wait for me." Joanna didn't even need to turn around to see who it was. She knew that voice very well. It was Chloe.

She jogged up to them, panting all the while. Chloe, who usually loved to talk, simply grasped Joanna's hand and began walking at a slow, steady pace. She must've sensed her friend's need for quiet. When they reached the schoolyard, Joanna suddenly stopped and took a deep breath. She hoped she wouldn't have to explain to everyone. Sure enough, scholars from all directions came running toward them, pounding her with questions.

"Where were you?" Matthew Riehl asked.

"What happened? Were you scared?" asked another schoolmate.

"Leave Joanna alone," Chloe declared protectively. "She doesn't want to talk about it, so just let her be," she repeated.

"I'll tell you what happened," Sadie Lapp announced, eager to share all that she knew with the whole class. "A huge, scary, *ferhoodled* man came up to her and grabbed her. He said ..."

Sadie's voice trailed off as Joanna and Chloe walked around the side of the schoolhouse. "*Ach,* Chloe, I'm trying to forget what happened, but it's so hard. I don't know what to do. That terrible man..." Joanna's voice pleaded softly for help.

"Never mind that Sadie Lapp. She always sticks her nose where it doesn't belong," Chloe said in disdain. "You can pray that *Der Herr* will help you forget," her friend suggested.

"*Jah,* I've done that already. But you don't understand, Chloe. Everywhere I go I'm afraid that man is going to come and take me away again. Every time I hear an *Englischer* car, I think it might be him."

"That isn't going to happen, Jo. Didn't you say that the police officer stopped him? I think the *Englischers* put people in jail for that sorta thing, *jah*? You're safe here. Besides," Chloe continued, "I don't think *Gott* will let that happen to you again. He saved you, *jah*?"

"*Jah,* He did," Joanna agreed.

"I'm sure you'll forget as time goes by. Just try not to think about it so much. Try to think about something *gut* – like the *boppli* that my *mamm* is going to have this fall." Chloe waited for Joanna's reaction.

"You're jokin'." Joanna smiled, questioning Chloe with her big blue eyes.

"No, I'm not," Chloe confirmed.

"*Ach*, Chloe, that's the best news. I bet you're excited." Joanna grinned broadly. And by the look in her eyes, Chloe agreed.

DONG…DONG…DONG…DONG, the school bell declared. At the familiar sound, both girls walked confidently into the schoolhouse with the other scholars.

During lunch time, Joanna and Chloe talked about the new *boppli* that would be born this winter.

"I hope it is a boy," Chloe said optimistically. "We have plenty of girls in the house. With me, Rachel, Anna, Abigail, and Ruthie, *Mamm* has enough help. But *Dat* only has Stephen to help him. I know *Dat* and Stephen both wouldn't mind havin' another man around to help out with farmin' and what not."

"*Jah*, a boy would be nice," Joanna agreed, and then noticed the other children playing. "Let's play hide and seek now. I'll count first and you go hide."

Joanna stood by the old oak tree and covered her eyes. She began counting; instinctively knowing Chloe would run off. "One…two…three…" Joanna counted while Chloe searched for good place to hide.

When Joanna finished counting, she set off looking for Chloe. "Ready or not, here I come." She stopped short when she noticed Chloe standing near the corner of the schoolhouse, in plain sight of all things. *Why is Chloe just standing there?*

Joanna thought, and slowly snuck up behind her. "You're it, Chloe," she exclaimed.

"Shh..." Chloe hissed. "Look, there's my sister Rachel and your brother Isaac – what are they doing?"

Joanna carefully peered around the back corner of the schoolhouse. Sure enough, Isaac and Rachel were standing by the back door. "They're talking and laughing," Joanna answered.

"Do you think they're sweet on each other?" Chloe puzzled, gaping at the sight.

"That's what it looks like to me," Joanna mused aloud. Her eyes suddenly grew wide. "Isaac just got his courtin' buggy. Maybe he's going to court our teacher, your sister..."

"Maybe they'll even get married...and then have *bopplin,*" Chloe added.

"Then we'd be related – like sisters!"

"It would be *wunderbaar* to have you for a sister, Jo." Chloe beamed at the prospect, her eyes sparkling. "That's the best kind of sister to have – your best friend."

"Sisters." The two girls celebrated the possibility.

"Sisters?" asked a familiar young man's voice. The girls whipped around and found Isaac and their teacher – both of them looking baffled. Joanna could feel heat rush to her cheeks.

"Oh, n-n-nothing," Chloe stammered, attempting to mask the discovery of her sister's possible secret courtship.

"We were j-just discussing Mary Esh's *b-boppli,*" Joanna stuttered.

"It'd be *gut* to have an-nother brother, rather than to have another sister, *jah*?" Chloe stumbled over the words as she spoke them. "B-b-because I have s-so many sisters already."

"Girls, why are you speaking that way? I've never heard either of you stutter before," Rachel asked quizzically, lowering her eyebrows. "Are you feeling all right?"

Neither girl explained, nor did they care to. Isaac and Rachel would surely both be nigh unto death with embarrassment if they had any idea what their sisters had been discussing.

"*Jah*, we're fine," both girls shrieked in unison before scampering back to the front schoolyard – leaving behind Rachel and Isaac, who were thoroughly bewildered and even more confused than before.

CHAPTER 6
The New Job

"Even a child is known by his doings, whether his work be pure, and whether it be right." Proverbs 20:11

Joanna happily hummed a hymn from the *Ausbund* as she sauntered into her bedroom to change for chorin' time. This was one of her favorite times of the day. She lifted her dark blue dress and apron off the hook on her wall. After removing her school dress and slipping into her chorin' dress, she then took the straight pins from her drawer and pinned on her apron.

Once Joanna had retrieved her basket, she skipped outside to the small chicken coop. This year her family only had fifty of the feathery fowl, twenty white, twenty-nine red, and a single rooster. She quickly gathered the eggs into the wire basket and scattered the feed for the chickens, trying to avoid the rooster which could sometimes cause trouble.

Next, she went into the barn to feed and water the horses. She walked through the two large barn doors that housed the large animals and went directly to one of the stalls. "*Hullo, Bloobier. Hiya,* Cinnamon," she greeted the content animals in a sing-song voice, "How are you doin', Barley?"

She fed Cinnamon some alfalfa by hand and the animal enjoyed Joanna's attention, always making the most of it. Joanna giggled. "You silly thing, you're all *ferhoodled* in your head – just the way I like you." Just then Barley snorted, as if he was trying to say, "What about me?" confirming his envy.

Joanna turned. "*Ach*, Barley. Why are you jealous? It's not as if you don't get plenty of attention," she said teasingly, over her shoulder. Then she walked across the narrow passageway to Barley's stall and stroked his mane, feeding him by hand just as she had with Cinnamon earlier. "You're so fast," she murmured to Barley, remembering when she and Chloe had raced him and Cayenne, one of the horses owned by the Esh family.

The girls wouldn't be allowed to ride horses anymore when they'd become ladies – just three years down the road. *Dat* and *Mamm* didn't like the idea of the girls racing, for fear she'd be injured. "Sometimes horses can be unpredictable animals, especially if spooked," *Dat* had warned. But that hadn't stopped Joanna and Chloe. They couldn't help but race the beautiful creatures, despite their parents' concerns. They did feel a bit guilty afterward, though. *The Bible did say to honor their parents... but why would God make horses if they couldn't race them in the first place?* After all, their parents hadn't outright forbidden them to ride...

Joanna shook herself from her musings and moved on to *Bloobier's* stall. They had named the white colt Blueberry because when she was born she had large, beautiful blue eyes the color of blueberries. *Bloobier* was her name in Pennsylvania Dutch, the nickname Joanna liked to use for the blue-eyed mare.

After feeding Blueberry, she continued on to the last occupied stall where the new horse stood waiting. Isaac's courting buggy horse they'd purchased at the auction. Joanna shivered as she remembered that day, then quickly pushed the thought aside and tried to focus on the magnificent animal before her. The horse appeared skittish and scared, probably not yet accustomed to her new surroundings. She snorted, throwing her head back. Joanna moved slowly so she wouldn't frighten the creature, and held out a long orange carrot. "*Kumm*," she spoke gently, and the horse gradually came near and began to nibble on the carrot. Feeling compassionate toward the new animal, she began to sing a *liede*. The horse had visibly calmed down and she was even eating grain from Joanna's hand. For this, she was pleased. "You are a nice horse, *jah*?" she encouraged, gently stroking her mane.

Joanna studied the large equine creature. Mainly black in color, except for the white star on her forehead and white socks on all four feet, the horse was very beautiful in build, strong and sleek. The sheen of her black coat was lovely as well. Just looking at it made her mind run wild with excitement. *Just wait until I get to race her...that is, if Isaac lets me.*

Joanna strolled into the kitchen where her mother was cooking supper. As she stepped into the room a delicious fragrance permeated the air. Joanna closed her eyes trying to guess what the menu was for the evening meal. She smiled, *fresh bread, roast beef, vegetables...*

"Joanna, I need you to set the table," Esther said.

"Sure, *Mamm*." Joanna took out six plates from the cabinets and six forks from a drawer which held the silverware. She headed toward the table and set the plates and forks down one by one.

Dat and Isaac had come in from the barn, after stomping the mud off their boots. They had just this week received a large order for a dining room set: a kitchen table, eight chairs, and a china hutch. Installing a telephone in the barn had really helped their family business. Now, they received calls for orders several times per week. Most of the Amish in their community didn't own telephones, neither were they allowed to. This was because they felt that having a telephone in the home was opening up a door to the *Englischers'* world, one that all too often lead to wickedness and a departure from the Amish church. Just one of the ways the church leadership attempted to keep members in the fold, thus preserving their unique way of life. The bishop and the other elders of their district did, however, sometimes allow telephones in the barn for business purposes.

Esther and Grace set the food out on the table: green beans, a creamed beef dish, and fresh-baked bread. *Oh well, at least my guess was close,* Joanna thought as she eyed the delicious feast. Oh, how Joanna loved fresh bread with slow-churned butter on top. Just the thought of it made her mouth water.

Gideon came and sat down at the head of the table, the place where an Amish father always sat, demonstrating his leadership in the home. Esther, his wife, sat next to him with each of the children beside, or across from her. After every family member was seated at the table, they all bowed their heads in silence. When Gideon was finished with the silent prayer, he cleared his throat. Each family member then served themselves a helping of food, with the exception of Jonathan, whom Esther helped in order to avoid disaster.

When the meal was finished, Gideon said another silent prayer, and then everyone was excused from the table. The women cleared the table, and Esther joined Gideon in the living room shortly thereafter. Grace and Joanna moved to the sink to wash the dishes, and then retired to the living room where the rest of the family was. In the evenings, the Fisher family would often read the Bible, play games, or read an Amish publication. This was the place where Joanna felt the safest, amongst her loved ones.

"Joanna," Gideon spoke, lifting his eyes from the newspaper, "are you still wantin' a job?"

"For sure and for certain!" Joanna replied with excitement. "What did you find, *Dat*?"

"It says here, 'Wanted: reliable person to deliver honey in Paradise. Part-Time. Please call (717)915-0027.' You could use your scooter to make the deliveries. Would you like me to call the number and find out where they're located?" Dat asked.

"Oh, yes. *Denki, Dat.*" Joanna smiled.

Gideon arose from his seat and headed toward the barn. He returned several minutes later. "Well, it looks like you may have yourself a job," her dad said encouragingly. "I'll have Isaac take you to meet the woman Friday after school. She seemed real nice. She said she had health problems and couldn't do the deliveries on her own anymore. I think the place may be just down the street from Phillip King's farm, so you shouldn't have any trouble finding it."

Joanna smiled...a job at last!

CHAPTER 7

A New Friend

"A man that hath friends must shew himself friendly: and there is a friend that sticketh closer than a brother." Proverbs 18:24

Isaac stood waiting next to his buggy as Joanna trudged out of the schoolhouse on Friday. Today they were going to see Joanna's new employer. Isaac helped her into his new courting buggy and soon they drove off. "Is there something wrong?" Isaac asked, noticing concern on her face. "I thought you'd be excited about your new job."

"Just nervous, I guess," Joanna replied. She didn't want to bother Isaac about her frequent nightmares. "I hope the lady that I'm working for will like me."

"*Dat* said she sounded real nice on the telephone. I think you'll be fine...besides, who wouldn't like a sweet eleven-year-old Amish girl?" Isaac said, trying to pull a smile from her lips.

"Don't overdo it, Isaac," she said, smiling. "But thanks for trying to encourage me."

"*Trying* to encourage you? I got you to smile, didn't I?" He grinned.

"*Jah. Denki, Bruder.*"

They rode along in silence now as they passed a few farms, drove over the covered bridge that stretched across Miller's Creek, and arrived on the outskirts of town. Right down the street and across the road from Philip King's herb shop was a small, dark-blue cottage with white trim and gables to match.

A lovely garden graced the front yard – a quarter of it contained culinary herbs such as parsley and dill, another portion grew young sprouting vegetable plants, in a beautiful third quarter bloomed colorful, fragile flowers in their beginning stages, and in the midst of the fourth section stood a large, sturdy oak tree. Its branches hung over the house as if to protect it, which would also provide plenty of shade in the summertime. An old wooden swing hung from one of the branches of the large oak tree. Joanna felt the house looked a bit spooky, especially when she saw the swing blow in the soft breeze.

Goose bumps suddenly emerged on Joanna's arms. "Tis some house, *jah,* Isaac?" Joanna commented. But Isaac didn't seem to think there was anything scary about it, at least he didn't act like it.

"*Jah*, I guess." Isaac couldn't understand her apprehension. "*Kumm*, Joanna. Let's meet your new boss." She looked around as they slowly walked up to the door. The cottage had a beautiful porch that seemed to wrap around the whole house – it was quite lovely. A small white wicker sofa with bright throw pillows decorated the porch. An empty rocking chair that sported the same design and colors gently rocked in the breeze. She took a deep breath before Isaac knocked on the door. *I'm glad I'll be working for a lady and not a man,* Joanna breathed a sigh of relief. She was still uncomfortable around strangers after her frightening ordeal.

A woman's voice sounded through the door, as they heard the click of the lock turning and a chain unlatching. "Just a minute, please." The door cracked open a little, and then finally opened all the way. The familiar woman peered out. "Joanna Fisher? Did *you* come here for the job I posted?" Naomi asked in disbelief.

"Naomi Fast, I can't believe it's you. I didn't know you sold honey." Joanna smiled at the pleasant surprise, relief flooding her soul.

Naomi chuckled. "Well, there are many things you don't know about me. Except that maybe I'm a crazy driver." She hoped bringing that up wouldn't bring back painful memories for Joanna.

Joanna and Isaac both laughed. "*Jah,* thank *Gott* for that. Now I know why your name is Naomi *FAST,*" Joanna replied, which made them all laugh even harder.

The playful banter subsided and they got down to business. "Let's go out back and I'll show you the bee hives," Naomi said. After quite a long walk to the edge of her property, they finally reached the hives. "This is where the honey is made; I thought you'd like to see it."

"I don't want to get too close, I've already been stung a couple of times," Joanna shared, hesitant to step forward to the many rows of white boxes.

"Well, it's not essential to be near the bees for your job, so don't worry. I just assumed you'd like to know a little bit about them and see where they are kept. They are actually fascinating creatures. Did you know that one honey bee only makes about 1/12 teaspoon of honey in its whole life?"

"*Ach*, no...and they're always so busy too," Joanna commented.

Isaac piped in curiously, "How much honey does each hive make?"

"Well, that depends on the weather. Normally, when it's not too damp, each hive will produce about fifty to sixty pounds of honey per year," Naomi answered.

"So, with twenty hives..." Isaac said, mentally counting, "that's about a thousand pounds or more a year? Wow! No wonder you need extra help."

"It's actually not as much as it sounds. For example, some of my customers buy five gallons at a time. That equates to about sixty pounds, and that's just for one customer," Naomi explained.

Naomi proceeded to show Joanna and Isaac around her property. It was mostly flatland with a small sloping hill toward the back of her fifty acres. The bee hives were kept close to the small hill because Naomi didn't want the children playing near them. Directly behind the house, she had about two acres that were fenced in. A long clothes line stretched from the back porch to one of the trees in the yard. The fenced area also housed some children's play equipment – a large wooden structure that had a slide, two swings, some plastic rocks to climb up, and a pole to slide down. There was also a colorful see-saw and a trampoline. Joanna had never seen so many unnecessary items. And although they looked like fun, she wondered who would ever have that much extra time to play on them.

Finally, they came back to the house. "Would the two of you like some lemonade?" the kind lady asked them.

"*Nee, denki.* I mean, no, thank you. We should be starting back home soon," Isaac answered for them both. Truthfully, he was eager to get home so he could prepare for his date with Rachel tonight.

"Do you have any questions about the job, Joanna?" Naomi looked at her.

"Well, I was wondering...would it be okay if my friend Chloe comes along with me? I'd rather not go out by myself anymore."

"I understand, and that would be perfectly fine with me. As a matter of fact, I think it's a wonderful idea. I have a lot of customers already and I get new ones every week," Naomi replied approvingly, and then added, "By the way, Joanna, I'm really glad it was *you* that came today. I have a feeling that we're going to become good friends."

"Denki, Naomi." Joanna smiled genuinely, looking into her eyes with affection. This would indeed be a good, safe place to work.

I can't wait to tell Mamm and Dat who I'll be working for, Joanna thought excitedly, as Cinnamon trotted along. *And Chloe.* She mused. *No, I won't tell Chloe. I'll keep it a secret and surprise her, too.*

"Did you hear me, Joanna?" Isaac asked, interrupting her thoughts.

"Hear what?"

"I guess you *didn't* hear me. I asked you about working for Naomi Fast. I said, don't you think it's a coincidence that your employer turned out to be Naomi, after all that's happened?"

"Do you think I'm workin' with Naomi for a special reason, Isaac?" The thought had never occurred to her.

"Could be." He shrugged.

They both sat quietly and pondered that for a while. Then Joanna spoke up, "Isaac, did you see any children there?"

Isaac thought about it. "No. Did you?"

"Nee. I didn't hear any either." Joanna looked straight ahead at the covered bridge they were about to tunnel.

Isaac slowed Barley as they entered the shaded enclosure. "They probably went somewhere with Naomi's husband, *jah*?" The sunshine beat warm on their shoulders while they continued toward home, passing neighboring houses and farms. Levi and Joshua Hostettler waved a hello from the back of a plow when they passed by the Hostettlers' farm and they waved back.

"There were a lot of toys in the backyard. I wonder how many *kinner* she's got."

"Maybe we should have asked her," Isaac replied.

"*Jah.* I'll ask her next time," Joanna said, as they pulled into their drive.

That evening, there was a knock at the door. Bishop Hostettler stood on the porch, his expression unreadable. "*Hullo,* Gideon. I hope you and your family are well this evening."

"We are," Joanna's father replied. "What brings you out tonight, Judah?" he asked his familiar friend.

"I actually wanted to speak with Joanna outside. Of course, you may come as well," the bishop stated matter-of-factly.

"Very well, I will get her." Gideon then proceeded to the living room and returned with Joanna. They all stepped outside onto the back porch, and then sat down.

The bishop cut to the chase. "Joanna, the reason I am here is to clarify a few things about your abduction. I understand that you were alone when the incident took place. Am I correct?"

"*Jah,*" Joanna answered timidly.

"How long were you alone for?" he asked, concern shown in his eyes.

"Not long at all. We heard Chloe's *mamm* call, but I needed to use the restroom. Chloe went to her *mamm*, and I turned to find the restroom, which wasn't far away. But as soon as I turned the corner, that's when..." Joanna's voice trailed off, she was unable to speak anymore, not willing to replay the scene in her head again.

"I do not wish to add to your distress, but I wanted to let you know that the elders are going to make an announcement at the Sunday-Go-To-Meeting in two days. We have learned something from this incident, as I am sure you have too." He paused, stroking his long, graying beard. Although Judah Hostettler wasn't much older than Gideon, his facial hair was much grayer. Joanna attributed the fact to the sometimes demanding role a bishop had in trying to juggle the needs of his family with the needs of the community. The position derived much sympathy from the People, especially when a bishop had an especially large family, as did Judah. "We want the People, especially our young people, to be kept safe. We have decided that no young person should ever be out in public alone, but always have another person with them. I believe this will prevent any more problems, such as the one you experienced."

"That sounds like a reasonable request," Gideon commented, looking from the bishop to his daughter.

"If you feel uncomfortable about attending Meeting on Sunday, you may stay home. I spoke with Brother Esh and he has agreed to allow Chloe to stay behind with you. Your *vadder* has already agreed to it, as well."

"*Denki.*" Joanna was grateful that her church district had a kindhearted bishop. She'd heard that they weren't very common amongst their People. And although he could be stern at times, he genuinely cared for the People of Paradise.

CHAPTER 8
Honey

"Pleasant words are as an honeycomb, sweet to the soul, and health to the bones." Proverbs 16:24

Joanna jumped out of her sleep at the rooster's crow. She sighed heavily as she sat up in her bed, wiping the sweat from her brow. She had, once again, been bombarded with frightening nightmares. *When will they ever go away?* She thought.

The dreadful man, by whom she was kidnapped, seemed to haunt her almost nightly. She saw herself riding with him in his truck again, but this time she was wearing the boys clothing that he had given her. He drove her out to a small, decrepit old house in the middle of nowhere. They got out of the truck and she looked around. She realized that there wasn't a single soul around for miles – she could scream, but nobody would hear. He took her arm roughly and they walked to the house and...

that's when she woke up, thankfully. She did not want to find out what would happen next, had her dream continued. It was too frightening. Tears filled her eyes and she began shivering. *Oh,* Gott, *please help me. Thank you that it was just a dream. It was just a dream,* she reminded herself.

She took a deep breath, and then managed to compose herself. Somehow, she had to push these ugly thoughts out of her mind. She was safe at home now, wasn't she? She arose quickly from her bed and donned her purple dress, black shoes and stockings, black apron and white prayer kapp – after pinning her hair up. It was only a little after five o'clock on Saturday. *Today I'm going to visit Naomi Fast and start my new job.* That was something positive to think about. *And if Chloe can go with me, she'll be able to earn money for her family, too. Yes, this will be a* gut *day.*

After breakfast and chores were completed, Joanna took her new green scooter from the barn and headed toward the Esh house. Her parents had given her the scooter as a birthday gift last year. *I hope Chloe's mamm will allow her to go with me,* she thought. As she rode into the Eshes' driveway, she saw Stephen, Chloe's only brother, in the field. She felt sorry for him. Since he was the only boy in the family, he had it pretty rough. There was a lot of work to do around the Esh farm and Peter Esh often hired other young Amish men to help work in the field. Daniel Esh, Chloe's grandfather, helped out some, but he was getting up in years. Even though Chloe was a tomboy, she seldom worked in the fields. Her father didn't want to burden the women folk in his home, as he felt the responsibility to provide rested on his shoulders. Joanna hoped the Esh family would be blessed with another boy, for Peter's and Stephen's sake.

Although Chloe sometimes played with Stephen, he still didn't have someone especially close to him. And even though he and Levi Hostettler seemed to be pretty *gut* friends, Joanna sensed he had no one that he could really confide in. Someone he could share his deepest, darkest secrets with and know they would never tell a soul. That's how it was with her and Chloe, and that's how she wanted it to stay. But perhaps boys didn't need that kind of companionship?

Joanna quickly parked her scooter and walked up the steps to the door. Just as soon as she knocked, the door flung open revealing Chloe's mother. Mary Esh looked rather piqued. "*Hullo,* Mary Esh. How are doing today?" Joanna asked politely.

"I'm feeling a bit tired today, but I'll get by," Chloe's mother answered.

Oh no, Joanna thought to herself. *She probably won't want Chloe to go.* She forged ahead anyway. "I'm starting my new job today delivering honey and I was hoping that Chloe could come along. She would be back by dinner time. After what happened at the mud sale, I-I'm afraid to go anywhere by myself," she pleaded. Oh, how she detested bringing up that wretched day!

Mary paused, sensing the poor girl's distress. "I think I can get along without her today," she answered compassionately. She turned from the door, inviting Joanna inside.

Mary went to the bottom of the stairs to summon Chloe. "Joanna wants you to go with her to her new job. You may go if your chores are done," she told her daughter as Chloe hasted down the stairs.

"I just finished them, *Mamm.*" Chloe smiled brightly, and then turned to her friend. "And I would love to go with you, Joanna. Let me get my scooter."

"*Denki,* Mary Esh," Joanna called, as they headed out to the barn. She wanted to tell her congratulations on her *boppli,* but that was not their way. Pregnancies were usually kept quiet until it was too obvious to keep secret anymore. Joanna felt privileged to be one of the few privy to the wonderful news.

While Joanna waited for Chloe to get her scooter, Abigail Esh walked up to her. "Joanna, may I go with you and Chloe?" she asked softly.

"Sorry, Abby, not this time. Chloe and I are starting a new job," Joanna replied. It was hard not say yes to sweet little Abby. She was little for six, had beautiful green eyes that bored right into you, strawberry-blond hair, and a smile that brightened the world.

"Abigail, go see if *Mamm* needs help with Ruthie," Chloe suggested. "I found my scooter. We're off now, *jah*?"

"*Jah,*" Joanna answered. "Goodbye, Abby. I'll see you when we get back, and then maybe we can swing, okay?"

The young girl's eyes brightened. "*Denki,* Joanna!"

Joanna and Chloe waved goodbye to Abigail and took off in a hurry. The girls rode through puddles and around rocks. The beauty of the countryside was everywhere. The trees seemed to scream, '*Look at me*' as they modeled the first faint flowers of spring. Joanna loved Paradise. It was where she was born and where she desired to stay forever.

"Let's race, Jo," Chloe challenged. Not waiting for an answer, she took off ahead of Joanna and dirt flew into Joanna's mouth, hitting her in the face.

"Chloe, stop! Ya got me all dirty," Joanna hollered after her friend.

Chloe stopped and waited patiently for Joanna to catch up with her. When Joanna did sidle up next to her friend, she was panting. "I guess racing was a bad idea," Chloe remarked and then giggled. "It looks like you've been making mud pies – and eating them too!"

Joanna couldn't help but laugh also. "Thanks to you. *Ach*, I must look a sight." She attempted to wipe the caked mud off of her face, only smearing it in the process.

"*Jah*, sorry about that," Chloe answered, removing a handkerchief from her sleeve. She helped Joanna clean her face and then they continued on to their destination at normal speeds.

I'm glad Naomi Fast is so nice. I'm going to like working for her. Joanna thought, as she and Chloe found the address and went into the driveway. *At least she doesn't live too far from my house.* Chloe tapped on the door and Joanna waited to see her reaction.

"Hello, Joanna," the familiar voice greeted her at the door. "And this is your friend Chloe, right?"

"Naomi Fast?" Chloe asked in disbelief.

"I do believe we have met already, Chloe." Naomi smiled, and then gestured with her hand. "Come on in, girls." She led the girls to the small sectional in her living room. "Let me get you some lemonade and you can sip on it while we go over your delivery schedule for the day."

"How many customers will we be delivering to today?" Joanna asked, taking note of the mostly plain furnishings. Naomi's place wasn't much different from her own home. She did have *electric* though, but there wasn't a television in the room like she'd once seen inside an *Englischer's* house. She'd heard most *Englisch* homes contained the wicked devices.

"You only have ten for this morning. I figured I would start you out slowly, and then as you get the hang of it, I'll add more customers to your route. Most of them are around here, so you won't have to go too far just yet."

"That sounds *gut,*" Joanna said.

"And I'd like the two of you to join me for lunch when you're done," Naomi insisted.

"That would be *wunderbaar,*" Joanna exclaimed, looking at Chloe, who agreed.

"Here is your list of customers. You have the Starks, which will be just down the street on the left-hand side; the Alcorns, which are across the street from them; the Kleins, the Hamms, and the Tuftses, which all live on Miller Road. I've written all of the addresses down in case you get mixed up. I'm pretty sure you know where the rest of the customers live – the Yoders, the Bontragers, the Zooks, the Millers, and the Gingriches."

"*Jah*, we know where they live." Chloe confirmed the names of the Amish that lived in their church district.

"Then it looks like you're all set," Naomi said.

Joanna and Chloe proceeded to take the honey and carefully loaded the amber filled jars into the front baskets of their scooters. In no time, they were off to deliver the honey to the names Naomi had written on the list. As they collected the money from each sale, Joanna placed it into an envelope and stuck it into her apron pocket.

Rumspringa, or the running-around years, typically begins when Amish boys and girls in the community turn sixteen. At this time, they are allowed to explore the outside world and then eventually decide if they want to be baptized and officially join the Amish church.

A young man's parents usually provide him with his own courting buggy in which he can begin to court a young woman. He will ask her permission, and then she'll let her beau drive her around in his buggy after Sunday night Singings – a special time when young folk gather together to sing, play games, and fellowship.

Likewise, at this age a young woman may receive a hope chest to store things that she'll use when she gets married: special quilts, tablecloths, tea sets, etc. Courtships are kept secret in the Amish communities. Sometimes the parents don't even know who their son or daughter is courting until just prior to the publishing, or public announcement, of their upcoming wedding. The wedding will normally take place within a few weeks after it's published, typically after the fall harvest.

Isaac Fisher and Rachel Esh rode past an open meadow in Isaac's new courting buggy. A gentle breeze flowed through the buggy bringing with it the delightful fragrances of spring flowers.

"How do you like it?" Isaac asked, gesturing to his new rig and attempting to quell the pride that threatened his being.

Rachel pulled her eyes away from the two butterflies flitting in the sunshine near a copse of trees. *Perhaps they are a match...I wonder if Isaac and I are a match as well.* She glanced over at Isaac and caught his smiling eyes under his straw hat and her heart leaped. "*Jah*, 'tis nice, Isaac."

Isaac attempted to calm his nerves, taking a deep breath. It wasn't easy riding with a girl a year older than him. Most likely, she'd already attended many singings and Isaac had no idea how many young men she'd already ridden home with, especially since the girls in their district were allowed to attend singings at fourteen. At this very moment, he didn't like that allowance. Why couldn't their girls start attending singings at sixteen like they did over in Bishop Bender's district? He wiped a sweaty palm on his trousers trying to summon enough courage to ask this beautiful woman to be his steady girl. "Rachel, I was hoping to ask you to go to the singing with me on Sunday."

"Are you *hopin'* to ask me, or are you asking me?" Rachel teased.

"*Ach,* quit teasing, Rachel." Isaac smiled. "I'm nervous enough as it is."

Rachel giggled. "I thought that might be why you've been so quiet. *Jah,* I will go to the singin' with ya, Isaac," she replied, blushing.

Isaac took a relieved breath and gently caught Rachel's hand. "*Gut.*"

"What'd you name your new horse?" She quickly changed the subject, lest her cheeks become brighter than the tomatoes she and *Mamm* canned last harvest. *He's holding my hand!*

"I was thinkin' of naming her Racer because she used to be a race horse. I couldn't come up with anything else. Unless you have any suggestions..." Isaac smiled at his girl.

Rachel pondered for a moment, assessing the large creature. "Well, she is black...how about Midnight?"

"I'd say Midnight fits her right fine with her shiny black coat and the star between her eyes. I like it. How do you like that, Midnight?" On cue, the horse snorted her reply, as if agreeing to the name. "Midnight it is." Isaac laughed along with Rachel, as they rode merrily through the countryside.

"You want to see how fast she can run?" Isaac asked, eager to try out his new horse.

"We can go a little faster, but I don't want to go full-speed. She looks like she can run a pretty fast clip," Rachel replied apprehensively.

Isaac clicked his tongue and slapped the reins. Midnight took off a little quicker than he'd expected. Isaac pulled on the reins, but Midnight did not slow down.

"Whoa, Midnight," Isaac called to the horse. Midnight began to slow until they drove near a leftover puddle from the last rain. The horse spooked at the sight of her reflection in the water and took off again. She abruptly veered to the right, which caused the buggy to swing into the other lane. Rachel hung on for dear life, while Isaac attempted to gain control of the frightened mare. The oncoming car slammed on the brakes, but could not stop...

At about 11:30, Joanna and Chloe returned to the Fast residence. "You girls finished the route a little quicker than I'd expected. I hope you didn't run into any problems," Naomi commented.

"*Nee,* we didn't," the girls said, reassuringly. "There was one customer though, Elsa Klein, that wanted us to stay and talk awhile. After about ten minutes, we told her we needed to get back."

"Sometimes I feel sorry for the elderly woman. She doesn't have any relatives to care for her, so she lives all alone there. She says the honey helps with her arthritis – she mixes it with apple cider vinegar and water, and then drinks it down. I try to visit her once in a while," Naomi replied.

"Perhaps we can visit her sometime, too," Joanna voiced her thoughts. "I guess living in an Amish community has its advantages. Our elderly people always have someone to care for them, even if they have no relatives living. We feel it is our responsibility to take care of them, like the Bible says."

"That's right. The Amish never put their loved ones in those homes for older folk," Chloe chimed in.

"I think Ms. Klein would like it very much if the two of you visited her." Naomi smiled.

Joanna thought she heard a baby crying. "Naomi, I think I heard something. A *boppli*?"

At first, Naomi looked puzzled. "Oh, you probably heard Katie. I guess she must have awakened from her nap. I'll just set the soup on the table, so you girls can help yourselves already." She quickly took three bowls and spoons from the kitchen and set them on the table next to the steaming pot of obviously homemade chicken noodle soup that smelled delightful. She then ran upstairs to her daughter.

"I didn't know she had a daughter. Did you?" Chloe asked, sitting down at the kitchen table.

"I figured she had children because of the toys in the backyard. I've been meaning to ask her about that," Joanna answered, as she dished out soup for the three of them.

Naomi walked slowly down the stairs leading a little girl with curly brown hair, caramel eyes, and little freckles that spotted her face. She looked like she was about two years old.

"Honeybee, this is Joanna and Chloe, they are going to be delivering honey for me. Say hi, Katie." Naomi prodded.

"Hi, Katie," the little girl answered shyly.

The ladies laughed in unison at Katie's innocent mistake.

"Honeybee – that's such a cute nickname," Joanna commented.

"And very appropriate too, with you being in the honey business. How many words does she know?" Chloe questioned.

"Well, not too many." Naomi thought aloud, "Let's see...she knows hi, bye, no, yes, food, and Mama. I think that's it. But sometimes she jabbers on and I have no idea what she's saying."

"No, Mama. No," Katie said, tugging at her mother's dress and trying to pull her to the kitchen.

"Are you hungry, Katie?" Naomi asked.

Katie nodded.

"All right, I'll get you some applesauce," Naomi said, walking into the kitchen with Katie clinging to her calf-length, pink floral cape dress. She returned a moment later with a small bowl and spoon, which she gave to Katie who happily began to feed herself.

"I noticed the playground outside. Do you have other children too?" Joanna asked curiously.

Naomi sighed. "Well, yes and no. You see, I did have twin girls: Faith and Charity. They were about your age. As a matter of fact, the two of you remind me a lot of them. My husband David and the girls passed away last year in a terrible automobile accident. Our car was hit head-on by a drunk driver."

Both girls looked at each other, then back at Naomi with sympathetic eyes. "Were you in the accident also?" Chloe asked.

"Yes, we all were. Katie and I were the only ones to survive. I guess God still has plans for us. Katie's car seat went through the window and landed on the side of the road. She escaped with just a few scratches, miraculously. I was in the hospital for a while and I had to have surgery on my back. That's why I decided to hire someone for the honey route. I'm not able to get around as well as I used to, and my blood circulation hasn't been the same since the accident. I try to exercise some, but it's not enough – my hands and feet still fall asleep often. The doctors can't help me, either."

"I'm sorry to hear about your husband and daughters," Joanna offered her condolences with tears in her eyes, "...and your health problems."

"Thank you, I appreciate that," Naomi said in a comforting tone, "but I'm not upset about it. I do miss them, but I take comfort in knowing that I'll see them in Heaven someday. God has already used the accident for good."

"What do you mean by that?" Chloe quizzed.

"Well, at the funeral there were several family members and friends that came to the Lord."

"You mean, they go to your church now?" Chloe looked at Joanna to see if she understood what Naomi was saying.

"No, I mean that they got saved. They are now on their way to Heaven." Naomi explained further, "When a person believes in Jesus Christ and trusts Him alone to save them, they are born again."

"But I don't understand..." Chloe looked confused. "I thought you had to be Plain to go to Heaven."

"Let me show you what the Bible says." Naomi took her King James Bible out of her purse and opened it to John 3:16. "'For God so loved the world, that he gave his only begotten Son, that whosoever believeth in him should not perish, but have everlasting life.' Does it say anything in this verse about being Plain?"

"No, it doesn't. It just says that you have to believe in God's Son," Chloe answered. "But I heard that it's prideful to say you're going to Heaven."

"It can't be prideful because there's nothing that *you* can do to get to Heaven. It's *only* through God's free gift that we can get there, like it says in Ephesians 2:8-9. Please don't take my word for it. Study God's Word for yourselves. If you want, I'll give you a list of Bible verses to look up," Naomi offered.

"We would like that. *Jah*, Chloe?" Joanna said, as she took her last bite of soup.

Naomi quickly wrote down some verses off the top of her head from John, Romans, Ephesians, Galatians, Titus, and Revelation. "When you girls come back again, we can discuss the verses and any other questions you have." She handed each of them a piece of paper.

The three of them stood up from the table and the girls offered to help with the dishes. Naomi declined the help and insisted the girls enjoy a chocolate chip cookie in the living room, while she cleaned Katie up. "You know, I was hoping to get to know you girls better today, but it seems like you've learned more about me." She laughed.

A loud screeching noise, followed by a boom brought their attention outside. The girls jumped up from the couch and hurried to the door to see what had happened, with Naomi close behind. "*Nee*, it looks like a buggy accident!" Chloe cried.

CHAPTER 9
The Crash

"He causeth the grass to grow for the cattle, and herb for the service of man..." Psalm 104:14a

Naomi and the girls ran to the site of the accident. A blue, mid-sized vehicle sat at an angle on the opposite side of the road. The front fender had been smashed in and black skid marks lined the road just up to where a black courting buggy lay turned on its side.

"It looks like Isaac's buggy," Joanna panted, fear evident in her voice. She looked closer and saw her older brother lying on the road beside the buggy, his leg bleeding profusely. "Quick, Chloe, go get Phillip King!" Joanna hollered. She removed her apron and placed it over Isaac's wound, applying pressure as she'd seen her father do with an injured horse one time.

Chloe took off on foot as fast as she could.

"Don't worry, Isaac. Chloe is getting help. You'll be fine." Joanna attempted to comfort her unconscious brother, tears streaming down her cheeks. She determined to remain calm for Isaac's sake. *Dear* Gott, *please let my brother be all right,* she continued praying silently.

Naomi emerged from around the opposite side of the buggy with her free arm around Rachel Esh, who appeared to be intact, but was obviously shaken. Chloe had not yet seen her sister, so she didn't know about her involvement in the accident. Isaac's new horse had gotten free and was now eating grass on the side of the road. The driver of the blue vehicle sat in his car with his cell phone to his ear. He appeared to be uninjured.

Chloe returned with Phillip, who carried a large black bag with him. Joanna moved away so Philip could take over. He quickly took out a sandwich-sized plastic bag that contained a red powdery substance, which he poured generously onto Isaac's bleeding leg. The bleeding stopped within a couple of minutes. Phillip then poured on a little more for good measure, and began to wrap the wound tightly. "He's still conscious, but appears to be in shock." Phillip took a small, brown, glass dropper bottle out of his bag and put a few drops into Isaac's mouth. Immediately, Isaac's eyes flew open.

"Water," Isaac begged. Phillip handed him a fresh bottle of water from his bag and he drank like a parched man in the middle of the desert.

Phillip turned to look at the ladies. "He'll be okay," he said confidently. Turning to Rachel, he asked, "Are you doing all right?"

Rachel replied, "*Jah*, I'm fine. *Denki* for helping Isaac," she said with a hint of concern in her voice. Rachel knelt down beside Isaac and he took her hand, giving her a weak reassuring smile.

"That's what I'm here for," Philip said. "You should probably go home now and get some rest," the kind herb doctor advised.

"But, Isaac –" Rachel protested, looking at his now-closed eyes.

"He'll be fine. He just needs some rest now," Philip reassured Rachel once again, and then turned to Chloe. "Make sure she gets plenty of rest as well."

Chloe nodded, and then she and her older sister set off on foot, after saying goodbye to Naomi and Joanna.

Phillip walked across the street to check on the man in the car. "Are you okay?"

"Yeah, I'm fine. Scared to death at first, though. I didn't know if the boy was going to make it, he looked pretty bad. I called 9-1-1," the man said.

Screaming sirens sounded, drawing their attention down the road. The noise brought back unwanted memories for Joanna, catapulting her back to that fearful day of her kidnapping. The image of her abductor grasping her arm replayed in her mind, seemingly forever seared in her consciousness. *Oh no, not again,* she thought dreadfully.

As the ambulance and a fire truck arrived on the scene, she was jolted back to reality once again. Joanna watched in a haze as the emergency medical attendants laid Isaac on a stretcher and put him into the ambulance. Naomi came alongside her and placed an arm around her waist. She asked if she would be all right, and then informed Joanna she needed to take Katie back inside the house. Joanna indicated that she would be in shortly, bidding Naomi farewell. The technicians shared a brief conversation with Philip King, and then whisked her brother off to the hospital.

Joanna walked silently to Midnight, who seemingly had no idea what was taking place. "Hey, how are you doing?" Joanna said while gently running her hands over Midnight's shiny black coat.

"Any damage?" Joanna turned to see Philip standing a few feet behind her.

"*Nee,* she seems fine. I think she's just scared. Would you like to check her?"

"Yes, I would." Philip began looking over Midnight, gingerly feeling for any damage. The horse didn't protest as Philip probed the animal, but responded well. "She's still shaken up a bit, but there appears to be no damage done. She should be fine by tomorrow. Would you like me to go to your house and let your parents know about the accident?" By then, several other buggies from their district had arrived to assess the scene. It was likely that her folks were already informed of the accident, but she couldn't be sure.

"*Jah,* that would be *gut. Denki*, Philip." Joanna was thankful to have a knowledgeable herbalist in their district.

"I can take Isaac's horse home if you'd like," Philip offered. Joanna nodded her consent, and Philip rode off on Midnight in the direction of the Fisher residence.

"Joanna, your family is here." Naomi gently shook Joanna awake where she lay on Naomi's couch. "They've asked me to drive to the hospital. We'll leave as soon as the babysitter arrives."

"*Denki*, tell them I'll be right there." Joanna shook herself from her weariness, then got up quickly and hurried to join her family. Esther, Gideon, Grace, and Jonathan all sat at Naomi's table with mugs of hot cocoa when Joanna walked into the dining room. Jonathan poked his index finger into his mug, pushing down the marshmallows that floated on top. He took one of the slippery white treats and popped it into his mouth, sucking the remainder of cocoa off his dripping fingers.

"*Ach,* Jonathan. Must you make a mess everywhere you go? Mind your manners now," Esther warned the boy.

"Is Isaac hurt badly?" Grace asked, paying no mind to her brother's foolishness.

"I don't know for sure. His leg didn't look too *gut.* Philip King stopped the bleeding and bandaged him up before the ambulance came," Joanna replied.

Gideon Fisher sighed in relief. "That's good to hear. Hopefully, he can come home with us tonight. Philip said he was going to the hospital to check on Isaac."

Just then, the front doorbell rang. "That must be the babysitter. Is everyone ready to go?" Naomi queried.

"*Jah*, we're ready," Esther answered, after helping Jonathan wash and dry his hands. They abruptly arose, heading to Naomi's vehicle. As soon as Naomi finished instructing the babysitter, they were off to the hospital.

Ding Ding. The elevator opened to the fourth floor of the hospital. Gideon strode up to the nurses' station while Naomi, Joanna, and the rest of her family walked to a nearby waiting room.

"They said he's in room 427. He can only have two visitors at a time, so your *mudder* and I will go in first. Grace, keep an eye on your *bruder*. Jonathan, you must be *gut*," Gideon dictated. "The doctor will come and give us an update in a little while and let us know whether he can come home with us tonight or not." Joanna's parents departed, turning down a corridor toward Isaac's hospital room.

The waiting room was decorated with colorful, abstract paintings. The blue chairs, that sat along the walls, somewhat matched the paintings and the carpet as well. A television blared in the upper corner of the room, and Naomi walked over to turn it down. Joanna and her siblings, along with Naomi

Fast and a handful of other *Englisch* visitors, whom she did not know, waited patiently for any news.

Gideon and Esther returned to the waiting room a few minutes later. "Isaac was asleep and we didn't want to wake him," Esther explained.

Philip King walked into the waiting room and shook Gideon's hand. "How's he doing?" Philip asked.

"We don't know yet. We're waiting to hear from the doctor," Gideon said, just as the doctor walked into the waiting room.

"Are Isaac Fisher's parents here?" the doctor asked.

"*Jah*. We are Isaac's parents," Esther informed the doctor.

"I just wanted to let you know that Isaac is doing well. Whoever treated him at the scene is to be commended. They possibly saved his life. The EMT workers said that the bleeding had already stopped before they even arrived. That's amazing considering his artery was cut open. He easily could have lost a lot more blood. Whoever patched him up knew what they were doing," the doctor said, marveling.

"'Twas a *gut* friend," Gideon stated, knowing that Philip wouldn't want his name mentioned. He nodded and smiled a 'thank you' to Philip. Philip briefly nodded back.

"Will Isaac be able to come home with us tonight?" Esther enquired.

"We'd like to keep him here overnight for observation. If all goes well, he'll be released to you in the morning," the doctor answered, shook their hands, and then left the room.

The group sat back down and began conversing amongst themselves, the rest of the visitors had cleared out of the waiting room. "Naomi Fast, have you met Philip King?" Gideon asked, remembering his manners.

"Well, I saw him at the scene of the accident...but no, we have never been formally introduced," she answered, purposely not mentioning the fact that she'd seen Philip at the Fishers' home on the night of Joanna's disappearance.

Philip stood up to shake her hand. "Naomi, is it? Nice to meet you."

"Nice to meet you too, Philip. Would you mind if I asked you a question?" Naomi quizzed. Philip nodded his consent. "What did you put on Isaac's leg to stop the bleeding?"

"Cayenne pepper." Philip smiled with a twinkle in his eye.

"Cayenne pepper, as in the spice?" Naomi cocked her head, looking confused.

Philip laughed. "I get that reaction a lot. Yes, cayenne is one of the greatest herbs that God has given to mankind. I would not be without it. It is excellent for many things...and one of those things is the blood."

"You mean helping the blood to clot, right?"

He nodded. "Yes, but it's also good for circulation. High blood pressure, low blood pressure, and even for heart attacks. It equalizes the blood," Philip answered assertively.

"Where can I get some for myself?" Naomi wondered.

"You can buy it at the health food store, or I'd be glad to bring you some," he offered.

Joanna interjected, “I work for Naomi, and she just lives down the street from you. I’ll be glad to bring her to the store after I’m done with my honey deliveries.”

“Honey?” Philip was taken aback. “Do you sell *raw* honey?” he asked Naomi, lifting his dark brows.

“Yes, I do. My deliveries have been increasing since the flowers started blooming – allergy season, you know.”

“Do you think you’d be able to supply the store? I usually have to order my honey from out of state, but I prefer locally harvested honey. That would be great to have a supplier nearby.” Philip chuckled. “And to think I’ve had a supplier just down the street all this time...I should really get to know my neighbors better.”

“That would work out just fine for me. Just let me know how much you’ll need.” Naomi was pleased; this meeting had to be providential. This single transaction would help her financial situation immensely. “Well, Joanna, it looks like we’ve just added a new customer to your delivery route.” Smiles abounded.

“We need to go check on Isaac again. Perhaps he will be awake now.” Gideon stated, returning to the issue at hand. He and Esther walked out of the room, leaving the others behind.

“*Dat, Mamm,* is that you?” Isaac called out as they stepped into room 427.

"*Jah*, Isaac. Tis us," Gideon confirmed. They rushed to his bedside to offer a hug. "How are ya feelin'?"

"Fine. My leg hurts a bit, though," Isaac answered. "How is Rachel?"

"Rachel?" Gideon and Esther looked at each other questioningly. Both were unaware of the secret courtship between Rachel and their son. Nobody had mentioned her involvement in the accident.

"*Jah*, Rachel Esh. She was in the buggy too. Didn't anyone tell you?" he said, panic-stricken. "Where is she? Is she all right? I need to see her!"

"No, we didn't know that she was in the accident. I'll be right back, *Sohn*." Esther quickly left the room and Joanna returned in her stead.

"Rachel is fine, Isaac. She wasn't injured in the accident, just a little shaken up. She's at home resting. Don't you remember?" Joanna reassured her brother.

A sigh of relief escaped Isaac's lips. "*Jah, jah*. I remember now. That's *gut*."

"The doctor said you'll probably get to go home tomorrow," Gideon said encouragingly. "*Mamm* will stay here with you tonight and she'll call me in the morning when you're to be released. You will be able to see the Esh girl soon enough. Rest now, my son." Gideon smiled inwardly, *so Isaac's found himself an* aldi.

CHAPTER 10
The Challenge

"Study to shew thyself approved unto God, a workman that needeth not to be ashamed, rightly dividing the word of truth." 2 Timothy 2:15

Monday dawned a new week, and Joanna was glad that the bishop's announcement was behind her. The People readily accepted the new proclamation and not one had protested. After all, the rules of the *Ordnung* were in place for their own benefit and safety. Like the rules God has in the Bible – they're not for God, but for our own good.

The prior day, the day of rest, was anything but restful. Joanna's family, with her, Esther, and Isaac excluded, had gone to the Sunday-Go-To-Meeting. Esther was still at the hospital with Isaac, and Chloe had come to stay with Joanna. They had a great time preparing for the evening meal together and chatting about the events of the past week.

"What do you think about Philip and Naomi?" Chloe asked unexpectedly.

Joanna's eyebrows arched slightly. "What do you mean?"

"Well, Philip needs a *fraa*..." Chloe mentioned slyly.

Joanna caught on, adding, "...and Naomi's not married!" The two girls laughed out loud. "Do you think it's possible, though? Naomi is a Mennonite."

"*Jah*, but she's still Plain for the most part. Besides, love conquers all things." Chloe smiled, remembering the line from a book she'd read. Both of the girls remained silent for a moment, pondering the situation.

"I have an idea," Joanna said excitedly. "Well, Philip will probably order a lot of honey, right?"

"*Jah*, I guess so. What does that have to do with anything?" Chloe looked confused.

"*We* can't deliver that much honey with our scooters..."

"So...?" Chloe still didn't catch her drift.

Joanna helped her out, "So Philip will have to come and pick it up himself."

"...And what if we just happen to tell him to come around lunch time?"

"Of course, Naomi wouldn't want to be rude and she'd invite him to eat with us." The girls continued to scheme until their folks arrived back home. Chloe went home with her parents and Joanna's family planned to pick Isaac up from the hospital.

Barrett awoke to find himself alone in a small white room with a tiny window on the door. *The Hole,* he thought. It was solitary confinement – the place where the worst prisoners go to get over their "negative" behavior.

There was no one to talk to, except God. And that was something that Barrett had no idea how to do, nor did he want to. As far as he was concerned, there was no God. After all, what did God ever do for him? He came from an abusive home with a mother that was always strung out on drugs and he had no idea who his father was. His whole young life, he'd been bounced around to countless foster homes where nobody really cared about him, or so he thought. The small flap opened on the door and a container of food was pushed in.

"Why am I in here?" Barrett asked angrily.

"They said you started a fight out in the yard," the guard answered.

"But I didn't –" Barrett heard the outer door slam closed. It was no use trying to talk to the guards when you're holed up in solitary confinement. *Maybe I should talk to God,* he mused, *if I don't I might go out of my mind in this place.*

After dinner, the whole family sat in the Fishers' living room. Isaac had come home with a set of crutches, which he laid beside him next to the couch. Gideon sat in his wooden chair with the Bible open on his lap, and began to read the Sermon on the

Mount from Matthew chapter five. In the Sunday services, the ministers read from the German Bible. However, certain passages of the King James Bible had been approved by the leadership for home reading, to which they were thankful.

Just then, Joanna remembered the scripture verses Naomi had given her. She waited for Gideon to finish reading, and then spoke, "*Dat*, I have some verses that I'd like to look up." She handed him a paper and they read each verse one by one.

Gideon read part of the last verse again, "Not by works of righteousness which we have done, but according to his mercy he saved us..." He stopped, pondering for a moment.

"What does that mean?" Jonathan asked innocently, stroking the blue-bellied lizard he'd found under the wood pile outside.

"I think it means that we are not saved by the good things we do, but by God's mercy," *Mamm* explained.

"What's mercy?" Jonathan asked, placing the reptile atop his head to nest in his hair.

Gideon chuckled at the sight, and then just shook his head. He attempted to gather his thoughts once again. "Mercy is when we don't get what we deserve," *Dat* answered. "Remember the verse we read about everyone being a sinner?"

"*Jah*," Jonathan answered, nodding solemnly, the lizard bobbing up and down with the motion.

"What do sinners deserve?" *Dat* asked.

"Nothin' at all. I think I got it now," the boy said, taking the lizard and letting it perch on his shoulder now. "Is Lizzy a sinner too, *Dat?*" Jonathan referred to his reptile.

Gideon held in a chuckle and patted the Bible. "*Nee*, this is for humans."

Jonathan nodded his understanding.

Isaac chimed in, "Wait a minute, didn't the verse say He 'saved' us? It's written in the past tense. That means that Titus *knew* that he was saved already."

"But I thought the bishop said that we can only *hope* for salvation? And it's prideful to say that you're saved." Grace looked to *Dat* and *Mamm*, clearly confused. Her question begged clarification. If the bishop and elders said one thing and the Bible said another, then who was right?

Joanna spoke up now, "Naomi Fast says it can't be prideful to say that you're saved, because there's nothing that *you* can do to get saved. She said the Bible teaches that Jesus is the *only* one who can do the saving, so *HE* is the one who gets all the glory, not us."

"I've never thought about that before, but I think she's right. Now it all makes sense." Gideon silently praised *Der Herr* for the new-found truth they had just discovered. "Let's study this more, so we can be certain it's true." They all agreed.

That evening they spent over two hours searching the scriptures in context. Alas, they came to the conclusion that Naomi had indeed been correct in her assertion. After bowing their heads in prayer once again, one by one, they each confessed

Jesus Christ as their saviour and asked forgiveness for trusting in their own works of righteousness.

"That means we can't be Amish no more, *ain't so*?" Jonathan asked *Dat*, rolling the poor lizard up in one of his front shirttails.

"Anymore," Grace corrected her younger brother.

"No, *Sohn*. It means that I need to pray, and then have a talk with Bishop Hostettler." *Dat* knew that might be a daunting task. *Judah is an understanding man. Surely he won't say anything against the Word of God,* Gideon reasoned within himself.

CHAPTER 11
The Unthinkable

"But I say unto you, Love your enemies..."
Matthew 5:44a

As Naomi's property came into view, Joanna and Chloe saw an Amish buggy leaving her house. Was it Philip King's buggy? The girls glanced at one another in disbelief and shared a grin. After parking their scooters on the side of the house, they ran up the steps to the front door.

"Hello girls, come inside," Naomi welcomed them.

"Was that Philip that just left here?" Joanna asked, her curiosity getting the better of her.

"Yes, it was. He was curious about the bee business, so I showed him the hives in the back. He also wanted to know when the honey would be delivered."

"How much honey did he order?" Chloe asked.

"He ordered two cases, which is twenty-four jars. He said they'll probably sell out in a couple of weeks."

"Naomi, how will we fit all of those jars in our baskets?" Joanna asked conspiratorially.

"Oh." Naomi laughed. "You girls won't be delivering them. Philip is going to come by on his lunch break and pick them up."

The girls looked at each other again in disbelief, both of their jaws hanging open. Perhaps God was already at work in Philip and Naomi's lives.

"Is something wrong girls?" Naomi asked, with a knowing grin on her face.

"Sorry, Naomi, we were just talking about something on the way over here and..." Joanna stopped, deciding she'd already said enough.

"Well, I'd like you girls to get going as soon as possible. You know how busy Saturdays can get. Besides, I'd like you to be back when Philip comes by. Here is your list. And would you tell Ms. Klein that I'll be by to see her on Monday?"

"*Jah*, Naomi, we will," the girls confirmed as they rode off.

Rachel Esh knocked on the back door of the Fisher home. "Just a minute," she heard a voice say from inside the house. The door was opened by Isaac's mother, Esther, who wore a welcoming smile. She hoped his mother didn't think it was too forward of her to come visit Isaac at his home – in broad daylight, of all things. But she figured her behavior would be acceptable considering the circumstances.

"*Kumm* in, Rachel." Esther's excitement bubbled over.

"*Mamm* and I baked lots of cookies this morning, so I thought I would bring them by and see how Isaac is doing," she said shyly with a hint of pink in her cheeks.

"I'll get him for you," Esther obliged. "Isaac...you have a caller," she called up the stairs, and then excused herself to the kitchen with a knowing smile playing on her lips.

Isaac slowly limped downstairs as he held onto the rail. His face lit up at the sight of Rachel. "Let's take a walk outside, jah?"

"But, your leg..." she protested.

"I'll be fine. I'm starting to get used to getting around with these crutches. Besides, there's more privacy out there," Isaac said, referring to his mother and sister in the kitchen.

"I brought you some cookies," Rachel said, pointing to the basket on the table. "Would you like one?"

"*Jah, denki.*" He sank his teeth into one. "Mmm...This is the best cookie I've ever tasted."

"Isaac Fisher, you're just tryin' to flatter me."

"Maybe so," he said teasingly, "but they are *gut.*" His countenance turned serious as he made eye contact. "Sorry about what happened. I'm so thankful to *Gott* that you weren't hurt. I'm afraid I won't be able to take you home from singings for a while. I can't get around too well just yet and my buggy is out of commission, as you know."

"That's okay, Isaac. It wasn't your fault...besides, I can wait for you." She smiled encouragingly, helping him down the back steps of the porch.

"You will?" Isaac couldn't believe his good fortune.

"I hope I didn't embarrass you by coming here today," she said sheepishly.

"*Nee.* It's fine, Rachel. I wouldn't mind if you came every day," he said, his neck darkening a shade.

They walked along in silence for a while, heading toward the wood shop. "There's something I'd like to show you in the shop," Isaac said excitedly. He opened the barn doors where there stood several chairs and a dining table.

"Did your *Dat* make these?" She ran her hand over the smooth table top and admired the intricately carved wooden chairs.

"*Dat* and I did, *jah,*" he said, trying not to sound too proud.

"This is the best I've seen in all of Lancaster County," she proclaimed.

"Now, who's trying to flatter?" He teased.

"No, Isaac. I really do mean it. These are *sehr gut.* Someday I hope to have..." her voice trailed off, dreaming of her future home as a married woman. She probably shouldn't voice those thoughts to Isaac just yet; he might think her too eager to marry. But isn't that what every girl secretly hopes for?

"What did ya say, Rachel?" Isaac probed.

She quickly changed the subject. "Is there going to be a funeral soon?" she asked, looking at the pine boxes that lined the wall.

"Na...The bishop just likes *Dat* to keep a couple extra boxes on hand," Isaac replied nonchalantly.

"Should we go inside now?" she asked, feeling eerie about the caskets, and noting that they probably shouldn't be alone in the barn.

Isaac set his crutch aside, and then gently pulled her into his arms. "Not yet." He leaned closer to Rachel, attempting a kiss. Their anticipation rose as their lips were mere inches apart.

"BOO!" Jonathan popped up out of a pine box, and the lid flew open. He giggled and took off running as fast as he could.

"Aah!" Rachel couldn't help but scream, she was so startled by the little rascal. Her heartbeat failed to slow.

"Jonathan!" Isaac hollered after him, disappointed his brother had ruined his opportunity to steal a kiss from his girl.

Isaac then looked into Rachel's bemused eyes and they both couldn't help but burst into laughter.

Philip locked up the herb shop and placed his sign on the door: *Closed for lunch. Be back at 1:00pm.* It had been a long time since he'd been invited to a woman's home for a meal – a very long time. In fact, he had been just seventeen and still in his *rumspringa* – his running around years. He and his friends had been out at the bowling alley, and that's where he met an *Englischer* named Karen. She was fun and full of life and for six whole months they spent nearly every Saturday evening together. When the relationship began turning serious, Philip realized he had a choice to make. He could leave the Amish forever and marry Karen, or he could fully commit his life to God and the church.

His younger sister Rebekah had been in a similar situation a few years after Philip's dilemma. Unfortunately, she did leave the Amish for the man she loved and moved away to California, causing their parents much heartbreak. Philip was certain that had played a factor in the early death of their folks; they just weren't the same after Rebekah left. With only having two children due to medical complications during pregnancy, their family was smaller than most, if not all, in their community.

It had been a painful decision to leave Karen all those years ago, but he knew he'd made the right one. He was doubly certain after his sister left. But now, just over thirty and still single, there was little chance he'd ever find someone to marry. He had been so busy with his work, that he hadn't even thought much about it. Until now.

It had been kind of Naomi to offer lunch, especially since he wouldn't have time to stop by his own house to make something. She had told him about the unfortunate accident that claimed the lives of her husband and daughters. *It must have been very painful for her*. He could only imagine. She still had her youngest daughter, but somehow she seemed lonely. He noticed how her eyes lit up when he took an interest in the bees. He wasn't sure if it was just his imagination or not, but had there been a spark between them? A common bond, perhaps? *What would it be like to hold Naomi in my arms?* Philip quickly chided himself for the improper thought. No, he must trust *Der Herr* with his future.

He clicked his tongue urging his horse to go faster. *Dear* Vadder Gott, *if it's Your will, please give Naomi and me a chance together. Let this lunch date go well, Lord. And please help me not to do anything stupid to mess it up. I've been lonely and I'd really like to find someone to marry. And be blessed with my own* kinner. *Nevertheless, Thy will be done. You know what's best for me, Lord. Help me to trust you. Amen.*

Naomi glanced at the clock on her wall – ten minutes till twelve. *I hope the girls get here before Philip does.* There was a knock on the door. She took a deep breath, and went to answer it. "Hello, Philip. The girls haven't returned from their route yet, so would you mind if we sit out on the porch?" she asked, wanting to abstain from all appearance of evil, as the Bible says. "I'll bring out some lemonade."

"That would be great," he said appreciatively, taking a seat on the rocker.

Naomi returned with a tray holding two glasses and a pitcher of lemonade. "I wanted to thank you for the cayenne. It makes such a difference. I have more energy, and I can stand on my feet a lot longer than before."

"It's a wonderful herb – one of the best God has made. I'm glad it's helping you," Philip concurred, sipping on the sweet beverage. "When you run out, just let me know. I always keep it in stock."

"Oh, I just remembered that I haven't paid you for it yet." Naomi arose from her white wicker chair and started toward the door.

"No need to. Please, consider it a gift from a friend." He smiled.

"Thank you, Philip. I appreciate that." Naomi sat back down, taken aback with his kindness. She noticed that the time was slipping by, and Philip would need to get back to his shop before too long. Naomi pondered the situation for a moment, weighing her options. "I don't want you to be late. You may have customers, and I wouldn't want you to keep them waiting. Why don't we go ahead and eat without the girls? I'm sure they'll be along soon."

Philip nodded in agreement, secretly thankful to have some one-on-one time with Naomi.

When they sat down at the table, Naomi asked Philip to say the blessing over the food. Naomi had prepared a simple lunch of salmon sandwiches, fruit salad, and pita chips with hummus. Philip commented on the food, "Salmon is one of my favorites. This sandwich is outstanding."

Naomi laughed. "You don't get out much, do you?" She teased and Philip laughed as well. "Seriously though, salmon is a favorite of mine too. I prepare it at least once a week."

"Well, then I hope you'll invite me over next week also." He teased back – kinda. To that, they both laughed.

Conversation continued in a comfortable flow as they spoke on different subjects. It seemed they had a lot in common. Neither Philip, nor Naomi, could believe how well they got along. It was as if they were old friends and had known each other for years. Their instant camaraderie was quite unexpected.

When Katie awoke from her morning nap, she instantly went to Philip. Naomi hadn't ever seen her daughter react that way with a man, but for some reason she liked Philip King. And Philip seemed to be a natural with children, too. Quite surprising since he had no *kinner* of his own.

Knock, knock, knock.

"That must be the girls." Naomi went to answer the door, a bit disappointed that their time alone together had come to an end.

"Sorry, Naomi, but Elsa Klein insisted that we stay and sing for her. We tried to get here sooner," Joanna attempted to explain, as the girls scampered through the door.

"That's okay. You girls just sit down and eat now. Philip will need to get back soon, and I want you to help him load the honey before he leaves," Naomi insisted, setting a plate for each girl.

"*Denki*, Naomi," the girls said, as they joined the adults at the table.

"I really enjoyed our time together," Philip ventured as he leaned toward Naomi, his voice low so he wouldn't be overheard by the girls on the porch.

Naomi realized she held his gaze a bit longer than she should have. "As did I, Philip."

"Let me know if you need anything from the herb shop." Philip smiled, as he sat back against the seat in his buggy.

"I will. And you inform me if you need more honey," she answered back, just before he signaled the horse with the click of his tongue.

"When do you think he'll be back?" Chloe asked curiously, the girls joining Naomi at the end of the walkway.

"Why do you ask?" Naomi responded.

"I think Philip King is nice. Don't you, Naomi?" Chloe hinted.

"Yes. Philip King is a nice man." *And smart...and funny... and handsome,* Naomi blushed at the thought. She hadn't considered any man since her husband's death, but perhaps...

"May I ask you a question?" Joanna said earnestly, rousing Naomi from her thoughts, as they sat alone on the front porch. Chloe had now gone around to the backyard to push Katie on the swing set.

"Sure." Naomi sat up in her chair, sensing Joanna had something important to say.

"How did you do it? I mean, when I listened to you talk about your accident, it seemed like you were okay about it," Joanna tried to explain what was on her mind.

"I *am* okay about it. I realized that even though I don't understand what God is doing, I can still trust him," Naomi said.

"But what about the drunk driver? Don't you want him to pay for what he did?" Joanna asked. Even knowing her own people taught unconditional forgiveness, the principal was still difficult for her to grasp.

"Her," Naomi stated, "the drunk driver was a woman. And she *is* paying for what she did. Every day she has to live with the fact that she killed three innocent people, and all because she made an unwise decision."

"How do you know that?" Joanna wondered.

"I know that because I go and visit her every week. Her name is Virginia," Naomi stated.

"You go and visit her? Why?" Joanna couldn't believe what she was hearing. It was unthinkable. How could Naomi spend time with the person responsible for her loved ones' deaths?

"God laid it on my heart to let her know that I had forgiven her. When I told her, she broke down in tears. I let her know that it was only by God's grace that I was able to forgive. I shared the Gospel with her and now she is saved. We meet once a week at the jail for Bible study."

"How could you forgive her?" Joanna was curious. "I mean, how did you do it? Weren't you angry with her?"

"I realized that if God could forgive any sin, why couldn't I? I'd be putting myself above God if I didn't forgive. Who am I to hold onto unforgiveness when I myself have been granted forgiveness freely? The Bible says that if we don't forgive others, then we will not be forgiven," Naomi stated.

"I want to forgive too, but I don't know if I can," Joanna said with a tear on her cheek.

Naomi realized she was talking about forgiving her abductor. "God can help you. He can place forgiveness in your heart," Naomi reassured. "Just ask him."

CHAPTER 12
Courage

"Be strong and of a good courage, fear not, nor be afraid of them: for the Lord thy God he it is that doth go with thee; he will not fail thee, nor forsake thee." Deuteronomy 31:6

The prison chaplain walked to Barrett Winston's cell. "Winston, is there anything I can do for you today?" the caring man asked.

"Na...there ain't nothin' you can do to help me." Barrett sat on the side of the small bed with his head down.

"Well, I can pray with you. Would you allow me to do that?" The chaplain peered through the steel bars.

"I guess it couldn't hurt none," Barrett consented.

The guard opened Barrett's cell and let the chaplain inside. He took a seat on the small mattress beside Barrett. "What would you like me to pray with you about?"

Barrett shrugged his shoulders.

"Didn't you just get out of the hole?" the chaplain asked.

Barrett nodded in affirmation. "Yep, third time this month."

"What for this time?"

"Same old thing. I supposedly started a fight," Barrett grumbled. "You know, it's funny that I'm the only one that gets pounded. The other prisoners just get away with beating on me and I'm the one that ends up in solitary. Not one scratch on the other guys. Life just ain't fair."

"I'm afraid that inmates don't look too favorably upon someone with your criminal background. Neither do the guards. Have you ever thought about a lifestyle change – with God's help?"

Barrett hung his head down low again. "I don't know how I can make it in here for twenty years. Honestly, I'm at the end of my rope. I wouldn't even know where to start."

The chaplain handed Barrett a Bible. "Start here," he said, and then bowed his head to pray.

Barrett prayed silently, *God, if you're really there and you care about me, give me a sign.*

Gideon Fisher arrived at the bishop's house just prior to three o'clock. Bishop Hostettler lived about two miles from the Fisher residence, just past Miller's Bridge. The Bishop and his wife lived in the main house alongside their son, who constructed

Amish buggies. Nathan Hostettler and his young wife resided in the small *dawdi haus*. The last time Gideon had been out to the Hostettlers' place was when he put in the order for Isaac's courting buggy. But today, he was not there to talk business. He would be discussing matters of faith with the bishop, and he could only pray that it would go well.

"Good afternoon, Gid. I hope everything is okay." Oftentimes, many of the People only visited the bishop when there was something wrong.

Gideon reassured Bishop Hostettler. "There are no problems, Judah. On the contrary, we're doing great."

"How is Isaac's leg?" the bishop asked.

"It's healing. Isaac is a little frustrated that he can't do more...especially since his courtin' buggy is damaged. Do ya think Nathan can repair it?"

"I'm sure that won't be a problem," he answered. "And how is Joanna doing?"

"My *dochder* appears to be doing okay, although I can tell that she is still bothered at times. I think the job that she's taken with Naomi Fast is helping her a lot."

"One does not get over an incident like that easily. It will take some time." Judah tugged on his beard.

"Judah, the reason I've come is to discuss something that's been on my mind." Gideon forged ahead.

"Let us go inside and sit down. I will have Lydia prepare some iced tea for us." the bishop said, leading the way into the house. They sat down in a small room off the side of the living area, which Gideon supposed was the bishop's counseling office. "Now, what would you like to discuss with me, Gid?"

"Do you have an English Bible in here?" Gideon asked, glancing at the bookshelf behind the bishop's desk.

"Yes, I do. Would you like me to get it out?" His eyes peered over his reading glasses.

"*Jah,* but not for me. I brought my own. There are some things that I have been reading." Gideon stopped talking when he heard a knock on the door.

"*Kumm* in, Lydia." The bishop's wife set two glasses of iced tea on the desk. "*Denki, Fraa,*" Judah remarked, as Lydia quietly exited the room.

Gideon opened his Bible and the bishop pulled his from off the shelf. "Judah, I read something the other day with my family and I wanted to hear your thoughts on it. It says here in Ephesians chapter two, verses eight and nine: 'For by grace are ye saved through faith; and that not of yourselves: it is the gift of God: Not of works, lest any man should boast.'"

The bishop nodded his head. "*Jah,* that is true."

"But it says that we can be saved. And that salvation is a gift. And that there are no works involved. Am I correct in my understanding?" Gideon questioned, wondering what the bishop's reaction would be.

"Are you implying that there is salvation outside the Amish church?" His forehead creased.

"The Scriptures imply – no, they *proclaim* that salvation and eternal life are gifts. Gifts free for the taking upon faith in

Christ. Romans chapter six and verse twenty-three states this also. There is no mention of being a church member or of being a good person," Gideon spoke passionately. "Salvation is available to all...Amish and *Englisch* alike."

"I do agree with what you are saying, Gideon. However, I don't think it would be wise to share your feelings with everyone. This teaching can divide our community, and I'm afraid that we already have an alarming number leaving our fold. It is our traditions that keep us strong and unified," the bishop asserted.

Gideon couldn't believe what he was hearing. "But Judah, we're talking about eternal life! The difference between Heaven and Hell. To simply believe in God is one thing, but to trust Jesus Christ alone for salvation is another. The Bible says there is no other way to be saved. Don't you want that for our People? Shouldn't the Truth be paramount to *any* man-made traditions, including the *Ordnung*?"

The bishop seemed to be contemplating Gideon's words. "I don't want to make any hasty decisions. Let me pray about this, and then I will get back to you on this matter." He paused for a moment, weighing his words. "Gideon, you do realize where this could lead if it's not accepted by the elders. We are *gut* friends, I would hate to see you and your family under the *Bann*." The concern in his eyes was evident.

"Likewise, I would hate for our People to be deprived of the Truth. Good day, Judah." He gave a brief nod, and then stepped out.

Gideon left the Hostettlers' feeling disappointed. But he wasn't totally dejected – there was still hope for their community. However, if they rejected the Scriptures, there could be dire consequences for not only the community, but for the Fisher family as well. Surely the bishop would not impose the *shunning* on them, would he? Standing for Truth hadn't been easy for their Anabaptist ancestors. As a matter of fact, it had cost them their very lives. If the Fishers had to face the *Bann* for taking the right stance, then so be it.

Joanna sat at the small corner desk in her room with pen and paper in hand. She sighed. *Dear* Gott, *please help me to do this. Give me the courage that I need.* She picked up the paper that Naomi had given her. It read: Barrett C. Winston 95648-073, FDC Philadelphia, Federal Detention Center, P.O. Box 562, Philadelphia, PA 19105. Naomi had been kind to find the information for her. Now, she'd have to figure out just what to write. She began the letter...

Barrett C. Winston,

I wanted to let you know that I have forgiven you. God loves you and He wants you to be saved. Please read John 3:16 from the Bible.

From,

The girl you kidnapped

Joanna folded the letter and placed it into an envelope. She addressed it to the man but kept the return address blank, not wanting him to find out who she was or where she lived. She would take the letter to Naomi, who would mail it for her when she went into Lancaster later in the week.

Isaac took a deep breath. "Rachel, you know that we've been good friends since we were *kinner.* I have loved you for as long as I can remember. I oftentimes find myself daydreaming about you, and wondering if you love me the same way I love you. I have been giving it great thought, and I would be honored if you would consent to be my wife."

Isaac glanced into the mirror and then looked at his reflection which frowned back at him. "No, that will never do. I have to think of something else..." He paused a moment. "Hmm... Okay, now I know." Clearing his throat he began again. "Rachel, I love you very much and I know it's a lot to ask, but will you at least consider becoming my wife? Please say yes, Rachel. You will make me the happiest man alive –"

A high-pitched voice echoed from behind him. "Oh Isaac, you're so wonderful. I would love to marry you." Startled, Isaac looked into the mirror and saw Jonathan batting his eyelashes behind him. Isaac's face turned beet red with embarrassment, and then anger. Jonathan giggled at his brother's foolishness.

"Jonathan Fisher...just wait until I get my hands on you!" Isaac grabbed his crutches and dashed out the door, hobbling down the stairs after Jonathan, who had already safely made it outside.

CHAPTER 13
Freedom

"If the Son therefore shall make you free, ye shall be free indeed." John 8:36

When Joanna awoke this morning, peace flooded her soul. She realized that she had not had a single nightmare since four weeks ago – the night she and her family received salvation. She no longer struggled with fear. *Thank you for your goodness, Lord,* she prayed silently. She donned her Sunday dress with a smile, and started downstairs to help with the morning meal.

After breakfast, the Fisher family took a lengthy drive to the Yoders' farm which was several miles away. The church meeting would be held in their house today. Everyone filed in to the large dwelling: first the men, then the women and children. After all the People were seated, the *Vorsinger* began singing and the rest of the congregation joined in. The bishop, the ministers, and the deacon retreated to an upstairs room.

Several songs were sung from the *Ausbund* until the leaders returned to the front of the room and sat down. Uncharacteristically, the bishop stood up and addressed the congregation in English, "A member of our flock came to me this week with a challenge. The challenge was from the Word of God. He showed me some very convincing scripture verses that have made me question what I have always taught and believed to be true. After examining the Scriptures on my own, I proceeded to meet with the other leaders in our district and shared my convictions with them. They too, thought the scriptures to be perplexing and convicting. With that said, today's services are going to be different from what we normally do. If you have any questions, please feel free to come and talk to one of the leaders after the meeting is over."

Gideon looked at Esther with a smile, and then at the bishop, who nodded his head.

Did the bishop get saved, too? Joanna wondered.

Chloe, who was sitting next to Joanna, threw a questioning glance her way. Joanna smiled and silently mouthed "Naomi" to her. It was obvious to Joanna that Chloe had no clue what she was talking about, so she leaned over and whispered, "Remember the Bible verses Naomi gave us?" Chloe finally understood.

After the service was over and everyone had eaten, two of the ministers walked over to Gideon. They both shook his hand and thanked him for having the courage to share the truth that God had shown him. "I'm glad it was received with an open heart. Many in other Amish communities have rejected this message."

One of the ministers commented, "And many are under the *Bann* because of it. Although we will still hold on to our traditional Amish ways, we also want to follow God's will for our People. And we believe that we have found it."

Gideon didn't see the other minister or Deacon Yoder after the service and wondered whether they had agreed with the decision of the others.

"Mail call!" a voice rang out down the corridors of the prison. The mail attendant handed several inmates small envelopes, probably letters from home. Barrett sighed as he heard each name called out. He often wondered if they called the names out loudly on purpose – just to remind him and other unfortunate souls that no one cared for them. He had to admit that mail call was the hardest time of the day. Just another reminder of his pitiful life thus far.

"Barrett C. Winston," the name echoed down the hall of the penitentiary, "you have mail today."

Barrett knew the attendant had to be pulling his leg. He sat stock still on his bed, tired of the jeers he'd received since his incarceration.

"Didn't ya hear me, Winston? Said ya got mail," the attendant said.

Barrett turned his head to see the man holding out an envelope. The gruff, stocky man shrugged his shoulders, stood to his feet, and walked to the front of his cell. *My family and friends couldn't care less about me. Most of them hate me. I wonder who would be writing to me.*

With a quizzical look on his face, he stuck one of his hands between the cold iron bars. The mail call attendant dropped a plain white envelope into his hand. No return address. He sat back down on his bunk and turned the letter over, then slipped his finger under the flap to break the seal. He slowly pulled out the folded lined paper and noticed only a few short sentences. He read the letter and couldn't believe the words on the page. He read it again to make sure his mind wasn't playing tricks on him. Hastily, he grabbed the Bible that had been given to him by the chaplain, opened it to John 3:16, and read the precious words. Barrett fell to his knees and wept like a new-born baby. *Please forgive me, God. I've always thought nobody ever loved me. I was wrong!*

The End

Amish Girls Series - Book 2
Danika's Journey
J.E.B. Spredemann

Danika's Journey

J.E.B. Spredemann

Amish Girls Series - Book 2

To our Loved Ones who have gone on before us...
Grandpa Alcorn, Grandpa and Grandma Tufts,
Grandma Klein, Uncle Hal, Cousin Bobby,
Oma and Opa Spredemann, Cousin Veronica
Your lives have touched us in ways we don't even realize
and you'll be forever remembered in our hearts

AUTHORS' NOTE

It should be noted that the Amish people and their communities differ one from another. There are, in fact, no two Amish communities exactly alike. It is this premise on which this book is written. We have taken cautious steps to assure the authenticity of Amish practices and customs. Both Old Order Amish and New Order Amish are portrayed in this work of fiction and may be inconsistent with some Amish communities.

We, as *Englischers*, can learn a lot from the Plain People and their simple way of life. Their hard work, close-knit family life, and concern for others are to be applauded. As the Lord wills, may this special culture continue to be respected and remain so for many centuries to come.

CHARACTERS IN DANIKA'S JOURNEY

Danika Morales – Main character

The King Family

Philip King – the herb doctor, Danika's uncle

Naomi King – Philip's wife

Katie King – Naomi's daughter

PJ King – Philip and Naomi's son

The Yoder Family

Deacon Yoder – the deacon from neighboring church district

Sarah Yoder – deacon's wife

Eli Yoder – deacon's son, friend

Annie Yoder – deacon's daughter

The Fisher Family

Joanna Fisher – Main character in Joanna's Struggle

Gideon Fisher – Joanna's dad

Esther Fisher – Joanna's mom

Isaac and Rachel Fisher – Joanna's older brother & his wife

Grace Fisher – Joanna's older sister, school teacher

Jonathan Fisher – Joanna's younger brother

The Hostettler Family

Judah Hostettler – the bishop

Lydia Hostettler – the bishop's wife

Joshua Hostettler – the bishop's son

Susanna Hostettler – the bishop's daughter

Other

Cindy – Danika's best friend in California

Chloe Esh – Joanna's best friend, main character in Chloe's Revelation

Sadie Lapp – Antagonist

CHAPTER 1
Tragedy

"To every thing there is a season, and a time to every purpose under the heaven: A time to be born, and a time to die..." Ecclesiastes 3:1-2a

R*i-i-i-i-ing.* The seventh-grade students at Lincoln Middle School all took their seats in Ms. Harris' classroom. "All right class, put your books away. Today we are going to have a math quiz." Danika Morales groaned along with the rest of the students. She felt a tap on her shoulder, and a piece of folded lined paper fell into her lap. Danika looked up to make sure Ms. Harris didn't see. She opened the note under her desk and read, *Is your cell on silent?* She quickly wrote back, *Yes,* and then passed the note back to Cindy as she placed her book in her desk and removed her pencil for the test. She felt her phone vibrate in the front pocket of her hoodie and took it out to glance at the text message. It read, *Math is so boring.*

Danika grinned. Cindy hated math as much as she did. *I know how you feel. I don't know how I'll ever make it through medical school! Can't wait till next period,* she quickly texted back.

"Hey, Dani, can you come to my house after school today?" Cindy asked during lunch.

She loved spending time with Cindy, especially since her parents owned a nice cottage a block from the beach. Many times the two of them would take their surfboards out to ride some waves, or just sit on the sand and watch the tides roll in. Danika thought for a moment. "No, I don't think I can today. My dad said I need to get caught up with my assignments. I hate homework." She rolled her eyes. "Besides," she added in a more serious tone, "Dad's having another treatment again today. I can't wait until he's done with all that stuff."

"Yeah, me too. I've heard it can be rough," her friend sympathized. "And now that you mention it, I should probably catch up on my homework too." Cindy sighed. "I can't believe my mom and dad are getting a divorce. They were getting along just fine. I don't know what happened. Why does life have to change?"

Danika hugged her friend. "I don't know. Don't worry. I won't change, I'll be your friend forever," she promised.

When Danika walked through the door of her suburban two-story home, she quickly dropped her backpack on the couch and walked to the refrigerator to find something to eat. After she finished making herself a PBJ sandwich, she picked up her backpack and headed for her room. *Since dad won't be home for a while, I can check my email real quick and then finish my homework,* Danika thought, as she searched through her backpack to find her smart-phone. She tried to keep her mind on her studies but her thoughts often drifted to her father. She couldn't help but worry about him.

He was at the hospital again today. He had been diagnosed with cancer six months ago and was having another chemo-therapy treatment session. The doctors said that the chemo would help him get better, but it definitely didn't make him feel or look any better. When he came home from his treatments, he seemed even worse: he was constantly vomiting, he could hardly eat, and he had begun to lose his hair too. She didn't understand how that could make him get better. It just didn't make any sense. But his oncologist insisted that this was the only way to go, that is, if he wanted to stay alive. Eventually, he'd said, her father's cancer should go into remission.

Danika sympathized with her dad; she couldn't help but bear some of the suffering he was going through. He didn't complain, but she could tell by the look in his eyes that he was in constant pain. She was sure he was just trying to be brave for her sake. After all, he was all she had left. Her mom had passed away in childbirth when Danika was eight years old. Not only did she lose her mother that day, but a much-anticipated baby brother as well. She couldn't bear to lose her father too. Where would she go? How would she survive on her own?

Two hours later, her dad came through the door, assisted by the neighbor who had taken him to his appointment. Today, he had come in using a walker for the first time. This was not a good sign. Danika rushed to him as she noticed his weakened state. "Are you okay, Dad?" she asked, her concern evident.

"I'll be all right, Pumpkin," he answered bravely. "I just need to go lie down and rest a while."

To Danika, it seemed as if that's all he ever did lately. He'd come home from his treatments, rest, get really sick, start to feel better again, and then go to another treatment. It was a vicious cycle.

"Danika, I want to talk to you about something. Please come and sit on the couch by me," her father requested as he rested on their tan sofa. The neighbor had left and promised to come back again when she was needed.

"What is it, Daddy?"

"Honey, I feel like my body is weakening. I...I don't know how much longer I'll be around." He paused, drawing a labored breath.

Tears filled Danika's eyes. "Please don't talk like that, Dad. You're going to be fine. The doctors said –"

"Shh...it'll be okay." Her father's hand gently stroked her thick nearly-black hair. "I love you, Pumpkin."

"I can't live without you, Daddy. Please don't leave me here by myself." She sobbed.

"Danika, I want you to listen to me. You have to be brave. You *will* get through this. Do you remember your Uncle Philip? He's your mom's brother – the one that came to Mom's funeral from Pennsylvania."

Danika tried to recall the man. "No, Dad, I don't remember."

"Philip is a good man. After I'm gone, I'd like you to go and live with him," her father stated wearily, taking her hand.

Danika shook her head in denial. "But Daddy, you're not going anywhere. You're staying here with me. You have to! You have to!" Danika cried, holding her father's now-limp hand. "Daddy? Daddy?" She shook his shoulder to try and wake him up, but there was no response. She panicked, breathing heavily. "No-o-o!" She wept uncontrollably, as she realized her father was gone.

CHAPTER 2
Pennsylvania

"...ask for the old paths, where is the good way, and walk therein, and ye shall find rest for your souls." Jeremiah 6:16b

As Danika stepped off the airplane and into the Harrisburg airport, she glanced around. Really, she didn't even know who she was looking for, just that his name was Philip and he was her uncle. A handsome man approached her wearing a full beard with a straw hat, a blue shirt, black pants, and a pair of suspenders. She could see her mother's kind face in his and instantly knew he was her uncle.

"You are Danika, *jah*?" the man asked in a slight Pennsylvania German accent.

Danika looked at the man with questioning eyes. "Yes, I am. And you're my Uncle Philip, right?"

The man nodded and held out his hand. “Yes, I am Philip King, your *mamm*’s *bruder. Gut* to meet ya.” He smiled.

“Hi.” Danika shook his hand timidly, choked with memories of her mom. *Uncle Philip looks so much like Mom. Oh, how I miss her!*

“I guess you probably don’t remember me. It’s been awhile. You’ve grown quite a bit too,” Philip said, as they headed toward the baggage claim area.

“Oh, there’s my bag,” Danika stated, pointing to a large pink suitcase with a hibiscus flower design. Philip grabbed the feminine bag off of the conveyor belt.

“My *gut* friend Tobias will be driving us to Lancaster. We’ll be picking up my rig from his place,” Philip said as they approached a black car. He placed Danika’s bag into the trunk and took the front seat next to Tobias. “We should be in Paradise within two hours.”

“Okay. Um...Uncle Philip, do you mind if I take a little nap? I’m kind of tired from the plane trip.” Danika couldn’t help the yawn that escaped her lips. In the two weeks since her father’s passing, she’d been too anxious to get a decent night’s sleep. Thoughts had continually swirled in her mind somewhere between the deep sense of loss over her father to the instability of her pending future, or lack thereof. She fastened her seat belt and leaned onto her small carry-on bag next to her. In minutes, her eyes drifted shut and the male voices in the front seat faded.

"Well, here we are," Philip announced as they pulled up to a white two-story in the country.

Danika sat up and rubbed her eyes. "Wow, I can't believe I slept the whole way."

"We're not home yet. We still need to drive to Paradise. Why don't you head on over to the barn and I will get your bags. You can wait in the rig if you'd like."

Danika shrugged. "Okay, cool." She walked over to the barn and opened the large door. She had to wait a minute until her eyes adjusted to the dimly lit interior. Her eyes roamed the barn in search of Philip's vehicle, but it was nowhere in sight.

Philip walked in behind her and noticed her looking around.

Danika turned to her uncle. "I don't see your truck anywhere," she said.

"Truck?" A puzzled look crossed Philip's face. He raised his eyebrows and nodded knowingly, then gestured to the far side of the barn. He walked up to an open black, horse-drawn carriage and placed the suitcase in the back seat. Danika's jaw dropped open and she just stood there, staring in disbelief. Philip escorted her to the buggy and helped her up onto the front seat.

"Oh wow!" she gushed, looking around inside the buggy. "This is so cool! I've always wanted to ride in one of these things. Did you rent this just to pick me up?"

Philip seemed to be at a loss for words. "Uh, well –" he stammered.

"You are so thoughtful! You really didn't have to go to all that trouble," Danika continued excitedly. "That is too sweet. Oh, this is awesome! I can't wait to tell Cindy about this."

"Well, I actually didn't rent the buggy – it belongs to me."

"Oh. So you give other people rides then? Could you give my friends and me a ride in it sometime? I've never ridden in carriage, so this will be my first time. I've seen them in movies before, and I've always wanted to, but I've never had the opportunity. This is going to be so cool!" She bounced on the seat felicitously.

Philip smiled at her enthusiasm, knowing it would be short lived. "I don't exactly give people rides, this is how we get around."

"Oh, so what about your car?" She cocked her head to one side. "Is it in the shop or something?"

"*Nee.* No. I mean, this is how we *always* get around," Philip said, as he clicked his tongue to signal the horse to move. The brown mare started out in a gentle trot, and then slowly picked up speed as they merged onto the road.

"Whoa whoa whoa...wait a minute, what do you mean?" Danika asked, not sure she was fully comprehending what he was trying to tell her.

"We – I don't own a car. We do not drive automobiles," Philip stated emphatically. "We use this spring buggy when the weather is nice and the enclosed gray buggy when it turns cold."

"You mean..." Realization slowly dawned on her. "*This* is your car?"

"In a way, yes," he affirmed.

"Oh, not as cool as I thought." She grimaced.

Wow! This is going to be interesting. I've got to call Cindy, Danika thought as they traveled toward Paradise...at a very slow pace, she realized. "Do you mind if I use your phone to call my friend when we get home? My cell phone is dead and I need to charge it," she asked.

"We don't have a telephone. However, there is one in the herb shop, but it has only been approved for business use. Considering the circumstances, I suppose it'll be okay for you to use it this one time," Philip offered, referring to the health food store that sat next to the house on their property.

"Nah, that's okay. I'll just shoot her an email," she said decidedly.

Philip shrugged.

No phone! Oh my, this is going to be an adjustment. First, no car. Then, no phone. What's next, no television? Danika felt herself spiraling into panic mode.

As they pulled into the yard, an obviously pregnant woman came out of the house with two small children in tow. One of them, a little girl, seemed to be about four or five years old. She was dressed in a plain, dark-green dress with a black apron that matched the woman's. The other child, a little boy that appeared to have just started walking, matched Philip – suspenders and all!

"Danika, this is my wife, Naomi. And this is Katie and Philip Jr. - we call him PJ for short," Philip said.

Naomi reached out her hand to shake Danika's. "Nice to meet you, Danika. Why don't you come on in and get settled?" the kind lady offered, as she led the way into the house.

As Danika followed Naomi into the house, she noticed that there were no lights on inside. Now she was really starting to worry. "Uh, Mrs. King, why are all the lights off?"

"You may call me Naomi."

"Why not Mrs. King?" Danika wondered.

"We don't use fancy *Englischer* titles. Just a simple name is fine."

"Fancy *Englischer*?" Danika questioned. "Oh, I'm not English. I'm half Hispanic, actually." She chuckled. "And I'd hardly call my jeans and t-shirt fancy."

"*Englischer* means non-Amish and *Englischers* are fancy compared to the Plain people."

"Okay, so I guess I am a fancy *Englischer*. I've never fancied myself fancy," she said, giggling again. "So, tell me why all the lights are off, Aunt Naomi. I may call you Aunt Naomi, right?"

"Yes, Aunt Naomi will be fine. We don't use electricity. We use God's light, the sun, for our light during the day," Naomi answered, "and at night, we use lanterns."

"Wow," Danika said under her breath. "You mean like lanterns for camping? I'm always afraid to light those things." She remembered a recent camping trip with Dad, before he'd been diagnosed with cancer. He'd asked her to light the lantern and gave her instructions on how to do it, warning about a possible explosion if she did it wrong. So, shakily, she lit a match and stuck it into the opening. The mantle inside the globe lit, while she held the match with eyes closed, and it gave out a 'poof' sound. Danika had screamed, thinking she'd blown something up. When she opened her eyes, the lantern burned brightly and Dad was chuckling. She told herself she'd never want to light one of those things again.

"*Jah*. I guess they're similar to those."

"What does 'yah' mean?"

"*Jah* is 'yes'. Would you like me to show you to your room now?" Naomi grinned.

"*Jah*," Danika answered, then giggled.

Naomi smiled. "Before you know it, you'll be a regular Amish girl."

"A what?"

"An Amish girl," Naomi repeated. "That's what we are – Amish."

"Oh. Well, let's not get the cart before the horse!" She smiled at her intended pun. "I'm still a fancy *Englischer, jah*?"

"*Jah*." Naomi smiled, enjoying her playful spirit. When Philip had explained the situation about his sister Rebekah's daughter needing a home, Naomi hadn't hesitated to welcome their new guest. But she did have reservations about bringing a teenage *Englisch* girl into their home, though. Philip had assured her that everything would work out according to God's plan.

Naomi couldn't help but think about the twin daughters she had lost, along with her first husband. They would've been the same age as Danika is now. Was God bringing Danika into her life as way to comfort her for the loss of her daughters? He'd already blessed her with Philip, who was the finest husband she could ever ask for, and then of course, little PJ and the babe she now carried in her womb. She could never have imagined her life would turn out like this. It seemed as if life was a cycle of heartaches and joys, mostly mountains and valleys with a plateau here and there.

As Naomi showed her niece to her room upstairs, Danika looked around taking everything in. She noticed the walls were mostly unadorned, except for a scenic calendar from Beiler's Hardware Store. "Where are your family pictures?"

"We don't take photographs. The Amish believe that they are graven images and do not allow them."

"Really?" Danika gulped. Her hand moved to her chest and clutched the heart locket that hung from her neck. It had been a precious gift to her from her parents on her eighth birthday, and contained a small wedding photo of her mother and father. *I could never part with my necklace,* she thought to herself worriedly, as tears sprang to her eyes.

After unpacking all of her belongings, Danika tried to figure out where to put her laptop. *Oh no, I don't have anywhere to plug it in,* she realized disappointedly. She sat the computer on the small desk and pushed the button to turn it on. The battery still had a full charge, so she'd be able to use it for a couple of hours. She quickly sent an email to her friend Cindy:

Hey Cin,

Just thought I'd let you know that I made it here safely. You would not believe this place. It's like I stepped out of the real world and into Little House on the Prairie!! Remember that show my dad used to want to watch all the time? And I'm not joking, either. It's weird. I'm trippin' out a little bit

Hey, if I don't email you back it's because my computer battery is dead. No electricity here! I told you, it's like I'm living in a different century. So, could you send me a letter via snail mail? I know it's kind of a pain, but it might be the only way for us to communicate. Oh, and my phone's dead too, but I think my uncle might let me charge it in his health food store. My aunt and uncle seem pretty cool – so far.

Chat later,

Dani

Danika closed her laptop and headed downstairs when she heard Naomi's call. She guessed it was probably time for dinner.

"Will you take the plates from the hutch and set the table?" Naomi requested.

Danika noticed a couple of different China sets. "Which ones?"

"Well, since it's a special day, let's use the pink floral set," Naomi remarked, as she set a delicious-smelling pot pie on the table with freshly-squeezed lemonade.

Philip came into the house with PJ toddling close behind him. He washed his hands before giving Naomi a brief peck on the cheek and rubbed her rounded belly. He picked up the little boy and put him in his lap as he sat at the table. PJ immediately bowed his head and waited. "Not just yet, PJ. Katie's still in the kitchen," Philip instructed and the little guy lifted his head.

Katie dried her hands, and made her way toward the table. When all were seated, Philip bowed his head signaling he was about to pray. The family all bowed as well. Danika frowned, confused at first, but eventually caught on and bowed her head also. Praying before meals had not been the norm in her childhood home. The silent prayer finished, Philip cleared his throat and everyone raised their heads, except Danika. She kept her head bowed. Philip cleared his throat again. Still, Danika's head was bowed in silence. Finally, Philip declared, "Amen" and Danika raised her head. Philip and Naomi briefly smiled at one another.

After dinner concluded and the dishes had been washed, dried, and put away, the family gathered in the living room. Katie sat primly on the loveseat beside her new house guest, and PJ sat next to his *daed* and *mamm* on the small tan sectional. "So, what do you guys do here without a TV?" Danika questioned, breaking the silence.

"What's a TV?" Katie asked.

"Oh, it's so cool! You can wat –" Danika began to explain, but was abruptly cut off when Philip held up his hand to silence her, sending a look of warning.

"It is *verboten*, Katie. You need not know of wicked *Englisch* devices."

"We spend time with our family. Such as playing games, reading books and talking," Naomi said, recovering the conversation.

"Games? Cool, I'll go grab my Game Boy!" Danika hopped up, headed for the stairs.

"Whoa, whoa, whoa!" Philip called. "Game Boy?"

"Yeah." Danika halted near the bottom step, looking at them as if they were aliens. "You *do* know what a Game Boy is, right?"

Philip and Naomi looked at each other and both shook their heads, adorable PJ mimicked them.

"Wow." Danika couldn't get over their deliberate ignorance of modern technological devices. "I know you know what a computer is. It's kinda like a small computer with electronic games on it."

"We don't play those kinds of games. We play *board* games," Philip clarified. "Danika, how much did your father tell you about us?" Philip asked curiously.

"Not much at all. I mean, I really didn't even know you guys existed until, like, a couple of weeks ago," she answered. "And I had no clue about the whole Amish thing. I just thought you guys were like regular normal people. No offense."

Philip sighed, scratching his chocolate-colored beard. "I expect this will not be an easy transition for you. We have certain standards that we live up to."

"You got that right. I'm already freakin' out about the no electricity thing. My cell's dead, so I don't know how I'll be able to charge it *or* my laptop. I won't be able to download any books on my Kindle now either. And how am I supposed to check my Facebook or post on Twitter? I'll be totally out of sync with my friends in Cali. Unless you guys have a Starbucks around here and I can use their Wi-Fi?"

With mouths agape, Philip and Naomi looked at each other trying to make sense of what was just said. Danika definitely spoke a different language than what they were used to. Naomi spoke up, "We were hoping you could make some new friends here."

"You mean Amish ones? I guess that might be sorta cool," Dani answered imperviously.

"Naomi can take you to town tomorrow to get some fabric for your dresses," Philip stated.

"Dresses? Oh no. I can't wear dresses, I look terrible in them. They make me look too fat," Danika protested.

Naomi and Philip glanced at each other again, puzzled. Naomi reassured Danika, "Nobody here will think you're fat.

We all dress the same, so you don't need to worry about being made fun of. Besides, you're not fat at all."

"You will begin school on Monday, so you'll need to get started making the dresses as soon as possible," Philip suggested.

"You want me to wear dresses to school?" Danika asked in disbelief. The last time she remembered wearing a dress to school was her first day of kindergarten. "And you want *me* to make them?" Her eyes widened.

"Naomi will help you if you'd like," Philip offered.

"*Help* me? Do you guys think that I can, like, sew or something? I've never touched a sewing machine in my life." Panic mode was setting in.

"There's not much to it. You'll learn quickly. I will show you how to do it step-by-step. No need to worry," Naomi comforted.

"Whew! Thanks." Danika sighed. "You guys were, like, totally scaring me there for a minute."

"Well, enough scaring Danika. Let's read for a while, then we can play some games," Philip stated.

"Oh, I love games! Dad and I used to play Checkers all the time." Danika perked up.

"Philip loves to play Checkers too." Naomi smiled at Dani. "It looks like you're going to make it here just fine."

CHAPTER 3
Adjustments

"Let all bitterness...be put away from you."
Ephesians 4:31

As Naomi maneuvered the shopping cart around the store, Danika seemed to take a keen interest in the *Englisch* clothing. She knew this transition was going to be terribly difficult for her niece and hoped that somehow she could make the adjustment more bearable for her. A girl Danika's age already had enough to deal with without adding on the extra burdens of losing a parent, moving to a foreign place, and having to adjust to an Amish lifestyle. Considering everything, Naomi knew Danika was handling things amazingly well. She prayed that God would give her and Philip patience with the girl.

"Naomi King. Well, I haven't seen you out lately," Esther Fisher greeted her friend.

"*Hullo*, Esther. I'd like you to meet my niece, Danika. She'll be living with Philip and me now," Naomi stated.

"*Ach, gut* to meet ya. This here's my Jonathan. He's our youngest." Esther patted Jonathan's back. "Jonathan, say hello to Danika."

Jonathan peered at Danika under his straw hat, pushing his bangs to the side. He nodded to Danika, then said, "Guess what? I got me six *aldi*s at school!"

Naomi and Esther both suppressed a chuckle.

"*Aldi*s?" Danika asked.

"It means girlfriends in *Englischer's* talk," Jonathan informed her.

"How many girls are there at school?" Danika asked.

"Eight. But one's my sister, so she didn't want to be my *aldi.*" Jonathan shrugged. "The other one is Susie Hostettler. She said she won't ever be my *aldi,* but I don't believe her. She's my best girl, but she don't like me none." Jonathan's shoulders now sagged.

"Oh, I'm sorry," Danika offered, feeling sorry for the boy.

Jonathan's eyes perked up. "Would you like to be my *aldi* too? I ain't never had an *Englisch aldi.*"

Naomi abruptly spoke up before Jonathan was able to continue his shenanigans, "Esther, I think Danika and I should get over to the sewing section now. We've got some dresses to make if Danika's going to make it to school next week."

After bidding the Fishers farewell, Naomi and Danika quickly found their desired area of the store. "Well, here's the fabric. Go ahead and pick out a few colors." Naomi stepped back so Danika could view the myriad of fabrics. Animal prints, calicoes, and television cartoon characters seemed to dominate the wall space, but many solid colors were present as well. "Wal-Mart usually has a decent selection."

"Yikes, that's a lot of material to choose from. Oh, here's a nice one," Danika exclaimed, pulling out a bolt of pink and white floral material.

"I'm sorry, but we only wear plain colors - no designs," Naomi stated apologetically.

"I could stick with red or fuchsia."

"We wear burgundy, dark green, dark blue, and purple."

"I guess it's purple then."

"You may get some of each if you'd like. I'm sure you don't want to wear the same color every day. We'll also need some black for your aprons and some white organdy for your prayer *kapp,*" Naomi stated, pointing to her own.

Oh, wow. I'm going to look so lame in one of those things, Danika thought to herself, then said in contrast, "Yeah, I guess that might be sort-of cool."

As Naomi sat at the treadle sewing machine, Danika leaned over her enthralled, watching every stitch. "Hey, that's pretty awesome. Do you really think I can learn to do it?" Dani asked, now thoroughly interested in the sewing project.

"*Jah.* It's really not that difficult once you get the hang of it. Would you like to try?" Naomi offered, as she stood up and moved the chair back.

"Sure, but what if I break it?" Danika said apprehensively as she sat in front of the machine.

"You won't," Naomi assured. "Okay, now place your feet on the treadle." Naomi pointed to the floor. "Now, put your right hand on the wheel and turn it toward you." Danika did as told, and the material started moving under the needle. "Now keep it going with your feet and guide the material with your left hand. Try to keep it straight. You're doing *gut,*" Naomi said, as Danika effortlessly moved the fabric and pumped the treadle simultaneously.

"Hey, I think I'm going to like this. It's kinda fun." Danika smiled.

"It usually takes a while to get the hang of it, but you appear to be a natural. You're pretty good at it too. Look at those stitches," Naomi encouraged.

By the end of the day, they had already completed one of Danika's dresses and an apron. Surprisingly, Dani was excited to try on her new threads. "Hey, I guess I don't look too fat in these after all," she said, as she modeled one of her dresses for Naomi and Katie.

After dinner that evening, Naomi and Danika washed, dried, and put the dishes away. Philip, Katie, and PJ waited in the living room for the ladies to finish up the chores. When they finally arrived, Philip began reading from the book of John. Danika listened intently, trying to understand every word. Although there had been a Bible at her home in California, she had never really read it for herself. "*Jesus answered and said unto him*," Philip read. "*Verily, verily, I say unto thee, Except a man be born again, he cannot see the kingdom of God.*"

"Uncle Philip," Danika asked genuinely, "what does that mean – *except a man be born again, he cannot see the kingdom of God*? Even if my mother was still alive, it would be physically impossible for me to be born a second time."

Philip chuckled. "That's what Nicodemus tried to tell Jesus – that physical rebirth was impossible. But Jesus wasn't talking about physical rebirth; he was speaking of spiritual birth."

"Spiritual birth?" asked Danika, eyebrows mirroring her perplexity.

"Yes." Naomi joined the conversation. "Verse five says, *except a man be born of water and of the Spirit, he cannot enter into the kingdom of God.*"

"Oh, I see – being 'born of water' means getting baptized," Dani said.

"No, not at all. Being born of water is to be born physically. Have you ever heard someone ask a woman in labor if her water broke?"

"No, but I've seen it on TV." Danika added, "So, that's the water this is talking about."

"That's right, the physical birth. And being born of the Spirit obviously means being born spiritually. Jesus explains this in verse six. When you are born of the Spirit, you are born again. When you accept Jesus as your Saviour, that's when you are born a second time – that's when you become a Christian."

Danika appeared baffled at Naomi's words. "But I was baptized when I was a baby, and Dad said that you become a Christian when you are baptized – at least, that's what the priest told him."

"Baptism doesn't make you a Christian; it shows you are a Christian."

"Oh, it's like Mom's and Dad's wedding rings – the rings didn't make them married, they just showed that they were married."

"Right. Heaven is God's Kingdom and to go to Heaven, Jesus said we must be born again."

"But the priest said that we must keep the sacraments. You know: go to mass, confirmation, partake of the Holy Eucharist, pray the rosary, and all that stuff, if we hope to make it into Heaven."

Philip and Naomi looked at each other in bewilderment. "We kind of used to think that way too. I mean, that by doing the right things we could earn our way to Heaven. But we were wrong. I'm afraid those things are all referred to as 'works of righteousness' in the Bible. Those things can never get us to

Heaven. Isaiah sixty-four says that 'all our righteousnesses are as filthy rags', they are detestable to God," Philip explained.

Naomi added, "If we try to make it to Heaven with our own works, that means that we've rejected God's gift – his precious Son – the only acceptable payment for our sins, and we're trying to pay for them ourselves, which is impossible."

"Wow!" Danika let it all sink in. "So there's nothing that I can do?"

"Just believe. Simply place your trust in the blood that Jesus shed for you when he died on the cross. He promises to wash away all your sins and give you eternal life," Philip offered. "If you could work your way to Heaven, then Jesus would have died for no reason at all."

"Dude, that's heavy," Danika commented as Philip and Naomi briefly locked eyes again.

"The only question is now that you know, what will you do about it?" Naomi questioned.

"I'll have to think about it, that's for sure...and for certain." She looked teasingly at Naomi and Philip and they smiled. "I'm going up to my room now. I'll think about it, I promise. Good night." She started up the stairs.

"Danika," Naomi called. Dani stopped and turned to face her aunt. "Please, don't put this decision off. It determines your eternal destiny," she pressed, with an urgent pleading tone in her voice.

In her room, Danika thought it over. *I'd like to go to Heaven. But, why did Mom and Dad have to die? I don't under-*

stand. I wish I could talk to them right now! She frowned as tears welled up in her eyes. She thought about her mom's and dad's deaths and the unfairness of it all, and the tears threatened to spill on her cheeks. *If God* really *loves me, why did he take my mom and dad away? It's just not fair.* Danika threw herself on her bed and cried until she couldn't cry anymore. She stared stonily at the door and allowed bitterness to creep in to her heart and take root. *Why should I have to do things His way? I hate God. And I won't ever forgive Him for taking Mom and Dad!* Exhausted, she fell into a troubled sleep.

CHAPTER 4
Chores

"The heart of the wise teacheth his mouth, and addeth learning to his lips." Proverbs 16:23

"Danika, wake up. Danika." Naomi firmly shook Dani's shoulder.

Danika moaned. "Who... where... wha..." She looked at Naomi who held up a lantern. Aside from the light emanating from Naomi's hand, Danika's room was completely dark. It was pitch-black outside her window as well, and cold.

"Danika, it's 5:15 already. Do you plan to sleep all day?" Naomi gently chided her.

"5:15? In the morning? Oh, leave me alone!" Danika murmured as she sank back onto her bed.

Naomi walked out of the room muttering, "You leave me no choice."

It seemed like only a minute had passed before Danika felt ice cold water being splashed in her face. "What the..." She sprang up out of bed, now fully awake.

"Good morning, bright eyes!" Naomi grinned with a dripping cup in her hand. "Works every time. All right, first of all, you'll make your bed. Next, you'll be helping Philip and Katie milk the goats and feed the chickens – after you get dressed, of course. And then you'll be helping me make breakfast, and afterward you and Katie will do the dishes," Naomi replied with a twinkle in her eyes.

"You know, you can be pretty bossy sometimes," Danika accused, rubbing the water from her face.

Naomi took this thought into consideration. "That's quite possible, but talking about it isn't going to do you any good – Amish life isn't exactly easy. You'd be hard-pressed to find a lazy Amish person." She smiled and announced, "All right, let's hurry now. You're burning daylight."

Danika grabbed her dress and quickly put it on. "I'm trying to hurry. It's more like I'm burning nightlight, five fifteen in the morning," she mumbled to herself as she put her stockings and shoes on. She hurried downstairs struggling with her prayer *kapp*, her hair flowing around her shoulders. Naomi saw Danika and rushed to her aid.

"Here, let me help you with that." Naomi quickly wrapped Danika's hair into a tight bun and fastened it with five stainless-steel hairpins. "You have incredibly thick hair, Danika. It's so beautiful and dark," Naomi commented as she helped Danika fasten her white prayer *kapp* over her hair.

"Dad said I have his hair and his eyes, but I have Mom's face."

"Well, you have your mother's nose for sure and for certain. Philip said that he and your mother had the same nose, and yours matches your uncle's. *Kumm,*" She motioned. "Take this lantern." Naomi thrust a lantern in Danika's left hand. "And a bucket." Naomi picked up a bucket and gave it to Danika who took it in her other hand. "There, now go out to the barn. Philip and Katie are waiting for you. They will show you how to milk the goats." Naomi shooed her out the door.

These people are psycho, she decided. Danika hurried toward the other building behind the house. She heard some goats crying inside and a girl's voice hushing and scolding them. "Hush up now, Buttercup. There's no need to cause a bunch of ruckus, you silly old goat."

"That's it, Katie – you're gettin' the hang of it. My little helper will soon be able to milk the goats all by herself," Philip praised Katie. "*Kumm,* Danika. Have a seat. Did you sleep all right?" Philip pulled up a small wooden stool for her.

She huffed and sat down. "Well, I was sleeping fine until –"

"Let me guess. The old water trick?" Philip laughed, smiling mischievously. Danika nodded in confirmation. "So, have you ever milked goats?" Danika shook her head. "Well, that's all right. You get to learn something new today. First of all..." he continued to explain all the steps and then showed her how to milk a goat.

"Okay, I'd like to give it a try now." Danika took one of the teats in her hand and started squeezing, not pulling, the way Philip had shown her.

"That's good. Just keep doing it the same way," Philip encouraged. When he wasn't looking, she pointed the teat at Philip and squirted some milk in his face.

"Oops! Sorry." Dani laughed, and Katie giggled too.

Philip responded with a smile, "An accident, huh?"

"Yeah, just like this," she proceeded to shoot him with a steady stream of goat's milk.

"Hey, now, let's not waste too much of that. We'll need it for breakfast and to make cheese later. Not to mention my customers who come in to the health food store to buy it," Philip cautioned, as milk flew onto his face and in his beard.

"Okay, okay." Danika resigned to milking the goats carefully.

Danika proudly carried the goats' milk into the house and Katie followed behind her with a basket of eggs. Naomi was kneading dough in the kitchen when she noticed Philip coming in through the back door. He still had a little milk dripping from his beard.

"What happened to you?" Naomi asked Philip.

Philip just nodded his head toward Danika who was wearing a mischievous grin.

"She got him good, Mama!" Katie divulged, and they all burst into laughter.

Danika heard a knock at the door. She called, "Naomi, there's someone at the door."

From the kitchen she heard Naomi reply, "Oh, that must be Joanna and Chloe."

"Don't worry, I'll get it." Dani stood up from the sofa, put down the book she was reading, and swiftly walked to the door. She opened it and saw two girls about her age standing outside the door. Both of the girls looked surprised at first, but quickly composed themselves. "Come in." Danika motioned with her hands.

As both of the girls came inside, one of them asked, "Is Naomi here?"

Danika nodded. "Yeah, she's here. Let me get her real quick." Naomi strode into the room with paper in hand.

"Good morning, Joanna. Good morning, Chloe."

"Good morning, Naomi," they replied in unison.

Joanna glanced at Danika and said to Naomi, "You have company, *jah*? I hope we didn't interrupt."

"Oh," Naomi replied. "No, this is Danika. She's Philip's niece. She's living with us now."

"Hello, Danika. I'm Joanna Fisher," She held out her hand.

"And I'm Chloe Esh. Nice to meet you."

"Where are you from?" Joanna asked curiously, noting she hadn't seen her around the area before.

"California," Dani stated.

"I didn't know there were any Amish settlements in California," Chloe piped in, eyeing her Amish garb.

"Danika was an *Englischer* before she came here," Naomi added. "But we can discuss that over lunch. Right now, you girls should be off." She handed a list to one of the girls and they hurried out the door.

Danika turned to Naomi, "What are they doing?"

"Oh, the girls deliver honey for me. They've been working for me for a couple of years now."

Danika appeared to be thinking. "Where did they get those scooters from?"

"There's an Amish man that owns a shop in town; it's called Beiler's Hardware. He's kin to the Fishers. Joanna's uncle, in fact. He makes them and sells them to the Amish and English."

"Naomi, when do I get my allowance?" Danika asked innocently.

"What do you mean?"

"Allowance. The money for doing my chores."

"Money for doing chores? Why, I've never heard of such a thing." Naomi laughed.

Danika frowned. "You've got to be kidding me, right?"

Naomi shook her head. "No, I'm quite serious."

"You mean, I've been doing all this work and I'm not even going to get paid for it." Danika's temper was visibly rising.

"You get to live in this house, eat all of your meals, and you have clothes to wear," Naomi reminded her.

"But I'm a kid, you guys are supposed to give me that stuff! How am I going to buy anything for myself?" Danika stated selfishly.

"We Amish live very simple lives. We don't need fancy things to make us happy. God provides for our needs, and that is sufficient," Naomi said contently.

"Oh, that's just great," Danika declared sarcastically. "I thought I was coming to Paradise, instead I end up in Amish Hell!" She spun herself around and startled when Philip stood directly in front of her. His arms crossed over his chest.

"Danika!" With calmness he didn't feel, Philip tried to choose his words carefully, "I am glad that you've come here to live with us. But I will not tolerate that kind of speech. You have spoken disrespectfully to Naomi and you will apologize to her."

"No, I will not!" Danika shouted, as she ran out the back door.

Exasperated, Naomi threw up her hands. "Philip, I've never been spoken to that way before. I'm afraid I don't know how to deal with an *Englisch* young person."

Philip embraced his trembling wife. Knowing this incident was causing undue stress for her pregnancy, he attempted to comfort her. "It will get easier, *Liewe*, I promise."

Danika ran until she could run no more. Tears streamed down her face, as she sat in the grass against a tall pine tree in a dense wooded area. Her energy spent, she lay down using her folded hands as a pillow and fell into an exhausted asleep.

Clip-clop, clip-clop, clip-clop. Danika shot up at the sound of the hoof beats, and looked around. Before her stood a young Amish man about her own age. He was dressed in suspenders and wearing a straw hat over what looked like a blond surfer haircut. *Wow, this guy's a babe!* she thought. He stared at her curiously.

"Hello," he said timidly.

"What are you doing out here?" she asked.

"I guess I should ask you the same thing. My name is Eli – Eli Yoder." He held out his hand.

"Danika," she answered, purposely withholding her last name.

"I haven't seen you around here before," he stated, questions evident on his handsome face.

"Well, I'm kinda new to the area. I live with the Kings. Just got here a few days ago," she shared.

"Welcome." He smiled "You live with Philip King, the herb *dokter*?"

"Uncle Philip's a doctor?" Danika was amazed by this newfound information.

"For these parts, *jah*...He's your uncle and you didn't know?" Eli asked in disbelief.

"Well, I thought he just owned a health food store. Nobody bothered to tell me anything about him being a doctor. How was I supposed to know?" she answered defensively.

"There's no need for you to get all upset about it."

"I'm sorry, I'm just a little on-edge right now," she apologized.

"I could sorta tell. Do you mind me asking what for?"

"It's kind of a long story," she said.

"I have some time, I don't mind," he said, offering his ear. He plopped down next to her.

Danika sighed. "I don't really know where to start. My mom died when I was eight years old. She was giving birth to my baby brother, and there were complications. We ended up losing my baby brother too." Eli looked at her with compassion in his light-blue eyes, but said nothing. She continued, "My Dad got cancer about six months ago, and now I've lost him too," she choked out the last words.

"I'm really sorry you had to go through all that, Danika," Eli sympathized.

"Now, I'm stuck here in Amishville. I had to leave my friends, my school, my home, and not to mention the beach in California to come to the middle of nowhere. Everybody here tells me what to do and when to do it, and I'm tired of it." She felt better after getting all of that off her chest.

Eli wasn't sure just what to say to her. Her story didn't relate to his at all. "Well, we all have things that we have to do whether we want to or not."

"What do you mean by that?" Danika lowered her eyebrows in question.

"Take Philip or my *vadder,* for example, they have to work hard at a job all day long to provide for their families. *Mamm* has to prepare meals for everyone and wash all the clothes. If you think about it, we have more freedom than they do," Eli explained.

"I guess I never thought about it that way before." Danika pondered his words.

"Danika, I can tell that losing your folks has been hard on you, and I'm sorry. But don't take it out on other people. Philip and Naomi are nice folks and I'm sure they just want what's best for you. Besides, I don't think they're used to having a stubborn *Englisch* girl living with them." He hoped to coax a smile out of her.

"Hey, how did you know I was an *Englischer*?"

"I can just tell," he simply replied.

"Is that bad or good?"

"Well..." He didn't dare answer that one. He looked at his horse and changed the subject. "Can I give you a ride home?"

"You didn't answer my question," she protested.

"A wise man knows when some things are better left unsaid." He smiled and hopped onto his horse. "Well, what do you say?" He patted the back of the horse and offered his hand.

"Sure, why not." Danika smiled, as she took his hand and carefully swung her leg over the back end of the horse.

"You may hold on to my shirt if you need to," he offered.

"Thanks for being a friend, Eli. I needed one. I'm glad I met you today," Dani said as they neared the King residence.

"Me, too. Will I see you in school on Monday?"

"Yeah, I think I'll be there."

"Danika, anytime you need someone to talk to..." Eli smiled.

"I'll remember that. Bye, Eli." She waved as he rode off.

As Danika walked into the house, she noticed the family was already sitting in the living room, as they did every evening after dinner. Philip and Naomi looked at one another, not knowing what to expect of Danika, before she came into the room. She ran to Naomi and wrapped her arms around her, tears streaming from her eyes. "I'm sorry, Naomi." Philip nodded his head at Naomi and gave her a smile behind Danika's back. She then turned to Philip. "Sorry, Uncle Philip."

"I kept some dinner warm for you, if you're hungry. It's on the stove," Naomi offered.

"But I haven't done my chores yet," Danika surprisingly responded.

"They have already been done. There will be plenty more tomorrow," Philip stated. "You may eat now."

Relieved, Danika scarfed down her food. She couldn't believe how hungry she was until she realized that she hadn't eaten since breakfast early this morning. When she had finished, she asked to retire to her room early where she collapsed on her bed, exhausted from the day's ordeal.

CHAPTER 5
Church

"Not forsaking the assembling of ourselves together, as the manner of some is; but exhorting one another..." Hebrews 10:25a

"Everybody's gone surfin', surfin' U.S.A." Danika sang reminiscently as she splashed water on herself in the bathtub. She heard a gentle knock on the door of the bathroom. "Just wait, please. I'm bathing right now."

From the other side of the door she heard a soft, high-pitched voice say, "It's me, Katie. I gotta go potty bad!"

Danika sighed with relief and replied, "Okay, you may come in, Katie."

The door opened and Katie walked in, quickly shutting the door behind her. Katie watched Danika curiously as she resumed her singing, "Inside, outside, U.S.A. Inside, outside,

U.S.A. Everybody's gone surfin', surfin' U.S.A." Danika noticed that Katie was watching her and stopped singing.

"Dani, what's surfin'?" Katie asked with large innocent eyes.

"You mean, you've never heard of surfing?"

Katie shook her head indicating she hadn't.

"Oh, yeah." Danika remembered. "You've never been to the beach. You poor thing," she sympathized and started to explain, "Well, okay, I guess the ocean is kind of like a big huge bathtub."

"You mean like Miller's Pond?"

Danika shrugged her shoulders, never having been to Miller's Pond. "Yeah, I guess so, but it's much bigger than a pond. You can't see the other side because it's thousands of miles away. It's so massive, it's unreal."

"But if it's not real, how can you see it?"

"No, no. I just mean that it's so big, it's amazing. Not that it isn't real."

"But you said –"

"Never mind what I said," Danika answered. "It's just really big."

"Wow, I think I'd be too scared to go in there."

"I know, I sometimes get scared too. The ocean has waves that go like this." Danika took her hand and moved the water around in a wave-like motion. "The waves are very powerful and they'll come crashing down on you – that is, if you don't know what to do. And if you're not really careful, the waves will carry you away and nobody will ever see you again. But if you know how to do it right, you can get on a surfboard and ride on top or inside of the waves."

"What's a surfboard?"

"It's a board made out of special material. People use them to stand on to ride the waves, like this." Danika put two of her fingers on top of a bar of soap as if they were surfing. "They have different sizes, but the one I used was about three feet taller than your daddy is. It is called a longboard. Surfing is a big deal in California, and it's so much fun! I've always been too scared to ride on the really big waves, but my friend Cindy does it all the time. She lives right next door to the beach..." Danika's voice trailed off and she was lost in her thoughts for a minute, but she soon snapped back. "Anyway, I better hurry up and get out of here so we won't be late."

Philip let one of the young men from their district lead their horse to the Fishers' barn. The Sunday-Go-To-Meetings were always held every other week at various homes in their church district. This week, Gideon and Esther Fisher would be hosting the service. The inside walls of the house had been removed and the porch had been closed in, with the benches set up inside.

Philip went to the barn to join the other men, and Danika was taken aback when she saw the men giving each other a kiss...on the lips! "Uh, Naomi, why are the guys kissing each other?" Danika asked as they headed toward the main house.

Naomi laughed. "The Bible says to greet one another with a holy kiss and they do it literally."

"Oh," Danika said worriedly. *I hope nobody tries to kiss me.*

Naomi and Danika stepped up onto the porch, entered through the back door, and came into the kitchen, which was bustling with Amish women. Naomi found Esther Fisher and offered her assistance. Dani noticed Joanna was helping prepare the food and asked if she could help.

"It's not necessary, but *denki.* I'm just about finished up now. Would ya like to sit with me and Chloe during meeting?" Joanna offered kindly.

"I'll have to ask my aunt first," Danika answered, and then walked over to Naomi. She returned a short while later with a disappointed look. "She said maybe next time. I guess she doesn't trust me yet."

"That's okay. We'll have plenty of time at the common meal after the meeting," Joanna encouraged.

Naomi joined Danika, when she noticed the men were heading toward the house, and they sat down on one of the wooden benches toward the back of the living room. The ladies with small children and babies often sat in the back in case they needed to get up and leave during the service. Oftentimes, diapers needed to be changed and the babies needed to be fed, so the women would go to an upstairs room to care for their little ones. Naomi's reason for sitting in the back was two-fold. She not only sat back there for PJ, but also for herself. Women who are 'in the family way', as they call it, often need to use the restroom much more frequently than others, Naomi had informed Danika.

The men, women, and children all dressed in their *for-gut* clothing, filed in and took their seats. Danika thought it odd that the men came in first, and that males and females sat on opposite sides facing each other. She noticed that the young, single men and women sat in the first couple of rows nearest the front. She would have been with them, had she not needed to sit near Naomi.

The *Ausbund* hymnals had been passed out prior to their arrival and an older man with a long white beard began singing in a slow chant-like style. The others joined in singing shortly thereafter. Danika had no clue what they were singing but she tried to follow along in the German hymnal which contained no musical notation. It seemed as though she tried to sing everything too quickly, so she kept her voice low. The church leaders congregated in an upstairs room, as the congregation sang.

After two long hours of singing, praying, and preaching had passed, Danika wondered if the service would ever come to an end. Her back started hurting and her bottom had fallen asleep. She thought about joining Naomi, who had gone upstairs with PJ, but she decided against it. She looked over to where the men and boys sat and tried to locate Eli, to no avail. She could see the backs of Joanna's and Chloe's prayer *kapps*. *Oh well, I guess if I can endure being in school all day then I can get through this.*

Finally, the service ended and the men moved some of the benches into make-shift tables with the benches for the seats. They filed outside and the women and older girls put a place setting out for each person, and set the food out on the tables. After patiently waiting for the men and older folk to eat, the women and children took their turns. Danika's stomach roared voraciously when the delicious smells assaulted her senses, making her doubly glad she had eaten an extra portion at breakfast.

Chloe and Joanna joined Danika after the meal. "Would ya like to play volleyball? Some of the young people set up a net and they're going to start a game soon," Chloe said.

"You guys actually play volleyball? Oh, I'd love to!" Danika's face brightened. "Naomi, may I please, please, please go play?" she begged.

"Go have fun, but don't get into trouble," Naomi said.

The girls scampered off to where the game was just getting started. They jumped in, and Danika spiked the ball down quickly to the opposing side of the net. The other players looked at each other in disbelief. When Danika's turn to serve came she pitched the ball flawlessly over the net, then jumped back in when the ball flew her way. She bumped the ball up to the front row where her teammate spiked it over to the other side, resulting in another point for their team.

After winning two games in a row, the girls decided to take a rest. "I didn't know you could play so well," Chloe complemented.

"We played all the time back home. Aside from surfing, volleyball is, like, my favorite sport," Danika stated.

"What's surfing?" Joanna asked.

"Well, it's not that easy to explain. Why don't you guys come over sometime and I'll show you?" Dani offered, and the girls nodded in affirmation. "How about today?"

"I'll have to ask my *dat,*" Joanna stated.

"*Jah,* me too." Chloe nodded.

"Dude, that would be so cool. You guys will love it." Danika smiled. "Hey, what are you guys going to be for Halloween?"

The girls now sat down on the grass, not far from Jonathan and his friends. "Halloween?" Joanna asked.

"*Ach,* she must mean the *Englischer* holiday," Chloe offered.

"Yeah. You know, when kids dress up in costumes and go door to door for candy," Dani explained.

"*Nee,* we do not do that. It is wrong to dress up as someone you are not. That is a very bad day. *Mamm* said it is a holiday for the devil," Chloe insisted.

Joanna changed the subject. "We will go ask if we can come over to Philip King's house now." She and Chloe stood up from their places in the grass, leaving Danika to ponder the differences between where she'd come from and this strange new place.

"Hey, Danika!"

Dani looked up to see Jonathan Fisher and his two friends standing near. "Yeah?"

"What is this Halloween?" Jonathan wanted to know.

"Well, most of the kids dress up in costumes and go around to people's houses and ask for candy," she said.

Jonathan's eyes lit up. "Candy?"

"Yes, they give you lots of candy," Danika said. "But I guess I won't be getting any this year, because it's coming up this Friday night and I don't even have a costume. Hey, I bet I could go dressed just like this and everybody would think I dressed up."

"Where do the *Englisch* children go to get all this candy?" Matthew Riehl asked, looking at Jonathan and Joshua, then back to Danika again.

"Just to the houses in town. I wish I could go, but I'm sure Uncle Philip wouldn't let me." She shrugged. "Well, I better go. It looks like they're getting in the buggy now."

Later on toward evening, Joanna and Chloe knocked on the door.

"I wonder who's here," Philip commented to Naomi.

"I'm not expecting anybody," Naomi stated.

Danika came running down the stairs toward the door and was nigh unto opening it when Philip spoke, "Whoa, there. Danika, did you invite somebody over?"

"Yes, I invited Joanna and Chloe," Danika stated.

"Next time, you need to ask us before inviting someone over," he stated, raising his eyebrows.

"Okay, sorry." Dani felt bad, having let her aunt and uncle down again.

There was another knock at the door and Philip nodded. "You may let them in."

As the girls came into the house, they greeted Philip, Naomi, and the children. Danika decided she'd better ask before taking the girls upstairs. "Do you mind if we go upstairs to my room?" she asked, looking at Philip with pleading eyes.

"I think that would be fine...for a little while." To that, the girls excitedly went up the stairs to Dani's room. They looked around and noticed her laptop and cell phone sitting on the desk. The girls looked at each other worriedly as Danika turned her computer on. They had been well informed that the devices transported wickedness and were forbidden in their district. They wondered if they should speak up in protest.

"You've got to see this really cool video that Cindy's brother shot of us surfing," Danika stated, her voice full of enthusiasm. "There we go," she said as the video started playing. In the distance, they could see two figures standing on long boards on top of a wave.

"That looks like fun," Chloe said looking at Joanna, who wasn't quite so sure.

As the video zoomed in close, the girls quickly looked away covering their eyes.

"What's wrong?" Danika asked looking confused.

"You're not wearing clothes," Joanna stated matter-of-factly.

"Oh, sure we are. We have our bathing suits on. See?" Danika pointed to their bikinis.

"No, those are undergarments...unmentionables. They're not appropriate to wear in public," Chloe said.

"Okay, okay, I'll turn it off." Danika felt disappointed that her new friends didn't share her love of surfing. "I don't see what the big deal is. Everybody wears bikinis at the beach."

"God does not want us to show our bodies to each other. *Mamm* said we are supposed to dress modestly so we don't tempt the boys into sinning with their eyes," Joanna explained.

"You guys talk an awful lot about God. I'm not so sure I even believe in God," Danika shared.

"How can you *not* believe in God?" Chloe was shocked.

"Well, I prayed to Him about something and He didn't answer me."

"How do you know He didn't answer you?" Joanna asked.

"Because He let my mom, my brother, and my dad die. I never even got to hold my baby brother," a tear spilled down Dani's cheek.

"*Gottes ville.* Sometimes God's answer is no. We have to accept that God knows what's best for us even when we don't understand. It's called faith." Joanna sat close to Danika and put her arm around her.

"I don't have faith," Dani stated sadly. "I can't understand why God would want to take my parents away and leave me all alone. It isn't fair. I don't think I can put faith in a God I can't see."

"You must trust Him, because He can see things we cannot. Maybe there was a reason He brought you here. God will give you faith if you ask Him," Chloe advised.

"I think I might try," Dani conceded.

That's when they all heard Naomi holler up the stairs, "Who wants cookies and milk?" At once, the girls smiled at each other and rushed downstairs for a treat.

After the girls had left and dinner was complete, Katie helped Naomi with the dishes and Danika cleared the table. Danika could hear Katie attempting to sing the Beach Boys song that she had been singing earlier in the bathtub. "Everybody can go surfing, surfing in the UFA," she sang aloud to Naomi's astonishment.

"Katie, where did you hear such a song?" Naomi thought of Danika and looked her way.

"Dani sings it, *Mamm*. And this is how you surf." She showed her mother as she put her two fingers on a plate and pushed it around in the dish water.

Naomi chided Danika, "*Ach*, do you have to bring your *Englischer* music into this house? Now she'll probably have that worldly song in her head her whole life."

"Sorry, Naomi. I wasn't thinking about that. I didn't think it was a big deal," Danika offered.

"Well, it is a big deal. We strive hard to keep worldliness out of our lives." Naomi turned to Katie and instructed her, "Katie, we don't sing *Englischer* music, especially on the Lord's day."

"We just sing the hymns from the *Ausbund, jah*?" Katie inquired.

"That's right," Naomi said, giving Danika a disapproving look.

Danika sighed to herself, *I can't do anything right around here.*

CHAPTER 6

First Day of School

"Teach me good judgment and knowledge..."
Psalm 119:66a

As promised, Joanna and Chloe showed up at the King residence early Monday morning. They had offered to escort their new friend to school on her first day. Today, they came on foot since Danika didn't own a scooter. "Maybe you can ask Philip to buy you a scooter," Joanna suggested as they left the house, lunch pails in hand.

"I'd like one, but I don't think I should ask him for anything just yet," she said as she thought about the eggshells she'd been walking on lately. She desperately wanted to please her aunt and uncle, but it seemed like everything she did landed her in trouble. She definitely was not accustomed to all the rules and regulations her new Amish community imposed. "Let's talk about something else. You guys probably have some stories to tell."

It looked as though Chloe was searching her brain for something interesting to say, but Joanna spoke first, "Do you like horses, Danika?"

"I guess. I've never really ridden one before. Except for the other day with El –" she stopped short, unsure of whether she wanted to divulge their secret meeting.

"Were you going to say Eli?" Chloe asked wide-eyed. "As in Eli Yoder?"

"Why do you ask that way? Is something wrong with him?" Danika wondered.

"*Nee*," Joanna answered. "He's in a different church district."

"So, who cares?" Danika obviously didn't see the point. She had been friends with people from all kinds of different churches back in California.

"It's a big deal," Chloe stated. "And I'm sure Philip and Naomi would care."

"So, you're saying that I can't be friends with Eli just because he goes to a different church? You guys really baffle me. I don't know if I'll ever understand this whole Amish thing."

"That's not it." Joanna attempted to explain, "A couple of years ago there was a huge church split. The bishop changed some rules to the *Ordnung* and Eli's father fought it tooth and nail."

"What's *Ordnung*?" Danika asked.

"The *Ordnung* are the rules that the Amish church abide by," Chloe stated.

"So, what was the big deal? Why did Eli's dad fight it?"

"Well, I guess he didn't agree with the changes. He wanted to hang on to the Old Ways, the way things have always been done. The bishop asked Philip to try to reason with him, and he attempted to explain how the new way would be better for his family. Well, Jacob Yoder became quite upset and ended up leaving our church district, convincing several other families to leave with him. They formed Bishop Mast's district as a result. He resented your uncle for trying to persuade him and his family and vowed to never speak to Philip King again," Joanna explained.

"Oh." Danika voiced her thoughts, "It didn't seem like Eli had anything against Philip."

"Oh no, Eli is real nice about it. I think he even secretly agrees with the new ways. It's just, I don't know how his *daed* would feel about him being friends with you – living in the same house and being Philip's niece and all."

"Bummer. Why does life have to be so difficult," Danika stated more than asked. "Everything seems so complicated here."

"So, you really like Eli, huh?" Chloe pried.

Danika ducked her head to escape their knowing eyes. "He's the first friend I made here. He's so nice and really smart too." Dani smiled as she relived the short time they'd spent talking in the woods.

Joanna and Chloe exchanged a meaningful glance. "Well, at least he still goes to the same school. Our school is a lot closer than the school in their church district, so his *daed* allowed him and the children to stay."

Danika blushed. "Really? You mean he'll be there today?" She'd forgotten about that. She couldn't wipe the smile off her face now. Danika lifted her eyes to see if the school was in sight yet. She was beginning to believe the stories her mother told about when she was young she'd had to walk five miles in the snow to get to school every day. "So, what were you guys saying about the horses?" she asked, realizing the need to change the subject before her friends noticed her obvious crush.

"Before we answer that, may I ask you something?" Chloe tilted her head.

"Sure, I guess."

"Why do you keep calling us 'guys'? We are girls, you know."

Danika laughed at Chloe's question. "It's just something we say back in California. You know, just like you guys, oops, I mean, the Amish have their sayings. Like 'for sure and for certain' and 'ain't'."

"Oh, I see. It just feels strange to be called by a man's title." Chloe shrugged. "Now about the horses...me and Joanna, we ride horses all the time."

"Race them too," Joanna added quietly. "Just don't tell anyone I said that."

"Your secret is safe with me. Remember, you guys know my secret too," Danika replied while pretending to zip her lips.

The girls giggled. "So, do you think you will like school here?" Chloe queried.

"I don't know. I'm awfully nervous but at least I have some friends." Danika sighed heavily. "It would be easier if my dad was here. He always encouraged me to do my best in school."

"What did your parents look like?" Joanna wondered.

"I have a picture of them. Just a minute." Danika felt around her neck and brought out a locket and opened it. It held two small photographs; one was a wedding photo of her parents embraced in each other's arms, and in the other photo Danika sat in between her mother and father. She'd been just two years old when the photo was taken, but she remembered it well.

"It's very pretty," Chloe commented, "but we're not allowed to have pictures...or jewelry."

Danika held up her hands in protest. "There's no way I'm giving up my locket. It's one of the few things I have left of my parents. Please don't tell anyone that I have it," Danika requested desperately.

"Sure, you don't have to worry about us telling anybody," Joanna spoke for both girls.

Danika was apprehensive when she first entered the schoolyard. She was unsure how she would be treated since she was an outsider. *Will I be judged because of my skin color*? she wondered privately, noting that she had the darkest hair and skin of all the students. It was different in California. There had been much diversity, so she felt comfortable. But here, she was clearly the only Mexican. She took a nervous breath.

The other scholars quickly turned around to take a peek at the new girl, Eli Yoder being one of them. He flashed a big smile and she noticed how perfectly straight his teeth were. And how handsome he was. She smiled back at him, and then quickly looked away as she felt her face flush. She could feel that his eyes were still on her as she walked up the steps into the classroom with Joanna and Chloe.

"Danika, this is our teacher, Grace," Chloe introduced. "She's Joanna's sister."

"Nice to meet you, Miss Fisher." Danika tried to be polite. *She doesn't look that much older than me,* she thought to herself.

"*Gut* to meet you too. And you may call me Grace," the teacher instructed. Danika then remembered that they didn't use *Englischer* titles. "I have an empty desk over here, where you can sit for now." Grace walked to the back of the classroom, showing Dani where she would be sitting.

"Thank you."

"What was the last grade you completed at your previous school?" Grace asked, trying to determine which books Danika required.

"I just started eighth grade."

"So, this will be your last year," Grace stated.

"Yeah, until high school," Danika said matter-of-factly, "and, of course, college."

Grace looked at Joanna and Chloe, who had no idea how to respond. "Amish only have school till eighth grade," Grace informed her.

"You've got to be kidding!" Danika noticed that she was the only one laughing, finding solemnity in the other faces. "Seriously?"

The three girls nodded their heads.

Oh no! "But, I planned on going to college. My mom and dad have been saving money since I was a baby. I'm going to be a medical doctor," Danika said in a somewhat defiant tone.

"Well, I'm afraid you're going to have to talk that over with your uncle Philip," Grace advised, walking to the front of the classroom to pull the school bell.

When the children filed in, Danika was pleased that Eli sat in the row next to hers, just one desk away. Joanna and Chloe sat fairly close as well, but they were a little further away, towards the front. When she glanced to her left, she noticed Jonathan Fisher who wore a mischievous grin. To her right was another girl about her age whom she did not know.

Jonathan leaned over and pointed to a girl a couple of rows over. "That's Susie, the one I told ya about. She's my best girl," he whispered.

Danika looked to where he pointed and noted the auburn-haired girl. "She's cute," Danika agreed.

"Yep, she's real cute. And I'm *gut* friends with her *bruder*. Matt's my friend too. We're gonna go –"

"Shh..." Matthew hissed from the desk next to him. "Don't tell her all our plans." Danika overheard him say. She couldn't imagine what kind of plans a couple of nine year old boys could have in this secluded community.

"Danika, will you please come to my desk?" Danika hoped she wasn't in trouble already. By Grace's calm demeanor, Dani figured she was about to receive her school books. She released a relieved sigh and headed toward the front.

While she was away, Jonathan pulled something out of his pocket and sneakily placed it into her desk. Since the other scholars were busy with their schoolwork, nobody had even noticed. Danika came back to her desk to place the books inside. As her desktop creaked open she spotted something moving inside. When she realized it was a snake, she screamed as loud as she could and ran to the other side of the room. The snake slithered out of her desk and onto the ground, causing all of the other girls to scream as well. Spying the snake, Eli nonchalantly picked it up, holding it out for the teacher to see.

Right away, Grace knew who had put it there. "Jonathan Fisher! How many times do I have to tell you not to bring creatures into the schoolhouse? I'm going to have to tell *Dat,* I mean, your *vadder* about this incident. Now apologize to Danika and go stand in the corner," she scolded her younger brother.

Jonathan hung his head as he walked to the corner and muttered, "Ah, it's just an old garter snake. It won't hurt no one."

"Anyone," the teacher corrected. "Eli, will you please deposit that poor snake outside?"

Eli quickly walked outside with the slithering reptile, returning a short while later. The girls had already taken their seats. Danika opened up her desk and searched for her favorite subject. When she noticed that her science book wasn't there, she quickly raised her hand.

"Yes, Danika?" Grace asked.

"You forgot to give me a science book," Danika informed her. Some of the other scholars began chuckling, which befuddled Danika.

"We don't study science," Grace said.

No science? I've never heard of a school that didn't teach science, Danika thought disappointedly. She took out her English book instead and started reading.

A folded piece of paper lay on the edge of her desk, and she quickly hid it between herself and the desk so the teacher wouldn't see. She quietly opened the note. It read: *May I walk you home after school today? - Eli.* She looked up to see Eli smiling diffidently. Danika cheerfully nodded her reply.

As the children were let out of school, most of them ran to their scooters and took off in a flurry. Danika had notified Joanna and Chloe that she wouldn't be walking home with them, but she didn't say why. She waited by the old oak tree behind the schoolhouse where Eli had instructed her to wait for him. From the tree, she could see him talking to a few younger children and pointing the opposite way. As he stepped away from them, a girl about Danika's age came rushing up to him. If Danika wasn't mistaken, it was the snobby blond girl that sat next to her in class. Her name was Sadie Lapp.

Danika waited at the tree for a while, until Eli could finally pull away from Sadie. After the girl took off, Eli jogged over to where Dani waited. "Sorry about that," he attempted to apologize, "Sadie is always trying to get my attention." They didn't realize that Sadie had been watching them from a distance as they walked off toward Danika's house.

"Oh," Danika said, not sure how to respond.

"Here, I can carry your books," Eli offered, holding out his arms.

"Thank you," Dani said timidly, as they walked along. "I told you about me the other day, but you didn't tell me much about you."

"Okay, what would you like to know?" He grinned.

"I didn't see you at the Fishers' for church on Sunday."

"Ow." He winced. "Sore subject. But if you really want to know, I'll tell you. Do you want the long or short version?"

"Well, since both of us have chores to do when we get home, why don't you tell me some other time?"

"*Jah*, that would be *gut*. So, what else would you like to know?"

"What do you mean what *else*? You haven't told me anything yet," she teased, producing a smile from Eli. Danika contemplated for a moment. "Hmm...How about your family?"

"Okay, my *dat* is Jacob Yoder and my *mamm* is Sarah Yoder. I have ten siblings: five brothers and five sisters. Two of my brothers and one of my sisters are married. There are four of us in school, and the others are either too young for school or have already completed it."

"Wow, I don't think I could keep track of that many brothers and sisters. The children that you were speaking to after school – are they your siblings?"

"*Jah*. Hannah, Annie, and Samuel."

"So, what do you want to be when you grow up?"

"My *vadder* wants me to farm like him. But I think I'd like to raise horses, or maybe have my own buggy shop. That's what Nathan Hostettler, the bishop's son, does."

"That would be cool, I guess. But..." She hesitated to speak her mind.

"But, what?"

"Well, did you ever want to do anything else? I mean, like something non-Amish?"

"But I *am* Amish. I don't ever plan on being anything else. I don't *want* to be anything else. I am happy here." He smiled, hoping she could understand.

"Don't you think you're missing out? I mean, I could never become a doctor living here."

"But your uncle Philip is the best doctor I know, and he is Amish."

How could she explain to a backwoods Amish guy that what her uncle did was just a bunch of silly nonsense? Old wives' fables, foolishness. That stuff didn't really work.

"What are you thinking?" Eli asked gently.

"Okay, if you really want to know, I'll tell you." She yielded.

"Say on," he urged.

"I'm going to say something that might offend you," she continued on slowly, "I don't believe in all that old wives' tales stuff; it's just a bunch of foolishness if you ask me."

"Do you mean using herbal medicine?"

"Yes."

"How do you know? Have you ever tried them?" he challenged.

"What? Well...no," she admitted.

"Did you ever meet Isaac Fisher, Joanna's older brother? He hurt his leg in a buggy accident two years ago and your uncle treated it with an herb of some sort. Now his leg is fine. It's as if the accident never happened. He might have even died if Philip hadn't arrived when he did. You should ask him sometime, he just lives across the street from the Kings."

"Wow. No, I never heard that."

Eli continued on, "Or, you should meet Martha Troyer. Her medical doctor told her that she had cancer and gave her six months to live. He wanted her to go through chemotherapy, which she adamantly refused, then decided to see Philip instead. He put her on a special diet, I think a lot of fresh juices and mostly fruits and vegetables. He gave her some herbs to take too. Philip told her that she would feel sick at first, and then she'd feel great, which happened just as he'd said. After about a year, she went back to her medical doctor. Guess what?"

"I don't know."

"They couldn't find any cancer in her body. It was gone. That was seven years ago," he stated.

"Wow!"

"You know there is a verse in the Bible that says something to the effect of 'when you answer something before hearing it, it will be a shame to you'."

Danika stopped in her tracks, and looked at him. "How do you do that?" Danika asked in astonishment.

"Do what?" Eli stood looking at her.

"It seems like you always have the right words to say to me. You get me to think about things that I have never thought about before. You make me change my mind about the way I feel. It's as if you can see into my soul. It's not fair," she complained.

"Wow, now that's a compliment." He smiled at her again. "I like you, Danika."

"I like you too, Eli." She grinned back.

"No, I mean, I really like you a lot. I...I care for you, Danika. In a special way, I mean," he said, exposing his heart. Eli took her hand; he seemed even more serious now. "Do you think you would be willing to wait for me?"

"What do you mean?" she asked, staring at her hand in his.

"I think we're meant to be together. I've never felt this way about anybody. I want you as my *aldi*. Will you let me court you when I turn sixteen?"

Danika's heart melted. "But your father and my uncle –"

"Shh..." He put his finger to her lips. "Don't worry. We'll work all that out, I promise."

She trembled and took a step back. "I-I..." She wanted to say yes, but was suddenly overwhelmed. *Eli wants me to be his girlfriend?* She'd never had a real boyfriend before.

"We can be friends now – just friends. We can get to know each other better. But I want to know that you'll wait for me." His eyes were pleading.

"Yes, I will," she managed to squeak out, her eyes intent on his.

"You seem happy. How was school today?" Naomi asked, as Danika walked in the door with an enormous smile.

"It was great!" she answered, running up the stairs to change into her work clothes.

"Was that Danika that just came in?" Philip asked, grabbing a quick snack out of the fridge before returning to the herb shop next door.

"*Jah.* She seemed excited. School must have gone well," Naomi stated.

Danika seemingly came down the stairs just as quickly as she'd gone up. She handed a bag to Naomi. "Here Naomi, I don't need these anymore. Do you think we can take them to the thrift store next time we go into town?"

Naomi peeked into the bag. "Your *Englischer* clothes?" She looked up at Philip, who also appeared surprised.

"*Jah,* I don't need them anymore," she stated, as she grabbed the milk pail off the kitchen counter to head outside. "Oh, and will you help me finish sewing up my dresses tonight? I'd like to wear my blue one tomorrow." And with that, she was off to milk the goats.

Philip and Naomi just stood there looking at each other, completely baffled.

CHAPTER 7
The Englisch Holiday

"Children, obey your parents in the Lord: for this is right." Ephesians 6:1

Jonathan, Matthew, and Joshua sat in the pony cart watching *Englisch* children dressed in strange clothing. They looked down at their own attire, hoping it would sufficiently accomplish their goal. Joshua tied the pony to a street sign and the boys determined which house to go to first.

"Okay. She said that they just knock on the *Englischers'* doors," Jonathan informed his friends.

"What should we say?" Matthew asked.

"I don't know," Jonathan said, shrugging. "I guess we just ask for candy."

"It will be strange to ask an *Englischer* we don't know for free candy. Maybe we should offer some money," Joshua suggested.

"*Jah,*" Matthew agreed. "I have a few quarters."

"Alright, let's stop talking and just go. I will knock first," Jonathan said.

The boys cautiously walked up to a door and Jonathan knocked confidently. A teenage boy with blue spiky hair opened the door, his face completely white. The boys stared wide-eyed at the strange looking boy. Jonathan gulped, but found his voice, "Can we have some candy?"

Matthew offered a quarter to the boy, but the teen simply stared at it. "Man, if my mom caught me taking money from a kid, I'd be in big trouble. Keep your money, kid." He then took a big handful from the bowl on the table next to him and held it out to Jonathan. Jonathan stood mesmerized. "Hey, didn't you bring a bag or something for your candy?"

Jonathan looked at Josh and Matt and they all shook their heads.

"Okay, then just hold out your shirt and I'll put the candy in there," the teen said. "Or I can put it in your hat."

With shirts full of candy, the boys followed the children in front of them to the next house. "This is fun!" Matthew said as he popped a small chocolate bar into his mouth.

The next door yielded a kind, normally dressed *Englisch* woman. Her eyes lit up and she called her daughter over. "Look at these boys here, Jessica. They're dressed Amish. Don't they look so cute? They remind me of the little boys at the farmer's market."

The boys stood smiling, as the woman looked over their 'costumes'.

"Didn't you boys bring something to put your treats in?" the woman asked. After the boys shook their heads, she turned to her daughter. "Jessica, go get three plastic grocery bags for these boys. It's a shame their mother would send them out with nothing to put their candy in."

They continued on to several more houses on the block. "Look at all the candy we've got and we've only been to five houses!" Joshua said excitedly, chomping on a stick of gum he found in his bag.

"And I still have all my quarters! It seems no one wants to take my money for some reason. I feel bad taking all this candy for free," Matthew said.

"*Ach*, it's okay. The *Englischers* like to give us the candy," Joshua said.

"*Jah* and I like to eat it!" Jonathan said, taking a lick from the lollipop in his mouth. "I can't wait to give some to Susie."

"I don't think my sister likes you none," Joshua said, "but she does like candy."

"Well then I'll just have to save lots of mine for her, so may-be she'll like me then," Jonathan said.

"You can give her a kiss," Matthew said.

"*Ach*, she'd hate 'im for sure if he tried to kiss her," Joshua said adamantly.

"No, I mean a candy kiss, *dummkopp*!" Matt said. He reached into his bag and pulled out a Hershey's Kiss and showed his friends. "See, it says 'kiss' right here. I got lots of 'em, so you probably do too. Girls like chocolate."

"Hey, we should probably go home before *Dat* notices I'm gone," Joshua said, noticing the late hour. "I don't feel like visiting the woodshed tonight."

"*Jah*, okay. Let's just go to one more house and then we'll go," Jonathan said.

The boys walked up to a dark house with only a single black light bulb emanating scant light. Scary howling sounds seemed to come from the windows and two jack-o-lanterns burned with a candle inside. The boys looked at each other wide-eyed, slowly inching their way to the door.

"You knock," Matt worriedly told Joshua.

Joshua looked at him, then at the abundance of spider webs and the skeleton hanging from the overhang and shook his head. "No, you."

Jonathan stepped forward and bravely knocked on the darkened door. As the door slowly creaked open, the three boys said, "Trick a tree."

An ugly green-faced witch with a large wart on her nose greeted the boys, sending out a loud cackling shrill. The boys slowly began inching backwards, then took off in a full sprint when the witch followed them out the door and reached for them with her long black fingernails. "Come back here! I eat little Amish boys for breakfast." They heard the frightening woman say.

When they arrived at their pony cart out of breath, they quickly unhitched Prancer and took off in a flurry.

"Whew, that was close!" Matthew said when they were safely on the road toward home.

"*Jah*, I almost had an accident," Joshua admitted.

"Me, too," Jonathan and Matthew said simultaneously.

"Do you really think she was gonna eat us for breakfast?" Matt asked wide-eyed.

Joshua shook his head. "I don't know. But I sure wasn't gonna stick around to find out!"

"*Ach*, look at all this candy!" Jonathan exclaimed.

"I wonder why all the kids say 'trick a tree'? How do you play a trick on a tree?" Matt wondered.

"I don't know. Maybe Jonathan can ask Danika about it," Josh suggested.

"*Jah*, I think I will," Jonathan agreed. "But I heard *Mamm* say one time that fruit is God's candy. And fruit grows on trees."

"Do you trick the tree when you take the fruit off it?" Matthew wondered.

"I don't know. Who can know about all the strange *Englischers'* customs?" Josh asked. "We just gotta ask Danika cuz she's *Englisch*. She'll know all about why they say 'trick a tree'. It don't make no sense to me."

Monday afternoon a large mountain of candy sat atop the school picnic table. Danika noticed Jonathan's huge smile and immediately she knew where the boys had gone Friday night. She didn't know how they did it, but she knew for a fact Bishop Hostettler would not have given his son permission to go trick-or-treating. She joined the boys at the table.

"Well, Danika, what do ya think of all our candy?" Jonathan asked proudly.

"I can't believe you guys actually went. It looks like they give out more candy here than in my neighborhood in California!"

"*Jah*, and we already ate a bunch!" Matthew declared.

Danika gasped. "You had your parents go through it first, right?"

"No way! If my folks knew I got a bunch of free candy from *Englischers* I wouldn't be able to sit here on this bench," Jonathan said. "Why would I tell them?"

"The witches," Danika simply said.

The boys all looked at each other wide-eyed and gulped. "What about the witches?" Joshua asked, remembering the one that wanted to eat them for breakfast.

"There are some really bad people that put razor blades and pieces of glass and stuff in Halloween candy. My dad always went through my candy to make sure it was safe to eat," she said.

The boys held their hands to their throats, horrific thoughts of razor blades cutting their insides filling their minds. "*Ach*, for real?" Jonathan asked.

"Yeah, but you guys aren't dead or anything, so it looks like nobody put any in yours. But I'd be careful if were you," she warned.

All three boys solemnly nodded their heads.

"Hey, may I have a Snickers bar?" Danika asked.

"Sure," Jonathan said.

"See, I told ya girls like chocolate," Matt said.

"Danika, why are we supposed to say 'trick a tree'?" Jonathan asked.

"What?" she asked.

"You know, trick a tree," Joshua explained. "How do you trick a tree, and what does it have to do with asking *Englischers* for candy?"

Danika couldn't help it. She burst into laughter, doubling over until her stomach ached. Every time she looked up at the boys' clueless expressions, she burst into laughter again. She couldn't get the images of three Amish boys going door to door saying 'trick a tree' out of her mind. When she finally calmed enough to explain to the boys that it was 'trick or treat' the other children had been saying, she also explained what she knew of the origins of the custom. Needless to say, she was sure that the boys had experienced their first and last ever celebration of Halloween.

CHAPTER 8
The Conflict

"Wrath is cruel, and anger is outrageous; but who is able to stand before envy?" Proverbs 27:4

Eli had walked Danika home nearly every day since she started school two months ago. She couldn't imagine life without him; he was her best friend. Danika knew somebody else was pining for Eli Yoder as well. Sadie Lapp. Anyone could see how she constantly flirted with him and she was beginning to get on Danika's nerves. Since the first day of school, Sadie had turned up her nose at Danika. So she thought it odd when Sadie Lapp approached her during lunch.

"Hey, Danika, I bet Eli's *daed* wouldn't be too happy if he knew how much time he was spending with an *Englischer*," Sadie threatened.

"Mind your own business, Sadie."

"Sarah Yoder and my *mamm* are *gut* friends. I'm sure that if I just dropped a little hint about Eli seeing Philip King's niece..."

"Sadie, I'm warning you for the last time. Keep your mouth shut and mind your own business." Danika could feel her temper rising, so she walked away.

Sadie didn't miss a beat and followed right behind Danika, taunting her. "Stay away from Eli," she threatened again.

Danika was unsure how it happened, but somehow her fist managed to find its way to Sadie's face. "I said mind your own business!"

"She's trying to kill me!" Sadie cried as loud as she could. When Grace heard the commotion, she came running to the scene with the other scholars behind her. Sadie was still sitting on the ground, conjuring up as much sympathy as she could get. Danika rolled her eyes.

"Danika, I'm going to have to ask you to go home. You're expelled for three days," the teacher stated in an even voice.

Danika tried to explain. "But she –"

"Violence is never acceptable. It is not our way. Go home now, please," Grace reiterated.

Danika heaved a deep sigh. As she grabbed her stuff from her desk and headed toward home, she glanced back at Eli who wore a clearly disappointed expression. He waved to her silently and she waved back. She peered down at the note in her hand, written by the teacher. *Great! Now what am I gonna do? How am I going to explain this to Naomi and Philip? They'll be disappointed in me...again. What will happen if Eli's dad finds out about us? Sadie will surely tell now.* She tried not to think about the trials that would certainly come her way.

"Why are you home so early?" Naomi asked when she saw Danika coming through the door just after one o'clock.

With her head down, she handed Naomi the note in her hand. "This will explain it all."

Naomi's eyes widened in horror. "You hit one of the other *kinner*? How could you do that?"

"She made me upset and she wouldn't leave me alone. I told her to mind her own business," Danika stated.

"Now you've been expelled for three days. Word will get out all over Paradise. You've given yourself and this family a bad name. I wish you would think a little further before you do something like this," Naomi reprimanded. "Take this note next door and show your uncle."

"Sorry, Naomi." But Danika wondered if she really was.

Danika took a deep breath while walking the short distance. *I wish I had just ignored that snippy Sadie Lapp. Now I'm the one in trouble. When am I ever going to learn to control my temper?* She opened the door of the herb shop and waited for Philip to finish up with his customer. When the coast was clear, she made her way toward her uncle and handed him the note. She didn't offer any explanation.

"I'm disappointed in you, Danika," his words cut to her heart.

Tears immediately sprang to her eyes, "I'm sorry Uncle Philip. I didn't mean to give us a bad name."

"Why did you do it?" he asked.

"I couldn't help it. That snippy Sadie Lapp wouldn't mind her own business. She kept threatening me about –" she stopped cold. *Oh no, I've said too much again,* she chided herself.

"Threatening you about what?" Philip wanted to know.

"About telling Eli's dad about me."

"Are you referring to Eli Yoder? Jacob Yoder's son?" Philip looked concerned now. "I don't understand."

"It's kinda complicated."

"I'm listening." Philip stood with his arms folded over his chest and feet firmly planted.

The words flowed freely from her lips, "Eli and I are...uh... good friends. Sadie likes Eli and doesn't want me to talk to him. She threatened to go tell Eli's dad about it because his dad doesn't like you. He'll probably tell Eli that we can't be friends anymore. I told her to mind her own business, but she wouldn't. She kept following me around with her big, fat, gossiping mouth and that's when I turned around and punched her."

Philip attempted to hide an amused grin, keeping an even countenance. "So, what are you going to do about it now?"

"Pray?" she asked, hoping to get some advice.

"Well, I think that would be a good start. What are you going to do to prevent this from happening again?" her uncle inquired.

"Stay as far away from Sadie Lapp as I can!"

Philip ceased his interrogation and allowed Danika to help out in the herb shop for the rest of the day. He figured poor Naomi could only handle so much.

When Danika returned to school, Sadie gave her a smart look, trying to egg her on. Danika ignored her and went straight to her desk and sat down. The scholars took their seats and Teacher Grace made a request, "Sadie, I want you to switch desks with Joanna." To that, Sadie turned and gave Danika a dirty look. Admiring the shiner she'd given Sadie, Danika just smiled back. *Good, she won't be able to see anymore when we pass notes.*

Sure enough, Dani found a note that had been slipped into her desk. It was in Eli's handwriting. It read:

Dear Danika,

My dat found out about us and he won't allow me to see you anymore. He thinks you are trouble, but I know better. I'm afraid we'll have to send letters to each other from now on. Please know that this is not my doing, nor is it your *fault. He threatened to send me to a different school if I don't keep my distance and I'm afraid that if he did that, we'd never be able to see each other. You know how I feel about you.*

Yours, Eli

Danika couldn't help it as the tears fell from her eyes. Eli looked back, his countenance defeated. It was evident he was deeply sorry. Well, at least they could still see each other in school; that was something to be happy about. She should have known that snippy Sadie would try to ruin it for them. The more she thought about it, the gladder she was about giving Sadie a black eye. If anybody ever deserved it, she did, she decided.

The walk home from school seemed to take forever. It just wasn't the same without Eli by her side. They had a lot of great talks on their many walks home. They discussed God and the Bible, and he helped her understand things that she never knew before. He had eased her through the grief caused by the loss of her family. He helped her to understand the Amish culture better and gave her perspective on where Philip and Naomi were coming from. Could it be, as Eli had said, that God brought him into her life right when she needed him most? Maybe God did love her and care for her.

As she came to the tall pine tree – the tree where she and Eli had first met – their tree, she stopped and sat down for a minute. She bowed her head and prayed, "Dear God, If you're there and you can hear me, I'd like to ask you for something.

Will you please restore the broken relationship between Uncle Philip and Eli's dad? I know it's a burden that Uncle Philip has had to carry, and now that burden is on mine and Eli's shoulders too. It seems that nobody wins when there's bitterness involved. Thank you, Lord. Amen."

She had thought about what she'd prayed, and she realized that *she* was still holding on to bitterness too. She was still mad at God for taking her parents. She still hadn't trusted in God's will for her life. Eli had said that God always knows what's best, that He sees the end from the beginning when we can't see two feet in front of us. Danika determined to speak with Philip and Naomi tonight after dinner.

"Okay, I'm ready." Danika smiled at Philip and Naomi who had no idea what she was talking about.

"Ready to play checkers?" Philip asked in puzzlement.

"No, I'm ready to be born again." She shared.

"Oh Danika, that's wonderful-*gut*!" Naomi came to give Danika a hug and they both felt a swift little kick coming from the inside of Naomi's belly. "I guess the little one wants to come out soon." They both laughed.

"Not just yet," Philip cautioned. "Danika, do you really want to be saved?" He wanted to be sure she was serious. He explained how their forefathers had been persecuted for their faith, and that it was not something to be taken lightly.

"*Jah*, for sure and for certain," she declared. "I'm ready."

Philip and Naomi proceeded to show her the various verses on salvation and the penalty for sin. After they had read the scriptures, Danika had become even more convinced of her decision. She bowed her head and prayed aloud that God would forgive her, save her, and help her to live righteously for Him. She was so happy. She decided to sit down and write her friend Cindy about her new found faith.

She went upstairs and turned her laptop on. She wrote:

Hey Cindy,

It's been awhile since we last spoke, hope everything is going well. So much has happened to me, I don't even know where to begin. I met a really great guy. His name is Eli and he has quickly become my best friend here. School is pretty cool, but there's this girl there that hates my guts. We got into a fight and I hit her and got expelled from school for a few days! I told you a lot has happened.

My Aunt Naomi will be having a baby in about a month and I can't wait! I found out that my Uncle Philip is an herb doctor. Not any of that voo-doo stuff, but natural herbal medicine that actually works. I've decided to forgo college and follow in his footsteps. Don't freak out, this suits me better. I get to start my internship as soon as I finish up with school this year, I'm so excited! The Amish don't to high school, but you'd never know it. Sometimes, I think they are years beyond some of the English folk.

Now for the most important thing: I got saved! That means that if I died right at this very moment that I would go to Heaven. Jesus forgave my sins and now I am clean. Oh Cindy, I can't describe to you how good it feels! All I had to do was trust in Jesus, and you can too. Let me know if you'd like to know more, okay?

Oh, and I got your email about coming to visit. Philip and Naomi said that would be fine, so I'll expect you in two months. This will be the last letter I email you because my battery is almost dead. Please snail mail me soon!

Love, Dani.

She pressed SEND then shut down her laptop and went to bed.

CHAPTER 9
Friends

"A friend loveth at all times..." Proverbs 17:17a

Danika opened the latest note from Eli and was thrilled by his written words:

Please meet me at our special place this Saturday at 2:00. I really want to see you for my birthday. Say you'll come...Eli.

Her heart skipped a beat. Finally, they would get to spend time alone together! But what if Eli's dad found out? She wouldn't worry about that right now; she wasn't going to let anything steal her happiness. She quickly nodded her reply to him as school was letting out, with a huge smile, of course.

Joanna and Chloe met up with her after school. "Would ya like to go ridin' with us after chores today?" Chloe asked eagerly.

It sounded like a lot of fun. "*Jah,* but I'll have to ask Naomi first." She didn't want to get herself into trouble again.

"All right then," Joanna declared, "we'll meet you at your house in about an hour or two."

"Sounds *gut.*"

Danika hurried home to finish up all of her chores, enthused about the time she'd spend with her friends. Naomi had given her the okay, so she was all set. Philip showed her which horse to ride, so she wouldn't have a hard time.

She was already outside when the girls came riding up on their horses. Philip had helped her saddle the horse, she'd practiced mounting it, and had even rode around a little bit. When Philip was sure she had enough confidence, he conceded to let her go as well.

"It's her first time riding; go easy on her, girls," Philip cautioned.

The girls rode up one of the dirt lanes at a leisurely pace since this was Danika's first time out with them.

"Are you still spending time with Eli?" Chloe asked curiously, wondering what had become of the ordeal with Sadie.

"His father has forbidden him to see me," Danika answered in a dejected tone, feeling a little guilty that she was planning to meet him secretly.

"*Ach,* that's too bad," Joanna tried to comfort her. "But maybe it's for the best."

"What do you mean?" Danika didn't understand her logic.

"Well, *Mamm* said it's not good to spend too much time alone with boys." Joanna continued, "She said that when you spend lots of time with them, you start longing for them in other ways."

"Huh?" Danika still didn't get it.

"She's talking about lip kissin'," Chloe blurted out. "Has Eli tried to kiss you?"

Danika felt a little uncomfortable talking about this. "No, not yet. But I hope he does," she said dreamily.

Both girls gasped at once.

"What did I say?" Danika asked innocently.

"I wanna save my kissin' for the man I marry," Joanna stated.

"*Jah,* me too," Chloe declared.

"Why?" Danika couldn't see the harm in a kiss.

"When you get married, how many girls do you want your husband to have kissed before you?" Joanna asked.

Now it was Danika's turn to gasp. "None! I don't want my husband to have been kissed by anyone else."

"Well, do you think your husband wants you to be kissin' someone else?" Chloe said.

"No, probably not. But Eli and I might get –" Danika hoped they'd marry someday.

"But you don't know for sure. Isn't it better to be safe than sorry?" Joanna offered. "When you give away one kiss, it's a lot easier to give away another, then another."

"The best gift you can give to your future spouse is your purity," Chloe declared, and the other girls agreed.

"Wow. The Amish have a whole different way of looking at things. It's so different from the *Englisch* world," Danika said.

"Well, not all Amish believe that, for sure and for certain. But that's how it is with us. And I'm sure some *Englischers* have high standards too, *jah?*" Joanna wanted to give them the benefit of the doubt.

"Maybe, but none that I know of," Danika shared, "and TV is a lot worse. No wonder you guys don't allow it."

Changing the subject, Joanna suggested, "Let's go a little faster, *jah*?" She was dying to race, or at least gallop.

"Just a little faster. Remember, this is my first time," Dani warned.

"Danika, someday you'll be racing with us," Chloe encouraged confidently.

The girls clicked their tongues and the horses sped up a bit. They rode down to Miller's Pond and sat by the shore for a while. The place was beautiful, peaceful. The pond was oval in shape and stretched across several hundred yards. Willow trees adorned the banks, making it an ideal place for children to play. Danika could imagine younger children swinging from the willow branches into the pond. The water sparkled as the light of the sun reflected off of it. She wondered why Eli had never taken her there. It would be a perfect place for a picnic...someday. She figured it was probably too visible to passersby for them to spend time there. If only Eli's father could patch things up with Philip.

"This whole pond turns to ice come winter time," Chloe stated.

"*Jah*, I can't wait to go ice skating," Joanna said excitedly.

"You guys get to go ice skating too? And here I thought the Amish were all boring." Danika couldn't believe it.

The girls laughed. "The Amish do dress plain and work hard, but we know how to have fun too," Joanna stated.

CHAPTER 10
The Secret Meeting

"...Be sure your sin will find you out."
Numbers 32:23b

Danika couldn't get over the butterflies in her stomach. Today she would meet with Eli. All day she could not get him out of her mind. Two o'clock, he'd said. It was now one-thirty and she had a picnic lunch all packed, complete with some fresh chocolate-chip cookies. She was ready to go. She quickly ran upstairs to retrieve her gift: a two-inch lock of her hair, tied fancy in a silky red ribbon.

Danika set out on foot to their special spot – the tall pine tree in the woods where they'd first met. So much had happened since that first encounter. Danika thought of how much her life had changed. *I have Eli to thank for that*, she thought, *he's been such a good friend.*

Eli was already there waiting when she arrived. His smile melted her heart. He held a small bouquet of wildflowers in his hand and quickly offered them to her.

"*Denki.*" She smiled broadly and blushed a bit. "How did ya get away?" she asked, concerned for his well-being.

"My *daed* gave me this new mare for my birthday. He said I could take her out for a ride."

Danika looked over the large creature, gently petting its coat. "She's beautiful," she said, noticing the stunning build of the exquisite painted horse.

"No, you're beautiful," he insisted, and gently grasped her hand in his, bringing it to his lips.

Immediately, her cheeks reddened. *How will I be able to stay pure at this rate?* she thought to herself, and then quickly put distance between them.

She walked over to the picnic basket and pulled out an old small quilt. After she spread it out over the grass under the tree, she patted the spot next to her. Eli took a seat beside her. "Did ya eat lunch already?" She knew he probably had, but thought she'd ask anyway.

"*Jah*, but I can always eat again." He smiled.

"I figured, so I didn't pack too much. Just a couple of sandwiches and what not." She removed the food from the basket. "I baked ya some fresh cookies, they're still a little warm."

"*Denki.*" He moved closer to her – too close. It was plain to see he wanted her affection as much as she longed for his. He took her hand and brought it to his lips again.

"*Ach*," she said, taking her hand away. "You are not making this easy."

"*Was iss letz*?" His brow furrowed in concern. "What is wrong?"

"I want to stay pure...for my future husband," she declared.

"But I *am* your future husband," he said, gently gliding his fingertips down her arm.

"Eli Yoder, you're killin' me," she said, feeling all flustered. "Well, you're not my husband yet."

"Just one more year and I'll be sixteen," he reminded. "And you'll be fourteen. Did ya know the bishop in your district allows girls to court at fourteen?"

"*Ach,* no. Really?" She wondered if he was making it up.

"Honest," he said. "And since our courtin's done in secret, *Daed* won't know I'm with you."

"Hey, I thought you were the same age as me. You mean to say you're fifteen today?"

"*Jah,* had to stay home for a while and help *Daed* with the crops. I missed out on quite a bit of school, so I'm making it up. I'm glad now, though. I might have missed out on you."

Danika stood up when she remembered the lock of hair and took it from her apron pocket. Shyly, she offered it to him. "Happy birthday, Eli. I don't really have anything to give you. 'Cept this."

As he stood up, he took the black tresses from her outstretched hand and brought it up to his nose. He wanted to remember her scent. "This is a piece of you, it is precious. I will always cherish it." He fingered the ribbon and felt the softness of her hair. "I'll put it in my pocket for safe keeping," he said, thinking he was glad his mother had sewn a pocket into this pair of pants.

"You are the best birthday gift I could ask for," he said, as he drew her into his arms. She could hear his heart beating rapidly, but this time she didn't pull away. Although she knew she shouldn't, she would let him enjoy this moment in time. It might just be their last time together for a while, but she didn't want to think about that just now.

"I need to tell ya somethin' important," Danika stated, and he let her go.

"What?" Eli asked, curiously.

"I accepted Jesus as my Saviour. I'm saved now, Eli!" Her white teeth gleamed, as she spread her lips in a smile.

"That's the best news I've heard in a long time. Now, I know you're mine – for sure and for certain," he teased.

"No, now I belong to Jesus," she declared.

"If we could only get my *daed* to see the light, I'm sure all of this foolishness would be over."

"And then you could walk me home every day, *jah*?" She hoped.

"*Jah*, if we can stand it." He thought for a moment. "Maybe it's a *gut* thing we don't see each other too much."

"That's what Joanna said," Danika remarked.

"Danika, are you talkin' to your friends about us?" He seemed a little disappointed.

"*Jah,* is it not okay?"

"It's just that courtin's supposed to be kept secret," he gently reminded her, stepping close once again.

Danika took a step back. "But we're not courtin' yet."

"Well, we would be if I had my way," he declared shamelessly. "Let me give ya a ride home, before I try to kiss you," his eyes gently pleaded.

"I think that will be all right," she agreed with a smile. "The ride, not the kiss," she clarified.

Eli chuckled. "I guess I'll settle for a ride, if that's all I can get."

They rode along in silence as they both contemplated their special time together. Danika held tight to Eli, not wanting to let him go. As he helped her down off the horse, he embraced her once again and gave her a gentle kiss on the cheek. "This is the best birthday I've ever had," he said, mounting his horse once again. Danika couldn't wipe the smile off her lips as she longingly watched her beloved ride away.

Danika happily entered the house, humming a love song stuck in her head from her *Englischer* days. She noticed Philip and Naomi sitting out on the porch, she froze and stood erect. *Oh no, did they just see me with Eli?* She chided herself for not being more careful. She quickly tip-toed toward the stairs, attempting to escape unnoticed. It didn't work.

"Danika." It was Philip calling from the porch.

"Coming. Be there in a minute," she said nervously, quickly sticking her wildflowers in a small Mason jar with water, and then headed to the porch. She could already hear what was coming.

"Come sit down, Danika. We need to have a talk," Philip suggested. Naomi went inside to rest a bit, and to avoid the drama that was sure to come. He continued on, "Did I just see you riding with Jacob Yoder's boy?"

"Eli, *jah,*" she affirmed shyly.

"I thought you said that you and Eli were 'friends'. It looked like there was a little more than friendship going on." Philip observed.

Danika sighed, unable to defend herself.

"What ever happened with Eli and his father?" Philip wondered.

"He forbid him to see me," she admitted.

"His *vadder* forbid him to see you?" he repeated her words, concern filling his eyes.

She nodded.

"And you *both* deliberately went behind his back and disobeyed his wishes?" Philip asked in disbelief, his voice rising a bit.

Danika hung her head low, knowing her goose was cooked. "It was his birthday," she simply stated, in an attempt to defend the both of them.

"Oh, so what you're saying is that it's okay to disobey your authorities on your birthday?"

Danika kept her eyes on the floor, trying to shield herself from the accusatory words spoken by her uncle.

"I want you to look at me, Danika. It's how we show respect. Now please answer my question," he commanded sternly.

She brought her eyes to his. She hated that look – the look of disappointment. Once again, she had let her uncle down. "No, it's not okay," she answered softly.

"What would happen if his father found out the two of you were meeting secretly?" She was unsure whether it was a threat or a simple question. "Have you thought about the consequences?"

Again, she nodded her head in affirmation. She knew if they'd been caught, his father would send him to another school. How could she have been so careless?

"And that's a risk you're willing to take, just to see him for a couple of hours?" It sounded so foolish now that he laid everything out.

"If that boy can't respect and obey his father, how can I trust him with you?" His words stung. She didn't like to hear him talking about her Eli like that.

Danika shrugged her shoulders, not knowing just what to say.

Philip sighed. "I really hate to do this, but you leave me no other choice." He continued, unrelenting, "Since you continue to push the boundaries, I'm going to have to put my foot down.

Other than school, you are to have no contact with Eli Yoder. That means no secret meetings, no letters, and no phone calls. If he gives you a letter, you are to return it unopened." Philip didn't think she'd be using the telephone in the herb shop, but figured he'd better cover all his bases.

Danika took a deep breath as tears sprung to her eyes. *How could he do this? How could he be so unmerciful?* She allowed her tears to fall freely. She tried to stop the barrage of words, but they kept coming, assaulting her emotions.

Philip was uncomfortable speaking to Danika this way, but how else could he protect her? "I also think you're too young. You will wait until you're sixteen, the proper age, to begin courting. As long as you are in my house, you will abide by my rules. Do I make myself clear?"

How could he expect this of her? This was too much for her to bear! Her shoulders slumped under the heavy burden; she could not stop the free-fall of tears. She put her hands over her face and sobbed.

He spoke to her in a more gentle tone now, "Danika, you know I only want what's best for you." He put his hand on her arm, attempting consolation.

Danika quickly pulled her arm away and lashed out in anger. "No you don't!" she cried. "You just want what's best for *you.* It's your fault that Eli's dad wouldn't let him see me. All of this is your fault. I hate you." She ran into the house and up the stairs, throwing herself face down onto her bed, and wept.

Well that certainly didn't go very well, Philip thought discouragingly.

CHAPTER 11
The Locket

"For where your treasure is, there will your heart be also." Luke 12:34

Dinner that evening was a solemn event. Philip and Danika were both silent while Naomi tried to make light conversation with Katie. Katie noticed a change in her father's countenance as well as in Danika. "*Mamm*, what's wrong with Dani? Why is she sad?" the little girl asked innocently. The words brought a fresh wave of tears to Danika's eyes. Just the thought of her current circumstances was dreadful.

"She'll be fine, Katie. You don't need to worry about it," Naomi chided.

"Why is *Dat* so quiet?" Katie naturally wondered.

"He's thinking. Now just eat your dinner, so we can have family time," Naomi suggested, rubbing her rapidly growing belly.

As Philip read the Bible that evening, the Word of God spoke to all of them. He was reading from the book of Ephesians chapter six. Verses one and two popped out at Danika, 'Children, obey your parents in the Lord: for this is right. Honour thy father and thy mother...' Danika's father and mother were gone, and there was nothing she could do about that. Her aunt and uncle were all she had now, so she supposed that the obeying part was still required of her. *Why does obedience have to be so hard? I haven't honored Uncle Philip at all,* she ashamedly thought to herself as he continued reading.

'And, ye fathers, provoke not your children to wrath: but bring them up in the nurture and admonition of the Lord.' Philip paused after reading that verse. *Have I been too hard on Danika? What I said definitely upset her. I don't want to cultivate a harvest of bitterness and hatred. I want this to be a home where love and forgiveness dwell. It must start with me.* To everyone's surprise, Philip closed the Bible and set it on the small table next to his straight-back wooden chair. He looked at Danika and noticed how saddened she was. He knew he was partly responsible for her grief.

"Dani," he humbly spoke, "I'm sorry that I spoke harshly with you today. I'm afraid I have 'provoked you to wrath', as God says not to do. I'm asking for your forgiveness."

Does he think of himself as my father? The thought brought comfort to her heart. Danika was definitely surprised by her uncle's admission. She admired him for his humility. "*Jah*, I think I can forgive you," she offered.

"*Denki.*" Philip knew he had asked a lot of her.

"I need to ask for your forgiveness too. I'm sorry that I said that I hate you." Her eyes began to cloud over, but she continued, "It's not true. I'm sorry that I disobeyed, I know it was wrong."

"I forgive you. But some of what you said *was* true. This rift between Jacob Yoder and I has gone on for far too long. It's not right that you have to suffer because of it. I will pray that God will bring a solution to the problem."

"Oh, *denki*, Uncle Philip." Danika said as she gave him a warm daughterly hug. Philip wore a satisfied smile.

"We will pray too," Naomi spoke for herself and the girls. Danika agreed.

Danika arrived at school early on Monday morning and sat down at her desk with paper and pen.

Dearest Eli,

It pains me to write this letter. My Uncle Philip saw us on Saturday. He gave me permission to write this letter, but it will be my last for the time being. He was not happy that we went against your father's wishes. He's also forbidden me to accept letters from you or spend time with you, aside from school. He said that I won't be allowed to court till

I'm sixteen. I am so sorry, I wish there was another way. I have cried many a tear over you, my love. Please know that I do not regret one second of the time we spent together. It was precious to me.

You hold my heart,

Danika

P.S. My uncle is seeking the Lord about making amends with your father. Please pray with us in this.

She folded the letter and slipped it into his desk just before the bell rang. When Eli sat down, he noticed her usually-happy demeanor was gone, and his smile faded too. He looked at her with concern, wishing they could talk. When the teacher began instruction, he opened his desk and found the letter she had written. He quickly removed it and slid it under his notebook. When the teacher turned her back, he quickly opened the letter and read the solemn words.

I can't even write her a note? No courting till she's sixteen? That seems like forever. No wonder she's so distraught. This is terrible. There has to be some way. I've never known Philip to be unreasonable like this. Maybe I can talk to him myself. Eli thought a moment. *No, he'd probably side with my father. Well, I guess if Jacob in the Bible could work seven years for Rachel, I can surely wait three years for my beloved Danika. Yes, Danika, I will pray with you. We will be together in spirit.* Eli felt a little better after coming up with a plan of action. He would pray. God can move mountains, the Bible says, and that's exactly what it would take to restore the broken relationship between Philip King and Jacob Yoder.

Day after day, at recess, lunch, and after school Danika had looked for it. But it was nowhere to be found. Joanna and Chloe noticed her searching one day and asked what she was looking for. "My locket, I've lost it," she whispered to them, as she desperately searched. The precious gift that her mother and father had given was now gone.

She figured it had probably fallen off during a volleyball game. She had to find it before the lawn was mowed, or worse, before snippy Sadie Lapp found it. For sure and for certain, she'd love to have something to tell on Danika about. Knowing Sadie, she'd probably tell Bishop Hostettler. Chloe, Joanna, and even Eli had helped her search for the necklace, to no avail. She was afraid it was lost forever.

Naomi thought she had heard something upstairs. Was it Danika? She walked to her room and knocked on the door. There was no answer, so she turned the knob and let herself in. Danika sat on her bed in tears. What was wrong today? She wasn't seeing Eli and she didn't have another confrontation with Philip, so what could it be?

"Danika, what's wrong?" Naomi gently asked.

"Nothing," she replied. "You wouldn't understand."

"Well, perhaps not, but I can listen if you'd like to talk," Naomi offered as she sat next to Danika and put her arm around her. "Besides, you might be surprised by what I understand."

Actually, Naomi and Danika were alike in many ways.

"Promise you won't get mad at me?" Danika pleaded.

"Should I be mad at you about something?" Naomi wondered, her eyebrows arched.

"No, I don't think so, but other people might," she said.

"You can talk to me about anything in confidence, Danika."

Danika took a chance; she desperately needed to talk to somebody. "My mom and dad gave me a special gift and I've lost it."

"Why would I be mad about that?" Naomi was puzzled.

"It was a necklace with a heart-shaped locket that held a photo of my mom and dad. It was very special to me. Now, I might never find it again," she explained, wiping the tears away with her palms.

"You may have lost the necklace, Danika, but you'll never lose the memories. Those are locked in here forever." Naomi pointed to Danika's heart. "Come with me. I'd like to show you something special to me." Danika followed Naomi to her bedroom downstairs.

"What is it?" Danika wondered as Naomi dug deep into her hope chest at the foot of the bed.

"This," Naomi said, pulling out a small photograph, "was my first family. My husband and twin daughters died in an automobile accident."

"*Ach*, Naomi. I'm sorry. I never knew. I thought you and Uncle Philip –"

"Had been married forever?" Naomi completed her sentence.

"But you seem like you love each other."

Naomi smiled, "We do love each other. But we only met and married less than two years ago."

"So Katie doesn't belong to Uncle Philip?" Danika asked with surprise.

"Biologically speaking, no. But she belongs to his heart. And isn't that what matters most?" Naomi smiled.

"But you have a photograph. I thought they weren't allowed." Danika was confused now.

"When we took the photo, I was not Amish. I joined because of Philip. You, Philip, and I are the only ones that know about this photo. He lets me keep it although I'm not supposed to." Naomi thought of Philip's kindness and compassion.

"So, I'm not the only one with secrets, *jah?*" Danika teased.

"*Jah*."

"Aunt Naomi, you and I do have a lot in common." Danika smiled at the realization. "Thanks for sharing this with me."

CHAPTER 12
Special Delivery

"Lo, children are an heritage of the Lord: and the fruit of the womb is his reward." Psalm 127:3

Philip had entrusted the herb shop to Danika's keeping again. It had gotten so he didn't even need to be around much when she was there, and he was able to spend more time with Naomi. Philip had taught her about each herb in the shop and its usage. They had even gone wildcrafting for fresh herbs. Danika had no idea that God had provided such a bounty for man in nature. She'd always thought the greenery growing everywhere was just weeds. Never would she have thought they could be used to heal and save lives.

The part Danika liked best about working in the herb shop was conversing with the customers. It was amazing to see how much her uncle had benefited the lives of his friends and neighbors through his knowledge of herbal medicine. Customer after customer had come in and bragged about Philip to her, and she loved hearing every word. She felt blessed to have this special knowledge and was excited that one day she might have her own herbal practice.

Naomi had been taking some herbs during her pregnancy too. Near the end of pregnancies, Philip would give expectant mothers an herbal tea blend that would help strengthen their bodies for delivery. Philip found that this tea also greatly cut down the time of labor for the women. Naomi would be going into labor someday soon, and Danika couldn't wait for the blessed event to occur. Philip said she could be in the house when the baby was born to keep an eye on the younger children.

Danika had just served the volleyball when Isaac Fisher, neighbor to the Kings, drove up in his buggy. He had driven up to the schoolhouse like a bolt of lightning, spewing dust into the school yard. "Is Danika here?" he hollered toward the crowd of young folk.

"*Jah*, I'm here." Danika emerged from the group. "Is somethin' wrong?"

"*Nee*, all is *gut*. Naomi's having her *boppli*!" Isaac replied excitedly. "Would ya like a ride?"

"*Jah*. Joanna, will you please tell Grace that I went home?" she said as she jumped into the buggy.

On the drive home, Danika sent up a silent prayer. *Dear Lord, Please keep Naomi and the baby safe. Please don't let anything go wrong, and give Uncle Philip wisdom to know what to do. Amen.*

When Danika walked into the house, she expected to hear a bunch of hollering like in the movies. This was completely different. The house was pretty quiet for the most part. Rachel, Isaac's new wife, was watching the children upstairs and she could hear them playing. She only heard Philip's gentle words coming from the bedroom as he coached and comforted his delivering wife. "Push," she heard him say about three times.

"Wh-a-a-a!" she heard a tiny voice echo through the door. She ran to the door and waited a few minutes, then asked if she could enter.

"*Kumm* in and meet your new baby cousin," Philip declared joyfully. "Her name is Rebekah, in memory of your mother."

Bittersweet tears filled her eyes. "Oh-h..." Danika cooed, as she held the small bundle in her arms. "She's so precious. And tiny, too. Look at her little nose, it looks like mine."

"You mean mine," Philip teased. "Okay, let's allow the little one to get to know her *mamm*. She's probably hungry."

Danika handed the new precious gift to her mother. "How are ya feelin', Aunt Naomi?"

"A little tired, but I feel *gut.*" She smiled at her new little girl.

"I prayed for ya." Dani smiled.

"*Denki,*" Naomi said, as she looked down at her suckling infant. "*Gott* blessed us, for sure and for certain."

Danika had been much happier since her new little cousin arrived – Rebekah, named after her mother and Philip's sister. School was steadily getting better too. Seeing Eli didn't hurt as much as it had, but she still wished things could be different. She was still praying for restoration between her uncle and Jacob Yoder, and she believed God would bring it about in His perfect timing.

Eli handed her an envelope during lunch and she longed to open it, but she could not disobey Uncle Philip and disappoint him again. "Please open it, Danika," Eli softly pleaded with her.

"Aw, you know I can't, Eli."

"It's not a letter," he coaxed once more.

"Okay, but I hope this won't get me into trouble," Danika warned.

She gently opened the envelope and out poured her lost necklace. She couldn't help but give him a hug out of gratitude. "Oh, Eli! How did ya find it?"

"When you gave up, I came back to the school and kept looking for it. I prayed and the Lord helped me find it. May I put it on ya?" he asked timidly, hoping she'd let him.

"*Jah.*"

Eli opened the clasp and gently placed the jewelry around Danika's neck. His hands lingered on her neck a moment and he fought the urge to kiss her.

"*Denki*, Eli. 'Tis a special thing you did for me."

CHAPTER 13
Cindy

"Thine own friend, and thy father's friend, forsake not..." Proverbs 27:10a

Danika could hardly contain her excitement. Cindy would be arriving today. The morning was filled with chores and house cleaning, making sure it was spotless for their special guest. Dani asked Naomi for a box in which she placed her computer, cell phone, and other worldly items to give away to Cindy. She knew she wouldn't use them anymore, she was Plain now. Surprisingly enough, she didn't even miss them. When Danika finished her chores, she and Philip rode to the airport to pick her friend up.

During the long ride to the airport, thoughts of Eli ran through her head. She contemplated the rift between Philip and Eli's father and hoped desperately that they could resolve their differences so she and Eli could remain friends. He was the best friend she'd ever known and she didn't want to lose him.

"What are you thinking about, Danika?" Philip asked, breaking the silence. He was surprised to see her looking so down when they were on their way to pick up her good friend.

"Eli," she simply said.

"I know what it's like to love someone you can't be with. It's very difficult, especially at your age." Philip tried to relate with his niece.

"What do you mean?" Dani asked.

"Well, when I was in my *rumspringa* I had an English *aldi.* I had to make one of the most difficult decisions in my life. Even though I still loved her, I decided to break things off and join the church. For a long time my heart ached and I'd wondered if I did the right thing. Now I realize that if I hadn't done that, then Naomi and I would've never married. And I may have never met Christ. Sometimes we just have to trust God to know what He's doing. If it's His will, then it will work out. If it's not, that just means He has something better planned."

"I guess I never thought about it quite like that, but you're right." Danika was grateful that Philip had shared a special part of his life with her.

"So, what do you think your friend will think of us?" Philip asked.

"She'll probably flip out at first like I did, but at least *she* got some type of warning."

Philip chuckled at her comment. "*Jah*, I guess that was a pretty big culture shock for you."

"*Jah*, for sure and for certain. But now I've come to love it and I hope Cindy will too."

"Wow, Danika. You guys are, like, totally old-fashioned," Cindy said, as the two of them entered Danika's bedroom.

"I know. Isn't it sorta cool?" Danika said. "Just wait till you get to milk goats with me tomorrow."

"Milk what?"

"Goats. It's a lot of fun, especially when you squirt the milk right into your mouth." Danika smiled.

"Oh, that is so gross!"

"You're funny, Cindy." Danika laughed.

"No, I think you're the funny one," Cindy bantered.

"So, have you been surfing without me?" Danika realized how much she missed it.

"Just went yesterday. There were some great waves, you would've loved it." Cindy reminisced.

"Bummer. I guess that's one of the things I miss most. But there's some really cool things to do here, too."

"Really? Like what?" Cindy doubted.

"Well, aside from spending time with Eli, which I'm not allowed to do now anyway, there's horseback riding, volleyball, and when the pond freezes over we're going to go ice skating."

"No way, real ice skating out on a pond? Now, I'm jealous," Cindy teased.

"Well, you can always come back and visit in January." Dani smiled. "By the way, how are your parents doing?"

"You wouldn't believe it. They're doing great now. As a matter of fact, they're on a romantic cruise in the Caribbean right now." Cindy beamed.

"That's wonderful-*gut*! What happened?"

"Well, they started going to this church and got counseling. They are so much happier now."

"Are you going to church too?"

"Well, I kinda have to because they won't let me stay home alone," Cindy stated.

"Did ya read what I wrote in the last email I sent?"

"Yes, I did. It was interesting. I never thought you'd get into all that religious stuff."

"Oh no, it's not religious stuff," Danika asserted.

"I don't get it."

"I trusted Jesus Christ to save me. I now have a relationship with my Heavenly Father. Religion is a lot different than a relationship."

"Hmm...well, I guess I'll have to think on that." Cindy clearly wasn't interested, to Danika's disappointment. She decided she would pray for her. "So, when do I get to meet this Eli?" Cindy inquired.

"*Ach*, I don't know! Maybe you can walk me to school on Monday, *jah*?"

"Sure. So, what am I going to do around here all day while you're off at school making puppy dog eyes at your boyfriend?" Cindy asked rudely.

"Well, first of all, he's not my beau yet. I can't even court till I'm sixteen. Secondly, contrary to popular belief, I actually do my schoolwork during school time. But I do sneak a look every now and then," Danika admitted. "And you will have your hands full helping Naomi with the little ones. You're so lucky; I wish I could stay home with the babies!"

"Little Rebekah is awfully cute. And PJ's adorable," Cindy agreed.

"Well, I guess I should go downstairs and help Naomi with dinner." Danika arose from her bed and headed toward the stairs.

"Wait for me. I'm coming too."

"Wow, I can't believe you guys walk this far to school every day," Cindy said as the four girls neared the school house.

"It's not that far. Just a couple of miles," Joanna replied nonchalantly.

"Well, I'd have a hot bod if I did this every day," Cindy replied. Danika laughed, sometimes Cindy could be so funny.

"A what?" Chloe asked.

"Never-mind," Cindy answered.

"You'd rather not know anyway," Danika assured her friends. She spotted Eli pushing his younger sister on the swing. "There's Eli." She smiled, blushing as she said his name.

"Wow, Girl, you've got it bad," Cindy remarked.

"Shh...he's coming this way," Danika said excitedly, as he walked toward them. Chloe and Joanna had gone into the schoolhouse.

Eli smiled at the two of them as he walked up, but his eyes lingered on Danika.

"Eli," Dani introduced, "this is my good friend Cindy from California."

"Nice to meet ya," he said politely.

"Nice to meet you too," she answered back.

"So, what do you think of Pennsylvania so far?" He tried to make conversation.

"It's beautiful. I love the abundance of trees and foliage," Cindy said.

"*Jah*, me too. How long are ya stayin'?"

"For a week, while my parents are on a cruise."

"Oh, that's *gut*. I'm sure you and Dani will have a fun time together. Well I hope you enjoy your time here. Don't let Danika get you into too much trouble," he teased. Eli winked at Danika, said goodbye to them both, and then headed to the schoolhouse.

As soon as he was out of site, Cindy turned to Danika. "Wow, he's a hottie!"

"Shh...I know, huh?" Danika whispered back. Just then the bell started to ring. "Well I guess I better get in there. You remember how to get back home, right?"

"Yeah, I'll find my way. Have fun. And try concentrating on your studies," Cindy said, as she started toward the King residence.

Danika laughed, knowing her hidden meaning. "Yeah, if I can," she said, just before catching Eli's eye.

CHAPTER 14
The Confrontation

"...for whatsoever a man soweth, that shall he also reap." Galatians 6:7c

A knock on the back door of the schoolhouse interrupted the class. An angry voice boomed, "Is Eli in here?"

"*Jah*, I'm here, *Dat*. What is it?" Eli gulped. Surely his father coming to find him at school couldn't be good.

"Come outside with me, boy!" he said as he glanced around the room, searching for the dark-haired girl. His lancinate stare permeated Danika's being as he cast an evil eye at her.

Oh no! Danika breathed silently. *This can't be good.*

Eli hesitantly walked outside with his father. "Your mother found this in your drawer today. What is it?" Jacob Yoder held out the lock of hair Danika had given to Eli.

"It's Danika's hair," he said trembling.

"The Kings' girl?" he asked upsettingly.

Eli nodded.

"I thought I told you not to see that girl anymore!" Jacob Yoder's words echoed through the classroom.

Danika could hear the words clearly from where she sat and immediately put her face in her hands. *Please God! This cannot be happening.*

"But I...we haven't –" Eli didn't want to lie to his father; he was in enough trouble as it is.

"When did you get this, boy?" he asked roughly.

Eli sighed. "On my birthday."

"You mean to tell me you saw that girl after I forbid you to?" Mad as a hornet's nest, anger dripped with every syllable.

"*Jah,* sorry *Dat,*" Eli squeaked.

"Oh, you'll be sorry all right," Jacob Yoder threatened. "We are going down to Philip King's right now and I'm going to have some words with him. Get in the buggy." Eli hesitated at his father's command. "Now!"

"No, *Dat,*" Eli dared to say. "I love Danika and I plan to marry her whether you like it or not."

Danika could feel the eyes of all of her classmates on her.

"Don't be a fool, Son. Get in the buggy, I said," Jacob demanded and roughly grasped his arm; Eli had no choice but to obey.

Danika jumped out of her seat and ran out of the schoolhouse. She raced home on foot as fast as she could. *Please,*

Lord, no! she silently prayed. *Please don't let this happen, I beg you!* Her heart had never been heavier.

Jacob Yoder came stomping into Philip's herb shop with Eli behind him. "King, I want to talk to you," Jacob said in a semi-controlled voice.

"Uh, let's step out back," Philip suggested, not wanting to startle his customers.

"I found this in my boy's drawer." He held out the lock of hair. "Your girl gave it to him," he said angrily.

Philip said nothing. He could see poor Eli was trembling.

"What kind of girl gives a gift like that?" he stated more than asked. "And black hair too. She's not our kind."

Jacob Yoder was definitely a different man now than who Philip had known in the past. It was plain to see that bitterness had gotten a hold of him. Just then Danika ran up, panting. She and Eli locked eyes in horror.

"Philip King, you've given me more trouble than –" Jacob grasped his heart, obviously in pain, fell to his knees, and his face began turning white.

"Danika, quick, get the cayenne. He's having a heart attack!" Philip called to Danika who was closest to the herb shop.

"No, *Dat*!" Eli cried.

Danika ran back with a glass full of something red, and they gave it to Jacob to drink. After he had drunk the entire glass, they moved him into the house where he could rest. Eli went and stayed by his father's side. "I'm sorry, *Dat.*" He sobbed on his father's shoulder, while he lay on the bed.

Philip walked up behind Eli and touched his arm. "It'll be okay, Son," he said comfortingly. Eli stood up and Philip embraced him while his tears flowed freely. "It's not your fault," he stated.

Danika stood in the kitchen explaining the whole situation to Naomi and Cindy. Afterward, she went outside alone and prayed, *Dear Lord, Please don't let Eli lose his dad. Not like this. It would be too much of a burden for him to carry. No matter what happens to Eli and me, please let his father live.*

"Hi, Danika," Eli said, as he came and sat by her on the porch swing. "It looks like *Dat's* going to be okay."

Danika gave him a big hug, and he held her tight. "I'm so glad, Eli."

"Your Uncle Philip is in there talking with him right now. He's sharing the Gospel, can you believe it?"

"We must pray that he gets saved. Jesus is the only one that can heal his heart," Danika stated. Eli took her hand and he prayed aloud.

Philip poked his head out the door, and informed Eli and Danika, "Jacob would like to see you now. Both of you."

They looked at each other with questioning eyes, then back at Philip.

"It's all right, *kumm*," he reassured them. They followed him into the quiet house and he led them to the living room, where Jacob now sat on the small couch.

Jacob still appeared a little frail, but his countenance had changed somehow. Eli and Danika sat down on the two wooden chairs in the room. Jacob looked at Danika as if to be studying her. She did not look away. He then looked at his son and began to speak, "Eli..." his voice cracked, "I have been wrong."

"'Tis okay, *Dat*."

"No, my behavior was not okay. I have let my own pride stand in the way of truth. Because of it, I have become a despicable man. I am not only ruining my own life, but also the lives of those around me. I am ashamed that it had to come to this before I opened my eyes. Will you please forgive me for the grief I have caused you?" he asked, his eyes pleading.

"For sure and for certain." Eli smiled at his dad.

Jacob then looked at Dani. "Danika, is it?"

She nodded her head.

"Please come here," he requested.

She came and stood before him, quickly glancing at Eli.

Jacob took her hand and searched her eyes. "Forgive me for misjudging you, I was wrong. You and your uncle have saved my life. I am indebted to you."

“All is forgiven,” she granted with misty eyes.

Philip broke his silence and spoke up, “Jacob, I would be honored if you and your family would join us for lunch this Sunday.”

“We would be honored to come,” he replied.

CHAPTER 15
The Surprise

"A merry heart doeth good like a medicine..." Proverbs 17:22a

Danika couldn't think of a time in her life when she had been happier. Eli had taken most of the week off from school to help out at home. On Friday, he returned to class with the rest of the scholars. It was difficult for both of them to keep their minds on their studies. They were looking forward to this Sunday when their families would share in fellowship.

Eli escorted Danika home from school with the blessing of his father and Philip. They recounted all of the things that had happened since that first day in the woods. They marveled in the wondrous things that God had wrought, and how he had answered their prayers. God had never seemed more real in their lives than now, and they knew that they could trust Him with their future.

Sunday came quicker than expected and Naomi, Danika, and Cindy were busy making preparations for the noon meal. Philip had brought an extra table into the kitchen to accommodate their guests and the ladies quickly set it. When the Yoders arrived, Jacob gave Philip a hearty bear hug. Smiles and laughter soon filled the house as friendships were restored.

When all of the guests were present and seated, Philip made an announcement, "Naomi and I have a surprise for Danika."

Danika looked at them both inquisitively, and then glanced around the table to see if anyone else knew about it. They looked just as curious as she was.

Philip went to the bedroom and brought out a shiny red scooter.

"What in the world?" Danika asked in surprise.

"The scooter is not the surprise. It's in the basket." Naomi smiled.

Danika reached into the basket and pulled out a white rectangular envelope. She quickly opened it, a little nervous that all eyes were on her. She pulled out a card and read it silently, then read the words that were written by hand aloud: "Danika, we love you and we hope that you will be happy to be called our daughter. You are now officially Danika Morales King. Love, Your new *Mamm* and *Dat*."

With tears in her eyes, Danika rushed to her new parents and embraced them. "*Denki,* I love you too."

The End

Amish Girls Series - Book 3
Chloe's Revelation
J.E.B. Spredemann

Chloe's Revelation

J.E.B. Spredemann

Amish Girls Series - Book 3

To Heins, the best husband and father in the world. God knew our plan all along.

AUTHORS' NOTE

It should be noted that the Amish people and their communities differ one from another. There are, in fact, no two Amish communities exactly alike. It is this premise on which this book is written. We have taken cautious steps to assure the authenticity of Amish practices and customs. Both Old Order Amish and New Order Amish are portrayed in this work of fiction and may be inconsistent with some Amish communities.

We, as *Englischers*, can learn a lot from the Plain People and their simple way of life. Their hard work, close-knit family life, and concern for others are to be applauded. As the Lord wills, may this special culture continue to be respected and remain so for many centuries to come.

CHAPTER 1
Anticipation

"A merry heart maketh a cheerful countenance..."
Proverbs 15:13a

Ada Esh gingerly picked up her birthing supply bag, waved a quick farewell to her husband Daniel, then headed from the *dawdi haus* to the larger dwelling next door. Her granddaughter Chloe would possibly be observing her first birth today and Ada hoped she would eventually take over her midwifery duties in Paradise. Ada had recently passed her sixty-fifth birthday and she figured it was due time to train someone from the younger generation and pass on the art of "catching babies." Since Chloe had shown interest, Ada knew she was the perfect candidate for the job. Her outgoing personality would be an excellent asset that would be helpful in putting anxious mothers at ease.

"*Hullo*, Mary!" Ada greeted her daughter-in-law. "Is Chloe ready?"

Mary dried her hands on a dish towel and offered Ada a hug. "*Jah*, she is thrilled. That *boppli* is all she's been talking about lately. She should be down in a bit."

Chloe quickly descended the stairs. "*Grossmudder!*" She threw her arms around her grandmother for a quick embrace. "This is going to be so exciting!"

"Well, the two of us better get going before that *boppli* arrives without us. You know if that happens, Isaac Fisher will be beside himself not knowing what to do. We don't want the new *dat* to worry," Ada warned.

"The buggy is all hitched up and ready to go!" Peter Esh hollered from the back door.

"*Denki, Sohn.*" Ada and Chloe tromped down the back steps of the porch.

Chloe grasped the sides of her apron with sweaty hands, emotions swirling in her mind. This was the most exciting time in her life. Today she would be assisting *Mammi* with her first birth, school was finally over and done with, she would be staying home and helping *Mamm* with the house and the *kinner*, and she would be attending her first Singing soon. Her transition from childhood to adulthood had finally begun and her expectations couldn't be higher. She quietly smiled to herself as she and Ada rode along in their buggy. Cayenne, her beautiful auburn-colored quarter horse, seemingly took forever to arrive at the Fisher residence, not at all how he usually performed when Chloe raced him with Joanna Fisher's Arabian stallion, Blueberry.

Upon their arrival, Chloe hopped down from the buggy. As Isaac took Cayenne out to the pasture, she and Ada hurried into the house to see Rachel. Chloe was surprised when she noticed her sister Rachel preparing a casserole for the evening meal. Rachel smiled at the two ladies as they entered her home.

"*Wilkom!*" Rachel's cheeks glowed with joy.

"How's *Mamm* and the *boppli* doing?" Ada asked.

"*Ach*, I thought he was ready to make his appearance, but it seems he or she has settled down now. I haven't had one contraction since Isaac called you." Rachel sighed disappointedly.

"Appears to be false labor. Happens all the time, so don't feel bad. The *boppli* will come when he's good and ready." Ada chuckled.

"Since you're here anyway, how about a cup of peppermint tea?" Rachel suggested.

Ada and Chloe glanced at one another and both agreed. "Might as well."

"Hey, *Dat*. What's Mother's Day?" Jonathan Fisher asked as he and his father walked toward Beiler's Hardware store.

Gideon rubbed his beard, confusion darkened his face. "Mother's Day? Why do you ask?"

"Well, I just saw a sign in the window of that store over there. It read 'Don't forget Mother's Day this Sunday'," the ten-year-old explained bright-eyed.

"I reckon Mother's Day is a day the *Englischers* celebrate their *mamms*." Gideon hoped his simple answer would suffice his son's curiosity.

"How come we don't celebrate Mother's Day, *Dat*?" he wondered aloud.

"Like I said, Mother's Day is a holiday for the *Englisch*. We don't need fancy days to show how much our loved ones mean to us. We show them every day by our actions."

While Jonathan thought that Mother's Day sounded like a good holiday to celebrate, he didn't argue with his father. Instead, he tried hard to think of something special he could give his mother to show her that he loved her. A smile slowly crept across his face when he came up with an idea.

"Jonathan, are you sure you know what you're doing?" Matthew Riehl asked nervously as the two boys entered the cemetery.

"Come on, Matthew. Don't ya wanna get somethin' nice for your *mamm*?" Jonathan thought of the look of delight on his mother's face when he would deliver his special gift, and smiled.

"*Jah,* I guess so. But are ya sure this is okay?" He cast a worried expression at Jonathan.

"*Jah,* of course. Matthew, do ya think I'd do something to get you in trouble?"

Matthew thought of the time when Jonathan talked him into helping him rope off the outhouse at school. Unbeknownst to Matthew, their friend Joshua Hostettler, also the bishop's son, was inside. Matthew had to stay after school a whole hour every day for the next week and write an essay about the 'Golden Rule'. "Well –"

"Of course, not," Jonathan assured him, surveying the many graves that contained flowers. "The people here are all dead. They won't care if we take the flowers. Besides, the men that work here just throw the flowers away anyhow." Jonathan spotted a large bouquet of brightly-colored artificial flowers and his eyes lit up. He quickly knelt down and took the flowers from the plastic vase.

"But, isn't that stealing?" Matthew gulped.

"Like I said, Matthew. The people are dead, they don't care about the flowers. Besides, isn't it better to give flowers to people that are living?"

"Well –"

"Just think of how happy your *mamm* will be when she sees the flowers. Unless, you'd rather give her one of those big candles with a picture of Jesus on it. Na... that would probably be a graven image. Besides, how do ya suppose they know what Jesus looks like?" Jonathan mused aloud, not waiting for Matthew's answer.

Jonathan knelt down next to a large angel headstone. "Here's some nice flowers and they're purple too. Didn't you say purple was your *mamm's* favorite color?" Jonathan held out a small bouquet of silk lilacs to Matthew.

"Uh...okay. Do you think we should go now?" Matthew furtively glanced around.

"*Jah*, I can't wait till tomorrow!" Jonathan smiled confidently as he and his friend walked out the cemetery gate.

CHAPTER 2
Mother's Day

"Her children arise up, and call her blessed..."
Proverbs 31:28a

The Sunday-Go-To-Meeting would be held at the Weaver residence today. Chloe enjoyed the Weaver place because they had a lovely sweeping wrap-around porch and a garden that overflowed with an abundance of beautiful flowers. Rumor had it that the Weavers planned on turning their home into a bed and breakfast where tourists could come to stay the night and enjoy a nice home-cooked breakfast. Chloe thought a bed and breakfast would be fitting for the Weaver family because Lavina loved to accommodate guests and got along well with both *Englischers* and the Amish.

The Weaver family also had an expansive barn where Noah ran a successful gazebo business. The Singing for the young folks would be held there tonight after the service had well disbanded. This would be Chloe's very first Singing so she was glad that her friends Joanna Fisher and Danika King would be in attendance. If it weren't for her friends, Chloe would be a ball of nerves. What if some handsome boy asked to take her home? She blushed at the thought, especially since Deacon Yoder announced that the young people from the next district over would be joining them tonight.

When the morning service ended, Chloe was quick to help the other ladies prepare the food to be served. The men quickly removed the backless benches from the house and took them outside to set up the tables where everyone would share the common meal. The men and the older folks were typically served first, with the women and children following, due to limited seating space. Since serving was a blessing and a virtue that Jesus exemplified, the women didn't mind the task.

As Chloe set the cold cuts on the table for the men, she glanced up and caught Levi Hostettler looking her way. He gave her a nervous smile then quickly looked away, his cheeks darkening in color.

While they had attended school together, she noticed that Levi had always been a little shy – especially around girls. Even though the bishop's son was a couple of years older than her, she had always thought he was handsome. She wondered if he'd be attending the Singing tonight.

"Who put these flowers on the table?" Esther Fisher eyed the Mason jar as she set the table for the evening meal.

"I did, *Mamm*!" Jonathan exclaimed with a broad smile, his eyes bright. "Happy Mother's Day! I hope you like 'em."

Esther looked at her youngest son. "Mother's Day?"

"*Jah*. I figured if the *Englischers* could get somethin' nice for their mothers, then I could too. Do ya like 'em, *Mamm*?" Jonathan asked in anticipation.

Esther hoped her face didn't betray her speech. "Why, they're...uh...lovely, *Sohn*. *Denki* for thinking of me." She gave Jonathan a quick hug to show her appreciation.

"They're special flowers too, *Mamm*. They don't need no water. And they never die, so you can keep 'em forever." Jonathan exuberated.

Esther inwardly groaned, but smiled nonetheless. "*Denki*."

"Where'd ya get the flowers from?" his oldest sister Grace asked.

"Got 'em from the *Englischer* cemetery." Jonathan grinned at his genius.

Esther gasped. "*Ach*, Jonathan!"

Gideon, who had been listening in on the conversation as he walked in for dinner, stated, "Did ya take it from one of the graves?"

"*Jah*, that's okay, no?" Jonathan asked innocently.

"No, Jonathan. That's not okay. You will take the flowers back first thing in the morning," Gideon said.

"But *Dat*, them dead folk don't care about no flowers. It's best to give flowers to folks that are alive, ain't?" Jonathan hung his head.

"You're right by wanting to honor your *Mamm*. I'm right pleased. But taking somthin' that doesn't belong to you is stealing."

"All right, *Dat*. I guess I'll take 'em back then." Jonathan's tone held defeat as he removed the flowers from the table. "Sorry, *Mamm*, but you can't keep these. I hope you're not too disappointed."

"I'll never be disappointed knowing that I have a son that loves me enough to honor me with a special gift. Thank you for your thoughtfulness, Jonathan. That's what really counts." Esther breathed a sigh of relief, thankful that the pitiful-looking plastic flowers would be gone by morning.

CHAPTER 3

Chloe's First Singing

"Praise ye the Lord. Sing unto the Lord a new song, and his praise in the congregation of the saints." Psalm 149:1

As Chloe and her older brother Stephen pulled up in his open courting buggy, she noticed that there were already many youth present at the young people's gathering. Chloe smiled and sighed in relief when she saw her friends Joanna and Danika heading her way. Joanna had been standing next to Danika and her beau Eli Yoder as they were watching a game of volleyball.

"Hey, Stephen. They're about to start another game of volleyball over there and I was about to jump in. Want to join us?" Eli offered.

"Sure, let's do it." Stephen smiled enthusiastically, rubbing his hands together.

"Girls, would you like to play too?" Eli winked at Danika and she smiled back.

The girls looked at each other and smiled in agreement. "*Jah,*" Danika replied for all of them.

Chloe noticed Levi Hostettler was playing too and smiled to herself. Unfortunately, they were on opposite teams but she was happy to be able to steal a glance every now and then. There were also several young people from their neighboring district playing.

When Chloe stepped up to serve the ball she heard a male voice. "Come on, Chloe! Let's get it over the net and put them out of business." Chloe glanced to her left and noticed it was Saul Brenneman from Bishop Mast's district. *Ach*, he was ever so handsome. His sparkling blue eyes caught hers and he flashed her a gorgeous smile. Distracted now, Chloe took a deep breath then served the ball directly into the net. She hung her head in embarrassment and waited for the opposing team to serve the ball before rotating back up to the front.

"Hey, that's okay, Chloe. You did your best." Saul touched her arm reassuringly. Chloe glanced at the opposite side of the net and noticed Levi watching the exchange.

Glad for the game to be over, Chloe quickly joined her friends while the guys stood around talking. Chloe noticed both Saul and Levi looking in her direction.

"Well, it seems like someone or should I say *two* someones have taken an interest in Chloe," Danika noted.

"Shh..." Chloe hushed her friend. "Let's go stand in the shade, *jah*?" She was desperate to flee the area lest someone spy her blushing cheeks. *Ach*, being near handsome *buwe* could be so unnerving!

"Looks as though poor Stephen will be riding home sisterless tonight," Danika continued her teasing.

"*Ach*! Quit joshing. Who knows if anyone will ask to take me home." Chloe took a deep breath attempting to bring calmness as her hands slightly shook in nervous anticipation. How could her friends be so at ease?

"I'm pretty sure at least one of them will ask you, Chloe. Saul Brenneman seems to be pretty outgoing," Joanna agreed.

"Not to mention cute." Danika glanced over at the boys. "But of course, not as handsome as Eli Yoder."

"Well, Levi's good looking too," Chloe said defensively.

"*Jah*, but Levi's shy. I haven't seen him take a girl home yet." Danika blushed when Eli caught her looking his way and she quickly turned. "Of course, I've only been coming for a few months now."

Changing the subject, Chloe suggested they go inside for a drink of water. After another game of volleyball, which Chloe opted out of, the young men filed into the Weavers' barn for the Singing. The young women followed and sat on the opposite side of the table facing the guys. The three girls sat together and Eli sat across from them along with some of the other young men from their district, Stephen and Levi included. Saul sat by some friends from his district and was about the tenth person down the line from where Chloe sat.

As the Singing started, the barn was filled with over one hundred beautiful voices singing in harmony all in a cappella. Chloe closed her eyes as she listened to the lovely sounds their voices made. *Surely, this is what Heaven will sound like,* she thought to herself. The next two hours flew by and before she knew it, the young people were indulging in snacks and cool drinks.

Chloe sipped on her glass of sweet tea when she noticed Saul coming her way. She nervously twisted her *kapp* string around her finger and bit her bottom lip. Attempting to calm her rapidly beating heart, she began talking to Joanna.

"Hey, Chloe." Saul smiled broadly. "Can we talk for a sec?" He nodded his head to the side indicating he wished to speak with her in private.

"Uh...*jah,* sure." Chloe anxiously glanced at her friends who both gave her a knowing smile. They took a few steps away from where her friends stood chatting.

Saul looked into her eyes, apparently a bit uneasy himself. "Chloe, I uh...I was hoping to give you a ride home tonight. That is, if you'd like to."

Chloe gulped then replied unsteadily, "*Jah*, sure."

"Great." Saul smiled. "I'll just hitch up my buggy then and meet you outside."

As Saul quickly left the barn, Chloe calmly told her brother Stephen that he didn't need to give her a ride home. Stephen gave her a questioning look, glanced at Levi, then quickly agreed. When she told Danika and Joanna goodbye, she glanced over her shoulder to see Levi now standing next to Stephen and looking her way again. Oh, she hoped she was making the right decision by agreeing to ride with Saul.

"Don't worry about Levi," Joanna suggested. "He'll get his chance too, *jah*?"

"*Jah*, Lord willing," Chloe replied before taking a deep breath and stepping outside to meet Saul.

As Saul's buggy joined a long line of others and pulled up near the entrance of Weavers' barn, Chloe walked toward it. Saul quickly leaned over and offered her a helping hand when he brought the vehicle to a halt. She took his hand and hopped up into his buggy. He clicked his tongue and flicked the reins gently, setting his horse in motion.

"You can move a little closer. I don't bite, you know," Saul teased.

Chloe hadn't noticed that she sat all the way to the opposite side of the seat, clenching the side support tightly with her hand. She had to release some of this tension. She laughed, lightening the mood. "That's not what I've heard." She inched closer to him.

He howled and they both burst into laughter.

"And you decided to ride with me anyway? You're a brave one. I like you already, Chloe," he proclaimed. "So, you're sixteen then?"

"*Nee*...fourteen," she corrected.

"That's right." He snapped his fingers. "Bishop Hostettler lets the girls from your district attend Singings at fourteen. I had forgotten." He didn't sound alarmed.

"And how old are you?" she queried.

"Seventeen."

"How many brothers and sisters do you have?" Chloe wondered aloud.

"Five brothers and two sisters. And you?"

"Two brothers and five sisters." She laughed. "I guess we're exact opposites."

"Well, you know what they say. Opposites attract." He winked and smiled at her.

Chloe blushed. She'd never known an Amish boy so openly flirtatious. Saul and Levi contrasted like buggies and *Englischer* cars.

"I'm not too familiar with this area, especially at night. Is there somewhere around here that we can park? I'd really like to get out and stretch my legs. Unless, you're hungry or something. Then we can grab a quick bite to eat." He rubbed the stubble on his chin.

"*Nee*, I'm fine," Chloe assured him. She'd snacked at the Weavers' and figured she was probably too anxious to eat anything now. "There's a path by the wooded area near the Yoders' farm. They just live a short ways from here. It's kinda dark though. Would you like to go to the meadow instead?"

"Sure, that sounds great! Nothin' better than being under a beautiful canopy of stars."

Chloe agreed and guided the way to the vast meadow. She glanced out into the immense field straining to see the beautiful wildflowers she'd spotted earlier in the week. With darkness covering the land it was nearly impossible to see anything. Fortunately, the stars were shining bright enough to see a little bit.

Saul parked the buggy and tethered his horse to a nearby tree. He lent Chloe a hand to help her down. He reached over the seat and grabbed a blanket from the back, and tucked it under his left arm. Unexpectedly, Saul took her hand in his as they walked toward the expansive green field. Chloe somehow felt comfortable with Saul, and his likable personality put her mind at ease.

When they reached the middle of the meadow, Saul suddenly halted. "This is the spot." He looked into her eyes for a moment then remembered the quilt he'd carried under his arm. He haphazardly unfolded the blanket and spread it out on the grass. "Let's sit a while."

Chloe sat down on the quilt and Saul plopped down next to her. The coolness of the grass seeped through the quilt, bringing refreshment after the warm day. The quiet evening transformed into a resounding symphony as the cicadas raised their voices in praise to their Maker.

Saul took a deep breath, enjoying the woodsy scents around them. "Tell me some more about yourself, Chloe."

"Okay. What would you like to know?"

"What are your interests?" He smiled.

"Oh wow. Do you want to know everything, or just my favorites?" She laughed.

"That many interests, huh? Well, since we only have a few hours..." He chuckled.

"Okay, I'll tell you my favorite if you promise not to tell anyone," she warned.

"Hmm...do I really want to keep a deep dark secret?" he teased. "All right, I guess I won't tell."

"Nope, not good enough." She crossed her arms defiantly.

"Okay, okay," Saul answered defeatedly, then ceremoniously raised his right hand. "I, Saul Brenneman, do solemnly swear that I will keep Chloe Esh's deep dark secret for as long as I shall live." He wriggled his eyebrows. "Is that good enough for you?"

"Hey, how did you know my last name? I never told you," she challenged.

"Wouldn't you like to know?" he teased.

"Really," she insisted.

"I have my ways." His eyes sparkled with mischief.

"I'm waiting..." She feigned impatience by crossing her arms and tapping her foot.

"Okay, I give up. You know the guy that was playing volleyball with us, the one on the opposite team with the brown hair? I think his name was Levi or something."

Chloe inwardly cringed. *Oh no, poor Levi!* "Levi told you my last name?"

"Uh, huh. So now...about my oath. Was that good enough?" he prodded.

"*Jah*, I guess." She shrugged.

"You guess? I promise to keep your secret until I die and that's not good enough for you? Maybe I *don't* want to know what it is." He chuckled.

"All right, then. My favorite thing to do is race my friends on horseback." Chloe smiled, thinking of the last time she, Danika, and Joanna competed. Cayenne had pulled through at the last minute, giving her the victory.

"No way! A girl that races horses." He smiled to himself in unbelief. "You're joshin'."

Chloe crossed her arms, clearly demonstrating her resentment. "Do you have a problem with that?"

"Whoa! No...no problems here." He held up his hands in surrender. "I actually find that quite intriguing." Saul smiled, thinking he really enjoyed this spirited girl.

Chloe relaxed and dropped her arms.

Saul took her hand, encasing it in his own larger one, and gently stroked it with his thumb. He slowly inched closer, gazing into her eyes.

Chloe gulped when she realized his intentions.

Saul leaned forward slightly until their lips met. He closed his eyes, enjoying the tender moment.

Chloe knew she should resist, especially since this was barely their first date, but she followed her heart instead and kissed Saul back. With this being her first experience with kissing, she hoped she was doing it the right way. Saul's eager response indicated she was doing just fine. Remembering the numerous warnings she'd received about fleeing temptation, she abruptly pulled away.

"That was nice," Saul admitted with a silly grin.

For a long moment, he gazed into the depths of her eyes. At this very moment she realized how difficult resisting temptation could be. Entranced, she wanted him to kiss her again. *What am I doing?* Taking a deep breath, she cleared her throat. "Maybe we should go now."

"Are you sure, Chloe?" He rubbed her forearm with the back of his fingers, still gazing longingly into her eyes. "I was hoping we could spend a little more time together. Let's enjoy this magnificent evening a little longer, *jah*?"

A firefly zoomed just inches in front of them, his luminescence mimicking the stars above. Oh, how she'd love to spend hours in this terrestrial Utopia enjoying Saul's company. "*Nee*, we'd better not. It's getting late." She stood up before she could talk herself into staying.

"Uh...Chloe, I didn't mean to make you uncomfortable or anything." Saul backpedaled. "I'm sorry if I was a little too forward. I should have asked before kissing you."

"*Nee*, 'tis okay, Saul. But we really should go now." She decided.

"All right, then. If that's what you want, Chloe."

No, it was not what she wanted, not one bit. But it was what was necessary.

Saul stooped down to gather up the blanket. They walked side by side back to the buggy, leaving their tranquil sanctuary behind.

When they reached the lane to the Esh residence, the buggy rolled to a stop and Saul took Chloe's hand. "So, I guess this is it?"

Chloe smiled as she glanced down at their intertwined fingers. "*Jah,* I guess so. I had a *gut* time, Saul."

Saul leaned toward Chloe and brushed her lips with his once again. "Me, too. May I take you to dinner on Saturday?"

"*Jah,* I think I'd enjoy that." She found herself saying.

"Great! I'll pick you up here at five then." He smiled, then hopped down to assist her exit from the carriage. He offered his hand and she daintily accepted his assistance.

Chloe's heart beat wildly as she walked up the lane toward her house. She thought of Saul's gorgeous blue eyes and his sweet smile. And his kisses. *Could it be that I'm falling in love with Saul Brenneman?* She quietly hummed a tune that she'd sung at the young people's gathering earlier this evening. Just when she thought life couldn't get better, it did!

CHAPTER 4
Plaisir d'Amour

"And let us consider one another to provoke unto love and good works:" Hebrews 10:24

Lost in thought, Chloe carried the basket of wet laundry out to the clothes line that stretched from the *dawdi haus* to the barn. Mondays had always been wash day and a day she'd always dreaded. But not today.

A slow smile crept across her features as she contemplated her time with Saul last night. No matter what she did, she couldn't seem to get him off her mind. *Dat* had even chided her about daydreaming at the breakfast table. She couldn't help envisioning herself preparing a meal for Saul. What would it be like to be married?

No wonder *Mamm* was able to find joy in the mundane. Preparing breakfast wasn't a burden when one considered you were bringing nourishment and satisfaction to loved ones. All of a sudden, hanging laundry didn't seem so boring. What if she could look to the barn in between loads and catch glimpses of Saul all day long? Chloe sighed in contentment.

"So, Chloe, who'd you ride home with last night?" Her brother Stephen broke through her reverie.

"None of your business, Stephen," Chloe answered defiantly. She reached for one of her brother's damp shirts and fastened it to the line.

Stephen huffed. "Well, I know who it wasn't."

"What's that supposed to mean?" She looked at her brother curiously, holding up a pair of trousers.

"Oh, come on, Chloe. You had to know Levi Hostettler has been interested in you. Even a blind person could see that," Stephen challenged.

Chloe remained silent for a moment, contemplating the situation with Levi. "Well, he didn't ask me. If he had, I might have gone with him," she replied defensively. "So, who did he take home?" she wondered aloud.

"Nobody. He went home alone." Stephen shot her a disappointed glare then walked inside.

As Stephen walked away, Chloe found herself feeling guilty about Levi going home alone. *Stop it, Chloe,* she chided herself. *It isn't my fault Levi didn't take a girl home. Besides, I had fun with Saul.* Chloe felt her cheeks flush when she thought again about the kisses he had given her. Her very first kiss!

Chloe's week went by quickly, as she contently helped *Mamm* with chores, baking, and tending to the *kinner.* She had also made several house calls with *Mammi* Ada, although her sister Rachel still hadn't delivered. The prospect of being present at the birth of her first niece or nephew brought excitement and a bit of trepidation. What would it be like to actually attend a live birth? *Mammi* informed her that births were sometimes unpredictable and first babies were often late.

Day after day, Chloe dreamt of Saul. Could she possibly have a future together with him? Would they one day become man and wife? Then just as quickly, Levi would pop into her mind. For some reason, Levi was still ever-present in her thoughts. Why? She wondered. Was her future supposed to be with him? Life could be so confusing sometimes.

Before she knew it, Saturday had come. Just before five, she walked up the lane to where it met the road. She looked up and caught Saul's gaze. He was standing next to his buggy looking handsome as ever. His cobalt blue shirt enhanced his piercing blue eyes. His black suspenders matched his broadfall trousers, and gently pressed against his chest, slightly defining his muscles. Saul held his straw hat in his hands and he strode toward Chloe with a spring in his step.

Saul placed his arm around her waist and gallantly helped her up into his buggy. He jogged around to the other side, then hopped up and slid next to her. "I've been looking forward to this all week." He grinned.

"Me, too," she admitted, bearing a little more of her heart.

"I hope you like Italian food."

"*Jah,* I think I've had it before." Chloe tried to recall what exactly Italian food was. Her family seldom went to restaurants.

"Well, you're in for a treat then. We're going to one of the finest restaurants in Pennsylvania," he said assertively.

When the buggy rolled up to the front of the restaurant, Chloe noticed there were no hitching posts nearby. She got the impression that not many Amish folk frequented the fancy establishment. She was about to mention it when Saul pulled the horse over to where a bike rack stood.

"This ought to work," he said. He tied the reins to the bicycle rack, helped her down, then took a bucket from the back of the buggy and filled it at a faucet nearby. After setting the bucket down for the horse, Saul held out his arm and Chloe happily placed her hand in the crook of his elbow. She felt so secure walking next to him. He seemed to be confident and mature for someone his age and Chloe admired that. Saul was Amish with an eighth grade education just as she, but his poised appearance indicated he was much more cultured and knowledgeable of things outside the Amish community. Chloe wondered if perhaps he had spent part of his *Rumspringa* among the *Englisch.*

When they entered the restaurant Chloe realized the establishment was small, but evidently not inexpensive. Unfamiliar, delicious smells wafted through the air indicating Saul knew what he was talking about. Chloe's mouth began to water and she couldn't wait to taste the food. After a waiter adorned in a fancy suit showed them to their table, Chloe turned to Saul. "Do you visit this place often?"

"Na...I've been here a few times with my parents. For special occasions, you know. I hope you like it." His eyes were sincere and Chloe recognized he sought to please her. She smiled, feeling as though she were the most special girl in the world.

"*Jah*, 'tis wonderful-*gut*." She glanced around taking in the quaint authentic Italian decor, including a painting of the *Mona Lisa*. A beautiful sound caught her attention and she noticed a sharply-dressed man with a thick dark mustache playing a wooden musical instrument.

Saul must have noticed her curious expression. "It's called a violin. He will come to our table and play something for us," he informed her, knowing that many Amish cared little about musical instruments since they were forbidden to them.

Chloe felt as though she were a princess. She opened the menu and couldn't help it when her mouth dropped open at the sight of the prices on the menu. "Saul...uh, maybe we should go somewhere else instead," she gently suggested.

Saul frowned. "But I thought you liked –" he stopped in mid-sentence when he realized she saw the prices. "Please, don't worry about that, Chloe. I have plenty, I promise." He placed his hand over hers and gently caressed it. She gazed up into his eyes and he reassured her, "Get anything you want."

"But I don't know what any of this is. What do you like?"

Saul perused the menu a moment and pointed at the entrees. “The fettuccini alfredo is outstanding. It’s a delicious pasta with white sauce. I also like the cheese and vegetable calzone.”

“I’ll just get whatever you’re having.”

Just then, the waiter approached the table with pen and pad in hand.

“We’ll have two orders of fettuccini alfredo,” Saul requested, handing the menus back to the waiter.

“Would you like anything to drink with that, Sir?” the waiter asked.

“I’ll have an iced tea and the lady will have...” Saul answered then looked to Chloe.

“I’d like water, please,” Chloe piped up.

“Very well, Miss,” the waiter agreed then retreated to the kitchen to place the order with the chefs.

The man with the violin neared their table and lifted the bow. “Excuse me, Sir, Miss. Do have any suggestions?” he asked in a strong Italian accent.

Chloe was at a loss. She looked to Saul for direction.

“Yes. Do you know ‘Plaisir d’Amour’?” Saul requested in his best French accent.

The violinist nodded his response then gently moved the bow of horse hair over the strings. The lovely music filled the air and Chloe’s heart filled with joy. She desired to ask Saul about the meaning of the song, but decided to wait until the violinist had finished the beautiful number.

By the pleased look on Chloe's face, Saul knew he had made a wise decision in bringing her to the restaurant.

As the man stepped away from their table to perform for the other patrons, Chloe leaned forward and asked Saul if he knew what the title of the song meant.

"*Jah.*" Saul smiled. "Plaisir d'Amour is French and it means the pleasure of love."

"It sounded a little familiar," she noted.

"There was a famous *Englischer*, Elvis Presley, who sang a song with a similar tune. Perhaps you've heard it on the radio while riding in an *Englischer*'s car. It's called 'I Can't Help Falling in Love with You.'"

Chloe's cheeks reddened when she realized the implications of the song's meaning and she was surprised to see Saul blush as well. Could *they* be falling in love? Chloe wasn't sure because she'd never been in love before. But she did know that she loved being in Saul's company. She knew the wonderful-*gut* feeling she had when she thought of Saul and their future together. Was that love?

After finishing only half of her amazing dinner, Chloe declared that she was stuffed. Saul offered dessert, but Chloe declined. "We'll share then," Saul insisted. "You have to try their Tiramisu. It's delicious."

When the dessert arrived, Chloe only took a few small bites but enjoyed every second of it. The smooth, rich dessert was a delightful end to a perfect evening. Saul didn't flinch when the bill came, but nonchalantly placed two large bills into the wallet provided by the waiter.

Saul stood up and offered his hand to Chloe, which she gladly took. They walked out of the restaurant into the cool night breeze and decided to take a walk along the store fronts. Hand in hand, they strolled along conversing easily. Chloe determined she could definitely spend the rest of her life with this amazing man beside her.

As they drove home, Saul asked Chloe if she would be his girl exclusively. *His aldi!* She agreed, and all thoughts of a courtship with Levi fell by the wayside. Saul promised to pick her up for the Singings in her district and offered to take her to the ones in his district as well. This worked out perfectly because their Singings were held on alternate Sundays, which meant that they would be guaranteed to see each other at least once a week.

When Saul's buggy came to a stop at the end of Chloe's lane, he tethered the horse to a nearby tree. He walked her halfway down the lane, and then pulled her into his warm embrace. They stood in silence for a couple of minutes as he held her in his arms. She felt so protected in his arms, and so cherished. "Until tomorrow, *Mei Lieb.*" Saul leaned down and once again met Chloe's lips with his.

Chloe pulled away when she thought she heard a noise from inside the house. "I'd better go now." Chloe reluctantly broke free of their intertwined fingers.

Saul stood looking after her as she traipsed down the lane and disappeared into the house. He sauntered back to his buggy and headed for home, whistling as he went.

As Chloe slipped through the door, she untied her shoes and carried them upstairs so as not to wake anybody. When she neared the top landing she noticed Stephen standing sentry, his arms crossed over his chest. He didn't appear happy.

"Excuse me," Chloe said, attempting to step around her older brother. He didn't budge.

"Getting home a little late, aren't you Chloe?"

"That's none of your business and you know it. Now if you'll let me pass." She attempted to step around him again. It seemed that ever since she'd become old enough to attend Singings, Stephen had taken it upon himself to become the overseer of her love life. Chloe did not appreciate the unwanted intrusion.

"No." He stood as though he were a statue.

"Okay, Stephen. What do you want?" Chloe resigned. "Make it fast because I'm tired."

"I saw you kissing that boy," he stated, raising his eyebrows.

"Boy? Stephen, Saul is seventeen, which is a year older than you," she informed him.

"Which is why you should be even more careful," Stephen asserted. "I know how boys my age think."

"You shouldn't have been spying on me." Chloe huffed.

"Chloe, please think about what you're doing. You are only fourteen. That's too young to be in serious relationship."

"What's your point?" she asked defiantly.

"I don't want to see my little sister get her heart broken. Or worse, get into trouble," he warned.

"Okay, I get it. May I go to bed now?"

Stephen stepped out of the way, shook his head, and sighed. Would his sister ever learn?

CHAPTER 5
Friendly Advice

"Let no man despise thy youth; but be thou an example of the believers, in word, in conversation, in charity, in spirit, in faith, in purity." 1Timothy 4:12

Joanna and Danika stood at the back door of the Esh home and rapped three times on the door. Mary Esh welcomed the two girls and invited them in for cookies and milk. She walked toward the stairs and hollered up to Chloe. Chloe descended the stairs with a towel wrapped turban style around her still-wet hair. She'd obviously just finished her shower.

After Mary Esh left the room, Chloe noticed her friends were anxious to talk. "We missed you at the taffy pull on Saturday," Joanna stated.

"Yeah, where were you?" Danika chimed in.

Chloe bit her bottom lip and her cheeks flooded with color.

"Were you with Saul again?" Danika raised her eyebrows and looked to Joanna then back to Chloe.

"*Jah,*" Chloe stated timidly. "We went to dinner."

Joanna and Danika shared a concerned look.

"Chloe," Joanna began slowly. "You haven't let him kiss you, have you?"

"You're starting to sound like Stephen now." Chloe crossed her arms.

"So, he *has* kissed you." Danika huffed. "Here Eli and I have been waiting nearly two years and you let Saul kiss you on the second date."

Chloe didn't admit that it was actually the *first* date. "I don't need a lecture. I'm a big girl, you know."

"Chloe, we're not trying to lecture you. We're your friends. We care about you." Joanna reminded her. "What about our promise to purity? I thought that's what we all wanted. Remember, no kissing till we're married?"

"Well, it's kinda too late for that. For the no kissing part anyway," Chloe stated without apology. "I actually enjoy kissing Saul. It feels wonderful-*gut.* Besides, you don't know how hard it is not to."

"Oh, trust me, Chloe. I know," Danika said defensively. "Do I ever know."

"Yeah, well it's even harder after you've already done it." Chloe sighed.

"Which is exactly why you shouldn't. You can't go back and undo what's already been done, but you can decide not to from this point on," Joanna suggested.

"But, I love Saul," Chloe blurted out. "And being with him just feels so...so right."

"You can't follow your emotions, Chloe. Remember what the Bible says: 'The heart is deceitful above all things, and desperately wicked...' Please don't follow your heart or your feelings. You are being deceived and it will lead you on a path you don't want to go down," Joanna warned.

Danika sipped her lemonade. "Eli and I love each other too. That is *why* we stay pure. Love is patient and longsuffering. It's worth waiting for. I think *Dat* was wise to not allow Eli and me to court till I'm older."

Chloe sighed noncommittally. "I promise I'll try."

"Do you really think that is good enough?" Joanna challenged.

"What do you want me to do? Because if it means I have to stop seeing Saul, that's out of the question," Chloe asserted.

"What if you decide that the two of you *not* be alone together? Make it a point to always have someone else around. Go on double dates," Joanna suggested.

"I can suggest it, but I don't know how Saul will feel about it," Chloe said, not sure how *she* even felt about it.

"If he loves you, then it shouldn't be a problem. *Jah*?" Danika challenged, raising her eyebrows.

Chloe shrugged. "*Jah*, I reckon."

Joanna thought a change of subject would be appropriate. "Hey, did you guys hear what my little brother did this time?"

Both Chloe and Danika perked their ears up as Joanna continued on. Jonathan Fisher had always been an interesting subject.

Joanna proceeded to tell them about the Mother's Day incident and how he had to return the flowers back to the cemetery. The girls laughed as she went on with the story. "Since Jonathan didn't get to give *Mamm* the flowers, he decided to make her a batch of cookies."

"Ah, that's so sweet." Chloe smiled.

"Well, he got the cookie dough all ready and then he decided to try a little to make sure it turned out right. It tasted so good that he proceeded to eat the entire bowl of cookie dough, making himself so sick that he threw up." Joanna went on while her friends burst into laughter. "After he felt better, he decided to make another batch of cookies for *Mamm*. But this time he didn't even want to *think* about putting the cookie dough into his mouth, so he didn't try any.

"Well, when *Mamm* came home there was a lovely plate of cookies waiting for her on the table. She was delighted until she popped one into her mouth. She quickly spewed it out of her mouth and ran for a drink of water. I guess Jonathan accidentally used salt instead of sugar.

"But the funniest part was when *Dat* thought he had done it on purpose. On the way to the woodshed, poor bewildered Jonathan quickly explained what had happened. We heard a roar of laughter coming from outside and there was *Dat,* sitting on a stump of wood and holding the rod in his hand, laughing so hard he had tears rolling down his cheeks. Then he told Jonathan to *please* NOT get him anything for Father's Day!"

After the girls recovered from their fit of laughter and dried their tears, Joanna and Danika said goodbye and thanked Mary Esh for the cookies and milk.

Danika leaned over and whispered in Chloe's ear, "If you need us to, *Dat* will probably allow me and Eli to ride home from the Singing with you and Saul."

"*Denki,*" Chloe whispered back.

As Chloe watched her companions walk off toward their homes, she sent God a quick prayer of thanks for giving her friends that care enough to tell the truth even when it hurts.

CHAPTER 6
Rejection

"Hope deferred maketh the heart sick: but when the desire cometh, it is a tree of life."
Proverbs 13:12

"D*at*, may I talk to you?" Levi approached his father, Bishop Hostettler, as he placed a harness back on to one of the racks in the barn.

"Sure, *Sohn*. What is it you'd like to talk about?" Judah brightened, pleased his son had come to him to talk.

Levi blew out a breath. "What do you know about the Brennemans?"

"The family from Bishop Mast's district?"

Levi nodded, absentmindedly removing his hat.

"Eb Brenneman owns a successful construction company. I believe they build children's play structures. They have several children, as do most of our Amish families. I think they have a boy about your age." Judah tugged on his beard.

"What do you know about him? Saul Brenneman," Levi said steadily.

"Why do you want to know, *Sohn*? Is there a problem I should know about?" Judah eyebrows furrowed in concern.

"Just wondering is all. He was asking about one of our girls." *My girl*, Levi thought ruefully.

The bishop began apprehensively, "You know I'm not one to spread rumors, so this needs to stay between you and me."

Levi nodded.

"Seems there was some concern a while back about him and a *maedel*. I guess he's had somewhat of a wild *Rumspringa* spending time with the *Englisch* and what not. His father didn't seem too concerned and assured Bishop Mast that his son would eventually join the church and take over the family business."

"Thanks, *Dat*." Levi placed his hat back on his head and decided to take a walk.

Levi's frustration mounted as he thought about Chloe with Saul Brenneman. Would he whisk her off to the *Englisch* world with him? *If only I'd asked her first,* he chided himself for being so reserved. Had he lost his only chance with Chloe because of his timidity?

Feeling hopelessness closing in, Levi decided to pray. He'd recently committed a verse to memory that had been helping him fight his insecurities. '*For God hath not given us the spirit of fear; but of power, of love, and of a sound mind.'* Once again, he drew strength from God's promises.

Maybe I should ask her anyway, he thought as he headed in the direction of the Esh farm. Levi took a deep breath, then strode up the lane to the Esh home. He really didn't have any idea what he would say to Chloe, but trusted that the words would be there when he needed them. As he came closer, he noticed Chloe outside entertaining some of her younger siblings. She looked so beautiful with her strawberry-blonde hair shining in the sun under her *kapp*. Her eyes brightened at the sight of him, sending a surge of hope through his being.

"*Guten Mayrie,* Levi." Her sweet smile took his breath away.

Levi removed his straw hat and nervously turned it in his hands. He cleared his throat and realized this was going to be more difficult than he'd thought. "*Hiya,* Chloe."

"Did you want to talk to Stephen?" she asked easily.

"Uh...no. I...I was...I wanted to ask you if maybe you'd let me drive you home after the next Singing." His eyes were pleading as he fumbled over his words.

Chloe lamented having to deny Levi's request when she saw the longing in his eyes. "I'm sorry, Levi. Really, I am. But I have a steady beau already."

In that moment, Levi felt as though a portion of his heart had been mercilessly ripped from his chest. He regretfully looked away from Chloe's apologetic eyes.

"I see. Uh...goodbye, Chloe," he said awkwardly. Trying to conceal his disappointment, he quickly nodded then turned away.

He didn't know what he'd been expecting to feel, but certainly not this. Rejection was surely the worst form of torture there was. As Levi pondered that for a moment, he couldn't help but wonder if this is how God feels when his beloved creation rejects him...or rather rejects his only begotten son, Jesus. The only way to Heaven.

It was late at night when Chloe heard the phone ringing. She raced out to the phone shanty in the darkness and caught the receiver just before the answering machine picked up. On the other end, Isaac Fisher, her brother-in-law, frantically conveyed that his wife was in labor and her contractions were five minutes apart and steady. Chloe quickly assured him that she and *Mammi* would be right over.

Chloe hung up the phone and rushed to the *dawdi haus,* hoping she wouldn't trip on anything that might be in her path. "*Mammi*, the *boppli's* coming!" she hollered, bursting through the side door. "Hurry! Rachel's in labor!"

After waking *Mammi* and hitching Cayenne, they hastily made their way to Isaac and Rachel's cottage. Chloe had been familiar with the property since she and Joanna delivered honey for Naomi Fast, now Naomi King, a few years ago. The place held fond memories for her and she enjoyed visiting her sister every chance she got. With a new niece or nephew on the way, she suspected that occurrence would happen much more often.

Isaac greeted them at the house and shooed them inside while he tethered the horse. Chloe heard Rachel moan from her bedroom when she stepped into the house. *Mammi* quickly removed her shawl, washed her hands, and set to work, sending Chloe into the kitchen with a list of things they would need.

Chloe quickly gathered the items on the list and rejoined *Mammi,* Rachel, and Isaac in the bedroom. Rachel cried out and gripped Isaac's hand. *Mammi* lifted up the sheet draped over Rachel's legs and explained to Chloe how to check how far labor has progressed. Feeling somewhat uncomfortable, Chloe turned away. *Mammi* assured her that this is how God designed a woman's body to work and giving birth was perfectly natural. "She is dilated to eight centimeters," *Mammi* stated in a satisfactory voice. "When she gets to ten, it will be time to push."

Mammi turned to Rachel. "Did you lose your bag of waters?"

"*Jah,* I think so," she said in between quick short breaths. She cried out again and tightened her grip on Isaac's arm, making him wince in pain. "Sorry."

"*Nee.* 'Tis okay, Rachel," he assured her, smoothing her hair. He bent down and kissed his wife's forehead. "*Ich liebe dich.*"

Chloe smiled, thankful her sister had found a *gut* man to share her life with. Would she and Saul experience this same love years down the road? She hoped so.

After a few more contractions and about a half hour of pushing, little Gideon Fisher junior made his appearance. Chloe was thrilled to be the first one to hold her nephew. She helped *Mammi* clean the baby some and swaddled him tightly before handing him to his delighted father. Isaac's eyes danced with joy as he gazed upon his first son. In short order, he placed the babe into his mother's arms. Rachel spoke lovingly to the little one, examining his fine features.

An hour later, Chloe and *Mammi* wearily headed for home. Thrilled about sharing the good news and getting a few hours asleep, they encouraged Cayenne to hurry along. Chloe crawled into bed just after one a.m. and dreamt of the day she and Saul would have a *boppli* of their own.

CHAPTER 7
Ocean City

"There hath no temptation taken you but such as is common to man: but God is faithful, who will not suffer you to be tempted above that ye are able; but will with the temptation also make a way to escape, that ye may be able to bear it." 1 Corinthians 10:13

Each time Chloe and Saul spent time together, it seemed they fell even more in love. At first, Chloe had been nervous about attending the Singings in Saul's church district. But soon she became comfortable around his friends too. Saul was more than willing to double date if that's what made Chloe happy. Only occasionally, they'd be alone together.

Such was one of those times on a mid-summer day. Chloe met Saul early one morning at the end of her lane. It wasn't often she'd been allowed to take an entire day off, so the prospect of no work *plus* time with her beau was thrilling. She expected to be gone the whole day, but had no idea what Saul had planned. It seemed he enjoyed surprising her and she was perfectly happy with that.

When she spotted a vehicle near the road, her curiosity peaked. Saul stepped out sporting a pair of sunglasses and opened the car door for her. As she sat down on the leather seat, she felt a blast of cold air issuing from the vents in front of her. It was so refreshing compared to the sweltering heat they'd been experiencing lately.

Beaming, Saul hopped in and turned to Chloe. "Do you know what today is?"

"Uh..." She racked her brain endeavoring to figure out the significance the day held. "I give up."

"It's our two month anniversary!" he exclaimed, then leaned over and gave her a gentle peck on the cheek.

Chloe smiled back at him. "So, how are we celebrating?"

"I'm taking you to Ocean City." His eyes sparkled.

"The Boardwalk?" She'd never been there before, but had heard many great things about it.

He smiled and nodded.

"How long will it take to get there?" she asked excitedly.

"About three hours or so. Plenty of time for us to talk." He winked and brought her hand to his lips, placing a gentle kiss on it.

"You're spoiling me, you know."

"I've never known anyone so worthy of spoiling," he charmed. "You're the most special girl I've ever met, Chloe."

Could Saul Brenneman have been any sweeter? Chloe didn't think so.

They began talking about the boardwalk and all of the rides they planned to enjoy when they arrived. Saul said he hoped there was a place to rent horses so they could ride them on the beach. Chloe's eyes lit up at the prospect, as Saul knew they would. He loved to see her exuberance and bring her happiness.

Chloe couldn't believe her good fortune in meeting Saul. He was everything she'd ever hoped for in a beau, and more.

When they finally arrived in Maryland, they were somewhat disappointed that the rides had not yet opened. Saul suggested they grab a bite to eat, so they both enjoyed some New England clam chowder in a sourdough bread bowl. The droves of thrill-seekers reminded Chloe of an Amish wedding. She hoped they wouldn't have to spend all their time waiting in line for rides.

As soon as the ticket window opened up, Saul purchased all-day wrist bands for both of them. As it turned out, the lines moved pretty quickly. The first ride on their agenda was the carousel. They sat side by side and held hands while the animals beneath them went up and down and round and round. Chloe enjoyed the happy music and watching the jovial faces of the *kinner* around them. She supposed the horses on this carousel may be the only ones many of these children would ever ride. Once again, she found herself thankful for her Amish farm home.

Next was the roller coaster where Chloe experienced the thrill of her life – and almost lost her lunch. Then the go-karts and the Ferris wheel. Although she felt a bit of trepidation, Chloe enjoyed being able to see for miles when they came to the top. Saul must have sensed her fear because he slipped his arm around her and moved closer. He, on the other hand, seemed perfectly at ease on the large revolving contraption.

As the day wore on, they shared a sticky pink mass of cotton candy. Chloe had never eaten it before and loved the way the fluffy sweetness melted in her mouth. Saul asked around about renting horses, to no avail. They decided to head back to Pennsylvania after they'd taken a long stroll on the beach.

Chloe reclined in her seat as they drove into Paradise. "*Denki* for taking me. I had a lot of fun today, Saul." Her sparkling eyes caught his.

"The day's not over yet," he reminded her. "I don't want to take you home, Chloe. Not yet, anyway."

"What do you want to do?"

"Spend more time with you. Alone." He smiled. "Is there a quiet place we can park?"

"*Jah.* Miller's Creek, near the covered bridge," she suggested.

When they reached the bridge, Saul pulled the car off the side of the road near an embankment. The water trickled by in front of them and the gentle sounds of gurgling water reached their ears. They sat in the vehicle and watched the stream of water as it weaved its way around rocks and through plants. Fortunately, it was cooler out now and they rolled the windows down to let the nice breeze in.

Saul moved close to Chloe and drew her into his arms. *Be careful, Chloe!* An alarm rang out in her conscience, but she ignored it. He gently placed tiny kisses along her neck making her giggle and sending chills up her spine all at the same time.

"I love you, Chloe," he whispered in her ear.

Before she knew it, her *kapp* was off and her hair flowed down around her shoulders with Saul's fingers running through it. *No, Chloe. Don't!* His mouth found hers and he kissed her more passionately than he ever had before. Chloe felt her senses sprout wings and take flight as she reveled in his embrace. *Ach,* she desired to follow her heart, but a voice inside her screamed in protest. *You must stop now!*

The internal battle was so fierce, Chloe was confused as to what she wanted to do. A verse instantly popped into her head, as if God Himself had placed it there. *There hath no temptation taken you but such as is common to man: but God is faithful, who will not suffer you to be tempted above that ye are able; but will with the temptation also make a way to escape, that ye may be able to bear it.*

"Saul," she said breathlessly.

"*Jah,* Chloe?" he asked dreamily, entranced in the moment.

"We need to stop." She heard herself say the words, but her actions indicated otherwise. As a drug addict desperate for his next fix, she could not break away. The Spirit was willing, but her flesh was so weak. *Please help me, God. Give me the strength to do the right thing.*

"Yes, we need to," he agreed as they continued to kiss.

"Stop, please," she said in a louder, more firm voice and finally forced herself away from him.

Levi could have sworn he heard voices as he neared the covered bridge. He was glad he had been traveling on foot or he may not have seen the car near the embankment. Perhaps the vehicle had crashed and they needed help, he thought worriedly.

He rushed down the side of the bridge but was totally caught off-guard at the scene before him. As he peered into the window of the vehicle, he heard a familiar woman's voice call out, "Stop, please." At the sound of his near footsteps, the couple in the vehicle looked up.

Levi's heart dropped at the sight of his beloved Chloe, her hair down and slightly disheveled. Her eyes radiated guilt, and her lips were...bright and full, as though they'd been kissed...a lot.

Levi swallowed a lump in his throat. Anger and jealousy simultaneously coursed through his veins. When he found his voice, he croaked out, "Chloe? Are...are you all right?" He instinctively reached out and grasped her hand protectively.

"*Jah*, Levi. I'm fine." She bit her bottom lip, clearly embarrassed, her eyes cast downward.

Skeptical, Levi protested, "But I heard you calling out. You said 'Stop, please'."

Leaning toward the window, Saul glared at Levi's hand on Chloe's, then into Levi's eyes. "Listen, she said she was fine. Levi, was it?"

Levi nodded, not caring for Saul's tone of voice.

"We're kind of having a private moment here, so if you don't mind," Saul pleaded, not so subtly insinuating that Levi should leave.

"Chloe, are you sure you'll be okay?" Levi asked one more time, his eyes darting from Saul to her. *Lord, help me to know what I should do,* Levi asked under his breath.

Saul sighed as he visibly grew impatient. "I understand that you care for Chloe. But Chloe is *my aldi.* Please leave us."

Levi nodded in assent, took one more forlorn look at Chloe, then reluctantly released her hand and walked back up the bank and onto the road. Now his blood was boiling. He'd never been so angry.

When Levi was out of their sight, he paced back and forth. Covert in a copse of trees adjacent to the creek, he wondered what the best course of action would be. He decided to stay put until the car left, which thankfully was only a couple of minutes after he had. He wasn't sure what he would have done had they stayed longer. And he was sure he didn't want to find out.

Chloe took an anxious breath as she watched Levi disappear into a nearby wooded area. *Denki for sending Levi, Lord,* Chloe prayed silently.

"*Ach,* Chloe. I'm really sorry, *Lieb.*" Saul apologized once again, softly combing her hair with his fingers. "It seems like when I'm alone with you, I tend to get carried away."

"What about Levi?" Chloe worried.

"I'm sure he'll get over it." Saul shrugged.

"But you don't understand, Saul. Levi is the bishop's son," she explained as calmly as she could.

"You don't think he'd squeal, do you?"

"I don't know. I don't think so," she said as she clumsily gathered her hair to put back into a bun.

"Well, he won't if he knows what's best for him," Saul threatened, then he grew serious when he saw her neck. "Oh no, Chloe. I gave you a mark."

"What?" Innocent, she had no idea what he was talking about.

"Look in the mirror. Look at your neck." He pulled down the visor, chiding himself. "*Ach,* Chloe. I'm sorry."

"*Ach,* Saul. How do I get it off?" she asked desperately as she surveyed the darkened spot that marred her ivory neck. "Please take it off."

"We can't." He sighed. "You'll have to wait until it goes away."

"When will it go away?" She looked in the mirror again, her hands trembled as she set her prayer *kapp* back in place.

"Probably in about a week or two." He grimaced.

"But Saul, I can't go to Meeting like this!" Chloe cried frantically and sheer panic gripped her. "I can't go anywhere. I can't even go home! What will I do?"

"Shh..." Saul pulled her into his strong arms to comfort her as the tears poured down her cheeks, drenching his shirt. "It's going to be okay, I promise."

CHAPTER 8
Punishment

"...and be sure your sin will find you out."
Numbers 32:23c

Too disturbed to go home, Levi figured the best thing he could do was share his concerns with someone. But who? *I don't think it would be wise to talk to Dat about this right now. But I need to talk to someone!* he thought. Racking his brain he tried to think of somebody – *anybody* – whom he could confide in.

Why of course! Why didn't I think of that before? Joanna was Chloe's best friend. Chloe wouldn't listen to him, but surely she would listen to what Joanna had to say. Picking up his pace, he walked quickly to the Fishers' farm.

Although it was near suppertime, Levi found Joanna working out in the vegetable garden. Sitting on a small stool, she was pulling weeds from between the tomato plants. She wiped the sweat off her brow with her apron and offered a greeting. "*Wie Ghets,* Levi?"

Levi paced back and forth, searching for the best way to form his words. He glanced around to be sure they were alone. "It's Chloe."

Joanna stood up and concern filled her features. "Is she all right?"

Levi sighed. "*Jah.* I mean no. I mean I don't know."

"What's going on? Is there something you need to talk about? We could go for a walk if you'd like," she suggested.

"*Jah,* that'd be *gut,*" he said as he nervously twirled his hat in his hands.

Joanna quickly wiped her soiled hands on her apron. "I'll be back. I just need to tell my *mamm* where I'm going." She returned a minute later and they strode toward a nearby hill on the property.

"Joanna, I'm concerned about Chloe. I was hoping you could talk to her," Levi stated evenly.

Joanna eyed him curiously. "About what?"

Levi sighed heavily, not really wanting to relive the disturbing scene he'd witnessed. "Well, a short while ago I happened upon her and Saul Brenneman. They were in a car near Miller's Creek and Chloe...her *kapp* was off, her hair was down. She was in his arms, and it was clear they were...uh...well, their behavior was inappropriate. She even had a red mark on her neck."

Heat crept into his cheeks again as he thought of Chloe with Saul. This was not an easy subject to discuss with a girl, by any means. He also didn't tell her that what he'd felt like doing was pulling Saul Brenneman out of the car and knocking his socks off! "I wasn't eavesdropping or anything. I came upon them quite by accident. I really had no idea that Chloe was in the car."

"*Ach*, Levi. I'm sorry you had to see that, but maybe it was a good thing that you came along when you did, *jah*?" Joanna frowned. "Danika and I tried to warn her about being alone with Saul. Not that he's a bad guy or anything. It's just that it's difficult to resist temptation when you're alone with someone you love."

Love? Levi felt as though he'd been slapped in the face. *Chloe can't love Saul!* "Do you truly think she loves him?" He wasn't sure whether he really wanted to hear the answer.

"*Jah*, I do. They've been seeing a lot of each other lately. I really think he cares for her too. I wouldn't be surprised if they marry." Joanna recognized Levi's concern and sympathized with him. She'd never realized how much Levi cared for Chloe, but lately it seemed he'd worn his heart on his sleeve. Notwithstanding, she didn't want to give him false hope.

Levi winced. How could he have let her slip away? "What do you think we should do?"

"I think the best thing *you* can do is pray. I'll go over and visit Chloe and try to talk some sense into her," Joanna promised.

"*Gut. Denki,* Joanna. I know if she'll listen to anyone, it'll be you," Levi said confidently. "I'll start praying now." He gave her a half-smile before he turned to go.

Joanna took a deep breath and prayed. "Lord, please help me to get through to Chloe. Please give me the words that she needs to hear. Thy will be done. Amen."

Chloe cautiously looked around as she entered her house. *Gut! No one is around.* She let out a sigh as she nervously fingered the chiffon scarf around her neck. Saul had purchased it for her after she fretted about the mark he unintentionally left on her. Although the gesture was kind, she felt ridiculous wearing a scarf in the middle of summer – even if it was a summer scarf. She quickly made her way up the stairs to her room, doing her best to go unnoticed.

When she reached the landing, Stephen stepped out of his room. "Finally home, huh? I wondered when you'd get back. Did you and what's-his-name – Hey, what's that around your neck?"

"It's just a scarf. It was a gift from a friend," she asserted.

"Well, I'm pretty sure *Dat* won't like you wearing it around here. You know how he feels about *Englischer* clothes." Stephen reached over and gave her scarf a playful tug. His eyes grew wide when he noticed the dark spot on her neck. "Chloe, what is that on your neck? Is that a gift from a 'friend' too?" He folded his arms and glared into her eyes, insistent on an answer.

Once again, tears welled up in her eyes. "You won't tell, will you, Stephen?" she pleaded.

Stephen took pity on his sister. "No, I won't. But I don't know how you're going to keep it hidden. *Dat* and *Mamm* weren't born yesterday." He gave her a stern look. "Chloe, I think you need to stop seeing him. You are going to get yourself into trouble."

"I love him, Stephen," she protested.

He rolled his eyes. "What do you know about love, Chloe? You're fourteen years old. Do you have any idea how much hot water you're going to be in when *Dat* sees that thing on your neck?"

"A lot. But there's nothing I can do about it now." She sighed.

"Hello," a familiar voice called from downstairs.

Chloe looked at Stephen, her eyebrows furrowed. "Joanna? Is that you?"

"*Jah*. Your *mamm* said you'd be upstairs and said to let myself in," she called up.

"Time for me to water the horse," Stephen said to Chloe before directing his steps outside. "I'm sure you girls would like to chat."

Joanna ran up the steps and joined Chloe in her room. She closed the door behind her.

"Chloe, Levi came and talked to me. He's concerned," Joanna unequivocally stated, hands on hips and clearly addled.

"*Ach*, Joanna. I don't know what to do." Chloe's hands covered her face in distress. She wiped away a tear.

Joanna wrapped her arms around her friend. "Have your parents seen your mark yet?"

"How did you know?" Chloe looked up.

"Levi."

"Oh no, Levi saw it too! I'm going to be in so much trouble." She sobbed and her body shook with fear.

"You know, he cares for you too," Joanna said softly, rubbing her forearm.

"*Ach*, Levi's so sweet." Chloe realized.

"Chloe, I know you and Saul love each other, but you're not married yet," Joanna gently reminded. "You're not even fifteen. Marriage could be years away. It seems to me you're movin' a little too fast, *jah*?"

"*Jah*, we are. I never knew how much desire a kiss could bring, Jo," Chloe agreed. "I shoulda listened to you and Dani."

"Do ya want me to stay for dinner? Maybe your *daed* won't be so harsh if I'm here," Joanna suggested.

"I don't know. It might just make things worse." Chloe gritted her teeth. "Who knows what *Dat* will say?"

"All right, then. Let me know if ya need anything." Joanna lovingly touched her shoulder, then left for home.

"Chloe, dinner's ready!" her sister Anna called up the stairs.

Chloe took a deep breath and sent up a silent plea. She descended the stairs and sat at her usual place at the table, attempting to appear as calm as possible.

The rest of the family was already seated and all eyes were on her. Or more accurately, her new scarf. Peter Esh bowed his head and gave the silent prayer, then spoke up. "Chloe, you know we don't wear fancy clothes in this home. Please remove the scarf."

Chloe took a deep breath and glanced at Stephen. With shaking hands, she bit her bottom lip and apprehensively untied the scarf, pulling it from around her neck.

Her father nodded his "*denki*" then gasped when he noticed her mark.

"What's that on your neck?" her sister Abigail blurted out.

All eyes once again turned to Chloe. Her mother sighed and shook her head in disappointment.

"I knows what it is!" six-year-old Ruthie volunteered. "It's called a monkey bite."

Mary gasped. "Where did you hear that, Child?"

"From Jonathan Fisher!" she happily shared. "He showed us at recess." She held out her arm and proudly showed her 'monkey bites' to her parents. "This is how ya do it!" She put her arm to her mouth to demonstrate, but was quickly halted by her father. Ruthie cocked her head in question and eyed Chloe's neck curiously. "Chloe, how did ya gots one there?"

"*Jah*, how indeed?" Her father raised his eyebrows disdainfully.

Chloe's cheeks reddened in embarrassment.

"Proceed with dinner, *kinner*. Chloe, *Mamm*, and I need to have a discussion. In private. Now." The children recognized their father's tone and hastily picked up their forks. Mary handed little Miriam to Anna.

Chloe gave Stephen a pleading look, but he shrugged his shoulders helplessly. She quietly followed her parents into the other room, bracing herself for the worst.

"Going somewhere with a friend, huh?" Her father frowned and cocked his head to the side. "Just exactly where did you go today and which 'friend' did you go with? The truth, please."

Chloe's hands began to tremble. "I...we went to Ocean City. Me and Saul."

"Saul?" Peter questioned. "Do we know a Saul?"

"Saul Brenneman. From Bishop Mast's district. You probably don't know him," Chloe quickly explained.

"He took you out of the state?" Her mother's incredulous voice rose an octave.

"*Jah*. Maryland," Chloe confessed quietly.

Her mother and father stared at each other in silence for what seemed like an eternity. Chloe wondered if some secret communication was passing through them.

Peter began as calmly as he could. "No daughter of mine will bring shame to this family. You will be confined to the house until your 'monkey bite', as your sister calls it, is gone. You are not allowed out of your room when visitors come over. All callers for you will be turned away," her father directed. "As for this Saul fellow, perhaps it's best if you stay away from him. It's obvious to me, he doesn't have your best interests in mind."

"No, *Dat*. I won't stay away from Saul. We love each other!" she wailed.

"You will NOT defy my authority!" Peter Esh boomed, glaring angrily at his daughter.

"Peter," his wife pleaded softly, attempting to be the voice of reason. "Maybe we should think this through before making any hasty decisions."

"Mary, have you seen our daughter?" He gestured to her neck. "Have you forgotten she's only fourteen years old?!"

"We met when I was fourteen," she gently reminded him.

After a few seconds, he released a surrendered sigh, then looked at Chloe. "After your confinement is over, you may attend Singings in our district only and you may ride home with Stephen. If you want to spend time with this Saul fellow, he'll have to come here so the two of you can be supervised."

"*Denki, Dat.*" She threw her arms around her father.

"Don't thank me. This is your *mamm*'s doing." He turned to his wife. "I think I need to take a ride out to Jonathan Fisher's place tonight and have a word with Gideon." He stood up to head back to the dinner table, then turned back around. "By the way, Chloe, go ahead and put that scarf back on."

CHAPTER 9
The Secret Mission

"Rejoice evermore." 1 Thessalonians 5:16

When the teacher, Grace Fisher, announced that it was time for recess, Jonathan sighed in relief. He jumped up and headed out the door with his friends. "Hey, Matt, Josh!" he called to them. They turned and looked at him inquisitively. "I saw Sadie Lapp writing in her notebook during class."

"So?" Matthew rolled his eyes.

"Well, guess what she wrote?"

"Do I want to know?" Joshua asked.

"She wrote 'Sadie and Eli' inside of a big red heart."

Matthew stopped near the side of the schoolhouse and crossed his arms skeptically. "I don't believe you."

"She did, she really did." Jonathan's head profusely bobbed up and down.

"Prove it," Matthew challenged.

"All right, I will." Jonathan marched to one of the windows. "Can't right now, Grace is still inside."

"Not for long." Matthew ran to the nearest tree he could find and quickly scrambled up in its branches.

"What are you doing?" asked Jonathan.

"Getting Grace out of the schoolhouse," he replied matter-of-factly.

"By climbing a tree?" Joshua stared up at him doubtingly.

"Sure, why not? Watch this!" Matthew dangerously wiggled on the branches as his friends looked on.

"Hey, be careful. You're gonna fall," Joshua warned.

No sooner had the words escaped his lips, did Matthew come crashing to the ground. He landed on his arm and let out a shriek. He held his scraped arm and cried in pain as the other scholars ran to gawk at him.

Levi and Joshua's younger sister, Susanna Hostettler saw him and screamed, "Grace, come quick! Matthew's hurt!"

"What's all the commotion?" Grace ran outside, her scoring pen still in hand.

"Good, here she comes!" Matthew whispered urgently to Jonathan and Joshua, before beginning to wail again. The students moved out of the way for Grace, who helped Matthew to his feet.

Matthew quieted down, whimpering softly, and wiped his feigned tears with the sleeve of his shirt.

Grace looked at him with concern and asked, "Are you all right?"

"*Jah*, I think so," he replied with a shaky voice. "I think I better go inside for a minute and sit down."

"All right, Matthew," Grace agreed.

Matthew turned and walked slowly to the schoolhouse, sniffling as he went and holding his 'injured' arm. From inside the schoolhouse near Sadie's desk, he heard Grace reassuring the students outside. "Now, children, Matthew's going to be all right, he just scraped his arm a little." When he was sure she wasn't looking, he opened Sadie's desk and grabbed her notebook. He stuffed it into his shirt and quietly slipped out the back door where Jonathan and Joshua were waiting.

"Here it is," he announced, holding it up without a tear in sight.

Joshua shook his head. "Well, what does it say? Open it!"

Matthew opened the notebook and saw several red hearts with professions of love written in them. He whistled. "You're right, Jonathan. Sadie Lapp has her *kapp* set on Eli Yoder. But he's in love with Danika King, and Danika likes him."

Joshua interjected, "Well, it's too bad Sadie doesn't know that."

"She does," Matthew said rolling his eyes. "She just doesn't care."

"But what if she thought..." Jonathan's eyes grew big. "...that Eli liked her?" he schemed aloud.

The other boys' faces brightened at the thought. "Oh, Jonathan, you are so good!" Matthew slapped him on the back.

"Now, here's what I have in mind. Joshua, you go to your brother's buggy shop and retrieve a sample of Eli's handwriting. Matthew, you make sure that notebook goes back exactly where you found it so Sadie won't suspect anything." Jonathan announced, "All right boys, we've got a mission to accomplish." He continued seriously with a hint of authority in his voice. "Meet me here at o-seven hundred hours!"

Matthew was confused. "What does o-seven something mean?"

Matthew looked to Joshua for an interpretation. Then Joshua, as baffled as his friend, shrugged and looked at Jonathan.

Jonathan sighed at his friends' military ignorance. "It's a military term. It means seven o'clock, before school starts. Ain't ya read them GI Joe comic books I gave ya?"

Matt and Josh nodded their heads. Joshua finally caught on and saluted Jonathan, with Matthew following his example. "Yes, Commander, Sir!" Joshua tested the words. "But we should get back to school before Grace comes to see how Matthew's arm is faring. By the way, Matt. That was great!"

"*Denki*. Come on, let's get inside."

Saul flicked the reins of the buggy and clicked his tongue for the horse to speed up. He would be meeting Chloe's family today and, quite frankly, he was a bit nervous. Not only because he'd given her a love bite last time they were together, but this was the first time he'd courted a girl and had to meet her parents. Typically, courting was done in secret, but sometimes the parents insisted knowing who their child was courting. Of course, he couldn't blame Chloe's folks for their reaction.

It was different with the girls in his district because he pretty much knew their families already. And it was also different because this was Chloe. *Chloe.* His lips turned up in a smile. Just thinking of her name caused his heart to somersault.

He had courted several girls already, but it had only taken one or two buggy rides to know those were not the girls for him. There was Rebekah Stoltz, Mary Lantz, Dorcus Yoder, Hannah Gingerich, and even Sarah Mast, the bishop's daughter. *And then there was Chloe.* A girl in a class all by herself. All it took was that one first night with her to realize that she was different than all the others. There was something about her that he just couldn't put his finger on. Maybe it was her jovial personality or the way she incessantly teased him while feigning stubbornness. Or perhaps it was her beautiful strawberry-blonde hair and her gorgeous green eyes. Whatever it was, she had him spellbound.

He knew she was *the one.* The one he would hopefully someday marry. The one who would someday bear his children – a whole houseful of them, if God allowed.

His heart lurched as he neared the entrance to her lane. The last two weeks away from Chloe had nearly driven him mad. He thanked God every day that her father hadn't forbidden them to see each other, but instead worked out a compromise. It was better this way. Because when he and Chloe were alone, well, look what happened last time. Yes, supervision would definitely be a good thing and a sure way to abstain from temptation.

Even with his apprehension, Saul was glad that he would be spending time with her family. He wanted to know what it was like in Chloe's world. He knew that if her family was anything like her that he would instantly fall in love with them as well. Chloe had warned him already that her older brother Stephen was cautious about him, but who could blame a guy for wanting to protect his sister? He was confident that, with God's help, he would be able to win her family over.

He slowly brought the buggy to a stop as he neared the hitching post by the barn. He took a deep breath and said a silent prayer as he dismounted the buggy. He scanned the property for signs of life and was thankful when an older Amish man with a red beard, whom he supposed was Chloe's father, approached. Now he knew where Chloe got her hair from.

The man wore an apprehensive look, but as he came near his countenance changed. "Are you–"

Saul reached out his hand and offered a winning smile. "Saul. Saul Brenneman."

"Peter Esh, Chloe's *vatter*." He shook Saul's hand then informed him, "You may put your horse out in the pasture, and then we can head inside for supper."

Chloe's brother Stephen emerged from the barn after Saul closed the gate to the pasture. Saul immediately recognized him as one of the young men near Levi at the Singing and couldn't help but wonder if perhaps they were good friends. Saul sighed, *another reason for him not to like me.* Saul offered his hand to Stephen as he approached, and although he shook his hand, Stephen gave him a curt nod.

After washing up at the large sink in the back room, the three men entered the kitchen. Chloe turned from the stove and met Saul's eyes. While they lovingly gazed at each other, Stephen, who was standing behind Saul, cleared his throat loudly. Saul's cheeks flushed and he quickly moved out of the way, giving Stephen an apology and allowing him to pass. Stephen looked at Chloe and rolled his eyes and she flashed him a look of warning.

Saul was taken by surprise when he felt a small hand in his. He looked down and saw an adorable little girl, whom he supposed to be about six years old. She flashed him a toothy smile and immediately started gabbing. "Are you Chloe's beau? Chloe said someone 'portent would be comin' for supper. Us womans made a special 'ussert too. *Mamm* said I'm 'upposed to be *gut* and not talk too much. Do you think –"

"Ruthie," her father warned.

She sighed in disappointment, and then immediately perked up again. "*Mamm,* can Chloe's beau sit by me?" Still holding his hand, she gave him a big smile. "I like him."

"You'll have to ask him," Mary Esh replied.

Ruthie turned to him, eyes large. "Chloe's beau, can I sit by you?"

Saul chuckled. "Yes, Chloe's beau would love to sit by you, Ruthie."

"His name is Saul, Ruthie," Stephen brusquely informed his young sister.

"Saul?" Her eyes widened as she stared at him in wonder. "Did you got blind?"

Saul gave her a confused look.

"She thinks you're Saul from the Bible." Stephen snickered. "We read from Acts chapter nine last night."

"Oh." He smiled, then crouched down next to Ruthie. "No, I was never blind, but my parents did name me after him. Were you named after Ruth from the Bible?"

Ruthie turned to her mother, as they sat down at the table. "*Mamm,* did ya gots my name from the Bible?"

"Yes, Child. Now settle down," Peter Esh said, and then cleared his throat to pray.

The family bowed their heads and soon there was a flurry of movement when dishes were passed around the table. Saul thought the food was delicious and made sure to say so. Silence reigned while everyone enjoyed the meal.

Saul spoke up after few minutes. "I see you've got corn and alfalfa planted. How many acres are there?" he asked Peter.

Peter's eyes brightened. "Forty of each."

"My *daed* farmed up until a few years ago. I always enjoyed it," Saul commented.

"Yeah right," Stephen sarcastically mumbled under his breath.

Chloe scowled at her brother.

"What's he do now?" Peter wondered aloud, not catching his children's exchange.

"He started a construction business. We build play structures for children. The farm wasn't large enough to support our family and *Daed* tried to find more land to purchase, but good land in these parts is scarce nowadays. Either that or it's outrageously priced." Saul shook his head.

"How is the construction business doing?" Peter queried.

"The new business is doing a lot better than he had hoped," Saul stated. "I still love farming, though. Nothin' better than working the land. I'd be happy to help out when the harvest comes in."

Peter raised his eyebrows, clearly impressed with Chloe's beau.

Stephen chimed in, "We can always use more hands at harvest time, *jah, Dat*?

"*Jah*. We'd be glad to have you, Saul," Peter agreed.

Saul smiled, and then looked to Chloe who was beaming. Saul couldn't help but think he'd be a perfect fit in this family. He also noticed that Chloe was still wearing the scarf he bought her. Ruthie must've noticed him looking at the scarf because she spoke up.

"*Dat* told Chloe that she could still wear the scarf even if hers monkey bite wents away." She held up her arm. "Mine wents away too, but I made 'nother one so I don't forgets how to do it. Jonathan Fisher showed me how," she chattered on. "*Dat* said he can't know how Chloe gots one on her neck and I can't know neither. Do you know how she gots it?"

Everybody looked at Saul and waited for an answer, his cheeks bright red.

Chloe came to his rescue. "Ruthie, let Saul eat, please."

Stephen spoke up, looking straight at Saul. "I'd like to hear what Saul has to say too. Saul, do you know how that 'monkey bite' got on Chloe's neck?" He raised his eyebrows accusingly.

Saul got the feeling that Stephen enjoyed watching him squirm.

"That's enough, *Sohn,*" Peter spoke up, giving Stephen a warning.

Saul gave a sigh of relief and quickly finished his food.

When everyone was done, Saul helped clear the table and offered to do the dishes with Chloe. Mary protested at first, then acquiesced when Saul recommended that she relax a bit and enjoy some time with her husband. The others gathered in the family room too, leaving Chloe and Saul in the kitchen to wash dishes. They stood at the kitchen sink conversing quietly while the dishes were cleaned. Saul glanced toward the living room to be sure no one was around before dropping his drying towel and pulling Chloe into his arms for a long-awaited kiss.

"Uh...hum!" Stephen cleared his throat loudly as he entered the kitchen. They quickly pulled away from each other. "Came in for a drink. You're lucky it was just me. Next time I'll send

Ruthie in." After he grabbed his water, he knowingly walked back into the living room with a smirk on his face.

"Now, where were we?" Saul turned back to Chloe with a sly smile.

"Saul, Chloe, are ya done yet?" Ruthie hollered a second later. "Hurry, I wanna play games but *Dat* says we gotsta wait for you."

Saul's eyes met Chloe's and he shrugged in defeat. "Looks like we better go play some games."

Joshua cautiously glanced around the buggy shop to be sure his older brother was nowhere near. He figured he was probably gone since he hadn't seen his buggy anywhere outside the shop. Eli appeared to be working alone. *Perfect.* "Hi, Eli. Where's my *bruder* Nathan?" he asked.

Eli looked up from the desk and replied, "He went to Lancaster to get more supplies."

"Oh. Well, since Nathan isn't here right now, do you think you can help me with my English assignment?" Joshua asked Eli.

"Sure, what's the problem?"

"I'm having trouble writing a business letter, can you show me how to write one?"

"*Jah*, it's not that difficult. I used to have trouble writing business letters in school too, but once I learned how to write one properly, it took hardly any effort at all." Eli smiled.

Jonathan, Matthew, and Joshua met behind the schoolhouse, as planned at seven o'clock, the next day. "Well, did you get it?" Jonathan asked excitedly.

"*Jah*, I did. What are we going to do with it?" Josh quizzed.

"We're going to write Sadie a letter from Eli," Jonathan divulged.

"Oh-h..." As the light dawned on Joshua and Matthew, their eyes sparkled with pure mischief.

"Jonathan, you are so-o good!" Matthew laughed.

CHAPTER 10
John Fisher

"Blessed are they that mourn: for they shall be comforted." Matthew 5:4

The brown mare that Levi sat upon sped through the dense wooded area near Deacon Yoder's farm. Soon Levi's horse would be topping the hill that led to the road near the Esh property. At any other time, Levi would be glad to make this visit, but not today. It was never any fun being the bearer of bad news.

As his horse trotted quickly down the lane, he spotted what he thought was two people on the porch swing. After tying the mare to the hitching post, he took long strides toward the house. Upon climbing the porch steps, he realized it was Chloe that sat on the porch swing. She was asleep and leaning on Saul, his arm draped over her shoulder. Next to him sat Chloe's three year old brother Little Daniel, who held his hand. The sight was enough to make Levi's stomach knot up with envy.

Charity envieth not, the Scriptures chided him.

Levi was about to speak when Saul held up a finger to his lips. "She was out all night with *Mammi.* Delivered a set of twins early this morning," he whispered.

Levi whispered back, "Her friend Joanna's *grossdawdi* passed away. I'll go in and tell the family." Levi moved toward the door.

"Wait. We should probably wake her up then. She'll want to know," Saul suggested, then gently squeezed her arm and spoke softly. "Chloe, *Liewi,* you need to wake up."

Chloe started to stir and slowly opened her eyes before yawning. Her eyes widened when she saw Levi standing on the porch. "Levi?" she said in question.

"*Hiya,* Chloe. I'm sorry, but *Dat* asked me to notify everyone. *Grossdawdi* John Fisher passed away this morning," Levi said regretfully.

"*Ach,* that's terrible." She stood up and stepped closer to Levi. "I need to go see Joanna. Does Isaac and Rachel know?"

"I was heading there next," Levi explained.

"Do you know how it happened?" Chloe asked as her eyes filled with tears.

Levi reached out and touched her arm, then glanced at Saul who didn't seem concerned about his friendly gesture. "*Mammi* Miriam woke up and he was gone. Must've died in his sleep. The doctor said he had something called Sleep Apnea. I guess he stopped breathing."

"Poor *Mammi*! How is the family taking it?" Chloe wondered.

"Jonathan is taking it the hardest. I guess he and *Dawdi* John were pretty close. It was quite unexpected," Levi said. "Will you let your folks know? I better head on over to Isaac's."

"Sure. *Denki,* Levi." She gave him a half smile. Levi dropped his hand and turned to go.

Chloe stepped into the kitchen at the Fishers' home. Many friends and neighbors had already arrived offering their condolences and bearing food gifts. Joanna sat on the couch with her arm around her grandmother, both with tears in their eyes. Chloe walked over and gave them both a long hug, then sat down next to Joanna.

Joanna dabbed her eyes with a handkerchief. "We were just talking about when *Dawdi* John took the boys fishing one time. Jonathan was just four years old. *Dawdi* had his fishing pole in the water and they could see a large fish swimming right by the hook trying to eat the worm. Jonathan got so excited, he decided to jump in and catch the fish himself. He grabbed hold of it in spite of the fact that he couldn't swim and he wouldn't let it go for nothin'. *Dawdi* John had to jump in to keep him from drowning. He kept that fish clutched in his hands until he got home and gave it to *Mammi*. He came in and said, "*Mammi, Mammi,* I caught fishy!" He was so proud of that fish.

"At dinner that night, we all enjoyed the fish... Well, everyone except Jonathan. When we told him we were eating the fish he caught, he cried for hours. *Dawdi* John explained to him that the reason they go fishing is so we'd have food to eat. When he finally understood, he and *Dawdi* John became the best of fishing buddies. Those two had a special relationship." She smiled.

"I think Jonathan reminded John of himself when he was younger. Jonathan was more than just his namesake." *Mammi* Miriam said, wiping away a tear. "He would be touched to see how the boy grieves for him now."

"Where is Jonathan?" Chloe asked, looking around the nearly-crowded living room.

"He's probably sitting up in the loft right now. He said he wanted to be alone." Joanna sighed. "I'm hoping maybe Joshua and Matthew can cheer him up when they get here."

Chloe noticed that Levi had arrived at the Fisher residence about an hour later with his family. When he stepped into the kitchen where the ladies set food out on the table, his eyes found Joanna. Chloe was surprised when Levi walked straight past her, with nary a glance in her direction. She then watched in dismay as he walked up to Joanna and folded her in a warm embrace. *Are Levi and Joanna sweet on each other?* Chloe wondered. Levi spoke with Joanna at length, but barely said two words to Chloe the entire visit, and for some peculiar reason she felt a pang of jealousy. *I love Saul. What do I care if Levi likes Joanna?*

"Hey, Jonathan! Are you up there?" Matthew called from the barn floor.

Jonathan quickly wiped his eyes and swallowed the lump in his throat. "*Jah,* I'm here."

Matthew climbed the ladder and popped up into the haymow, Joshua close behind him. "Your *mamm* said you were up here. I'm sorry about your *grossdawdi.*"

"*Jah*, me too," Joshua offered.

Tears began forming in Jonathan's eyes and Joshua thought it would be wise to change the subject. "Hey, Jonathan. Did you get that letter finished?" he asked enthusiastically.

Jonathan's eyes brightened. "*Jah*, I got it up in my room. Wanna see it?"

"Let's go!" Matthew urged.

The three boys scrambled down the ladder and into the house. They nearly flew past the visitors in the house and up to Jonathan's room.

Chloe turned to Joanna. "I guess you were right about Joshua and Matthew cheering him up."

"*Jah*, I just hope they're not up to mischief!" Joanna laughed.

CHAPTER 11
The Letter

"...Let us not love in word, neither in tongue; but in deed and in truth." 1 John 3:18

Saul walked between the half-grown stalks of corn with Peter Esh in the row beside him. He was pleased with the Esh family and glad that even Stephen had become somewhat companionable. The compromise Peter agreed to with his daughter turned out to be a blessing in disguise. A hot gentle wind blew, causing the stalks to sway.

"I'm glad my Chloe found you, *Sohn,*" Peter spoke.

Did I hear correctly? Is Chloe's father giving me his approval? Maybe this is my opportunity to ask. Saul found his voice. "Me, too. Chloe is a blessing. I hope that someday we can be hitched," he declared boldly.

"I don't think I'd be opposed to that." Peter smiled. "Just not too soon."

"I was hoping we could marry when she's sixteen. I know that's still a bit young, but I'll be nineteen then. It will give us nearly two years together. Plenty of time to join the church," Saul ventured.

"*Jah.* Sixteen is a bit young. Let's see how things go," Peter suggested. "Shall we head to the house for a glass of cool lemonade?"

"That sounds great!" Saul declared, excited to share the news with Chloe.

"My *vatter* said that?" Chloe squealed as she and Saul sat on the back porch.

Saul smiled and stood up, offering Chloe his hand. "Come, let's go for a walk."

They walked hand in hand through the field and over the hill to the other side. The giant oak trees provided cool shade from the sweltering heat. When they came to a fallen tree, they sat down for a break.

As they sat on the log facing each other, Saul reached for Chloe's hand. "Chloe, I know it's still a couple of years off, but I want to ask you now. If you'll be my wife, you'll make me the happiest man alive."

"Saul." Tears welled up in Chloe's eyes and she was unable to speak. "I couldn't think of anyone I'd rather marry more. I'd love to be your wife." She leaned forward and kissed him on the lips.

"I love you, Chloe. My future *fraa*." Saul smiled. He stood up and reached for her hand again and they strode back to the house, not wanting to alarm anyone with their absence. When they stepped out of the wooded area, Ruthie stood there smiling.

She began chanting, "Saul and Chloe sittin' on a tree. K-i-s-s-i-n-g. First comes love. Then comes marriage. Then comes the *boppli* in the *boppli* carriage!"

"That's right!" Saul looked down and smiled at Ruthie, then took her small hand in his other one and the three of them contently walked back to the house.

Eli Yoder helped his younger siblings down from the buggy and they trudged into the schoolhouse to drop off their lunch boxes before heading outside to play. As he pulled away from the schoolhouse, Sadie Lapp waved at him and flashed him a huge smile as usual. Eli waved back kindly and headed toward Nathan Hostettler's buggy shop to work.

Jonathan, Matthew, and Joshua stood outside the schoolhouse and peered through the window as Sadie sat down at her desk. All three of them were having trouble containing their gleefulness when they saw her open the top of her desk. They watched as she grabbed the letter and thrusted it into her apron pocket. With all thirty of her pearly whites showing, she bounced outside and made a beeline to a large tree and sat under it.

The boys stood behind the nearby outhouse and watched as she read the letter. Did she have tears of joy streaming down her face? Jonathan looked at his two friends and they struggled to remain silent, wanting to burst into laughter. This was by far the best prank they'd thought of yet!

Sadie opened the letter and read the words silently.

Dearest Sadie,

I find myself thinking of you often. I've come to realize that you are my one true love. Please don't tell Danika yet, because I'd like to let her down easy. She is a nice girl, but I cannot continue to see her when my heart belongs to you. I hope to see you after church on Sunday. I will be counting the days until then.

Sincerely yours,

Eli

Sadie reread the letter, folded it, and placed it back in the envelope. She held it to her heart and smiled. *Yes! Eli does love me. I can't wait until Danika hears of it,* she thought with a wicked grin spread across her face.

CHAPTER 12
The Best Prank

"Even a child is known by his doings, whether his work be pure, and whether it be right."
Proverbs 20:11

Jonathan sat quietly on the backless bench in the Kings' house. Sitting next to his friends, he intently watched every move that Minister Bontrager's hands made. He was getting anxious. Would Minister Bontrager ever drink his water? Jonathan hoped he would before Bishop Hostettler got up to speak. Having the bishop drink the water wasn't such a great idea.

"Hey, Jonathan," Matthew quietly voiced his thoughts, sounding desperate. "What do we do if Bishop drinks it?"

"I won't ever forget it if he does," Joshua answered nervously, knowing his father wouldn't be too pleased if he knew what they'd done.

"Shh..." Jonathan replied quietly.

"Ye are the salt of the earth," Minister Bontrager recited, before gulping down his water.

Jonathan, Matthew, and Joshua looked at each other wide eyed. Did he know about their prank?

The Minister suddenly sputtered, causing all eyes to turn to him. Coughing and choking, he managed to squeak out, "Bishop, can you take over now, please?"

Jonathan coughed to cover his giggles. This was just too funny!

As the bishop walked to the center of the room, Minister Bontrager leaned toward him and whispered, "There's salt in the water."

The bishop's head immediately spun around to where Jonathan sat. Everyone knew that Jonathan Fisher was a prankster. He shrank down on the bench, with a guilty Joshua and Matthew following his lead. Jonathan was certain that the woodshed was probably the first place he'd be going to when he got home.

Jonathan, Matthew, and Joshua hid inside one of the enclosed buggies parked near where Danika sat outside.

"Oh, good! Here she comes!" Jonathan announced quietly as Sadie walked up to Danika.

"Hey, Danika, whatcha doin'?" Sadie asked smugly, holding the letter in her hand at her side.

Danika stared at Sadie and replied, "Waiting for Eli."

"I don't know why you bother. Eli doesn't love you, ya know," Sadie continued.

"Whatever, Sadie." Danika rolled her eyes. "Of course Eli loves me."

"If he loves *you* so much, then why did he write *me* a love letter?" Sadie gloated, bringing her precious letter to her chest.

"What?" Danika stood up. A cold pang shot through her heart when she thought she recognized Eli's handwriting.

"It's right here!" Sadie smirked triumphantly at Danika and handed her the letter.

Danika yanked it from Sadie's outstretched hand and hurriedly opened it. She hastily pulled out the letter and quickly scanned it. *This* is *Eli's handwriting! No, this can't be true. I know Eli loves me. But...*She gasped, second-guessing herself.

"See? I told you so," Sadie bragged.

Danika's enraged fist found its way to Sadie's face and she fell to the ground. Sadie jumped back up and yanked off Danika's prayer *kapp*, pulling her hair as well. Danika gritted her teeth at the pain and twirled around quickly jabbing Sadie in the stomach. Sadie let go of Danika's hair and scratched her across the face. Danika and Sadie exchanged several punches and slaps before Eli ran between them acting as a referee.

Jonathan, Matthew, and Joshua looked at each other in amazement. "Wow, this is even better than I thought!" Jonathan exclaimed.

"Whoa, whoa, whoa girls! There's no need for fighting. Let's just talk this out like civilized human be –" Danika aimed her fist at Sadie's face and missed it, hitting Eli squarely in the nose and interrupting his speech. "Ow, my nose! I think it's broken."

Jonathan gulped. "Uh, oh."

"I don't care if it is!" Danika yelled.

"What did you hit me for, Danika?" Eli said in shock.

"Oh, you know. Don't play dumb with me, Eli Yoder! You're a heartless, two-faced, double-crossing, two-timing, male chauvinist pig! That's why," Danika screamed at him, her *Englischer* roots returning full-force. "And I was actually aiming for Sadie before you so rudely interrupted."

"Wait a minute, what did I do?" Eli asked in bewilderment, his bloody nose dripping down his now-stained shirt.

"Stop playing dumb. Have you forgotten the love letter you wrote to Sadie? *My dearest Sadie,*" Danika mockingly recited what she remembered of the letter to refresh his memory. "*I find myself thinking of you often* –"

"I haven't written any letters to anyone except you, Danika!" Eli protested.

"Uh...huh. – *You are my true love, the one I have loved all along* –" Danika continued on.

"But Eli, of course you love me. You have to!" Sadie's alarmed voice rang out. "Here's the letter you wrote to me."

Eli took the crumpled letter, amazed that the handwriting almost perfectly mirrored his.

"Danika, *you* are the only one I love. I didn't write a letter to Sadie or anybody." That's when Eli spotted a trio of heads peeping up from inside a nearby buggy, doubling over in laughter. "But I think I know who did!"

Eli stomped to where the three boys crouched. The laughter quieted as Eli approached. "Get out of that buggy!" Eli fought to control his voice. "Joshua, you wrote that letter, didn't you? I want the truth."

"N...no, Eli. I...I didn't write that letter," Joshua stammered.

"Then which one of you did?" Eli asked, looking from Joshua to Matthew to Jonathan.

After a moment of awkward silence, Jonathan shrugged and admitted, "I did."

Eli forgot about controlling himself, roughly grabbed Jonathan by the collar, and escorted him to where his father stood talking to the bishop.

Oh no, Jonathan thought. *The bishop's telling him about the salt water right now too!*

"I believe your son has some confessing to do," Eli said angrily.

Gideon noticed the blood running down from Eli's nose. His eyes widened. "Jonathan, did you hit Eli?"

"No," Eli stated. "Danika did!"

"What's all this about?" Gideon asked brusquely.

Jonathan explained the prank, leaving his two friends out of it. Gideon proceeded to gather his family to drive them home. Once they arrived, he promptly escorted Jonathan to the woodshed.

CHAPTER 13
Heartbreak

"Be not deceived; God is not mocked: for whatsoever a man soweth, that shall he also reap." Galatians 6:7

Saul and his father Eb had just closed up the shop for the day when Saul spotted a buggy driving up their lane. He identified the carriage as belonging to Bishop Mast. He noticed two people riding in the buggy. The bishop and his daughter Sarah. Bishop Mast's face was grim when he descended the buggy.

"Eb, I'd like to have a word with you and your son," he stated evenly.

Saul glanced at Sarah, who sat in the buggy with her head down. The bishop's eyes were piercing like a dagger and a cold chill ran up Saul's spine. *What could be wrong? Had Sarah told her father about the Englischer party we attended sever-*

al months back? Saul wore a confused expression as the three men sat on a bench near the barn.

"I don't know any other way to say this, so I'll be frank," the bishop said, keeping his gaze on Saul. "My Sarah is in the family way and she claims the child is yours."

A blow to the abdomen wouldn't have caught Saul more off-guard. "Wh...what? That can't be." Saul's head began to spin. "No, that can't be true." He shook his head in unbelief, denying the bishop's words.

"My Sarah isn't a liar," the bishop insisted. "She said the two of you attended a party where you both became intoxicated. Whether you *intended* to conceive a child or not is beside the point. The fact is that my Sarah is with child and *you* are the father. She hasn't been courted by anyone else."

Saul's breath came in short gasps. As he came to grips with reality, his eyes filled with tears. "No. This cannot be happening. I...I'm betrothed to be married to Chloe Esh." He still shook his head, disbelieving.

Saul's father turned to him. "If the child is yours, you must take responsibility for it."

"I can't! Give the baby up for adoption, I don't want it," he stated apathetically. "I don't love Sarah."

"Son, you know that is not our way. You must marry the girl," his father insisted.

"*Dat,* I can't marry someone I don't love," he said desperately. He felt as though he'd been put in box with the lid on tight. He had to escape.

"I'm afraid you have no choice, Son," the bishop stated matter-of-factually.

"There has to be some mistake," Saul insisted.

"There is no mistake. We must accept this as God's will," Bishop Mast declared. "You will marry as soon as possible."

"I...I have to go. I need some time to think." Saul bounded toward the barn, saddled a horse and abruptly rode off.

"Saul!" his father called after him.

The bishop placed a hand on Eb's shoulder. "Let him go. I'm confident he will make the right decision."

Saul rode for what seemed like hours. He couldn't understand. His life was perfect. *Perfect.* He had finally found the love of his life. The one person he was sure would complete him. Their future was bright. Her father already consented to their union. *Maybe we should run away. Chloe and I could marry and we could go on with life as planned.* But she was still just fourteen. *And would she even want me, knowing what I've done?*

Hot tears stung his face as reality set in. He would never marry Chloe. He couldn't imagine his future now. Marrying someone he didn't care for. Raising a child he didn't want. If only he could go back in time and change things. If only he hadn't gone to that party. If only...

Saul swallowed hard. He suddenly realized he had no one to blame but himself. He *did* have a choice and he had made it months ago. He's the one who took Sarah to the party in the first place, knowing there would be alcohol present. And while he never intended for anything to happen between them, it did. He'd been so foolish. But his father was right, he realized. He was responsible whether he liked it or not. It was the ugly truth, and he hated himself for it. If only he had known what the future held, if only he'd been thinking.

Why? Why did God allow him to meet Chloe? Why was he being punished so harshly? And what did Chloe ever do to deserve this? As he questioned God, the answers came flooding to his mind. *This is the natural consequence of sin.* When he chose to follow his own will rather than God's perfect will, there was a price to pay. And oh, was he paying dearly for it now! And not only him, but others around him too. In choosing his own way, he had managed to hurt the one he loved most.

How would he ever be able to explain this to Chloe? Would she ever be able to forgive him? He couldn't bear the thought of hurting her. Tears once again pricked his eyes as he thought of his beloved. She would never be able to understand.

Peter Esh smiled as he saw Saul riding up on his horse. He was looking forward to having the young man as his son-in-law and was certain he would make a good husband for Chloe. Peter thought it a bit odd for Saul to be visiting in the middle of the week, though. As the horse neared the hitching post, it was evident the young man was in distress.

"Saul, what brings you by today? Is everything all right?" Peter asked, sensing his need to talk.

"No. Everything is not all right. I need to speak with Chloe," Saul insisted.

"She is in the house, *Sohn,*" Peter said.

Saul cringed at the last word.

Saul strode up to the house and knocked on the door. Chloe happily answered it, then her countenance fell when she saw Saul's sullen face. "Saul, is something wrong?" She searched his face for the answer. It was evident he'd been shedding tears. *Saul crying?*

"We need to talk, Chloe," Saul stated dismally. "Can we go for a walk?"

"*Jah,* sure," she said as she hesitantly stepped outside. "What is it, Saul? You're scaring me."

"Not here," he insisted, then nodded toward the road.

They walked in silence until they were a good distance from the house. Saul stopped abruptly and turned to Chloe. He gently took her hands in his and searched her eyes. "Chloe, I want you to know that you mean everything to me," he said as his eyes brimmed with tears. "I love you and you only."

"Wh...what are you saying, Saul?" Chloe squeaked out nervously.

"I'm sorry, Chloe, but I never meant to hurt you like this, you've got to believe me," he said sadly. "I...I can't marry you.

We can't see each other anymore." Oh, the words were so difficult to say!

"Why not?" Her heart sank, and tears immediately surfaced.

"Because I'm an idiot. Before I met you..." He couldn't finish the sentence.

"Before you met me, *what*?" She dreaded to hear the words, but asked anyway.

"I just found out that I'm a father," he said shaking his head. "The bishop's daughter is in the family way. We never even intended to do anything. I never even loved her. We went to a party and had too much to drink. One thing led to another. It was before you and I met."

"How could you, Saul?" Chloe cried aloud, hitting his chest with her palms. "It was perfect. I loved you and you loved me. We were going to get married." She sobbed, falling into his open arms.

He held her tight against his chest. "I'm sorry, Chloe." He wept, still holding her. "I'm so sorry!"

They stood there and cried in each other's arms for several minutes. A feeling of helplessness engulfed them both. The heartache was excruciating. Reality was suffocating them and there was nothing either of them could do. Nothing they could do...but pray. Pray for healing and for God to work all things for good.

Saul gave Chloe one last hug and swiped the tears from her eyes with his thumbs. He placed a gentle kiss on her lips to bid her farewell. He hoped that assuring her of his love would make the blow easier, but somehow it seemed worse. "Someday, we will have all the answers, Chloe. Right now, we need to trust God to know what he's doing." He said the words, but he wasn't sure if he fully grasped them himself.

"We have no choice, *jah*?" she said as tears once again filled her eyes. She attempted to put her bravest face forward.

"I don't know what it is Chloe, but God has a plan for you," Saul stated confidently atop his horse.

"And for you too, *jah*?" she said.

"*Jah*." He nodded. "Goodbye, Chloe. I won't ever forget you." Saul's voice wavered as he said the words. Then turning his horse around, he rode out of Chloe's life.

CHAPTER 14
Mourning

"The Lord is nigh unto them that are of a broken heart..." Psalm 34:18a

It had been over three weeks since Saul said goodbye, but it seemed like just yesterday. The excruciating pain in her heart would not subside and Chloe wondered if she'd ever be able to live normally again. The first week had been the worst. She spent nearly every waking moment in tears. Barely able to leave her bed and the miserable comfort of her blankets. Unable to eat more than a few bites.

Everything was a reminder of Saul. A reminder of something that could never be. She knew she was not the only one affected, though. Ruthie asked about Saul constantly. She also asked why Chloe was so sad all the time. She didn't understand. How could a six year old understand that her beloved had been snatched away? Chloe still couldn't comprehend it herself. It all just made no sense.

She abstained from church and insisted she didn't want any visitors. Not even her friends. Especially not her friends. Danika still had Eli. Now Joanna had Levi. And she...she had nobody. She wanted nobody, but Saul. But that was now impossible.

Her *mamm* and *dat* worried about her. They were afraid the grief she was experiencing was too much for her to handle and they were correct. Her sense of loss was overwhelming and she wasn't sure she'd be able to go on living. Could a person really die of a broken heart? She certainly thought it could be true. For that's how she felt.

When her parents spoke with Bishop Hostettler, he recommended she see a grief counselor from the Plain community. Chloe refused to leave the house, so the counselor came to them. The counselor explained to her parents that the grief she was feeling was akin to the loss of a loved one. Chloe had, in fact, lost a loved one, although not to death. She explained the five stages of grief and suggested that what Chloe needed most was time to heal. Right now, she was in the depression stage which was a difficult but necessary step to the final stage, which was acceptance. Eventually, she would accept things as they are and move on with her life.

News of Saul's marriage came to Peter's ears via Bishop Hostettler. He wondered if it would be wise to let Chloe know and asked the grief counselor for her advice. She recommended that he should indeed share the news with Chloe. She said it would bring more pain at first, but eventually she would see that Saul was able to move on with his life. And she, too, would be able to move on with hers. The counselor also encouraged them to have Chloe spend time outside every day. She said that the Vitamin D provided by sunshine was monumental in helping those experiencing depression.

"Levi." Judah Hostettler approached his son. "I recall you were asking about a young man from Bishop Mast's district a while back."

"*Jah*, Saul Brenneman. Why do you mention it?" Levi had heard that he and Chloe had stopped seeing each other and wondered if his father might know why.

"Saul and Bishop Mast's daughter Sarah were married this week," the bishop stated.

Levi's eyes grew wide. He wouldn't ask his father why, but he only knew of one reason a young couple would get married so abruptly and not during the normal wedding season. *Poor Chloe! Had Saul been unfaithful to her? How could he hurt her like that?* Once again, Levi's wrath rose up in him. He had to go see her. Surely she was heartbroken over the whole matter. Joanna had said that Chloe and Saul loved each other and that they would probably marry.

At that moment, Levi determined that he would go see Chloe. She needed him whether she realized it or not. She deserved someone she could count on. Someone that would love her and be faithful to her. Even if she would only accept his friendship, that would be good enough for him. It would have to be.

Chloe was sitting on a bench in the yard soaking up the sunshine when Levi walked up. His brown hair was slightly peeking out from under his straw hat, his hazel eyes concerned. Levi was one of the kindest boys Chloe knew, but she had lost her chance with him when she fell for Saul. Now Levi cared for her friend Joanna.

"Mind if I sit down?" Levi asked, stopping in front of her and blocking out the sun rays.

"No," she simply said.

They both sat there in awkward silence for a moment gazing out into the field. Levi searched for the right words to say. "How are you doing, Chloe?" He scanned her red-rimmed eyes.

Chloe's bottom lip began to tremble.

Levi placed his hand over Chloe's. "It's all right," he gently reassured her. "You don't have to say anything if you don't want to."

Chloe nodded her head in thankful silence as tears slid down her cheeks. Levi wished he could kiss them away, then chided himself for the inappropriate thought.

After a few moments of quiet, Levi was desperate for something to say or do. "Is...is there anything I can do for you?"

"You're doing it right now."

"Would you like to take a walk?" Levi offered.

"*Jah.*" She stood up from the bench. Chloe was thankful for Levi's companionship.

They walked side by side toward the field where the corn was now head high. Soon harvest time would come and Saul would not be there to help. But Levi would. Levi and his family helped out every year, just as the Esh family usually assisted the Hostettlers when the time for their harvest came. Levi was steady. He was dependable. And Chloe realized that he was exactly what she needed. But he belonged to Joanna.

She glanced his way and he smiled back at her. Her heart fluttered. That was something she thought she would never feel again. A ray of hope entered her soul. She stole another glance and noticed his hazel eyes reflected the dark green of his shirt. In the middle of the cornfield, Levi stopped. Chloe looked up at him inquisitively.

Levi took a deep breath. "Chloe..." He halted, but willed himself to go on. "I'd like to be your friend." He stopped again, removed his straw hat, and nervously raked his hand through his hair. "No, that's not entirely true. I'd like to be more than just your friend...when you're ready." There. He said it.

Chloe's eyebrows furrowed. "What about Joanna?"

"What do you mean?" Levi raised his eyebrows.

"Joanna. Aren't you courting Joanna?" she asked in confusion.

"Whatever made you think that?" he wondered aloud.

"Well, when *Dawdi* John passed, I saw you hugging Joanna. And you chatted with her for a long time, but barely said two words to me."

Levi wanted to chuckle, but he didn't. Was Chloe jealous? "I'll admit that I was a bit upset after seeing you and Saul in the car." His faced contorted as he thought about that day and how upset he'd been. "I didn't think you'd be jealous of me speaking with Joanna, though."

"No? Isn't that what you were aiming for?" she challenged.

"I'd hoped," he admitted.

"Levi Hostettler!" She huffed. A smile crossed her lips. It was the first time she'd smiled since she'd been with Saul and it felt good. "Okay," she simply said.

"Okay, what?" he asked.

"You may court me," she boldly declared.

"But I didn't ask to court you."

"No, but you wanted to. And if I have to wait around for you to ask, it may just never happen," she teased. "And you may take me home after the Singing on Sunday."

Levi grinned, shaking his head in disbelief.

Chloe smiled, stepped up on her tiptoes, and kissed his cheek. Then she turned around and confidently walked through the cornfield toward the house.

Levi beamed, touching his cheek where she'd kissed him. Taking off his hat once again, he tossed it in the air then shouted, "Thank You, God!

CHAPTER 15
Pure Love

"Flee also youthful lusts: but follow after righteousness, faith, charity, peace, with them that call on the Lord out of a pure heart." 2 Timothy 2:22

Jonathan and his friends sat underneath a tall oak tree on the side of their one-room schoolhouse, planning their next mission. At times, Jonathan would stop talking and get a far-away look in his eye. Joshua and Matthew knew that he was remembering his *grossdawdi,* so when his eyes would begin to cloud, they would tell him that his *grossdawdi* was in a better place and that he was happy. Sometimes this would comfort Jonathan, and at other times he would ask, "You mean, he'd rather not be with me?" His friends didn't know how to answer that question, so they kept silent and usually changed the subject.

"So, Jonathan, what's our next mission going to be?" Joshua asked curiously.

"I know!" Matthew replied. "Let's put worms in Grace's lunch box."

"No." Joshua sighed. "Why don't we tie the strings of the girls' prayer *kapps* together?"

Now Jonathan, who had been silent, spoke up. "I found some baby mice in the field the other day. We could let them loose in school."

"Hey, that's a great idea!" Matthew exclaimed happily.

The boys walked toward the schoolhouse, but were stopped by Sadie entering their path. Sadie reached out to slap Jonathan, but he stealthily ducked and dodged her hand.

"Well, hello, Jonathan," Sadie said sweetly, as if nothing had happened.

"What do you want, Sadie?" Jonathan answered coolly, ignoring Sadie's greeting.

"I just wanted to tell you that I hope you got a good spanking for what you did on Sunday," she sneered.

"Oh, yes, I did, Sadie," Jonathan replied, meeting Sadie's narrow eyes, one of which was black. "And I would gladly get fifty more to see the look on your face when you read that letter!"

"Well, I never..." Sadie stomped off in a huff, ignoring the laughter behind her.

"Jonathan, you're a natural," Joshua said. The three boys walked into the schoolhouse chatting happily.

Levi clicked his tongue and flicked the reigns to set his horse in motion. Chloe proudly sat beside him in the buggy seat. The last Singing she had been to, she'd left with Saul Brenneman and Levi had left alone. But now it seemed that God had brought them together at last.

Chloe scooted closer to Levi and leaned on his shoulder. While Levi felt a bit uncomfortable with her forwardness, he allowed her to do so. At that moment, he realized that courting Chloe could turn out to be quite a struggle. He had kept himself pure, while she on the other hand, had no doubt kissed Saul many times.

"Did Joanna ride home with your brother tonight?" Levi asked, recalling the two of them conversing at the Singing.

"*Ach*, I don't know." She sat up. "Did you see them together?"

"I just saw them talking is all." He maneuvered the buggy onto the main road.

"Oh." She glanced toward the road in front of them. "Are we going somewhere?"

"Just driving around. Is that all right?" He wasn't sure what she had come to expect and since this was officially his first time courting a girl, he was a little nervous.

"*Jah*, that's fine." She shrugged.

Levi sighed.

"What's wrong, Levi?" Chloe asked, wondering why he didn't seem as content as she felt.

"I just hope you won't compare me to him."

"Why would you think that?"

"Well, uh..." Levi attempted to find the best way to explain himself. "We have different standards."

"*Jah*, I know that."

Levi pulled his buggy off the road and stopped on the shoulder. A small car whizzed around them, honking its horn, but Levi didn't care. He turned in the seat to look into Chloe's eyes. "I just want you to know, Chloe, that I don't ever intend on leaving you." He wanted her to have reassurance. Levi realized that her heart had been damaged and her trust in him was essential.

"Neither did Saul," she said glumly, then whispered, "But he did."

"I'm not Saul," he stated adamantly. The edge to his voice didn't go undetected.

"No, you're not." She smiled and leaned close to him. Too close for comfort. She leaned forward to kiss him, but Levi turned his face away and backed up.

"*Ach*, Chloe. You're not going to make this easy on me, are you?" Her nearness caused his heart to beat rapidly. With all his might, he fought the urge to kiss her. Perhaps stopping on a public road in an open buggy wasn't such a great idea.

"What do you mean?" She cocked her head.

He cradled her face in his hands and intently searched her eyes. "You have no idea how badly I'd love to kiss you." His desire grew as the words escaped his mouth, and he longed to pull her close. Realizing his weakness, he quickly dropped his hands and forced himself to look away.

"But?" She reached up and turned his face, forcing him to look her in the eye once again.

"I can't...we can't," he insisted.

"Levi, I assure you we can. I can show you how," she offered boldly.

"No, Chloe. That's not it." Levi sighed. "Have you forgotten how much trouble we could get into?"

"No, I haven't." She pouted. "But couldn't we get into just a tiny bit of trouble?"

"Chlo-e," he said in a warning tone. "Besides, it just ain't right."

"Well, how long will we have to wait?" she wondered aloud.

"Until we're married," he stated firmly.

"That long?" She stuck her bottom lip out again.

"Unless you think that I'm not worth it." Levi lifted his brow.

"Well, why don't we try just one little time then I'll know?" She sure was tempting.

"Hey, that's a great idea!" he said sardonically.

"It is?" she asked wide-eyed, not catching his sarcasm.

"Sure. And afterward we can stick our feet under my buggy wheel and run them over!" He drove his point home.

"Levi!" She was clearly shocked. "Why would you suggest such a thing?"

"Well," he quoted her, "If we 'just try it one little time, then we'll know' whether we like it or not."

Chloe was clearly becoming annoyed. "I really don't appreciate your sarcasm, Levi."

"I'm not making fun of you, Chloe. But do you see my logic? 'How do you know you won't like it if you don't try it?' doesn't fly in the face of reality. One sweet little kiss can turn into so much more. I'm afraid that if we started then we...I...wouldn't be able to stop. The consequences could be so much worse than having our feet crushed by a buggy wheel. I wouldn't want to hurt you and the last thing I want to do is dishonor God," Levi gently explained. "Do you understand now?"

She nodded her head, but Levi still sensed a little disappointment.

"Do you have any idea how long I've loved you? How long I've been waiting already?" he asked gently.

Chloe shook her head.

"Remember the first day of school about eight years ago?" He smiled.

She mentally figured the math in her head. "That would have been my very first day of school." She smiled.

"Well, that year there was one extra student. Do you remember?" He waited for her response.

"*Jah*, I do." She looked at him in question, willing him to continue.

"I remember that you raised your hand and volunteered to give up your seat so the other girl could sit down. You even said that you wouldn't mind standing up that day." He smiled. "That was the day I first fell in love with you."

Chloe gasped.

Levi continued, "Year after year while we were in school, I watched you. You've always cared for people, Chloe. Offering your pencil when someone didn't have one...even if it was Jonathan Fisher and he just played a prank on you the day before. Helping the younger *kinner* when they didn't understand." He smiled recalling all the things he loved about her. "I always knew that you were the one for me. I knew you would make the perfect Amish wife."

"But you never said anything. I had no idea," she said in amazement.

"That's because I was always so shy," he explained. "Before tonight, I had never taken anyone home from a Singing. Not because I was timid, though, but because I've been waiting for you. And I'll continue to wait for you as long as it takes. And I won't take kisses from you because they're not mine to take, they belong to your husband."

"But I've already given Saul..." her voice trailed off as guilt took over. Had Saul stolen what was rightfully Levi's, or her future husband's?

"I know, Chloe. Saul took a lot more than he should have. But God still forgives and so will I. I thought I'd lost my chance when Saul Brenneman came along. You can't imagine how my heart ached for you, Chloe. But I still prayed for you. I knew that if God planned for us to be together, then He would make it happen."

"He was right," Chloe stated.

"Who?" Confusion adorned Levi's face.

"Saul. He said that God has a plan for each of us and we can trust Him even when we don't have all the answers. I see it now, Levi. I still can't say that I understand it all, but I can see it. And I know I can trust God with my life." Chloe smiled and Levi knew she was truly content. Content to be his for now, and content to trust God's will for her life.

After Levi dropped Chloe off at home that night, she sent up a prayer of thanks to God. With His help, she and Levi would stay pure to God and to each other and perhaps one day become husband and wife. Because she knew she'd always consider Saul her first love, she felt bad for Levi's sake. While Chloe would never regret meeting Saul, she recognized she'd given him more of her heart than she should have.

At this moment, Chloe couldn't help but wonder how Saul was dealing with the consequences of his past choices. What was God's plan for his life? And why had she been a part of it? Chloe guessed that she'd probably never know the answers to some questions, and realized that was okay. Saul was now a part of her past, and she would look to the future for God's perfect plan.

The End

Amish Girls Series - Book 4
Susanna's Surprise
J.E.B. Spredemann

Susanna's Surprise

J.E.B. Spredemann

Amish Girls Series - Book 4

AUTHORS' NOTE

It should be noted that the Amish people and their communities differ one from another. There are, in fact, no two Amish communities exactly alike. It is this premise on which this book is written. We have taken cautious steps to assure the authenticity of Amish practices and customs. Both Old Order Amish and New Order Amish are portrayed in this work of fiction and may be inconsistent with some Amish communities.

We, as *Englischers*, can learn a lot from the Plain People and their simple way of life. Their hard work, close-knit family life, and concern for others are to be applauded. As the Lord wills, may this special culture continue to be respected and remain so for many centuries to come, and may the light of God's salvation reach their hearts.

CHARACTERS IN SUSANNA'S SURPRISE

The Hostettler Family

Judah – father, bishop of Paradise

Lydia – mother

Nathan – oldest brother

Levi – older brother, protagonist of Chloe's Revelation

Joshua – Susie's older brother

Susanna – protagonist

Paul, Elizabeth, Ella, Micah, and Yonnie – other siblings

The Thompson Family

Katrina – mother

Andrea – daughter

The Fisher family

Gideon – father

Esther – mother

Isaac & Rachel – oldest son & wife

Grace – oldest daughter

Joanna – protagonist of Joanna's Struggle, youngest daughter

Jonathan – youngest son, instigator of mischief

The King Family

Philip – father

Naomi – mother

Danika – daughter, protagonist of Danika's Journey

Katie – daughter

P.J. – son

The Yoder Family

Jacob – deacon, father

Sarah – mother

Eli – son, protagonist of Danika's Journey

Annie – daughter, Susanna's best friend

The Lapp family

Sadie – oldest daughter

Andrew – oldest son

Others

Matthew Riehl – boy Susie likes

Chloe Esh – protagonist of Chloe's Revelation, Levi's *aldi*

Brandi – Katrina's co-worker

Angela – Brandi's daughter and Andrea's friend

CHAPTER 1
Boys

"...he deviseth mischief continually..."
Proverbs 6:14b

Susanna Hostettler sat on a rock in the school yard, deep in thought. Lunch was nearly over and she yearned for some quiet time. It seemed the older she became, the more she relished time alone. Of course, growing up in the home of the bishop, along with eight other siblings, scarcely provided moments for reflection. She had to take what she could get, even if it occasionally meant separating herself from her friends.

"Hey!" came a loud voice from behind her. She jumped slightly and whirled around to face Jonathan Fisher, who was grinning earlobe to earlobe. Why did Jonathan *always* have to ruin her peace and quiet?

"Scared ya." Jonathan timidly held out a small wildflower. He obviously fancied Susie, but to his disappointment, she had no interest in him at all.

"What do you want, Jonathan?" Susie was quickly becoming annoyed at the distraction. She wasn't usually rude, but lately Jonathan had been getting on her nerves. She never knew what Jonathan would do next or whether or not he was up to mischief, and she certainly didn't want to find out.

"I just wanted to give ya this flower," he answered sweetly.

"*Nee, denki.* If I wanted a flower I would have picked one myself." She flounced over to her friend Annie, who'd been sitting on the steps of the school house observing Jonathan's antics. Susanna felt just a twinge of guilt when Jonathan hung his head and walked away.

Jonathan glanced back at Susie wondering what else he could do to get her attention. Sooner or later, he was determined to make Susanna Hostettler his girl. And she would be, he knew, she just didn't know it yet.

"You're so lucky, Susie," Annie said wistfully. She evidently had heard what had happened. "I wish I was as perty as you. How come you don't like Jonathan? He's the handsomest boy in school," Annie blurted out.

"You, Annie Yoder, are *ferhoodled.*" Susie rolled her eyes. Everybody knew Annie was the prettiest girl in school. Nobody had beautiful flaxen blonde hair like hers. Susie often wondered why Jonathan didn't fancy her friend instead.

"Why does it seem that everyone likes Jonathan except for you?" Annie's hands rested on her slim hips.

"I'm not interested in him. Besides, I don't *have to* like someone. I'm only twelve, you know."

"Almost thirteen. And that's only three years away from courtin' age. And you'll be goin' to singings in a year. You're so lucky," Annie reminded Susie.

Although they were best friends, Annie was nearly two years younger than Susie. And in Susanna's opinion, definitely too young to be thinking about boys.

Annie released a drawn out sigh. "Someday, when I have the courage, I'm gonna march right up to him and say, 'I like you, Jonathan Fisher.'"

Susanna spotted Jonathan out of the corner of her eye. "Well, here's your chance. He's coming this way," Susie teased.

When the bell from the schoolhouse rang, Jonathan purposefully walked toward the steps behind his friend Matthew. His previous disappointment had vanished and was now replaced with a mischievous grin.

"*Ach*, I can't believe you, Susanna Hostettler! You know I wouldn't *really* do that." Annie's cheeks flamed red and she scurried into the schoolhouse before Jonathan caught her discomfiture.

Susanna laughed and then quickly regained her placid demeanor as Jonathan neared. She wouldn't want him to believe they were talking about him. That was the last thing she needed. If he thought she had an inkling of an interest in him, he'd never leave her alone.

With a knowing look, Jonathan walked past Susie into the schoolhouse, tipping his hat toward her. Susie rolled her eyes and sighed.

Katrina Thompson sat in the staff room at Lancaster County Hospital finishing off the last of the tuna sandwich her daughter had prepared for her. Her workplace held bittersweet memories. This had been where she had become completely overwhelmed with grief when her first daughter was stillborn. And it was the place she held her daughter Andrea for the first time. She was so perfect and small when she was born, just a little under five pounds. She gave a faint smile at the cherished memory.

"Hey Trina, does Andrea have another big game today?" Her co-worker Brandi walked into the lunchroom, searching the refrigerator for a yogurt.

"Yes, they're playing over in Harrisburg. That's why I'm leaving early."

"That girl sure can pitch. Did you say they were going to the State Championships?" Brandi asked.

"It looks like it so far. Andrea's so excited," Katrina replied enthusiastically.

"How old is that girl now?"

"She'll be thirteen next week. Would you like to bring the girls and meet us at the Dairy Queen next Saturday night? I'm sure Andrea would love to see you on her birthday."

"That sounds like fun, but I'll have to check our schedule," her friend replied.

"Ella, Lizzy, Paul, I don't want you getting too far ahead of me," Susanna called to her younger siblings. Since her brother Joshua had recently finished eighth grade, she was the oldest one in the family attending school now, so it was her responsibility to watch the younger children. That could be a bother sometimes, but her *mamm* always said, 'You are blessed to have so many brothers and sisters.' Susie didn't feel very blessed when she found out that Lizzy had 'borrowed' her *for gut* stockings and returned them with a hole torn in them.

It was nice to have other brothers and sisters to play with and share the chores, she had to admit. Still, there were times she felt like she was missing something or someone. She couldn't quite place her finger on it, but there was a certain emptiness inside her heart that she couldn't describe. It was something that she could only talk to God about.

When Susie reached her house, she quickly changed her from dark-green school dress into her brown chorin' dress. She went downstairs where she joined her other siblings and they all headed to the barn for milking time. After they finished, she and her sisters would help *Mamm* with the laundry. Lots of Amish folks washed their laundry on Mondays, but with such a large family one day was not enough for the Hostettlers.

"Do you need any help with your math today, Paul?" Susie asked once they had reached the barn and settled down on their three-legged milkin' stools. Some folks used milkin' machines, but since they didn't have too many cows, they still milked them by hand.

"*Nee*, David promised to help me," Paul expressed, referring to his *gut* friend, David Lapp. Instead of rinsing out the milk buckets like he should be doing, her brother gazed out the window.

That's strange; I usually help him with his math. "Well, I'm here if you need me," she replied kindly. Susie did well in school and hoped to become a teacher someday. She looked at her brother from behind the cow's rump and shrugged. *I reckon he's just growing up. Something's probably on Paul's mind. He's most likely thinking about his hunting trip tomorrow.*

Something was *always* on Susie's mind when she was milking. She'd rather have a book in her hand, but that was not possible while milking. She'd tried it once and accidentally dropped her book into the milk bucket. It wouldn't have been as bad if it hadn't been a school book. And, of course, she'd had to give the milk to the mouse catchers.

Today she thought about school and the situation with Jonathan Fisher. She wondered why he had to like *her*. Annie said it was because she was pretty. She wasn't that pretty, was she? She'd been endowed with wavy auburn hair, brown eyes, which *Mamm* said had gold flecks in them, and a few freckles on her tan skin. She was taller than most girls her age and was quickly turning into a young woman. That part, she didn't care much for. It was kind of embarrassing. But thankfully, *her* body wasn't the only one going through changes. She'd noticed the same type of things in other girls her age.

In Susie's eyes, Annie was just as pretty as she was – even prettier. Stock-straight flaxen blonde hair, big, light blue eyes, and surprisingly light skin. She was a sweet, sensitive girl.

Susie remembered perfectly the day when she and Annie walked down to the creek and Annie tricked her into thinking that there was a fish in the water. As soon as she leaned over to look, Annie pushed her into the creek. Susie never did find the prayer *kapp* that she had lost that day, but at least she got Annie back by pulling her in when she was trying to help her out.

"Are ya going to milk that cow forever, or are ya gonna get started on a different one? Poor Gertie's probably sore by now," Ella's voice startled her out of her thoughts.

"I'm coming. I'm coming," she grumbled, leaving Gertrude and moving on to Hilde. Susie settled onto her three-legged stool again.

I definitely don't like Jonathan in a romantic way, she mused. *Sure, he's good-looking, but he is so immature – always pulling pranks, pushing the limits, and sometimes he's downright exasperating. He does make me laugh though, I have to give him credit for that.* Besides, if her looks were the only reason Jonathan liked her, it wasn't good enough. She laughed as she was reminded of the wooden plaque that hung in her *grossmudder's* kitchen: 'Kissin' don't last, cooking do.' *Ach*, she couldn't imagine a boy kissing her – especially Jonathan Fisher.

Matthew was a different story. He was one of the Riehl boys – nice, handsome, serious, and always a good student. One time she saw him helping a little boy that had fallen from a tree and noticed how caring he was. That's when she decided he was worthy of liking. She just needed to get his attention and let him know she liked him. Somehow. There was one problem, though. Jonathan and Matthew were best friends.

Susie continued on to the other cows until they were all milked. She then handed the bucket to Paul, who poured the creamy liquid into freshly-sterilized jars. After she churned the cream on top, it would make a rich butter to spread on fresh baked bread. My, was she looking forward to dinner tonight.

Susanna was glad it was now Friday. That meant no school till Monday and Sunday-Go-To-Meeting would be this week. Her favorite part was the common meal that followed the meeting when she and her friends could spend time together. This week the meeting would be held at the Millers' home. Out of all the places Meeting was held, the Millers' was the favorite for the children. Miller's Pond is where they would go to swim in the summer and ice skate in the winter when the pond would freeze over. *Maybe Annie and I could use one of the Millers' boats and spend some time out on the pond next Saturday - my birthday.* Susie smiled, thinking of the fun they'd have.

CHAPTER 2
Jonathan Fisher

"Foolishness is bound in the heart of a child, but the rod of correction will drive it far from him." Proverbs 22:15

Sunday morning Susanna put on her blue *for-gut* dress and her white apron. She placed her prayer *kapp* over the tight bun at the nape of her neck. *I hope Matthew's there today*, she thought as she glanced into the mirror making sure her hair was just right. Susanna had to admit to herself that she was thinking about boys a little more, now that she was getting older. She pulled up her black stockings and tied her black shoes, ready now for breakfast.

"Someone's having a birthday soon," Judah Hostettler commented to his daughter as she bounced down the stairs.

"Thirteen," she reminded her father with a half-smile.

"And you've become such a beautiful young lady." His eyes shown pride. "Takin' after your *mamm*, you are."

"*Ach, Daed,* do ya have to talk that way in front of them?" Susie blushed, referencing her siblings. "It's vanity, you know."

Judah laughed. "*Ach,* listen to that. The bishop being reproved by his own *dochder*. 'Tis true, you are beautiful. Nothin' wrong with a *vatter* admitting that. And you *are* growin' up." He smiled.

Mamm interjected, saving her daughter from further embarrassment, "Have you thought about the sermon today?"

"*Jah*. Susie's birthday's got me thinkin' on some things from the past. About growin' in the Lord and the necessary changes that must come, whether good or bad." Judah glanced at his wife and they shared a look Susie couldn't comprehend.

"What do you mean by that?" Susanna's eyebrows lowered. "Why would my birthday make you think of changes?"

Judah caught Lydia's disapproving look, receiving her signal.

"Just pay attention to the teaching today," her father suggested.

Lydia gave a sigh of relief. There were some things that were better left unsaid. No need to bring up things that couldn't be changed anyway; especially this close to Susanna' birthday.

The sermon her father had given today had been interesting, to say the least. Why did Susanna feel there was something her parents were keeping from her? Between her mother's odd behavior at breakfast and her father's sermon, she couldn't shake the feeling that something was not quite right.

"Let's go over to the pond," Annie Yoder urged, pulling her by the arm. "We can take off our shoes and walk along the shore."

"*Jah*, that would be *gut*," Susie agreed and they started in that direction. The other children were already getting wet and playing games.

It was Jonathan Fisher's turn to swing out into the pond. He always drew a crowd because he was constantly trying something crazy and new. He loved to show off, so Susanna tried to completely ignore him, pulling Annie in the opposite direction. She wouldn't give him the satisfaction of knowing she was watching him pull his stunts. It did not impress her in the least. As a matter of fact, she wondered if he knew it had the opposite of his desired effect. She couldn't stand it when boys were prideful, it wasn't the way of her people.

"No, Susie, let's watch the boys," Annie protested pulling her nearer to the other spectators. Susanna relented to satisfy her friend and plopped down next to Annie on the shore.

This time, Jonathan ran and jumped up to grasp one of the long willow branches. He let out a 'whoop' as he swung high in the air, then let go as he catapulted himself head over heels into a mid-air somersault. Impressed, the children on the shore gasped and aahed. But when Jonathan hit the water, his body lay there still and lifeless.

"It's Jonathan!" One of the girls shrieked. "Something's wrong."

Concerned, Susanna and Annie stood up and walked closer to the water.

Four boys hurried out to the middle of the pond and swam back with Jonathan's limbs linked in their arms. They lay his body on the bank of the pond, and many children and adults gathered around. Susanna was near too, feeling helpless. She immediately felt bad for the way she'd been treating him. *What if something is terribly wrong?*

"Oh, Jonathan!" she said desperately. "Please be all right," she begged as she leaned over him.

Just then, Jonathan reached his hand up behind her prayer *kapp* and quickly pulled her face down to his, kissing her squarely on the lips.

"I'm just fine, now," he said slyly as he opened his eyes, then raised his eyebrows with a huge grin embellishing his face.

"Jonathan Fisher!" Susie's face instantly turned beet red as she looked around and noticed the crowd of at least forty Amish folks watching – her father, Bishop Hostettler, being one of them. Furious, Susanna ran off, thoroughly humiliated by Jonathan's tasteless prank.

Jonathan hopped up to follow after her, and a few of the other boys slapped his back in congratulations. He was suddenly halted by a firm grasp on each arm. He looked up to see

Bishop Hostettler and his father glaring at him. Undaunted, Jonathan remarked, "Pretty sneaky, huh?" A mischievous grin swanked on his face. Both men found it necessary to look away to keep from displaying their true emotions. *That Jonathan Fisher is something else, that boy's got more gumption than the next ten boys,* Judah thought. They both shook their heads in disbelief.

Isaac Fisher would be sitting at his father's table for supper this evening, along with his small family. Jonathan was glad, for once, that the attention would be off of him. He had received a pretty stern warning from the bishop about the pond incident with his daughter, Susanna. *Oh Susanna!* The punishment he'd received when he returned home was well worth the feel of Susie's soft lips on his. Jonathan didn't know why exactly, but he was head over heels for the bishop's daughter.

Gideon Fisher emerged from the woodshed with his youngest son. He was indeed a challenge, that Jonathan. They walked up the back steps and into the kitchen, where Isaac, his expecting wife Rachel, and their three-year-old son sat waiting. Jonathan was still wincing and rubbing his backside when he came to the table.

"What'd you do this time, Jonathan?" his older brother chuckled, reminiscing bygone days with his younger brother.

"You mean, you didn't hear what happened after the meeting down at Millers' pond?" his sister Grace queried.

Isaac looked to Jonathan, who gave him an impish grin and wiggled his eyebrows.

"Poor Susanna Hostettler –" Grace continued, but was abruptly warned by her father.

"We don't need to be discussing your brother's foolishness. Now, let's just eat," Gideon declared in a huff, then bowed his head for the silent blessing.

"Esther," Gideon called to his wife, "I need to go over and talk to the bishop."

"*Mamm's* in her room with Rachel," his daughter Joanna answered.

"Tell your *mamm* I went to talk with Judah; be back before too long," he instructed and Joanna agreed. "Somethin's got to be done about that boy," he mumbled under his breath.

"Come here, Giddy. Let's go outside with Uncle Jonathan," Jonathan said to his young nephew.

The little boy looked to his father for approval, who nodded his head giving the okay. "Now Jonathan, I don't want you workin' your wiles on my boy," his older brother warned.

"*Ach*, don't worry about us, we'll be fine," Jonathan said as he happily swung his nephew onto his shoulders and headed toward the door.

"Judah, I'm pulling my hair out over that boy," Gideon confided in his bishop friend. "It seems like I don't have enough work to keep him out of trouble. I'm worried he'll be out of control come time for *Rumspringa*. I don't want to lose him to the world."

"A boy like that needs more than just work to keep him out of trouble," Judah commented.

"If it's discipline you're referring to, he gets his fair share."

"No, I was thinking something else. Gideon, what kind of boy were you growing up?"

"I was a good boy and stayed out of trouble for the most part. Nothing like my Jonathan. I was more like Isaac," Gideon asserted.

"That's what I thought." Judah pondered the situation, scratching his beard. "How would you feel if your boy came and worked for me part-time? I think I may be able to relate to the boy. You wouldn't know it by looking at me now, but I was just like Jonathan when I was his age. Wild and crazy. I did anything and everything for attention." He gave a slight smile.

"Really? You?" This admission thoroughly surprised Gide-on.

Judah nodded. "I think your Jonathan has the makings of a fine preacher, if that's the Lord's will for him."

Gideon mulled over the proposition. "But what about your daughter?" he hesitated.

"Oh, he won't be seeing too much of Susanna. She'll be helping her mother in the house and I'll have Jonathan busy working on the farm. Besides, would it be such a terrible thing if our two ended up together?"

Gideon had to smile. He and Judah had been good friends for years. Why not family too? "I'll send him over during the week after school and chores are done." The two men shook hands and Gideon headed toward home feeling somewhat confident.

Isaac Fisher opened the side door and walked out of the house. He cupped his hands and called, "All right, Jonathan. Where are you and my son hiding? It's time to come in now."

He heard his younger brother's voice yell, "We're back here – out by the garden."

Isaac walked behind the house toward the garden. He stopped short when he saw his brother and son. Both were inside a small mud hole and they were completely covered in mud – from the tops of their heads to the soles of their feet. The only places that weren't covered in mud were their eyes and their teeth.

Little Gid happily threw some mud at Jonathan, who in return playfully threw a dirt clod back. Jonathan noticed his brother watching them. He smiled, showing his white teeth. "Well, how do you like our mud hole?"

Isaac crossed his arms in front of his chest. "I like the bathtub better. Come on, get out of there now." His annoyed voice sounded. "You're lucky he's not wearing his *for-gut* clothes. His mother would have your hide."

CHAPTER 3
The Secret

"For nothing is secret, that shall not be made manifest..." Luke 8:17a

Jonathan searched for Susie on the playground at school and found her on one of the swings. Susanna saw him too and paid no attention to him. "Susie, I'm sorry for what I did on Sunday. Will you forgive me?"

Susanna kept swinging, not even acknowledging his presence.

"Susie, please don't be mad at me."

Susanna still said nothing.

"Susie, don't ignore me."

She stared straight ahead.

"Won't you at least talk to me? At least say something," he pleaded.

Susie stopped the swing and stood up. Looking Jonathan straight in the eye, she coldly stated, "You and I aren't exactly on speaking terms." Then she walked away without another word.

Jonathan forlornly stared after her.

"She must be really mad at me," Jonathan muttered to himself.

"She is," a voice piped up behind him. Startled, Jonathan turned and saw Annie staring at him.

"I don't know what to do." He sighed in defeat.

"Seems to me too much doin' is what got ya in trouble in the first place. Maybe you don't have to do anything."

"What do you mean?"

"Maybe God has something else in mind."

"Oh, like what?" Jonathan cocked his head to one side.

"I don't know. Something." Annie walked off leaving Jonathan wondering.

Matthew Riehl caught up with Susanna as she was on her way home from school. "Hey Susie, how are you doing?"

"All right, I guess." She hoped he didn't want to talk about Jonathan right now.

"Well, I was wondering...um, isn't your birthday coming up soon?"

"*Jah,* it is," she said shyly wondering why he was asking.

"Would you let me take you on a boat ride on Miller's Pond... and maybe we could have a picnic too?"

Susie blushed a bit. *Matthew wants to spend time with me!* "*Jah*, 'twould be fine. When?"

"Do you think you can get away after school on Friday?" he asked.

"I can probably meet you there after chorin' time," she suggested.

"*Wonderful-gut!*" Matthew said excitedly. "I'll see ya at school tomorrow." He waved quickly and sauntered off toward his house.

Jonathan walked into the barn feeling dejected. *Susanna didn't speak to me at all today, except for, of course, the fact that she informed me that she wasn't speaking to me. What should I do?*

Gideon noticed his son's unusually distraught countenance and felt concerned. It was so unlike Jonathan to be down, he was always happy-go-lucky. "What's wrong? You look like your world has been turned upside down."

"I'd rather not talk about it right now." He sighed heavily.

"You know, Jonathan, you can talk to me about anything," his father offered.

Jonathan held up his hand for him to stop, and let him know he was not interested in conversing at this moment.

"Jonathan, I have something I need to tell ya. I met with Judah on Sunday, and he would like you to begin working for him. Today."

Suddenly, Jonathan's eyes brightened and his head shot up. "Are you serious?" He couldn't believe his good fortune.

His father nodded his head in affirmation.

All of a sudden Jonathan ran past Gideon. He ran up and down the hill near his *daed's* farm, spinning cartwheels and yelling, "Who-hoo!" with a smile as big as Texas. Gideon couldn't help but laugh. Jonathan always did everything in a big way.

Esther joined Gideon in the barn. "What's going on with Jonathan?"

"I just informed him he'll be working for Judah."

Esther gasped. "Oh my. Are you sure that's such a *gut* idea?"

"The bishop suggested it." Gideon shrugged his shoulders and looked at his wife. "And who am I to question the man of God?"

Lydia sat at the treadle sewing machine mending a pair of the boys' pants. "Susie, will you fetch the box of buttons out of my dower chest?"

"*Jah, Mamm.*" Susanna meandered into her mother's room and rummaged around in the large cedar box. "Where is it, *Mamm*? I don't see it anywhere," she hollered back to her mother.

"Check under the quilt on the right side. I think it might be under there."

Susie removed the quilt and stopped when she noticed an unfamiliar package with her name written on it. She quietly unwrapped the thick kraft-colored paper and discovered a small white baby gown. She lifted it up to take a better look and discovered an identical gown beneath it. *Why would Mamm keep two gowns for me?* Susanna wondered, since her *mamm* usually only kept one baby item per child. She hunted around more and discovered her mother did indeed only keep one item for everyone except her. *What does this mean?*

"*Mamm*, what's this?" Susie innocently inquired of her mother. "I found it in your hope chest. Why are there two?" She searched her mother's eyes.

A wave of panic ran through Lydia, paralyzing her thoughts.

"*Mamm*, are you all right?" Susanna said with concern, noticing her blanched demeanor.

"*Jah*, I'll be fine, *Dochder*." Lydia walked over to the living room and sat down on the couch. "*Kumm*, sit down by me. We need to have a talk."

"I don't understand." Susie puzzled.

Her mother began to explain. "When you were born, you had a twin sister."

To this, Susanna gasped. "But *Mamm* you never –"

"We never told you because we didn't want you to be saddened. She died shortly after being born," Lydia stated sadly.

"So that explains it," Susie simply said.

"Explains what?"

"Lately, I've felt that I've been missing something or someone. Now, I realize it's my twin sister. Where is she buried, *Mamm*? I'd like to go see her grave."

CHAPTER 4

Birthday

"Every good gift and every perfect gift is from above..." James 1:17a

Jonathan practically ran to the Hostettlers' house after all his chores were finished. He spotted the bishop and slowed his pace, walking up to him as calmly as he could – though he felt anything but calm. The bishop noticed him coming and he greeted him. "Hello, Jonathan. Glad you made it. I've been expecting you." He showed Jonathan around the farm and the work he'd be doing.

When the bishop stopped talking, Jonathan eagerly asked, "Where's Susie?"

The bishop chuckled and told him, "Susanna's inside with her *mamm* sewing. If you hurry, you'll be finished working by the time she's done. But I expect you to do a good job, and you are not allowed to see or speak with her until you've finished all your work. Is that clear?"

"Yes, Bishop. I'll get started right away."

Judah was working out in the field when his wife and daughter drove up in their buggy. "To what do I owe this pleasant surprise?" The bishop tipped his hat toward his wife.

"Susie found the baby gowns in my hope chest. She knows about Maryanna; I told her. She wanted to go see her grave, so I'm taking her to the cemetery," Lydia stated matter-of-factly.

Judah's face pained when he saw Susie's crestfallen countenance. "I'm sorry, *Liewi*." He placed a hand on his daughter's arm.

"'Tis okay, *Dat*. I understand," Susie said. Just then, she noticed a young man out in the cornfield. "Who's that?"

"That would be Jonathan. I've hired him to help me around here," Judah stated.

"But, why? You already have Josh and Levi to help." Susie could not understand how her father could think this was a good idea.

"Don't you worry about it. I have my reasons." He smiled.

"*Ach, Dat* –" Susie protested.

"I know he's sweet on you. Don't worry, I'll keep him busy. Now you ladies go about your business and leave us men here to do the work." He smiled, sending his wife a wink.

"If I didn't know any better, I'd say your *vatter's* up to something," Lydia commented to her daughter.

"I'd rather not discuss it right now, *Mamm*," Susie replied.

"Sooner or later, you're going to have to face that boy," her mother advised.

"I know, *Mamm*. I'm just thinking of my sister right now. I'll never get to know her. My heart aches for the life we've missed together." Her eyes misted.

"I understand. I'm just glad that the Lord allowed us to keep you," Lydia said, as she put her arm around her daughter.

They pulled up to the graveyard and dismounted the buggy. Lydia walked over to the where the small child was buried and identified the grave marker. "She was buried here," she said, pointing to the small engraved stone marker. "I'll wait for you in the buggy. Take as long as you need."

Susie slowly walked up to the grave. She knelt down and cleared the weeds that had grown around the small white stone. It simply read: *Maryanna Hostettler. Born and Died on Sept. 29 to Judah and Lydia Hostettler.* Tears welled up in Susanna's eyes and she couldn't help but grieve for the sister she would never know.

"Why *Gott*?" she wondered aloud. "It doesn't make any sense." There was no use asking questions she would probably never get the answers to, she figured. At least not this side of eternity.

She pulled a small cloth doll out of her apron pocket. *Mamm* had given it to her when she was younger and, being the first girl after a string of boys, she'd always pretended it was her sister. She now realized Maryanna was the sister she'd been missing. Although it was not their way, she lovingly placed it near the headstone, wiping away her tears. After a couple of minutes, she got up and returned to the buggy with her mother and they headed home.

Every day after chorin' time, Jonathan would head to the Hostettlers' farm to work with Judah. He'd been there for five days already and had only been able to catch a glimpse of Susanna. He knew her birthday was coming up and hoped he would be invited to the small celebration. Just in case, he had purchased a special gift for the occasion.

As he was working in the field, he noticed Susie walking alone down the lane with a small picnic basket. *I wonder where she's going*. Jonathan thought. *I should follow her.* He left the plow and crept out of the field so as not to be noticed. He stayed back a distance, so Susie wouldn't see him.

When he had followed Susie to Miller's Pond, he noticed Matthew Riehl standing by a tree. *Oh, no.* Jonathan sighed. They were talking to each other, but he was too far away to understand what they were saying. The couple walked over to the small dock and Matthew stepped into an aluminum fishing boat and held out his hand. Susie handed him the picnic basket, then took his hand and stepped into the boat. Jonathan didn't miss the radiant smile she'd given Matt. Matthew pushed off from the dock using oars to propel them away from the shore.

Jonathan's heart sank. He couldn't let Matthew steal his girl, but what could he do? He felt like walking up to Matthew Riehl and punching his lights out. But, if he made a scene, Susie would hate him even more. Besides, he and Matthew were *gut* friends. He would just have to wait for a good time then approach her and try to seek forgiveness. Right now, though, he had to get back to the Hostettlers' farm. It wouldn't do for Judah to find him gone when he was supposed to be there working. Besides, he couldn't stay there and watch Susie and Matthew together, it was just too much.

He had to get his mind off of her, so he drove the team harder. He'd have to wait until Susie returned. He hoped to have a chance to speak with her and straighten things out. He finished the chores Judah had given him and started toward the barn. Just his luck, Susie was in the barn with the mouse catchers. She didn't notice as he walked into the barn and he didn't want to startle her. He cleared his throat.

"Hello, Susie," he said shyly.

Susie walked straight up to Jonathan without a word and slapped him on the cheek. He couldn't have been more shocked.

"That was for what you did at the Millers' on Sunday," she stated in an even, satisfied voice.

Jonathan smiled at her with pleading eyes. "Does this mean you've forgiven me and we're on speaking terms now?" He hoped it was true.

"*Jah,* I guess so." She shrugged.

"*Wonderful-gut*!" he exclaimed and smiled widely, briefly gazing into her eyes.

Susanna didn't want to admit it to herself, but she felt her heart slightly flutter as Jonathan gazed at her with his piercing blue eyes.

He then turned and started toward home; Susanna watched him go. All of a sudden, he stopped, then turned around as though he'd forgotten something. He walked back toward her a little ways.

"By the way, Susie, where'd you go earlier when I saw ya walkin' down the lane?" He already knew the answer, but he wanted to hear it from her.

Oh no, I can't tell him I was with Matthew. I don't want to hurt his feelings. She stammered, "I...uh...it was nowhere important."

"*Ach, gut.* Well, I guess I'll see ya tomorrow then," Jonathan carried on. "It's your birthday, *ain't so*?"

"Tomorrow, *jah,*" she said timidly. *Why does he want to know?*

He stood there searching her eyes for a moment, drinking in her beauty. She sure was something. "Bye, Susie." He then turned and started toward home, whistling as he went.

Susanna shook her head in amazement. *That was the most pleasant conversation I've ever had with Jonathan.*

On Saturday evening, Lydia prepared yumaseti for Susanna's birthday dinner. Each of the Hostettler *kinner* received a special meal for their birthday. Most of the family was present, except for Levi, who they figured was probably out courting someone. Jonathan was still out working in the field when the family sat down to eat.

After the delicious meal, Lydia brought out a chocolate cake, which was Susie's favorite, and set it on the table. Just then, there was a knock at the back door. Judah arose from his seat and moved to open it. He didn't miss the tinge of color on Jonathan's face when the door creaked open.

"Sorry, for botherin' you, Bishop. Just wanted to let you know that I finished up in the barn and I'll be headin' home now." Jonathan informed him as he did at the end of each day. Normally, Judah and his sons would be out in the field as well, but today they'd been dismissed early in light of Susanna's birthday. Jonathan had been invited too, but he didn't feel it was his place to intrude on Susie's special day with her family.

Judah turned and glanced back at the table. "We're celebrating Susanna's birthday with a chocolate cake right now. Why don't you join us, Jonathan?" he urged.

"Well, I don't know how Susie would feel about it." Jonathan hesitated. "I don't want to intrude and ruin her special day."

He watched Judah walk to the table and whisper something in Susanna's ear. Susie glanced toward the door, then nodded her head. "She said it would be fine with her." Judah smiled.

Jonathan followed him to the table and sat down at the opposite end of Judah across from seven-year-old Lizzie. She peered at him from beneath her brown lashes holding a steady gaze. Jonathan returned the stare until Lizzie stuck out her tongue. He smirked, dismissed her foolishness, and then refocused his attention on the chocolate cake Susanna's *mudder* served.

Lydia served up a large slice of chocolate cake and passed it down to Jonathan with a big glass of milk. "*Denki.*" Jonathan had never tasted better cake in his life. Of course, that may have been because he sat at the same table with the girl of his dreams. What he wouldn't give to become a permanent part of this wonderful family. He didn't know if she was just being polite, but he did see Susie glance his way a couple of times. *Wouldn't Matthew be jealous.* He smiled to himself.

After Susie had opened up her gifts, Jonathan excused himself to go home. "*Mamm* might be getting worried now," he explained.

To his surprise, Susie seemed disappointed.

Judah spoke up. "Susie will walk you out," he offered, and immediately a rush of color filled her cheeks.

Jonathan removed his hat from the peg on the wall and held the door open for Susanna. They walked outside and noticed a heavenly canopy of stars above them.

"*Ach*, it's so pretty!" Susanna said as she gazed into the heavens.

"Which constellation is your favorite?" Jonathan wondered, looking up at the beauty surrounding them.

"I'd have to say Ursa Major," she stated confidently.

"The Big Dipper? That's my favorite too," he said in amazement, looking at the attractive girl. Oh, how he longed to kiss her again. Susie's sing-song voice shook him out of his foolish reverie.

"*Ach*, you're just sayin' that, Jonathan Fisher," she challenged, wondering if it was really true.

"No, honest, it's been my favorite since the first time I noticed it. It always reminded me of *Mamm's* ladle – the one she always serves soup with. And you know I loved to eat!" He wriggled his eyebrows.

Susanna laughed, then again turned to gaze up at God's gorgeous handiwork.

"Susie, I hope ya don't mind, but I got ya a little somethin' for your birthday," he said timidly. He reached into his pocket and handed her a small package. "I wrapped it myself," he informed her proudly.

She looked at the delicately-wrapped package and removed the pink daisy on top. She sniffed it to see if it held any fragrance. "Where'd ya get the pretty flower?" she asked curiously.

"From my *mamm's* garden," he stated, hoping she liked it.

Uh, oh. "Did ya ask her first?"

"*Nee*. But I'm sure she wouldn't have minded," he reassured her. "She'd just be happy that I didn't get it from the cemetery."

Susie giggled. She pulled off the twine and slowly unfolded the tissue paper. She removed a fancy thin white handkerchief with lace edges. She noticed her first initial embroidered in pink onto one of the corners and she gently fingered it. "This is real nice, Jonathan. *Denki.*"

"I had Joanna put your initial on there. I hope ya like pink." He was glad that it was dark and Susie couldn't see that *he* was the one that was pink.

"Pink is my favorite color. How did ya know?"

He shrugged. "Just guessed. I just figured if I were a girl, what color I would like."

Susanna giggled again. "You're so funny sometimes, Jonathan."

"Well, I guess I better go now," he said as he started to leave.

"*Denki,* again, Jonathan. 'Tis real special," she said as she held up her handkerchief.

"Guten nacht," he called back.

Today has been a wonderful-gut *day!* Susanna and Jonathan unknowingly both agreed in thought.

CHAPTER 5
The Unexpected

"And the peace of God, which passeth all understanding, shall keep your hearts and minds through Christ Jesus." Philippians 4:7

Andrea Thompson sat at a large corner booth in the Dairy Queen surrounded by her mother and several friends. She was excited to be celebrating her thirteenth birthday. Katrina, her mother, brought out a cake and placed thirteen candles on top.

"Oh good, you made my favorite!" She smiled at her mother, eying the chocolate cake hungrily.

Katrina took out a match and lit the candles. The group started singing "Happy Birthday" and the other Dairy Queen customers turned to see the hullabaloo.

A couple of booths down, sat three young Amish couples, appearing to be having a good time. One of the young men looked at Andrea curiously as if he recognized her from somewhere. She tried not to stare, but somehow he kind of looked familiar to her as well. Did she know him from somewhere?

Joanna Fisher, Chloe Esh, and Danika King, along with Andrew Lapp, Levi Hostettler, and Eli Yoder, sat at a side booth in the Dairy Queen waiting for their banana splits to arrive. It wasn't every day that the couples triple dated, so this was a special treat. Chloe wondered why Levi had been staring at the corner booth until she turned around and looked for herself. Her eyes almost popped out of her head.

"That looks like Susie!" she stated in disbelief.

Levi just stared as though he were in shock.

"What's wrong, Levi?" Eli Yoder asked, taking the time to look away from his *aldi* to see what was going on.

"Today is Susanna's birthday," he stated calmly.

They all turned and looked at the girl in the booth to whom they sang "Happy Birthday" to. There was an amazing resemblance to Levi's sister – no, an exact replication. The girl glanced over and they all quickly turned around again.

"Susanna was a twin," Levi stated. "Do you think it's just a coincidence?" He glanced back at the girl who was surely Susie's twin.

"I don't know. What do you think we should do?" Danika King asked.

"I've got the car," Andrew Lapp said. "We could follow them and see where they go."

"Let's do it," Levi agreed eagerly.

The three Amish couples hurriedly finished up their desserts and scrambled to the car. They sat there discussing their plans for about ten minutes before the girl and her company had finally left the restaurant. A woman and the girl hopped into a white sports car and headed toward Lancaster. Andrew followed at a distance, not wanting to be noticed.

"How long should we follow them for?" Chloe asked, a little worried about the time.

"Just until we find out where they're going. It's late, so they're bound to go home," Levi stated confidently.

"Make sure you don't get too close," Eli warned Andrew. "It wouldn't be *gut* if they noticed someone was following them."

The white car took an exit off the highway and headed into a residential area. It stopped in front of a large apartment building and Andrew pulled behind a car on the side of the road about a block away. He quickly turned off the headlights.

"Can you see from here?" he asked Levi, who had the best view.

"*Jah.* I wish I had some binoculars, though," he stated, as he watched them enter the apartment complex.

"I think they're inside now. Let's sneak up and take a look at the car," Andrew suggested.

"You two go," Eli stated. "I'll stay here with the girls." He smiled at Danika as he took her hand in his.

Levi and Andrew quickly walked to where the white car was parked, trying not to look conspicuous. They peered into the windows, searching for some sort of clue. "Do you see it?" Levi asked Andrew.

"See what?" Andrew asked, peering into the window.

Just then, they heard the sound of a lock turning and then a door opened from one the apartments. They flew behind the bushes that bordered the large apartment building. Their hearts pounded as they crouched down until the woman closed her car door, set the alarm, and went back inside.

"Whew! That was close. Let's get out of here," Levi said. They took off toward their car as quickly as possible and left to head home.

"Levi, what did you see in that lady's car?" Andrew asked as he drove toward Paradise.

"It was a parking pass for the hospital. She must work there. That is where Susanna was born," Levi stated as everyone in the car wondered in amazement.

"What will you do now?" Chloe asked her beau.

"I'm still thinkin' on it. But I need you to promise you won't say anything to anybody about this," he warned, looking at them all.

"We wouldn't dream of telling anyone," Danika stated for the group. "Besides, we'd have to tell them we were out in an *Englischer* car if we did. *Dat* and *Mamm* would never approve."

The others agreed to silence, and they all went home wondering whether they'd be able to sleep tonight.

CHAPTER 6
The Revelation

"For there is nothing covered, that shall not be revealed..." Luke 12:2a

Annie Yoder hurried over to Susanna as she entered the school yard with her siblings. "Is it true?" she asked excitedly.

"Is what true?" Susie's confusion was apparent.

"Is Jonathan working for your *daed*?" Annie asked enviously. Boy, did she wish she was Susie.

"*Jah*, 'tis true," she stated, attempting to hide her feelings. She didn't even like to admit it to herself, but it was hard not to notice how her heart palpitated when Jonathan talked to her.

"You're so lucky." Annie's gaze floated heavenward, and a wistful sigh escaped her lips. "So, how did your birthday go?" Annie inquired.

"'Twas nice."

"Was Jonathan there?" her friend asked with wide eyes.

"*Jah.*" Susie smiled fondly, remembering their moment under the stars.

"Did he get ya somethin'?" Annie wondered.

"Did anybody ever tell you that you ask too many questions?" Susie asked, not wanting to disappoint her friend by giving her the answer to her question.

"*Jah, Dat* says it all the time. So, did he get ya anything?" She wasn't about to give up.

Susanna sighed and carefully pulled the handkerchief out of her apron pocket and showed her friend.

Annie gasped. "Oh Susie, you're so –"

"Lucky," she finished her sentiment. "I know." Annie caught the twinkle in her eye.

"Susie Hostettler, are you fallin' for Jonathan Fisher?" Annie asked with her eyes wide again.

"Shh...not so loud. Besides, we're just friends," Susie stated calmly.

"I wish I had a friend that would give me a special gift like that." Annie's voice returned to its wistful tone.

"I'll get you one for your birthday," Susie stated, teasing her friend.

"Oh Susanna, you know that's not what I mean."

Just then, the school bell rang and Jonathan walked past the girls, tipping his hat to Susanna. This time her heart fluttered for sure and for certain.

Levi wondered what he should do with his new-found information. He decided it would be best to confide in his father about the matter. After all, he didn't need to tell him the whole story – just the necessary details. He walked out to the field where his father presently worked.

"*Daed*," he started off slowly, "I'd like to talk to you about something."

"What is it, Son?" Judah stopped the team of mules and wiped the sweat from his brow.

"I don't really know how to say this..." He hesitated a moment, wringing his hands anxiously.

"You can share anything with me, Son." Judah attempted to offer Levi the confidence he needed to continue.

"I think I saw Susie's twin."

To that, Judah raised an eyebrow. "We buried Maryanna thirteen years ago. That's impossible."

"I know this sounds crazy, but I saw a girl at the Dairy Queen last night that looked exactly like our Susanna." Levi paused for a moment, then looked his dad in the eye. "She was celebrating her thirteenth birthday, *Daed*."

"But Susie's thirteenth birthday was yesterday," Judah stated in disbelief.

"The car had a parking pass for the hospital. The lady that was with her works at the hospital where Susanna was born, I'm sure of it."

"How could that be?" Judah scratched his beard, clearly confounded.

"I wouldn't believe it myself if I hadn't seen her with my own two eyes," Levi stated wryly.

Judah removed his hat, then placed it back on his head. "It's hard to know what to do in a situation like this. I'll have to pray about it. Let's not mention anything to anyone else just yet."

Judah was working in the field when he noticed a young man ride up on a horse. He made his way toward the barn and soon recognized the young man as Eli Yoder. "Good afternoon, Eli," the bishop offered a handshake. "What brings you out today?"

Eli took a deep breath, then slowly began. "I wish to marry Danika King this fall. We were both baptized last year," he reminded the bishop.

This was no surprise to Judah, for rumor had it that Eli and Danika had been sweet on each other for years now. Some things were difficult to keep secret. "Danika is only seventeen, still a bit young. Have you approached your folks on the subject?"

"*Jah*, the Kings were over for supper last Sunday and Philip and *Dat* both gave their blessing. And I know she's young, but we've already been waiting four years for this," he said twirling his hat between his hands.

"Do you have a date in mind?" the bishop asked, as if to be looking at a calendar in his brain.

"As soon as possible," Eli eagerly replied.

To this, the bishop chuckled. "I know the feeling. How does the first Tuesday in November sound?"

"Wonderful-*gut*!" Eli replied with a huge smile.

"I will ride out to Philip's house this evening to confirm the plans then," Judah said, then inquired about work. "How's business for you and Nathan at the buggy shop?"

"*Gut*. We've gotten two orders just this week," Eli said confidently.

"Greet my son for me next time you see him. We've both been a little busy lately and I haven't seen him since our last Sunday meeting," Judah requested.

"*Jah*. Okay, I'll be seein' him on Monday. I'll be sure to give Nathan your message." Eli turned to go then looked back with a lopsided grin. "*Denki*, Bishop!" he proclaimed.

CHAPTER 7

The Resemblance

"Ointment and perfume rejoice the heart: so doth the sweetness of a man's friend by hearty counsel." Proverbs 27:9

Katrina couldn't help fidgeting at work on Sunday. It had been a while since she'd ran into the Amish. *Why did that Amish boy keep looking at my Andrea?* She wondered about it all day.

"Is something wrong?" her friend Brandi asked. "You seem a little jumpy today."

"No, I'm fine," she stated flatly.

"Nervous about Andrea's game today?"

"Yes." That was a truthful answer, but not for the same reasons Brandi was thinking. *What if those Amish people show up at Andrea's game? She was in her uniform at the Dairy*

Queen. Now they know she plays softball. Katrina began to panic. *What am I going to do if we see them again?*

Matthew Riehl approached Susanna as she exited the schoolhouse on Monday. "Susie, would you mind if I walked you home today?" he asked sheepishly.

"*Jah*, I guess that would be fine," Susie agreed.

Matthew fell into step next to her and offered to carry her books.

They started toward her house with her younger siblings in tow. Susanna glanced over her shoulder and noticed Jonathan coming out of the schoolhouse. She caught his eye, but he quickly looked away. She didn't miss the way Jonathan's shoulders drooped at the sight of her and Matthew walking side by side. A pang of guilt shot through her heart when she saw his crestfallen countenance. She desired to turn around and go talk to him, but decided against it.

Later that day when Jonathan came to work for her father, he didn't seem the same. The usually cheerful Jonathan was gone. Even when she glanced his way as she hung up the clothes outside, he never even turned to see if she might be there. Normally, he was looking up from his work every now and again to get a glimpse of her. Nothing today.

Susanna wondered what she should do. She had been craving Matthew Riehl's attention for months and now he was finally taking notice of her. Isn't that what she had wanted all along? Now, she wasn't sure. Why did life have to be so confusing at times?

Judah Hostettler figured it was time to pay a visit to his good friend Gideon. *He* was the one in need of advice this time. Gideon had been hand-sanding a small table when Judah entered his woodworking shop.

Gideon glanced up. "Judah, how are you doing this fine morning?" Gideon seemed more cheerful than usual. "I hope my boy's not causing any trouble for you."

"On the contrary, Jonathan has been a huge blessing around the farm. Have you noticed a change in him at all?" Judah asked.

"*Jah.* I don't know what you're doin' with him, but I'm indebted to you. It seems as if he's grown up quite a bit in the last couple of weeks." Gideon thanked the bishop.

"That's *gut.* He's a good boy, your Jonathan."

"I'm guessing your visit has to do with something else?" Gideon inquired.

"You're correct in your assumption. You see, Levi thinks he's seen Susanna's twin," he stated.

"How can that be?" His friend seemed shocked.

Judah shook his head. "I don't know. He said that he was at the Dairy Queen yesterday and he saw a girl who looked identical to Susanna and she was celebrating her thirteenth birthday. Susanna's thirteenth birthday was yesterday. Levi also said that the car that they rode in had a parking pass, so it appears the woman that the girl was with works at the hospital. And that hospital happens to be the exact same one Susanna was born in."

"Does Lydia know yet?"

"*Nee*, I don't want to upset her. It was the most painful thing we've ever had to deal with – the loss of our daughter. If Susanna hadn't been there, I don't know how my wife would've survived."

"I understand, Judah." Gideon put a comforting hand on his shoulder, knowing that he wasn't just speaking for his wife, but for himself also.

"I'm just at a loss at what to do now."

Gideon whistled. "Well, I've never been put in a situation like this before. Looks like you've got quite a puzzle on your hands."

"*Jah*, indeed. What do you think I should do?" Judah queried his friend earnestly.

Gideon stroked his beard. Finally he told him, "The only thing I can think of for the time being is to pray. Then, maybe look into it. I mean, if it really is your daughter, then you need to have a lot of questions answered. And it will take wisdom getting' those answers."

Judah nodded. "*Jah*, I think I will do that. *Denki*, Gideon."

"*Ach,* it was nothing. Besides, I'm grateful to you for helping my Jonathan," he mentioned thankfully. "Judah, know that I'll be prayin' for ya too."

Judah was reminded of a verse. *Ointment and perfume rejoice the heart: so doth the sweetness of a man's friend by hearty counsel.* Judah gave his friend an appreciative smile and turned to go.

"Why do you suppose that Amish boy was staring at you the other night?" Brandi's daughter Angela asked Andrea.

"Did you notice that too?" Andrea thought maybe she was just imagining it.

"Do you know him from somewhere?" Angela inquired.

"Not that I know of, but somehow he seemed very familiar."

"You know what? Now that you mention it, he kind of looked like you. Like you could be related somehow." Angela said thoughtfully. "Do you have an Amish cousin or something?"

"Mom's never said anything about it. I guess I could ask her."

"How about your father? Was he Amish?"

"Definitely not."

CHAPTER 8

The Decision

"Wherefore be ye not unwise, but understanding what the will of the Lord is." Ephesians 5:17

"So, Danika, is it true that you and your *mamm* have celery planted?" Chloe teased. All Amish know that a large crop of celery was a tell-tale sign of an upcoming wedding.

Danika held up her finger to her lips to signal a secret.

"Leave her alone, Chloe," Joanna warned. "We've all known it was bound to happen sooner or later; Eli's liked her from the first time he laid eyes on her." She smiled.

"So what about you guys?" Danika asked Chloe. "It seems like you and Levi Hostettler have been courtin' for a while too."

"Well, as soon as *I* hear anything, you two will be the first to know." Chloe smiled. "But between you and me, it will probably be next year."

"What about you, Joanna?" Danika asked. "Are you and Andrew getting serious?"

"Well, we've only been courting for a couple of months so it's hard to tell," Joanna said. "Andrew's nice, it's just...I don't know."

"One thing's for sure, though. You need to think long and hard about having Sadie as a sister-in-law," Chloe blurted out, making all three girls snicker. Sadie was definitely a challenge to get along with. "She'll probably be crying at your wedding, Danika!" She laughed out loud.

"Well, who wouldn't be? I've got the cream of the crop," Danika teased.

Andrea opened the door to her mom's car and climbed in. "How was school today, honey?" her mother asked.

Andrea closed the door with a bang. "It was okay, I guess."

"Are you all right, Andrea?" Katrina's mouth puckered.

"I just have a lot on my mind. Mom, do I have an Amish cousin?"

Katrina stiffened, but then answered shortly, "No, we don't. Why would you ask something like that?"

"Did it seem to you like that young Amish man at the Dairy Queen was staring at me kind of funny?"

Her mom teased, "Maybe he thought you were pretty."

"Oh, Mom! Seriously." Andrea rolled her eyes. "Could you see me with an Amish guy? Not gonna happen."

"I did notice that too." Katrina shrugged. "Don't worry about it, Honey. The Amish have some strange customs." She brushed her daughter off.

That seemed to satisfy Andrea for now. *Whew! What am I going to do if we run into them again?* Katrina thought.

"Jonathan, are you all right?" Susie gently asked Jonathan at school.

He quickly glanced over at Matthew and frowned. "Yeah, I'm fine."

"Well, it's just that you don't seem to be acting normal lately," she stated flatly.

"What is normal, anyway?"

"You're usually different. You know, telling jokes, playing pranks on people –" She was about to add 'always smiling' before he interrupted her.

"It seems to me that some people don't like my 'normal' self." His disillusioned gaze briefly met hers, then he quickly headed into the schoolhouse early.

Susie's heart ached and her eyes misted. *What have I done to him?*

A week had passed by since Gideon and Judah last spoke of the matter of his daughter. Gideon Fisher walked out to the bishop as he stood on his plow. "Have you come to a decision yet, Judah?"

"*Jah*. Do you think you'd allow Jonathan to come to a ball game with me and Levi this week? I'd like to spend some more time with him. It seems he's been a little down lately."

"*Jah*, I've noticed that too. I guess I don't see any harm in that, as long as he's with you. What's your plan?"

"Well, Levi said the girl was wearing some kind of baseball uniform. There's a middle school in Lancaster that has the same emblem that was on her uniform. I'm going to call the school and inquire about their games."

"Good thinking, Judah. What will you do if you see her?" Gideon wondered.

"Well, first things first. I need to see her with my own eyes before I make any decisions. Then, I'll figure out my course of action after that."

"Let me know when you're going to go. I'll be prayin' for wisdom for ya," Gideon offered.

"*Denki*, I'm going to need it," Judah replied with a sigh.

CHAPTER 9
The Announcement

"...rejoice with the wife of thy youth."
Proverbs 5:18b

Judah Hostettler did not seem the same at the Sunday-Go-To-Meeting. When he got up to speak his mind seemed to be preoccupied with something else. He was clearly having trouble keeping his focus and uncharacteristically cut the message short. He almost forgot to make the announcements until he spotted Eli Yoder and remembered he was supposed to "publish" their wedding.

"Eli Yoder and Danika King will be uniting in holy matrimony on the first Tuesday in November at the Fisher residence," the bishop stated and all the people smiled.

Eli's smile couldn't have been bigger as he got up to go inform Danika that their wedding had been officially published. She had been awaiting the announcement at home, as was their custom. Now the planning would begin.

After Eli arrived, he and Danika celebrated the announcement with some coffee and hot apple pie. Afterward, Danika quickly sat down and penned a letter to her friend Cindy in California. Cindy called the herb shop the same day Danika's letter arrived offering her congratulations and confirming her attendance.

Katrina quickly attempted to shield her face as she saw the three Amish men approaching the bleachers where she sat. She quickly identified one of them as the young man at the Dairy Queen. *This can't be a coincidence. Oh no! What am I going to do?* The man with the beard seemed to be looking at the pitcher's mound where Andrea was. It was then that she noticed him – Andrea's father! Her heart beat rapidly as she tried to figure out what she would do. Thoughts of being thrown in prison for kidnapping crossed her mind. *We have to leave. Today!* She decided.

Andrea slowly walked to the pitcher's mound. Nervous and excited thoughts filled her mind. *If we win this last game, we get to go to the State Championships. The State Championships! We can make it to state!* Her team was out on the field. *Okay, calm down. It's another game, just another regular game. You can do this. Swing your arm back and pitch the ball.* She told herself. Andrea pitched the ball directly over the plate with amazing speed and strength. "Strike one!" the umpire called. *Good job, Andrea.* She encouraged herself, *Keep it up.*

Jonathan sat down on one of the benches. He looked out onto the field, scanning the players. He gasped as he looked at the girl who was pitching. His eyes grew in amazement. "Bishop, it's Susie! What's she doing here? You let her play baseball? I didn't know she could throw a ball like that. No wonder my face hurt when she slapped me."

Judah and Levi were taken aback and looked at Jonathan with questioning eyes.

"Don't worry, I deserved it," Jonathan quickly assured them, then diverted his attention to the game. "Hey, Susie, over here. It's me, Jonathan," he yelled, waving his arms.

The girl turned around and looked at Jonathan with a strange expression.

"Jonathan, please don't yell," Levi said, pulling him back down onto the bleachers. "People are looking at us. They'll think you've gone *ferhoodled.*"

But Jonathan didn't care, he was excited. "Did you see that? She acted like she didn't even know me," he exclaimed. "Did she get a new hair style or does it just look different because she's wearing that hat?"

"That isn't Susie," Judah leaned over and quietly informed Jonathan.

"What?" He looked closer. "Not Susie? Yes it is, she looks just like her."

Levi leaned over and whispered something in Jonathan's ear. Jonathan looked back at Levi in astonishment. "Really?"

He turned to Judah with inquisitive eyes. Judah nodded his head and that's when Jonathan noticed there were tears in his eyes. Realization finally dawned on him. This was Judah's daughter...and apparently Susie's twin sister!

Andrea tried to keep her attention on the game, but found it extremely difficult. The Amish boy from the Dairy Queen was in the stands watching her with two other Plain people. *Why are they here?* She wondered. She heard the younger Amish boy calling someone named Susie, but he was looking directly at her. *They must have mistaken me for someone else*, she thought. Mom was right, those Amish people have some strange customs.

After the game was over, Katrina scrambled through the crowd to get to Andrea. "Andrea, we need to leave quickly. Please hurry," her mother said, looking over her shoulder.

"But Mom, the coach wants to take us out for pizza to celebrate," she protested.

"Not today; we've got somewhere to go," her mother persisted.

"Okay, I'll tell the coach I won't be able to go," Andrea said disappointedly.

The Amish men headed toward their direction, and Katrina pulled Andrea's arm and started in the opposite direction as quickly as she could. "Get in the car," she said desperately.

"Mom, what's going on?" Andrea asked as she opened the car door to get in.

"I'll tell you when we get home," Katrina stated, as she placed the car in gear and took off in a hurry.

"Why were those Amish people following us? I don't understand." Andrea's voice wavered and she began to worry. "Are you in some sort of trouble, Mom?"

Katrina kept silent and didn't answer. Andrea couldn't figure out for the life of her what was going on.

As they entered the apartment, Katrina insisted, "We're leaving today. Go pack your things and don't ask questions," her mother advised.

Completely perplexed, Andrea stood with her mouth agape, staring at her mother. *What is going on?*

Discouraged couldn't even begin to describe how Judah felt. He didn't get to talk to the woman that was with Maryanna. He desperately needed some questions answered.

Apparently, so did Jonathan. "I hope you don't mind, Bishop, but may I ask you something?" He didn't wait for a reply. "You remember that girl playing baseball? How can she be Susie's twin? I don't get it...I mean...well, can you explain?"

Judah sighed. "Lydia was at the hospital when Susanna was born. She gave birth to what we thought were fraternal twin girls. There were some complications, so she wasn't able to see her babies. The twins were immediately whisked off to the hospital nursery. When I got to the nursery, we'd been told one of our daughters didn't make it. So we buried the baby, and asked the community not to tell anyone. It was kept a secret."

"Oh. I bet that was hard. Why did you keep it a secret?" Jonathan asked.

"We decided not to tell anyone because we didn't want any more heartache. No need to cause pain for little Susanna and the younger *kinner*. Thought it would be best if we just forgot about it and moved on." Judah sighed, remembering that the secrecy didn't ease his or Lydia's sorrow, and they certainly hadn't forgotten.

"But Susie's twin is alive; how is that possible?"

"I don't know, but that's our Maryanna for certain. And I'm almost positive that the lady she was with is the nurse that was on duty at the hospital when Susie was born," Judah stated.

"What do we do now?" Jonathan questioned.

"I don't know. But if we don't do something quick, we might never see Maryanna again." Desperation infused Judah's voice.

Levi bit his lip, wondering if he should chance getting into trouble. "*Dat*, I know where she lives," Levi admitted.

"How?" Judah raised his eyebrows.

"We followed her home," he replied sheepishly.

"You what?" Judah frowned at his son. "No matter. I guess *Gott* has had His hand in this."

"Well, what are we waiting for?" Jonathan asked. "Let's go!"

Judah shook his head muttering, "The things young people do in *Rumspringa*."

Katrina heard a knock at the door. She quickly peeked out the curtain and her heart sank. "It's the Amish guys."

Andrea picked up the phone. "Should I call the police?"

"No, no, no! I'll talk to them and see what they want."

"You sure, Mom?"

Katrina took a deep breath. "Yes, I'm sure."

"Okay, I'm coming with you." Andrea determined to protect her mother. "I'll get the bat." She left the room to retrieve her weapon.

Katrina slowly opened the door and in a voice as calm as she could muster asked, "May I help you with something?"

"I have some questions that I think you have the answers to," the bearded man replied softly.

Realizing there was no way out, Katrina sighed. "Please, come in."

The youngest one who appeared near Andrea's age eyed Andrea as she held the bat. He gulped and stammered, "I…I hope you're not planning on using that."

"Andrea, you may put the bat down now." Katrina permitted.

Andrea released her batting position, but held the bat close to her side, just in case.

The three Amish men entered the small apartment and looked around at the many pictures of Andrea that adorned the wall.

Andrea whispered, "Mom, why are these men here?"

"I think you're about to find out," Katrina whispered back.

The oldest man stared at Andrea for several seconds. "The resemblance is amazing," he finally spoke.

"I don't understand." Andrea frowned.

When they were seated on a small couch, the man spoke again. "Thirteen years ago, my wife gave birth to two daughters. Twins. We were told that one of them died. But now, I don't think that was the truth."

"Mom, what's going on? What's he talking about?" Andrea asked. She obviously had no clue as to what was unfolding before her eyes.

"Andrea, sweetheart, go to your room," Katrina wearily told her.

As she obediently turned to go, the bearded man said gently, "No. Let her stay. She deserves to know the truth."

Katrina nodded. Tears filled her eyes and she began to weep silently.

The bearded man spoke again. “It was you who told us that our other daughter died, and so we took home a dead baby thinking that she was our Maryanna. But our daughter wasn’t dead, was she? My other daughter is right here.” His hopeful gaze rested on Andrea.

Andrea gasped. “What? That’s crazy. You’re not my father. My dad took off before I was born. This is my mom. Mom, tell them.” Andrea worriedly looked at Katrina and saw that she was crying. “Mom?”

“I’m sorry, Andrea.” Katrina sobbed. “What he’s saying is true. I am not your real mother. I birthed a still-born daughter and I was told that I could never have any more children. Then I saw a woman who had birthed two healthy little girls. In sheer desperation I switched the babies. You are this man’s daughter.”

“You mean, I was born Amish?” she asked in disbelief. “This can’t be true.”

The youngest one spoke again. “Cool, huh?”

Andrea shot him a cold glare and held up her fist.

He shrank back and shook his head in disbelief. “You’re just like your twin sister, Susie.”

The room went completely silent for a moment.

Finally, Levi chimed in and held out his hand with a smile. “*Gut* to meet you, Sister. Welcome to the family. I’m your brother, Levi.”

"Hello, Levi." Andrea shook his hand timidly. Then she glanced at Jonathan and asked, "Is he my brother, too?"

Levi shook his head. "No."

A relieved sigh escaped Andrea's lips. "Whew!"

Katrina scolded, "Andrea, don't be rude."

"Exactly like her, for sure and for certain," Jonathan added.

To that, Andrea smiled.

"I think we should arrange for Maryanna to see her mother. She would love to meet you and so would your sister," Judah stated. "Would the two of you come and have a meal at our home with us?"

Katrina was taken aback at his kindness. "You're not going to call the police?"

Judah shook his head. "No, we're not. That is not our way. We don't include *Englischers* in our affairs unless it's absolutely necessary. So, will you come over? Maybe tomorrow around noon?"

Katrina looked at Andrea who nodded her head in affirmation. "I'd like to meet my twin, Mom."

"Then it's settled," Judah stated. He arose from the couch and handed Katrina a slip of paper. "Here is our address. We'll be going now." The three of them made their way to the door. Judah turned around one last time and met Andrea's eyes. "I am so glad you are alive, *Dochder*."

Neither Katrina nor Andrea missed the tears that clouded his eyes.

CHAPTER 10
The Discovery

"For ye are our glory and joy."
1 Thessalonians 2:20

When the men finally pulled into the Hostettlers' drive, it had already been dark for hours. Judah noticed that Gideon's buggy was parked near the hitching post. Lydia came out the back door, worry written all over her face.

Judah spoke up. "Sorry, *Liewe*. But you'll forgive me when I give you the good news." Judah looked at Gideon and gave a warm smile. "Let's go inside and I'll tell you all about it."

The group entered the house and Judah looked around. "Are the children awake?"

"I think Susanna and Joshua are probably still awake, but the young ones have been down for hours now," Lydia stated.

"I'll go get Susie and Josh," Levi offered and disappeared up the stairs.

"Sit down, Lydia. This news will come as a shock to you, I am certain." Judah waited until the older children descended the stairs and sat down at the kitchen table. The others were already seated, including Gideon and Jonathan.

Jonathan looked in Susie's direction and couldn't help but notice she was in her nightgown with her long auburn tresses cascading down her back and around her shoulders. She looked absolutely breathtaking as she descended the stairs and Jonathan felt his knees weaken. It was a good thing he was sitting down. She flashed him a smile and their eyes locked for far too long. He thought he had died and gone to Heaven.

"Well, I guess there's no use in dragging this out any longer. Our Maryanna is still alive." Judah smiled at his wife and daughter, waiting for their reaction.

"What?" Lydia was clearly confused.

"Maryanna, Susanna's twin sister, is alive." His eyes sparkled with excitement.

"How?" Lydia asked, her mind still trying to register the information.

"The *dot* baby that we brought home from the hospital was not ours. It belonged to a nurse that worked at the hospital. She switched our Maryanna with her deceased baby. Maryanna has lived in Lancaster all this time with the nurse."

"I can't believe my twin sister is still alive!" Susie said with a huge smile and looked at Jonathan.

Jonathan added, "She looks just like you, too."

"May God be praised! When can we see her?" Lydia asked as it dawned on her that this was not a dream, but indeed real.

"They're coming over for lunch tomorrow," Judah informed them.

"*Ach*, but there's so much to be done before tomorrow," Lydia protested.

"We'll think about that tomorrow. For now let's bow our heads and praise God for what He's done." After they gave thanks, Judah asked, "Gid, do you think you can spare Jonathan tomorrow morning? I need him to help me here on the farm."

"*Jah*." Gideon nodded. "I suppose 'twould be fine."

Susie sighed. Her mother was right; there was a lot to do around the house. Susie did the dishes while her mother did other chores around the house, and then she helped her mother with scrubbing the floor.

"Here, Susanna. Take these rugs outside and shake the dust out of them. Hurry, we don't have much time." Susie took the first rug outside and shook it out, dust swirled around her. She placed the clothes pins over the rug and fastened it to the clothes line and began to beat it with a broom.

Susanna glanced out into the yard and noticed Jonathan playing in the grass with her brothers. He crouched down on all fours and allowed the two youngest boys, Micah and Yonnie, to crawl up on his back. They held on to his suspenders as he trotted around on the grass as though he were a colt. He was so gentle with the little ones as he carefully rolled to the side to let them down. He then took them by the hand and played something akin to Ring-Around-The-Rosie. When he fell down he put on a big show which caused the two small boys to giggle loudly.

Susie watched in admiration, thinking, *he's going to make a good daddy someday*. Jonathan looked up and noticed that Susie was watching him and she waved his way. He gave her a genuine smile and she felt her cheeks redden. *Who would've thought that I'd fall for Jonathan Fisher!* She had to smile in spite of herself.

Wow! I can't believe I have a twin sister. Andrea thought to herself as she dressed to go meet her new family. She called out to Katrina, "What should I wear, Mom?"

Katrina was glad that she was still calling her 'Mom'. She knew Andrea was still upset with her for keeping the truth from her. "Something conservative would be my guess," she called to her daughter.

"Well, what are you going to wear?" Andrea inquired.

"My long floral dress. The black one that goes to my knees."

"Okay, I guess I can wear my skirt then." She sighed. "Sometimes choosing clothes can be such a pain."

"Are you nervous?" Katrina asked.

"Yes, I'm terrified. What if they don't like me?"

"You don't have to worry about that. They already *love* you," her mom reassured her.

"So, how many brothers and sisters do you think I have?"

"I don't know, but we'll find out really soon."

"Okay, Danika. Now that you and Eli are really getting married, we need to celebrate," Joanna suggested enthusiastically as the three girls sat on Danika's bed in her room.

"What do you mean?"

"Let's do something really fun, just the three of us girls. After you're married, we probably won't get to spend much time together. You'll be fussin' over your man," Joanna said.

Danika laughed. "Yeah, you're probably right."

"So let's do something fun," Chloe agreed.

"You mean like a Bachelorette party?" Danika asked, disbelief showing in her wide eyes.

"A what?" Joanna questioned.

"Never mind." Danika figured it would be better not to explain.

"Hey, I know what we can do!" Chloe smiled brightly. "Let's go horse racing one last time."

The three girls looked at each other in agreement. "Let's do it!" Danika squealed.

CHAPTER 11
The Accident

"In my distress I cried unto the Lord, and he heard me." Psalm 120:1

Not long after Jonathan had bidden Susie farewell, she heard a noise and stared toward the direction from whence it came. She spied a white sports car coming down the driveway. "They're here! *Mamm*, they're here," She excitedly called and raced toward the house to inform everyone. She then ran out to the driveway and waited for the vehicle to roll to a stop.

Slowly, a young girl emerged from the car. Susie was blown away when she saw a girl who indeed looked exactly like her, but *Englisch*. The girl stared at her in disbelief, then glanced back at her *Englisch* mother who smiled also. Her double slowly walked toward her. Then, at the same time, both girls ran toward each other and embraced as though they would never let go. No words were spoken. Finally, they stepped away from each other for a little bit, looking one another over.

"Welcome, Sister. I'm Susanna." Susie shyly smiled.

The other girl smiled at her. "Hi, Susanna. I'm Andrea. I can't believe it!"

Lydia chimed in, "Let me look at you, *Dochder.* How I've missed you so." Her eyes began to mist.

"Hello, Mom." Andrea smiled and gave Lydia a hug.

Lydia looked over at Katrina, beckoning her to join them. "Let's go inside. Susie and I just made some fresh sticky buns."

"We've never been on an Amish farm before," Katrina admitted. "This place is really nice." She glanced around when they entered the large dwelling. She had only ever lived in small apartments, so the over-sized farmhouse seemed like a mansion to her, even though it was sparsely furnished.

Andrea sat at the kitchen table when the rest of the children came in from outside with Judah. She looked at all of them in amazement, mentally counting each one.

"Maryanna," Judah insisted calling her by her Amish name. He started down the line from oldest to youngest. "These are your brothers and sisters. You've already met Levi, he's eighteen. Joshua is fifteen. Susanna is, of course, thirteen, like you. Paul is eleven. Elizabeth is seven. Ella is six. Micah is four. And little Yonnie is three."

"Wow. I've always wanted siblings." She smiled in astonishment. "I never expected to have this many."

"And let's not forget Nathan too," Lydia added. "He's your eldest brother. He's married and has four of his own *kinner*."

"So, I'm an aunt too?"

"That's right." Levi smiled at his newly-found sister.

The family sat around the table talking for hours after lunch as they all got to know each other a little better. Judah opened the Bible and shared some of his favorite passages with them, particularly verses on salvation and God's love for them.

"Do you have a church background?" he asked Katrina.

"No. I never really believed in God myself," she stated flatly. "And if there is a God, he doesn't care about me."

"You are wrong," he said gently. "God loves all people, including you. That's why he sent Jesus to die on the cross."

"What kind of God would let his own son die? It doesn't make sense," she challenged.

"A merciful God would. He knew that it was the *only* way to save his precious creation," Judah said.

"But there are lots of religions out there," Katrina reminded defiantly.

"That's true. But only one way to Heaven: Jesus Christ," he asserted.

"I don't understand. What's the difference?" she questioned.

"Jesus Christ is the only begotten son of God. He's the only one that lived a perfectly sinless life. He's the only one that triumphed victoriously over the grave. He's the only one that can redeem us. That is the difference."

Katrina sat there for a minute, allowing Judah's words to sink in. She then looked at him and asked, "Are you some sort of preacher or something?"

"My husband is the bishop," Lydia stated, looking at her husband with admiration.

"Would you and Maryanna like to join us for Meeting on Sunday?" Judah offered.

Katrina looked to Andrea for an answer and she smiled at her mother. "We would love to go!" Andrea stated for both of them.

"*Dat, Mamm,*" Danika beseeched her parents, "Joanna, Chloe, and I would like to spend the day together – just the three of us – before the wedding. Do you mind?" She asked in a pleading tone.

"I guess that would be okay. Just don't go gettin' into any trouble," Philip King answered kindly.

"We won't," Danika called back, as she ran out the door to the barn.

Danika quickly saddled Sunshine, her beautiful Palomino mare. This would probably be her last race, since she'd be getting married to Eli soon. Her carefree single days would be gone forever. Not that she minded, of course. She was marrying the man of her dreams – kind, fun-loving Eli Yoder – her best friend. She was one blessed girl. Danika and Sunshine galloped to their designated meeting place and waited for the others.

Chloe arrived next on Cayenne, the Eshes' auburn-colored Quarter horse. Chloe would most likely win the race since quarter horses were known for speed. Not that they only raced to win; feeling the wind rush past you was akin to flying, or so they had imagined. "Hi Chloe, where's Jo?"

"She was gettin' ready when I saw her last. She should be here really soon." Chloe smiled. She straightened in her saddle and turned when Joanna rode up on her white Arabian stallion, Blueberry, named after the color of his eyes. The horses whinnied to each other in greeting, causing the girls to laugh.

"I'm here. Let's race now?" Joanna said eagerly. "Now Danika, you know that we're not going to let you win just because it's your last time riding," she teased.

To that Danika smirked. "We'll see."

"Okay, here are the rules: we'll start at this line and race all the way to those two trees about an acre away. No bumping or trying to get someone off course." Chloe continued, "Okay, let's line up. Are you girls ready?" Danika and Joanna both answered affirmatively. "On your marks...get set...go!"

The animals sprang forward as the girls squeezed their legs and slapped the reins, urging their horses on. Chloe took the lead with the other girls close behind.

"Faster, Sunshine, faster," Danika urged, and her horse leaped forward with a burst of energy that surprised them all.

Danika grinned, she was in the lead. She held on to the reins tightly, and she leaned over the saddle the way she was taught. The hoof beats were so loud she couldn't hear herself breathing. Danika eyed a large rock on the path and she attempted to maneuver Sunshine around it. The horse stumbled over the object and Danika was instantly thrown from the saddle and landed about fifteen feet away.

"Danika!" Chloe screamed, desperately yanking her reins and jumping off her horse as it slowed. "Joanna, go get help." She rushed to Danika who was lying on the ground, unconscious.

Joanna quickly turned her horse around and dug her heels into Blueberry's side. "Go, Blueberry, faster," she yelled, galloping at full speed through the meadow, her heart pounding loudly. She raced Blueberry down the lane and up to the herb shop and ran inside. "Philip, there's been an accident," she caught her breath and rushed on, "in the meadow. It's Danika. Is Eli here?"

Philip listened intently. "No, he's at his folks' place today. I need to use your horse." She obediently gave him the reins. Philip swung into the saddle. "Joanna, go get Eli and the bishop." He took off as quickly as possible, herb bag in hand.

Joanna notified Naomi, then ran as quickly as she could to her brother's house that sat just across the street. "Isaac, I need to borrow Midnight! There's been an accident...it's Danika. I'm on my way to get Bishop and Eli."

"You go get the bishop. I'll ride out to Eli's *daed's* house," he suggested.

Joanna saddled Midnight and took off one way, while Isaac drove his buggy in the other direction. Joanna rode as fast as she could with thoughts flying through her mind about Danika and Eli's future. "Please, Lord! Let Danika be okay. Eli would be lost without her." She desperately pleaded, "I don't want to lose my *gut* friend."

"Danika, can you hear me?" Chloe gently nudged her friend's shoulder. "Danika?" She felt for a pulse and was relieved when she felt a faint twitching under her skin. But Danika didn't move. She just lay there still and lifeless.

"Eli, you need to come with me right now!" Isaac demanded, his face fraught with emotion.

"What wrong? What's going on?" Eli asked, searching his eyes. "Is it Danika?"

Isaac nodded with tears in his eyes, unable to speak.

"Dear God, please. No!" Eli looked to the heavens, pleading for mercy. "Please don't take my girl...my wife." He could scarcely breathe as though the wind had been knocked out of him.

"*Kumm,* make haste." Isaac patted the seat next to him and Eli hopped in the buggy.

The bishop quickly made his way to the house when he noticed Joanna Fisher ride up on a horse – a sure sign that something was not right. "*Was iss letz?*" Judah asked what was wrong.

"Danika King has been injured. She was thrown from a horse. She's lying in the meadow," she said, out of breath.

The entire Hostettler family had come out when they heard the commotion, including Susanna and her twin sister. Katrina quickly spoke up, "Where is she? I'm a nurse. I might be able to help. I'll call 9-1-1, they can get her to the hospital faster than I can. Besides, if she was thrown from a horse she probably shouldn't be moved. There could be injuries to her head and neck, or her back. Get into my car and I'll drive you to her, it'll be faster," she urged the bishop.

Judah looked at Joanna. "Where was she riding?"

"Over by the meadow."

"That's not too far off the road. Let's go," he said and got into Katrina's vehicle.

Philip had already administered some herbs before the others arrived. The cayenne tincture made Danika come to, awaking her from unconsciousness. Chloe sighed with relief. "Is she going to be all right?"

"Well, she's alive. We won't know the extent of her injuries until she receives an x-ray," Philip stated glumly.

Eli and Isaac drove up and Eli ran to Danika. "Is she okay?" he asked.

Philip answered, "Like I told Chloe, we won't know the extent of her injuries until we get her to the hospital. But we can thank *Gott* that she's alive."

Eli knelt over his beloved, and gently took her hand.

Danika's eyes met Eli's. "Where am I?"

Eli answered, "You were thrown from your horse, *Mein Liewe*. The ambulance is coming now to take you to the hospital. Can you hear the sirens?"

"*Jah*. I hear."

He looked into her eyes. "You're going to be okay, Danika. God has spared you. I won't leave you, I promise."

The others arrived at the scene just before the ambulance. Eli and Philip rode along in the ambulance with Danika. Katrina took the bishop and the girls to the hospital, and Isaac notified the community about what had happened. Rachel, Isaac's wife, offered to watch Philip and Naomi's children so she could visit Danika.

Philip and Eli had to stay in the waiting room until the physicians finished their examination and x-rays. Eli paced back and forth, half worrying and half praying. Danika was still in the x-ray room when the others arrived. Naomi ran to Philip and they embraced for a moment, "Have you heard anything yet?"

"No. Nothing. She's having a CT scan now," Philip said placidly.

"When will they have the results?" she asked.

"We don't know yet, but I have a feeling the doctor will give us a fairly quick response."

"How did she look to you?" Naomi searched her husband's eyes.

"She seemed worried. The wedding isn't that far off," he reminded her, and then added, "It's hard to tell without an x-ray, but I was able to administer some nervine herbs to feed her nervous system. If there's any damage to her body, it would probably stem from her central nervous system."

Alarm showed on Naomi's features. "Did she complain of any paralysis?"

"No, but I think she was still in a bit of shock."

Katrina came into the waiting room after inquiring about Danika's condition. "They've got her settled into a room now if you'd like to see her. She's in room 301."

As soon as Eli heard that, he flew down the hallway to Danika's room. He opened the door and rushed to her side. He took her hand in his. "How do you feel, Love?" His eyes queried hers intently.

She gave him a reassuring smile. “Eli, please don’t look so worried. You’re breaking my heart.”

“*Ach*, but I can’t help it. I don’t know what I would have done if I would have lost you today,” his voice wavered and tears began to form in his eyes.

“I love you, Eli Yoder.” She looked deeply into his eyes and spoke directly to his soul. “But remember, our hope lies in Christ. Please don’t place me above Him. Whether you would’ve lost me or not, God would have carried you through. You must be strong and trust His will.”

“You are a remarkable woman, Danika King.”

Eli heard steps behind him.

“Yes, she is.” It was Philip’s voice. “And the doctor said she should make a full recovery. The wedding will continue as planned.” He beamed.

Eli could hardly contain his excitement. He leaned over Danika as if to kiss her on the lips, then was interrupted by Philip loudly clearing his throat. “Let’s save that for November six,” he advised, quickly reminding Eli of their purity covenant.

“Uh..yeah. I guess I got a little carried away there. Sorry, Dani.” Eli’s cheeks blazed.

Danika couldn’t help but laugh, which quickly turned into a groan when she suddenly felt all her bruises at once. “I guess it might take a little time to recover.”

CHAPTER 12
Sisters

"For the same cause also do ye joy, and rejoice with me." Philippians 2:18

"I hope that girl is okay," Andrea said to Susanna as they sat high in the haymow.

"Danika is her name. *Dat* just published her and Eli's wedding," Susie stated.

"Published?"

"*Jah*, that's when the Amish community finds out about the wedding. It was announced at the Sunday-Go-To-Meeting."

"Is that church?"

"*Jah*." Susie thought aloud. "I wonder if they'll still be able to have their wedding in November. I hope so. Eli works with my brother, Nathan."

"You mean *our* brother Nathan," Andrea reminded her with a smile. "It's so strange to me having a houseful of brothers and sisters all of a sudden."

"*Jah*, I can imagine. And a twin sister too," Susie said. "Did you know that I just recently found out that *I* was a twin?"

"Really? Your parents never told you before?"

"You mean *our* parents," Susanna reminded Andrea this time. "And no. They didn't want me to be sad about it, I guess, because they thought my twin had died."

"And low and behold, here I am."

"Would you like me to call you Andrea or Maryanna?" Susie wondered.

"Well, I'm definitely more used to being called Andrea. But since I'm supposed to be Amish, you may call me Maryanna. At least when I'm here."

"Okay, Maryanna." Susanna smiled. "Did you ever feel that there was a part of you missing before? I mean, even though I didn't know I had a twin, I've always felt that something was missing in my life. It's hard to describe."

"Now that you mention it, I did feel that I was missing something. But I always attributed that to not having a father," Maryanna stated. "You know, it's kind of exciting having two families now. I actually have a father, and he seems like he's really nice too."

"*Dat* is a *gut* man, for sure and for certain," Susie said. "So what is your *Englisch* life like?"

"My *Englisch* life?"

"*Jah,* non-Amish."

"Well, when I first saw our Dad, I was playing softball. I'm the pitcher for our team. We're going to the State Championships!" she said enthusiastically.

"What does that mean?" Susie asked innocently.

"That means that our team has done really well. We've beat most of the schools in our area and now we have to compete against the best teams in the state. The team that does the best becomes the State Champions."

"Wow. I could see how that could make one prideful," Susie stated quietly.

"Yeah, we're real proud. We might just come out as the best," Maryanna stated with a huge smile.

"*Dat* says pride's not *gut.* 'Tis what made the devil fall. Pride goeth before destruction."

"Well, then I guess I'll have to try not to become too prideful."

"*Gut.*"

"So, what about you? I don't know hardly anything about the Amish," Maryanna asked.

"What do you want to know?"

"Everything." She smiled.

"That could take a while." Susie laughed, then began to explain, "Okay, the Amish are known for their plain and simple lifestyle. We dress Amish, we drive Amish, we have Amish schools, we marry Amish, and we have a very close-knit community. We help our Amish brothers and sisters anytime it's needed. For example, *Mamm* is probably makin' a meal right now to take to the Kings. Since they are at the hospital, Naomi won't have time to cook."

"That sounds nice. I don't know if I'd be able to give up my clothes though."

"The Plain lifestyle is not for everybody, for sure and for certain. There have been some *Englischers* that have tried to become Amish, but they usually leave because they're not used to our way of life," Susanna informed her twin. "Danika was once an *Englischer.*"

"The girl in the accident?" Maryanna asked and Susie nodded a yes. "Why did she become Amish?" she wondered.

"Her folks died and she had to come and live with her aunt and uncle. They adopted her as their daughter. Now she's marrying Amish." Susie smiled, thinking of her future with Jonathan.

Maryanna noticed the dreamy look on her face. "What are you thinking about?"

"A boy." She smiled. "Jonathan Fisher."

"Is that the boy that was with your, I mean, *our* dad and brother?" Her eyes grew wide.

"*Jah,* that's Jonathan all right." She grinned.

"Wow, he was so annoying," she blabbed, then quickly added, "but I guess he's sort of cute."

"Trust me, I know exactly what you mean!" Susie smiled. "But since I've gotten to know him better...well." She reached into her apron pocket and pulled out the handkerchief that

Jonathan had given to her. "He gave me this for my birthday." She blushed.

"Oh, that's so sweet," Maryanna agreed.

"*Jah*. He can be real sweet."

"Susanna, Maryanna, supper's ready," Lizzie called from outside the barn.

The girls quickly climbed down the ladder and headed into the house.

"Joanna's home now," Jonathan called to his folks from the top of the stairs. From the balcony, he had seen his sister being dropped off by Maryanna's *Englischer* mother. He walked down the stairs to find out the latest news.

"Danika will get to go home next week," his sister informed the family. "The doctor said she shouldn't have any permanent damage."

"That's wonderful-*gut* news." Esther smiled. "Now I hope this has taught you girls a lesson about racing horses. I was always afraid something like this would happen," she chided.

"Oh Esther, the girls were just havin' fun. You can't fault them for that. Besides, we can't protect them from everything. Seems to me we ought to be trustin' the Good Lord a little more," Gideon suggested.

"I guess you're right. I just couldn't imagine how I'd feel if it was our Joanna in that hospital instead of Danika." She shook her head. "What poor Naomi must be going through."

"Well, we just need to be thankin' *Gott* that she's okay," Gideon reminded. He then looked at Jonathan and noticed his mind was elsewhere. "Did you have something to say Jonathan?"

Jonathan spoke up, "*Dat,* may I speak with you outside? Man to man."

To that, the girls giggled.

Gideon's disapproving look caused their smiles to quickly fade. "*Jah*, Son. Let's go." The two men headed outside and sat on the back porch swing. "What is it you would like to discuss, Jonathan?"

"Well, how old were you when you knew you wanted to marry *Mamm*?" he asked seriously.

Gideon tried not to smile. "Seems like I was about your age, I suppose. Maybe a year or two older."

Jonathan nodded his head. "So, when I get hitched, will this place be mine?"

Gideon chuckled. "Well, I guess if you're willin' to take care of your *Mamm* and me."

"I think I'd like to do that," Jonathan stated. "How soon can I get married?"

Gideon practically choked on the sip of water he'd taken. Jonathan was dead serious, which brought him concern. "Well, you may get baptized and join the church when you're sixteen if you'd like. But marriage and caring for a family is a big responsibility. You need to think long and hard about it before you make any decisions. It is something you'll have to live with for the rest of your life. It deserves some considering."

"Thanks, *Dat,*" Jonathan simply stated, then stood up to go back inside.

Gideon spoke up, "Are you thinkin' on Susanna Hostettler?"

"*Jah,* I am."

"I think she'd be a good choice, Son," Gideon said approvingly with a smile.

This time Jonathan went inside and Gideon sat alone on the porch for a moment. *These* kinner *just grow up way too fast.* He shook his head in wonderment.

"Well, I guess we'll be seeing you tomorrow for church then," Katrina said as she and Andrea prepared to leave.

"We have an empty *dawdi haus* that you're welcome to stay in if you'd like," Judah offered. "I'd hate for you to have to travel all the way back into Lancaster tonight."

"Yes, it's all ready if you and Maryanna would like to stay the night," Lydia agreed. "There's a bath in there that you're welcome to use. And you may join us for breakfast in the morning."

"Well," Katrina looked at Andrea, who wore a big smile, "I guess it would be a lot better than going back home tonight. I am pretty tired."

Lydia showed them to the small dwelling next door that had remained empty since her parents had passed on. They'd been overwhelmed at the Hostettlers' hospitality. After Lydia had returned to the main house, Katrina turned to her daughter and smiled. "You know, I really like your new Amish family."

"Yeah, me too." Andrea smiled before putting out the light.

CHAPTER 13
Amish Life

"...my heart shall rejoice in thy salvation."
Psalm 13:5b

"Eli, you may go home now," Philip told Eli as he came into Danika's hospital room.

"No. I'm staying here as long as Danika stays," he said adamantly. "I'm not leaving her."

"But you need to go home and get some rest. What about work on Monday?" Philip asked.

"I will call Nathan about work, he won't mind if I take a few days off. If I went home I wouldn't be able to rest anyway. Besides, I told Danika that I wouldn't leave her and I meant it," Eli reminded Philip.

"Okay, Son, if you insist. You just make sure to let her get some rest," Philip advised.

"Philip, next time you come, would you mind bringing my Bible? I'd like to read some passages with Danika while she's here, especially since we won't be at the Sunday-Go-To-Meeting tomorrow."

"*Jah,* you'll have one by tomorrow," he promised. "Get some rest now. Naomi and I are going home for the night. The children are still with Rachel and I'm sure she's probably ready for sleep herself."

"*Denki,* Philip. *Guten nacht.*"

Knock, knock, knock.

"What's that noise, Mom?" Andrea asked sleepily, as she rolled over underneath the over-sized quilt.

Katrina pushed the top button on her cell phone to light up the time. "It's 5:45. My guess is that your Amish family eats breakfast early. I'll get the door," she said as she rolled out of bed. She stumbled in the darkness to find the light switch. "Oh yeah, no electricity," she mumbled to herself. Another knock. "Coming," she hollered. She used the light on her cell phone to find her way to the door.

"*Guten mariye*!" Susanna said cheerfully with bright eyes. She looked around and noticed there were no lights on, then saw Katrina holding up her cell phone. "Oh, the lamps are in the kitchen. I'll light one for you." She rushed in out of the cold and made her way to the small kitchen. She set the lamp on the table and struck a match, carefully lighting the wick in the lantern. The soft glow of the lamp quickly lit up the dark room. "'Tis much warmer in the house. Breakfast should be on the table in a few minutes. Better get up, Sister. I'll see ya in a bit," Susie said, then left for the main house.

"How do these Amish people do this? She looks like she's been up for hours," Katrina commented, then heard a snore come from beneath Andrea's covers. She walked over to her bed, holding up the lantern, and shook Andrea's shoulder. "Come on, Andrea, you've got to get up now. Your Amish family is waiting for us."

Andrea finally opened her eyes. "Okay, I'm up." She slowly lifted herself out of bed, then swung her bare feet onto the floor. "Ah, it's ice cold in here," she complained as shivers ran through her body.

"Your sister said it was warm in the big house, so hurry up and get dressed and we'll go over there. Breakfast is probably ready and waiting."

When Katrina and Andrea entered the house, it was indeed warmer than the *dawdi haus*. The family sat at the long kitchen table waiting patiently for them to take their seats. Andrea and Katrina glanced at each other, feeling somewhat guilty for their tardiness.

"Sorry," Katrina said, as they sat down at the table.

Judah bowed his head to say the silent prayer. Andrea and Katrina quickly caught on and bowed their heads along with the rest of the family. After Judah cleared his throat, the feast of coffee, juice, eggs, bacon, ham, pancakes, potatoes, and sticky buns were offered to their guests and passed around the table.

"The Sunday-Go-To-Meetings are usually pretty long for *Englischers*," Susanna warned her sister as they pulled up to the Yoders' homestead. "I'll sit in the back with you and your *Englisch mamm*. I will try to translate for you."

"Translate?" Maryanna queried her twin.

"*Jah*. The service is in German. Sometimes though, when *Englischers* are present, *Dat* will talk in *Englisch*," Susie explained.

"So, is this where you always have church?"

"No, every other Sunday it is at a different house. This is where Annie lives – she's my best friend and Eli's sister. Eli's the one that's gettin' married to Danika," Susie informed her. They made their way into the house and sat down on one of the benches near the back.

Maryanna attempted to take it all in. "So, you don't have a church building?"

"*Nee.* God's church is the people, not the building. The building is not important, it's just a place to meet," Susie said quietly as the *Vorsinger* began the first hymn.

"Wow, I wasn't sure I was going to make it through that service," Maryanna told Susanna.

"*Jah,* did you see *Grossdawdi* Hostettler? He fell asleep," Susie said with a smile.

"Was that the older man sitting by our brother Nathan?"

"*Jah.*"

"Susie, I wanted to ask you something about what Dad was saying in church," Maryanna said.

"Let's go sit under the oak tree and talk," Susie suggested, and she led the way out to the tree.

"About what Dad was saying the other night and again in church today; is that true?" Maryanna asked. "I mean the part that you have to know Jesus to get to Heaven. And that good people can still go to Hell."

"*Jah.* 'Tis true. God wrote it in the Bible. Every word in the Bible is true," Susie confirmed.

"But how can it be? How can good people go to Hell?" Maryanna baffled. "It seems unfair."

"It's like this. God is perfect and Heaven is perfect. There cannot be sin in Heaven or it wouldn't be Heaven."

"Okay, I understand that."

"A 'good' person by our standards still has sin by God's standards. Do you think that there's anybody that has ever lived that has not told a lie?"

"Probably not."

"Okay, then that would mean that every person that has ever lived is a liar. They all have sinned, which is what the Bible says. That is why 'good' people do not go to Heaven. They are not good in God's eyes; they are sinners."

"But isn't that wrong?"

"No, it's not. God sent Jesus to die for every person that has lived and will ever live. He has already paid for their sins, but they won't receive forgiveness unless they ask. Every person is without excuse because their debt has already been paid. All a person has to do is believe in Jesus to save them, then they will receive God's free gift of eternal life. 'Good' people don't go to Heaven, only saved people do."

"I want to go to Heaven," Maryanna stated.

"Then tell God. Ask Him to save you. He promises that He will," Susie said.

"Right now?"

"*Jah,* just pray and tell God what's in your heart. There are no special words to say."

"Okay." She bowed her head silently for a moment, then looked up at Susanna and smiled. "I'm going to Heaven now."

Susie gave her a big hug. "Now we're sisters twice!"

"What do you mean?"

"Well, we have the same Earthly father and the same Heavenly Father."

"Yeah, you're right." Maryanna smiled, peacefulness flooded her heart.

CHAPTER 14
The Wedding

"And the LORD God said, It is not good that man should be alone; I will make him an help meet for him." Genesis 2:18

A few days after Danika was released from the hospital, Eli traveled all around Lancaster and other nearby counties to invite their friends and relatives for the big day. As the day dawned closer, Danika and Naomi, along with Joanna, Chloe, Esther Fisher, Mary Esh, and Sarah Yoder all spent many hours cleaning the King home for the wedding supper. Eli and Jacob, his father, helped Philip *redd* up the outside of the King farm, trimming trees and bushes and cleaning up the barn. Not many days hence, the house would be teaming with Amish folk, all there to celebrate their happy occasion.

"I'm so glad your *Englisch mamm* lets you come and visit often," Susanna told Maryanna.

"Well, I guess she feels kind of bad because I missed out on so much. I love my new Amish family, especially my twin sister." She smiled.

"I bet it's a lot different than the *Englisch* world, *jah*?" Susie asked.

"Yes, in many ways. But not so different in other ways. I mean people are pretty much the same for the most part. Even Jonathan Fisher said *we* were a lot alike."

"I guess we are." Susie thought for a moment. "Hey, I wonder what you would look like in Amish clothes."

Maryanna squealed excitedly. "Oh, I would love to try on your clothes. That would be so much fun."

"Do you think we'd be able to fool anybody?" Susanna asked.

"They'd probably be able to tell the difference in the way we talk, *jah*?" Maryanna joked.

Susanna took a matching dress off of a peg on the wall. "Here, wear this purple one and the black apron like mine."

Maryanna quickly changed into the dress, then Susanna pinned up her hair in a bun, placing a prayer *kapp* over her hair. The girls both looked into the small mirror that sat on Susie's dresser. "Oh wow!" Maryanna said, "It's hard for *me* to tell us apart."

"This is going to be fun." Susanna smiled. "Let's go downstairs and show *Mamm*."

The girls hurried downstairs excitedly and Maryanna slowly came into the kitchen, while Susie waited in the living room.

"Susie, will you dry these dishes?" Lydia asked Maryanna.

"Sure, *Mamm*," she replied in her best Pennsylvania Dutch accent. She grabbed a towel and began drying a tea cup.

Susie then walked into the kitchen. "Hi, *Mamm*."

Lydia did a double take, then started laughing. "You girls sure had me fooled. Susie, will you help your sister *Maryanna* do the dishes?" *Mamm* said, then gave both girls a quick hug.

Jonathan was in a hurry to get to the Hostettlers' farm as usual. As he went into the barn, he spotted Susie petting a mouse catcher. When she heard him come in, she stood up and turned around to face him. Jonathan rushed over to her with a big smile and reached for her hand.

"Susie, do you want to go to Miller's Pond with me after I finish working for your *daed* today?" he asked earnestly.

"But I –" Maryanna tried hard not to laugh as Jonathan grasped her hand.

"Please don't say no, Susie. Just think about it," he quickly added interrupting her.

"But I –"

Jonathan interjected again, "I know Matthew likes you too, but –"

"Jonathan Fisher, what are you doing?" Susie came into the barn and interrupted this time. She looked at Jonathan while he held Maryanna's hand and gasped, sending him a disapproving glare.

Jonathan looked at Susie, then he looked back at Maryanna. Then he looked at them both again, completely dumfounded. Suddenly, he dropped Maryanna's hand and his cheeks blushed furiously. Both of the girls couldn't help laughing, and Jonathan turned around and walked out of the barn shaking his head. He had never been so embarrassed in his life.

"Finally." Susie laughed. "Jonathan Fisher is getting a taste of his own medicine."

Danika's friend Cindy had arrived by taxi a couple of days prior to the wedding. It was a lot of fun catching up on all of the things that had happened in their lives since they last spoke. Cindy had informed Danika that she had gotten saved while attending her parents' church. Not only that, but there was a nice young man that had his sights set on her. Danika was amazed when Cindy told her that her fiancé had every intention of becoming a preacher. Imagine that, Cindy becoming a preacher's wife! Who would have thought? But God was in the business of miracles, this Danika knew first hand.

This was the day Danika had dreamed about since she first fell for Eli Yoder. The young couple rose up early in the morning, before the break of dawn, along with their wedding attendants: Chloe, Levi, Joanna, and Andrew. They dressed in their wedding attire and headed over to the Fisher residence where the ceremony was to be held at nine o'clock.

The previous day had been filled with a flurry of activity as many couples came to prepare the wedding feast. The celery had been cleaned for the creamed celery dish always prevalent in Amish weddings, potatoes had been washed and peeled, and Eli, the bridegroom, had decapitated the fowls for the delicious meal as per their custom. Make-shift tables had been made and the house had even received a fresh coat of paint, including the *dawdi haus* where Eli and Danika would be spending their wedding night. Everything was set and ready to go.

Danika and Eli, along with their attendants, took their seats up front and waited for the guests to begin arriving. When the guests had arrived and the singing started, Eli and Danika followed Bishop Hostettler and the other ministers to an upstairs room where they had given them counsel on the duties of a husband and wife in a marriage relationship according to the Word of God. The couple returned holding hands and took their seats up front with their attendants.

After the long sermon highlighting Biblical examples of Godly marriages, the bishop pronounced a blessing over the couple, recited marriage vows, then pronounced them man and wife. Eli and Danika, along with their attending couples, headed to the Kings' residence for the marriage feast.

The bridal party took their seats at the Eck, a small corner table in the living room, which was filled with several beautifully decorated cakes and lots of candies. Many young guests were paired up at the tables surrounding them, and Susie and Jonathan sat across from each other. After the bishop said the blessing over the food, the guests enjoyed the elaborate wedding feast. When all of the guests had returned home after the long, fun-filled day, Danika and Eli retired to their wedding suite where they shared their first kiss.

CHAPTER 15
The Choice

"In all thy ways acknowledge him and he shall direct thy paths." Proverbs 3:6

"Wasn't Eli and Danika's wedding so romantic?" Annie asked Susanna at school.

"*Jah*, your brother looked really happy. So did his wife." Susie smiled.

"They're so lucky. I hope I can find someone that special someday," Annie said dreamily.

"Oh, you will. Just wait and *Gott* will bring along the right one," Susie said with confidence.

"You mean like you and Jonathan?" Annie winked at her friend.

"Annie, I'm only thirteen. I don't know what or who God has planned for me yet. Maybe it's Jonathan and maybe it's not. We'll just have to wait and see," Susie said, but she hoped the former were true.

"*Jah*, I guess you're right." Annie thought for a moment, then changed the subject. "What do you think of your new sister?"

"I love her, she's great." Susanna smiled.

"Well, is she going to come and live here with your family? I mean, you are her *real* family."

"I don't know. We haven't discussed that yet," Susie replied, pondering the thought.

As school let out, Susie grabbed her lunch box and started outside. Matthew Riehl approached her on the steps and asked if he could walk her home. "Sorry, Matthew, but I'm walking home with Jonathan today. But I'm sure Annie would like to go with you," Susanna replied, looking back to the schoolhouse where her friend was.

"Okay, maybe next time," Matthew said, feeling slightly rejected, then apparently went back into the schoolhouse to seek Annie.

Jonathan had overheard the conversation and told Susie, "I hope you're not expecting me to walk you home today, I already told Annie Yoder that I'd walk her home," he teased, but he kept his expression sober.

Susie's heart sank. *Jonathan and Annie? Was I wrong about Jonathan and me?* Susie started home alone, wondering how she'd been mistaken about Jonathan's feelings toward her.

Jonathan realized that she didn't catch his joke. "Susanna." He followed after her, then matched her stride. "I was just joshing."

She looked at him in all seriousness. "Jonathan Fisher, that isn't funny."

"But Susie, you know you're the only girl for me. I already talked to *Dat* and he said that I would get the farm when we're hitched," Jonathan jabbered on.

Susanna stopped and looked him in the eye, squinting from the sun. "Jonathan Fisher, you are *ferhoodled*."

"Maybe so, but I'm *ferhoodled* over you." He smiled confidently.

"Are you sure you're *ferhoodled* over me and not my sister?" she teased.

Jonathan stopped in his tracks and looked at her, remembering the embarrassing moment in the barn. "Susanna Hostettler, that's not funny."

"I've been thinking about the situation, Lydia." Katrina confided in her daughter's Amish mother.

"*Jah*?"

"Well, I want to do the right thing by Andrea and your family," she stated.

"Let's talk to Judah about it. He's coming in right now." Lydia could hear Judah's footsteps on the back stoop.

"Good afternoon, ladies," Judah said as he entered the Hostettler home.

"Judah, Katrina would like to discuss something with the two of us," Lydia informed her husband.

"Well, I've been thinking about Andrea, I mean, Maryanna. I want to do the right thing about the situation. But I'm not sure what the right thing is to do," Katrina stated.

Judah perceived that the situation perplexed the woman. "What are you thinking?"

"She is rightfully your daughter," she stated with tears in her eyes.

"Yes, that is true. But she has lived with you her whole life. A drastic change could have a damaging effect on her, especially at this age," Judah advised.

"Why don't we discuss this with Maryanna and allow her to make the decision?" Lydia suggested.

Katrina and Lydia looked to Judah, who appeared to be contemplating the situation. Judah spoke up, "Let us pray and seek the Lord on this matter. He knows what is best." The women agreed, and they all bowed their heads in silent prayer.

The girls came bounding through the back door in laughter, not realizing the solemn meeting that had been taking place inside. "Girls, come sit down. There is something we'd like to discuss," Judah stated.

The girls took their seats and waited for him to continue.

"We've been praying about a certain matter. Katrina here wants what's best for our Maryanna." He paused looking at his *Englisch* daughter. "We've chosen to let you decide, Maryanna, whether you'd like to become Amish or no."

Maryanna sat quiet for a moment and looked at them all. "I love you all. But, I couldn't leave Mom by herself, she'd be too lonely. Besides, I'm not ready to decide whether I'd like to become Amish or not, it's all so new to me."

"That is quite all right, *Dochder*. You don't have to decide now. Just pray about it," Judah offered.

"I have an idea," Katrina suggested. "Didn't I pass a little house that was for sale on my way over?"

"*Jah*, Abe Beiler's old place. Seems like Jacob Yoder was going to purchase it for his son Eli, but decided against it because it was too small," Judah stated.

"I have some money in my savings account that would make a nice down payment on the place." Katrina proposed, looking to her daughter. "What do you think, Andrea? Would you like to move to Paradise?"

"Yes, Mom, I would love to. For sure and for certain!"

Susanna embraced her twin and gave thanks to *Der Herr* for his loving kindness.

The End

Learning to Love
Saul's Story
Including Chloe's Revelation from the Amish Girls Series
J.E.B. Spredemann

Find out who Joanna marries and discover the surprises that await Jonathan and Susie! Follow your favorite characters to see how they learn to trust in God as their lives progress. And, of course, meet some new characters along the way.

Coming to paperback Fall 2014

Introducing:

Amish Fairly Tales

Cindy's Story

A fun novelette for adults!

Prologue

Ella stood near her father's grave. *He's really gone.* Tears welled in her eyes and dripped onto the ribbon of her prayer *kapp* as she thought of *Mamm*'s funeral several years earlier. She'd been just three then, but she still remembered *Mamm's* beautiful smile and kind words. Although her father had remarried, the gaping hole left by her mother's death had never been filled.

A cold hand on her arm demanded her attention. "*Mother said we need to go now,*" her stepsister Priscilla said in Pennsylvania Dutch.

Ella nodded and brushed her tears away. She followed Priscilla to the family buggy and stared out at the gray sky as she, her stepmother, and two older stepsisters traveled toward home. The clip-clop of the horse's hooves didn't soothe her the way they usually did.

"We are moving tomorrow," Mother Clara declared. "I have no need of this large farm and with no man around, we won't be able to keep up with it. I've already accepted an offer which is more than generous. We will be able to buy something much smaller that will suit our needs."

Nine-year-old Matilda bounced excitedly. "Where will we move, *Mamm*?"

"I thought Indiana might be a nice place. Since it's so cold up north, I plan to join one of the smaller settlements in the south," she answered satisfactorily.

"But I'd have to leave *Dat* and *Mamm*," Ella worried aloud.

Mother Clara squeezed her hand tightly and Ella winced. "We won't have any bad attitudes about this. Do you hear me, Ella? Your parents are dead now. You can stop your nonsense."

Ella nodded silently as moisture gathered in the corners of her eyes.

"*Gut.* Girls, you must begin packing immediately. Ella, you will tend to the animals. You may eat your supper when the chores are completed."

Ella wanted to protest and ask when she would have time to pack up *her* things, but she wouldn't risk more of her stepmother's reproof. She guessed she'd be packing while the rest of the house slept in peace. Just as long as she could take her *Mamm's* special chest with her. Right now, that's all that mattered.

Chapter 1

Ten years later...

"*Donner wetter!* You *ferhoodled* horse – get back here!" Nathaniel called out. He leaped onto Winsome's back and charged after the wild steed. "Go get him, girl."

Nat watched in dismay from atop Winsome as the white stallion jumped their pasture fence and raced down the lane. If he didn't reach him before he reached the main highway...

He wouldn't allow his thoughts to ponder that possibility. Besides, that was several miles away. Surely the horse would be in his secure grasp long before then. He hoped...and prayed.

"Whoa! Whoa!" Nathaniel called out to the new horse. Winsome began to slow down. "No, not you girl!" He squeezed his thighs, urging his horse to continue forward. "I knew I should have kept Bishop in his pen. Stupid dog," he uttered under his breath.

“Prince, you’ve got to slow down!” he hollered as he watched the frightened horse fade from his view. *God, I need your help. You’ve got to stop that horse…*

Available NOW at participating online bookstores!

www.ingramcontent.com/pod-product-compliance
Lightning Source LLC
Chambersburg PA
CBHW031024030726
47497CB00004B/992
* 9 7 8 1 9 4 0 4 9 2 0 2 5 *